System Finale

The Final Book (book 12) of the System Apocalypse

by

Tao Wong

License Notes

System Finale

A Starlit Publishing Book
Published by Starlit Publishing
PO Box 30035
High Park PO
Toronto, ON
M6P 3K0
Canada

www.starlitpublishing.com

Ebook ISBN: 9781990491269
Paperback ISBN: 9781990491832
Hardcover ISBN: 9781990491849

Books in the
System Apocalypse Universe

Main Storyline

Life in the North

Redeemer of the Dead

The Cost of Survival

Cities in Chains

Coast on Fire

World Unbound

Stars Awoken

Rebel Star

Stars Asunder

Broken Council

Forbidden Zone

System Finale

System Apocalypse: Relentless

A Fist Full of Credits

System Apocalypse: Australia

Town Under

Flat Out

Anthologies and Short stories

System Apocalypse Short Story Anthology Volume 1

Valentines in an Apocalypse

A New Script

Daily Jobs, Coffee and an Awfully Big Adventure

Adventures in Clothing

Questing for Titles

Blue Screens of Death

My Grandmother's Tea Club

The Great Black Sea

A Game of Koopash (Newsletter exclusive)

Lana's story (Newsletter exclusive)

Debts and Dances (Newsletter exclusive)

Comic Series

The System Apocalypse Comics (7 Issues)

Contents

What Happened Before

Traitor. Rebel. Heretic.

John Lee is all those things. Betraying Earth and turning on them with the Galactic Council vote has set Earth free of the political games it was forced to play, but at the cost of violence and war. Rebelling against the Galactic Council and revealing their deepest secrets has seen him marked for capture, torture, and worse. As a heretic, John has departed from the normal lines of inquiry for the System Quest and, in so doing, become one of the few to breach the mythical 91% completion rate for the Quest.

Forced to flee the capital of the Galactic Council, Irvina, John Lee and the rest of the crew runs and fights for months in the Forbidden Zone. There, they encounter outcasts, loners, and beings of great and frightening power. Among them is a sapient Golem who entrusts John with his legacy, a sentient, modified golem named Ezz. Further help arrives in the form of the Systemers, a religious group who believes the System itself is God and seek to free it from the clutches of the System Administrators. When the Galactic Council finds John and his friends, the Systemers sacrifice their island. Endila, child-prodigy mechanic, stows away on the *Nothing's Heartbreak*.

Unfortunately, for all their running, their final goal was always known. Breaking into the solar system that Xy'largh, home and birthplace of the dragons that populate the universe, was always going to be a challenge. With all eyes on them, the team manages to breach the protective barrier and enter the solar system, the Galactic Council's fleet right behind them.

Mere hours away from reaching the planet and some modicum of safety, John and his team is betrayed. Dornalor, Pirate Captain and trusted pilot, turns them in to save himself and the other crew members, all but Mikito and John.

Luckily, his betrayal was foreseen and Mikito escapes to meet with an old party member.

Playing bait once again, John allows himself to be captured and taken by the System Administrators, his fate yet to be determined.

Chapter 1

I almost prefer the torture sessions to this. At least when they're sticking flesh-eating worms under my skin or extracting bones from my extremities, the results are focused, and the intentions of my torturers are easy to guard against.

This is just so much more insidious.

"Well, what do you think?" Merdof asks impatiently.

"A little too bitter," I answer at last, swallowing the lump of chocolate.

"It's chocolate. Of course it's bitter!"

"It's only sixty percent cocoa. You added a bunch of sugar and milk to it too, to give it creaminess, but still managed to make it too bitter. I'd expect it to be that bitter and rich at around eighty or ninety percent," I reply, pocketing the remaining piece of chocolate.

"You're still taking it."

"Of course I am. It's chocolate." I lean back in the chair, fixing the man across from me with my stare. I'm told it's unnerving when I just look at people. Something about the simmering anger or the way a part of me—the part that has blossomed and grown thanks to the System and a lot of Intelligence points—runs the numbers and angles if I need to take someone apart.

Maybe it says something about my life that the need is all too common.

"What?"

I shrug, letting my gaze roam over the industrial kitchen we're in. It looks similar to what I'd expect a full-sized industrial kitchen would look like, with multiple stoves, burners, gleaming metal appliances, and kitchen sinks. Of course, the sinks are sonic disruptors, and the stoves are convection ovens that generate heat via Mana Stones, but outside of those details, a typical commercial kitchen.

"No, seriously, what?" he asks.

"Just trying to figure out your play."

"Chocolate."

I give him a flat stare and he shrugs.

"You're a smart human. You know what the play is."

"Yeah, I do. Good cop, bad cop." I raise one stump of a hand, the fingers and wrist still growing back from the latest session. "Torture, pain, mutilation, and death." I raise my untouched other hand. "Chocolate, friendly conversations, and betrayal."

"Exactly."

"But what makes you think I know anything worth all this effort?" I shake my head. "We've been at this for what, nearly a year now?"

I've kind of lost track of time. The Administrators cheat a little, twisting how much time passes in this dimensional plane they're keeping me in. I know, via the Administrative Interface I still have a modicum of access to, that I'm still attached to Xy'largh and time compressed, but I don't know exactly how much.

"In your Earth years, yes." A pause, then the grin again. "Just over, in truth."

"Can't be cheap. I know the System doesn't like when you waste so many resources putting up a time compressed zone. Hell, our experience gains have been hammered because of it."

"But still good, do you not think so?"

"In a sense."

I have to admit he's right. One of the reasons why they let me have my System access is to let me code solutions for the System. I'm still gaining experience from it, though it's incredibly heavily discounted. But considering when I'm not being tortured, I have nothing better to do half the time, I've been a good little worker bee.

It amuses me that the other Administrators thus far have yet to patch the cheat Mikito and I found. It's not as if it's not staring all of us in the face when we access the System Ticketing Board. Sometimes, I wonder if they're using it to track her. I can't think of how, but for all my skill and ability to absorb information, the System literally runs everything in our lives, and I've had only a few years to work out how to use it. Some of the other Administrators have had literal centuries.

"You are correct, however," Merdof says. "Every day that you delay us, it grows harder to justify keeping you alive."

"Then don't." I shrug. "I mean, I'm not exactly wanting to die, but considering my other options…"

"And what if I said that rather than death, the other hand gets you? For eternity."

"Eternity's a long time."

"We have Skills."

I grunt, closing my eyes for a second. It's a sign of weakness, of them getting to me. A year ago, I wouldn't have even given them that much. A year ago, I was all piss and vinegar, ready to take everything they could throw at me with the confidence that I'd come out swinging.

A year ago, I hadn't been put through hell and back.

Truth is, pain—constant pain—and the things it does to a person is impossible to predict. You never know how you'll react, what you'll do when your daily existence can change on a whim. One moment, you're working on a new ticket, the next, you're screaming your head off.

And I do scream. I might not have broken, I won't break—at least not yet, though the gods know what it'd be like a thousand years down the road—but I do scream. Holding it in is worthless, since by that point, they've stripped everything from me anyway—skin, organs, dignity….

A year ago, I would have not given them this much. But all this time has stripped me down, burnt out foolish egoistical things like not screaming.

Sure, I'll think about telling them all I know. I'll flinch. They know it, I know it, so why bother hiding?

But...

"I guess I'll be screaming a long time then."

A grim nod. "He's not your friend."

"I never thought he was," I reply.

"The Prime Administrator will not save you," he continues.

"Didn't figure him to."

"And we will capture your friends."

"I'm sure you will try." I return his heated gaze with my own, taunting him.

He stands, fast and hard, and the mask falls away. I'm not surprised. They keep changing the good cop, hoping at some point they'll find someone that works. They've tried it all—big and ugly but friendly to thin and cute and perky. At least five different sexes at last count, just under a dozen races. Some don't last more than a few days, others like Merdof last months.

They all break eventually.

I guess if I had a skill, it'd be pissing people off.

He claps his hands and they come, dragging me out. I could fight, but what's the point? The bracers on my hands short-circuit any of my Skill use. And the moment I try, they'll drain me of Mana, shut down my link to the System, and beat me even more.

More importantly, I've never managed to kill the guards before I'm caught.

So I wait for the time when my friends come and rescue me.

And even if they do drag me into the room—gods, the room—and truss me up for my latest round of torture, I wait. Knowing that somewhere, sometime, they'll come for me.

I just have to hold out.

***

When they throw me back into my cell—and it is a cell, with about nine feet of space both ways—I'm left bleeding and broken. The System of course does its thing, and within ten minutes, I'm back to normal, albeit without a shred of functioning clothing. It doesn't bother me anymore, recreating my wild youth on Wreck Beach.

More interesting for me is the way the System works on my mind. Constant torture has rewired certain parts of me, the anticipation of pain nearly as bad as the pain itself. Chemicals—both good and bad—flood my body, some to dull what happened, others to ready me for another long bout. I could name them—stupid Intelligence—but that kind of data has been side-slotted somewhere in the System and I'm content to leave it.

No, what's more interesting for me is the way the System slowly clears some of the chemicals and memories, taking the "bite" out of them. It doesn't remove the memories—in fact, again with the evil Intelligence boosts, I can remember all of the sessions in vivid detail—but the emotional impact gets dulled. The memories themselves are slowly moved away from my mind to something else, the part of me that the System has boosted and changed ever since I started increasing the Intelligence attribute.

For a very, very long time, I believed—the Questors believe—that the System can't really read our minds. It can—at best—read the flashes in our brains—or the alien equivalent of our mushy organ—and interpret that for its own use. It's capable enough that when it injects information into us—like our Skills or Classes—it can read how we take it all in, make adjustments, and ensure that when we need to trigger them, they work. Sort of like strapping electrodes to a brain and watching the MRI imaging. You can see the parts flash up for arousal, boredom, logical thinking, and you can make guesses, but the exact details? That's impossible to guess.

That's why, we always believed, the Shop doesn't sell information in our heads. Because the System doesn't have it—and if it doesn't have it, it can't sell it. However, the past year has me wondering about all that.

The way the System pulls memories of my torture sessions, dulls my feelings and the emotional impact, sideloading them just like my Skills so that they're accessible but no longer directly affecting me... It begs the question. How can it do that if it can't read my thoughts?

Obvious answer—it's recording where everything goes in high-stress situations, then pulling all of it aside later to shunt away. It's why PTSD and nightmares are less common. At first, that was my prevailing theory. It lined up with all the information the Library has, it didn't break the prevailing theories and tests that had been run, and well, it was comforting. To know that the System had limits, that there were places in our minds, in our existence, where we were safe.

Unfortunately, the longer I'm subjected to all this, the more I doubt the theories. Reflecting on how easily the System manages things like adjusting the size, spacing, and alterations of where and when spells fall, how Skills are triggered, and even things like putting Portals in the right place, I have to wonder—how does the System know all this without reading our minds?

More to the point, with how easily it extracts the memories of the pain and fear and humiliation, leaving but portions of the emotional toll behind, the way it smooths things out, I can't help but think there's something more going on. A series of deliberate choices to aid an individual. Not necessarily to heal them all the way, but to keep them functioning.

Functioning and processing Mana and Leveling, which as far as I can tell—and everyone agrees—is what the System really cares about. The intake of unaspected Mana and processing of it through our bodies—and how and why we do that is a mindfuck of its own that someone else can deal with—is what the System wants. Everything else—from Dungeon Worlds to Levels to Statuses—seems to be built around that. Even Levels are just a method of slowly pushing individuals to take in more Mana.

Of course, one does wonder why not just force us all to take in as much unaspected Mana as we can and call it a day? Outside of the very real barriers that physical bodies, unused to the rigors of processing such levels, would fail—and trust me, you don't want to see those experiments—something else is holding back the System.

After all, there's nothing to stop it from slowly fattening us up from birth, adding more and more Mana processing ability until we're all pulling in Mana like Legendarys and cycling it back to the System. There's no reason it can't do that, at least from the experiments the Corrupt Questors have undertaken.

Yeah, they stole children—or in some cases, bred them specially—just so they could then slowly force the kids to take in more and more Mana. It's a little disgusting really, and a lot of the failed experiments are the ones you don't want in your head. But with the right Classes, spells, and enchanted locations, it's possible to get a few kids to process unaspected Mana at incredibly high levels.

Most of those experiments ended badly. The other aspect of being able to process so much unaspected Mana is the ability to wield it. Most end up with weird System Classes, twisted and unique, almost all focused on spell work. Which they then wield on their captors, more often than not, since most of their captors and the Questors aren't the loving, kind father figures you'd want around.

One experiment took heed of the cautionary tales and managed to bring up a kid who had the power of a Legendary—well, the Mana pool (and regeneration rate at least)—while still a Basic Class. He even loved his "parents" and stood by them when the Galactic Council found their little hideout. They all perished that day, of course.

You don't defy the Council and expect to live.

Which is why, when my brain finally stops wibbling in the corner and I have some control over my body and emotions again, I limp over to the showers. Walking without the toes of one foot sucks, but at least they left me the other one this time. I hate crawling to the showers.

Once I'm clean and the nubs of my toes are regrowing—yay for the Body's Resolve Class Skill—I grab some dinner and pop open my only form of entertainment in this area.

I know, I know, in prison, you're supposed to be pumping metal and getting buff. But genetic cleansing has made me buff already, along with the System, and pumping weights is entirely unimportant when your Strength is mostly derived from the System. It's more of a mental and willpower driven thing, to alter where and how my Strength plays out, than anything actually physical. If anything, training how to shift more and more of my Strength to something as simple as physical strength would be more useful.

Except, you know, there are weird-ass equations that deal with damage and rely on you using certain System-enabled Strength modifier scores, and they work against an individual's Constitution and Agility scores to calculate actual damage which then translates to what Health is.

So actually altering your Strength score too much can work against you if you're trying to do damage, especially by swinging a sword. It's one of the reasons why melee weapons are still favored—those Strength scores offer additional damage against an individual that a flat beam weapon doesn't.

Of course, the Erethrans have a simple solution to that.

Bigger guns and more people carrying bigger guns.

I chew through the grassy, seaweed-looking purple and yellow "food" they supply me with, making a face at the texture and taste but resolutely eating. Starving to death is a weird, weird thing under the System and not something I necessarily want to experience again. All that healing requires resources, and while the System offers a large chunk of it in Mana, a large portion does come from us.

Not having food can leave one gaunt, hollow, and perpetually starving—even as the System keeps you alive. Supposedly, it's possible to starve people to death even at the higher Levels, but it's a very long, very slow process as Mana Regeneration gets impacted more and more, as we cannibalize what we give to the System. At some point, it just stops being a net benefit for the System to have us alive.

Then we die.

All in all, as I said, not something I want to experience—even partially—again. So I eat my seaweed that tastes like bleu cheese with one bite and rotten meat the next, as my brain attempts to process and assign a taste to the truly alien molecules going through my mouth—and get to work.

Not just to keep the nightmares and dreams away, but also because it's my only line to Mikito.

Chapter 2

Mind you, it's not as though we've got a text chat open, communicating with one another. It's more like me reading her footprints in the sand on a beach, after the tide has run over them a couple of times. Not a lot of information, always old and easily confused with others.

Yet for all those caveats, it's what I have and what I grasp hold of with an intensity that's more than a little crazed.

Welcome to System Administrator Ticket Board 3.2.8PoL Middle System Administrator John Lee

The 189th request to revoke access to Ticketing Board and Middle System Administrator role has been denied by Root Administrator. Would you like to read the ticket notes (Y/N)

I snort, tabbing no immediately. I've read the notes before, multiple times. I still do every tenth request, just to make sure nothing useful or informative has been sneaked in. There hasn't been, at least not yet. I still hold out hopes, that he/she/it will communicate with me. Then again, considering the other System Administrators are just waiting for that to happen, I can see why the Root Administrator hasn't.

After a moment, I shake my head and move on. After all, I've noticed the next notification and it does make me smile a little.

Level Up! You are now a Level 27 Middle System Administrator

Well, it looks like one of the tickets I fixed has finished propagating and pushed me over the edge. Of course, I don't get a Class Skill point, what with my hidden Class having overtaken my other Class and its automatic assignment of the point to System Edit.

Very annoying.

So's the brain freeze as data is dumped into my mind when the Class Skill goes up a level. Distantly, I feel my head bounce off the table, but I've got other things to worry about than bouncing my skull off metal. Instead, I swim through System Edit options, the vast database of code that has been provided to me.

The code database is immense, probably half the size of the Library in my noggin. The database holds the best solutions, the most elegant methods of solving problems that thousands of System Administrators before me have created.

The more I see of the System, the more I'm surprised at how it manages to hold itself together. Think of the most complicated pre-System program you've ever encountered. Now, keep adding hardware, accessories, new programs that hook into the main operating system over the course of tens of thousands of years. Complication after complication, layered on top of one another, conflicting with each other. New systems, new Classes, new Skills, all added to give sapient creatures a chance to survive and produce more Mana.

The information flowing through me tells a story, one I've heard before, of the history of the Galactic Council and the System. How there wasn't even a Council before, no settlement system, no Shops, not even Classes or differentiated Level gains. Time and need sees the System change.

Too much choice sees individuals, often caught in dangerous situations, freeze. Too many combinations end up being the wrong ones, or cities and societies over-specialize on the "good" combinations, never exploring additional ones, only to find themselves side-swiped by something new that upends their system. Not that Classes don't do that too, but because the Classes are so restrictive in their own way, people might game the optimal methods within a Class, but they're also likely to explore other Classes for an advantage.

The Shop system, the settlement system, even entire Classes built around Artisans and crafting; all of that are just add-on services. As technology is lost and reproduced, new Classes come into play, new Skills that twist and warp reality and create their own strained principles on the System.

I draw in the data, read the Code and the resolutions to a million and one errors, and realize why so many of the damn Administrators suck at their job. Why bother learning when it's easier to put a Class Skill point into your System Edit Skill and get even more information, even more codes? Why bother re-working things when everyone before you has done something just as good—or close enough?

Sure, there are those brilliant and driven individuals, but many are driven in the wrong way too. After all, you can't get a System Administrator Class before you hit Master Class at the least. And even then, it's hard. The kind of people who reach that far, they're mostly geared and focused on something else.

Being an Administrator is an add-on.

At least for most of them.

The exceptions though, those are the guys who climb the ranks, I bet. Not that I've met many yet. And the few I have met, I've killed.

Eventually the flow of data stops, the code base levels out, and my brain stops feeling as if someone took a spanner to it. Unsurprisingly, once I get a glass of water—no alcohol here, and certainly nothing System-augmented—I pull up the ticketing board. The glass of water I hold trembles a little, but I ignore the shaking in my hand. It'll go away in time.

You have 29832 Tickets Assigned to you.
Would you like to view the tickets?

Looks as if they've been busy foisting their dirt upon me. I acknowledge the prompt, not even bothering to read the details before I pull up the first three tickets.

Conflict: No Sunshine Skill vs Cloud Cover spell

Mana spillage during conflicting Skill and spell currently at 4.128% over acceptable parameters...

Dungeon Overflow Guidelines for Morisson Grubs in Conflict with Alterations in Grimsey Overrides and Vermin Grower (Grubs) Dungeon Keeper Class

Overflow Guidelines are currently underestimating number of denizens by a factor of 3819%, creating multiple Dungeon spillage events and throttling Mana flow to Dungeon by...

Conflict: Erethran Standard Issue Marine Blaster Rifle v3881.91v9 issuing a 0.00173% damage increase when combined with Skill: Call to Arms (Unique Empire Skill)

Urgent rectification required, as on-going conflict has created an estimated 281984 estimated overflow and use of System Mana while conflict is in play. Rectification and reduction with code...

My mind splits a little as I get to work. That's the fun part about Intelligence and, I realize, the System Edit Skill. With the new point in the Skill, I can split my mind more easily than ever, grabbing a review of the code and conflicting details, even having the ability to hold the code in its own test section in my brain to run for conflicts.

Not exactly my brain of course, though a part of me is always there. The System aids me in all this, running data and analysis faster than I could normally, an attachment that is so smooth that if I didn't know there was no way I could have done this before my score upgrades, it never would have occurred to me it wasn't just me.

I get to work clearing out tickets, the Overrides the easiest since I have a bunch of new code to refer to while fixing it. The moment a ticket is done, I pull up another ticket and keep going.

While I'm doing that, looking through the notification windows and ticketing board that glow in my vision, I take in my cell. Not really a cell, though it's not exactly luxurious either. It's like a bachelor's suite, with a cordoned off shower / bath and a single door leading out. Not much to go on. I know we're down deep enough that trying to dig my way out will just hit earth.

Yeah, I tried that early on. They left me buried in the collapsed earth for the better part of two days before they dug me out. I'd nearly asphyxiated before they dragged me out and interrogated me. I admit, that was probably the first time I talked. Not that a long diatribe about movies—mostly B-movies—I'd watched that involved people being buried alive was that helpful to anyone.

Hey, I never said I was a film critic.

The doorway leads to a hallway. Two doors in that hallway, the first being a full-on security door that I would have to break through. No idea what's behind that since the door is enchanted and made to handle Heroics. I could cut through given enough time, but that I do not have.

The second door?

It's a room I know all too well. One that knows me too well, since large portions of me have ended up scattered all across the room in one way or the other. That it's normally entirely bare until my Heroic Class Galactic Spy Breaker enters and makes use of the nannites to form whatever tools he needs makes it even less useful for escape purposes.

I'm hemmed in, trapped with no way to enter or exit. No idea of where I am, no information on the layout of the prison itself nor the other half-dozen—at least—security measures they must have in place to stop me from escaping.

And most importantly, without my most trusted, most worthy of all allies.

Ali's gone and has been, ever since they banished him.

***

It's surprising how much I miss that floating ball of sarcasm. In more ways than one, he's kept me grounded. Without him, I feel a little more unhinged, a little more angry, a little more sad. Without him to discuss bad '70s and '80s TV shows—who watches all the versions of *Ultraman?*—and torture me with his lustful thoughts about *Baywatch*, I find myself spiraling.

The only thing that keeps me halfway sane is the ticketing board and the work within. In the hours I've been sitting, limping, and lying down on the table, I've crossed off a couple hundred tickets. Mostly, the work is easy, routine things that any Administrator worth his salt could do.

Drudge work.

The experience flows in anyway, 50 XP here, 100 XP there, a few thousand sometimes if I'm lucky. Nothing like going out and stomping on a couple of monsters, but stuck as I am, it's my only method of leveling.

I do wonder if they realize I'm using the ticketing board as a lifesaver. Or if they do realize it, and realize without it, I might just break. Except not the useful, give them the information I don't have way, but the kind of breakdown that would make the Root Administrator walk away.

Because that's what they want. They want Root to come out, to talk to me, to do something to them. Which means to me that the Root

Administrator is not their friend, potentially someone they might have direct conflict with. I sometimes wonder why they don't lock out everyone else if they are the Root Administrator.

Then I get another blip from the ticketing board, another cascade of information and the resulting rush of tickets. And I know why.

Because the System is too big, too unwieldly for any single individual to handle. The System itself, in its own inorganic way, can handle and fix problems. Pave them over with excess Mana and processing power or whatever it uses. Unfortunately, the more it does that, the less it has to control the functions of the rest of the System, to hold back and process unaspected Mana.

Which means that unaspected Mana grows faster, putting more pressure on the System and the System Galaxy. The Forbidden Zone grows, and more people die. Which leads to less Mana being processed which means the Zone grows faster.

Starting a cascade of failure and bringing down the entire house of cards. The entire system, and System, are all tottering from one failure point to another, the System Administrators patching things together where they can.

Not to say they aren't skimming off the top, benefiting themselves wherever they can. Feasting on the slowly rotting corpse while the world burns. That's kind of the way with sapients, no matter if they're billionaire humans or Legendary Class mages. Fools, all of them, happy to keep running a system that works for them, no matter how many are crushed beneath their feet.

And in truth, I don't blame them. I probably wouldn't be any better if I was in their place. I don't even really care about them.

Torture has a cleansing effect on an individual. Cleans out all kinds of things—lungs, nerves, foolish morals. In the end, you end up with just the things you truly value. Heart, brain, and a driving need to know.

What is the System?

And can I punch it in the face?

***

Digging through the tickets and clearing them is just one of the things my mind does. Pondering about the System, trying to pry its secrets clear from the myriad pieces of information I've been given, and tying it all together with the knowledge downloaded into my head by Feh'ral—and damn, but I miss that creepy librarian—is another. The other part is looking for the breadcrumbs left behind by Mikito as she goes through the world.

The obvious one is the fact that the ticket feeding her my XP is still active. That's a good indication that she's alive. Considering how rare a combination we are—unique, in fact—the moment she—or I—dies, this ticket would close. No point worrying about it ever happening again.

That's just the first indicator of course. There are others. Like over here—a spike in Mana use, Heroic Level Skills being used to take down a couple of monsters. Level 98 Ng'itter Scavengers—monsters that are a real pest on Xy'largh. They sneak into dragon nests, eat their eggs, thus enraging the dragons while they run away, camouflage in full bore. Then everyone else has to deal with the grieving Level 140+ monster. And that's a young, still fertile dragon.

Oh yeah, did you know that there are multiple strains of dragons? Some are egg layers, some pop out children like mammals. It's one of those weird evolutionary facts of being hundreds of thousands years old, being able to polymorph, and also living in the middle of a Forbidden Zone. Mutations everywhere!

I'm not even going to talk about the dragons' weird-ass social structure, the way different breeds and purity levels create differing castes and structures and how the Dragon Knights—and Dragon Lords—fit into all of that.

Yeah, old societies with giant living calamities living alongside them—and part of them—create some truly screwed up worlds. Especially when you realize that most dragons don't even consider others of their kind actual members of their society until they pass a few hundred years and Level 150. Everything beneath that is just another monster.

As I said, really screwed up.

Anyway, the point is, I can see when Mikito uses her Skills in large bursts. It shifts the Mana output flows and triggers more than a few subroutines since she's using Skills that have no place on this planet. She has basically a unique Class—not really, but for this solar system's purpose, yes—and it triggers even more reports.

Of course, that's not even counting all the different kinds of trouble and reports that flow in when she encounters the hunters going after her. The only good news is, because Xy'largh is so screwed up, the Galactic Council can't send everyone they want against her.

Not that they can afford to either—there is a minor Galactic War going on, and a major one brewing. Pulling enough people to handle a pair of skilled Heroic Classes on a planet that eats Master Classes for breakfast and asks for more is tough.

The fact that any major incursion would also annoy the dragons and other high-standing members of Xy'largh is something else the Council has to be careful about. The Shadow Council might not have a Legendary Dragon whatever on hand, but there are more than a few Dragons sitting about in the Level 200+ range. They just can't be bothered to deal with anything outside of their planet.

And everyone wants to keep it that way, trust me.

Which leaves, as always, the Galactic Council having to be somewhat discreet, employing whoever they can to hunt down Mikito and Bolo while the pair runs around the planet doing…

Something.

I'm a little hazy about what their plans are. Both by necessity and planning. All I know is that they're bouncing around the planet killing monsters, occasionally taking part in Arena fights, and once, they even went so far as to down a dragon that got too big for its scales.

Still, knowing they're alive and running around gives me hope. The day they get caught, the day her ticket goes dark…

That's the day when all hope will be lost.

On that day, I might even give them what they want, if it'd get me closer to what I really want.

An answer.

Chapter 3

Days pass, or the subjective displaced realm equivalent of days, before they come for me. I complete hundreds of tickets, not needing to sleep, but the pile keeps growing. The war going on out there, the one I get only sideways information on as I deal with fluctuating Mana levels and massive experience dump events, is going badly.

For who, you might say? Everyone, as far as I can tell. Administrators are going to the front lines, their tricky and unknown abilities causing death and destruction to Master and Heroic Classes. When your Skills suddenly shut down, when you aren't able to flee when you need to, it's never a good thing. Battles between Heroic Classes in particular are seat-of-the-pants, death-defying events. Or one-sided stomps. Not much space in between.

Tilt the battlefield one way and you suddenly see a lot more deaths. That, of course, has resulted in the "real" Council—or the rebels, depending on which side you ask—deploying countermeasures. Specifically, they've started hunting down Administrators.

It's not as though the Administrators and their anomalous Classes, slower Leveling speed, and just overall weirdness haven't been noticed. When a bunch of somebodies all back one another up and start showing up at fights, all of whom are in the late Master or Heroic Classes, some of whom have no reason to be in the battlefields, it twigs the professionally paranoid that something is up. Individuals who might have been a curious anomaly on a statistical model are now a potential threat. With some of the more vicious groups—the Truinnar and Movana in particular—just the suspicion of being an Administrator is a good way to have their assassins come after you.

More chaos. More destruction. More Mana not being churned.

And more System Administrators falling, which means there's even more work to handle. The System isn't teetering on the brink of failure since there are enough safeguards in place—including the numerous Dungeon Worlds—but the Forbidden Zone is encroaching faster.

Of course, faster is relative. Instead of taking fifty years to overtake the next habitable planet, it's only thirty-four years. It's more dangerous for planets in the Restricted Zone, the ones already fighting a losing battle to keep from being consumed. More Mana flooding through means more monsters on already beleaguered planets, many of which are low on combat personnel due to the wars.

If the wars last too long, there will be a massive loss of life and planets. System integration will speed up for many planets that aren't already part of us, though in most cases, it's just adding barren planets to the system. But there are a few populated planets that, within the next century, might find themselves introduced to the System in a less than stellar way.

I see all this from charts and tickets and aid requests, piece it all together along with the historical knowledge gifted to me. I feel a little bit of guilt, knowing I set this off, but while I'm arrogant, I'm not certain I'm arrogant enough to believe that this war is just because of me.

Days on end of clearing tickets, understanding what is happening, until finally, someone shows up. I'm a little surprised by who it is, considering I haven't seen her since my initial capture. The blue-skinned, sleek, and copper-plated-faced mermaid Administrator is a known sight, if one I detest. She's not alone either, a pair of guards beside her. Normally, not enough to stop me from trying my hand at bashing her head in, but being out of Skill abilities, thanks to the pair of nice little bracers and the collar they've locked onto me, I don't really stand much of a chance.

"Senior System Administrator Sephra. What do I owe the displeasure of seeing you?" I say, letting all the venom I can muster drip with each word.

"Why, your stubbornness of course." Sephra saunters over and sits down on empty air. Nannites form out of the floor at eye-blinding speed, creating the chair she needs, which she then lounges back into. Positioning herself only a few steps into the room and right in front of the door shows me how little she wants to be here.

It also alerts me to the change in the room. I eye the corners and quickly note the almost invisible force screen that has sprung up between us. She really isn't taking any chances with me.

Smart, considering if I get a chance, I'll end her. Or at least try. I have a bone or two to pick with her after all. Something, something, killing my friends, something, something torture. You know, the usual.

"Well, that's not new." I yawn theatrically.

"Am I boring you?" Sephra says, her voice caustically sweet. "Should I ask Yewa to come see you again? Perhaps you'd like his company more."

"He's certainly more interesting than you."

There's a flicker of irritation on her face before she smooths it out. I count that as a score, though a part of me wonders how much of it is real. You don't grow to our Levels without some level of politicking. And even if most of what I do is aided by the Subterfuge Perk I picked up all too long ago—which has been, I'll admit, pulling its weight on the backend of all my interactions—I still have learned a few things myself. Part of which includes never taking anything for granted.

She lapses into silence, studying me. I consider playing the silent glaring game with her, but after a moment, I decide I'm too mature for that. Instead, I pull up a couple of tickets and work on them while I wait.

It takes only a few minutes for her to break, what with me studiously ignoring her while I finish the latest ticket.

"You know, certain factions are considering keeping you here, alive and quiet. Working for us, fixing the problems you have caused us. They say that a good worker like you could free more important personages," Sephra says.

"Not hard to do a better job than you people." I snort. "You'd think none of you ever took a Coding 101 course." I rub the back of my neck while I add, "I'll admit, you're like most coders I knew. None of you ever put notes in your code. Bloody amateurs, one and all."

This time, I don't get the reaction I expect. Instead, a long-suffering look crosses her face. "I tell them all the time. How are we supposed to know what you changed if you don't note it down… but they're all, 'The System knows!' Like I want to browse through System changelogs when you could just take another five minutes and…" She splutters to a stop, realizing what and who she's speaking to.

I finish her sentence for her. "Put in some proper comments. It's not hard, but then again, idiots are more likely to just revert to an old version and restart than try to work out what the previous idiot did, and then they just introduce a new problem."

There's a long-suffering sigh from Sephra, and for a moment, we have a moment of shared exasperation. It only lasts a moment before she shakes her head.

"It's because you might actually be useful in the long run that we're making this offer," Sephra says, her voice growing colder. "We—"

"I've heard it before."

"Then listen again," she says frostily.

I yawn, but when the pair of guards shift and tap the big truncheons by their side, I take the smarter course and stay silent. See? I can learn.

"Join us. All those questions you have about the System? We can answer them."

"Bullshit." I can't help but say that, since this is the first time I've heard this particular pitch. Wait… actually, no. Third time. I just discounted the other two times since they were mentioned in the middle of a get-to-know-your-organs session.

"I do not understand your human fascination with excrement," Sephra says. "Do you eat it?"

"What? No!"

"I'm sure I've seen something about humans—"

"FETISH!" I place a hand over my eyes, groaning. Seriously, what is wrong with the English and culture pack downloads going out these days?

"Well, okay." There's doubt in her voice, and when she sees my rather suspicious glare, she shrugs. "It's not exactly a unique dietary requirement."

"I did not need to know that."

Another shrug. "To the point—your questions about the System? They can be answered."

"I don't believe you."

That's when she drops the bombshell. A simple notification box that she shares to me and changes my world.

System Quest Completion Rate: 99.99%

"You're nearly there," I say in disbelief.

"I am there."

"I'm sure math isn't your thing, but normally completion is one hundred percent," I say. "You know, all of it."

"No one gets a hundred percent," Sephra says. "But trust me, the answers we get? They're more than enough."

I snort, but I have to admit, the difference between full completion and what she has is so thin, if the Quest was a cake, you couldn't feed a mouse the crumb of difference. It should be enough for most reasonable people.

"It's not complete."

"And you're going to stand on that principle alone? Be tortured and punished because of less than a fraction of a percent?"

I shrug.

Sephra smiles then, one that is almost painfully gleeful. "I told them. Anyone stupid enough to take us on would never bend, not even a bit. And here you are, doing everything I said you'd do. All those old Admins, thinking they know better. I told them."

"That's nice. I'll get you a trophy. About five feet long, with a point, and I'll make sure to deliver it to you."

The pair of bodyguards stir, but she waves them down. "Don't worry, the mad dog can bark, but he cannot do anything. We defanged him." I growl at her, and she laughs. "See?"

I draw a deep breath, forcing down my irritation. My fist unclenches slowly as I breathe out and I realize there's something I do want from them, something I might be able to get. An answer, after all the lies I've been told. It might be more lies, but I need to ask it anyway.

"Why do you want me on your side so much anyway?" I say.

"You know why."

"The Root Administrator."

A nod, blue gills opening and closing in the air. She pauses, running a hand across her neck, and I feel Mana flow, running along her hands and across it. A second later, she lowers her hand, still smiling at me as though what she has done is of no consequence.

"They're your Root Administrator. Surely you communicate with him all the time," I say, fishing. My guess is they don't actually. That's why they're desperate to hear from him, to track him down. Maybe even deal with him and take away his access, so one of their own can be the Root.

"Oh, we do." I blink, and she smiles at my surprise. "We communicate with them all the time. It's us who they don't communicate with. They don't talk to most Administrators. In fact, they don't talk to anyone unless they need to. Except for you."

"Except for me," I repeat. "And that's what you want, me to lure them out. To play bait."

"Yes."

Something rings false in her answer. Maybe it's the angle of her body, the way she blinks, the twitch in her gills. The skill set for alien body language I downloaded, the years I spent working with aliens and creatures that aren't human, the Intelligence increases, and the Subterfuge Perk, it all combines to tell me there's something more than her answer. Something she won't tell me.

"What makes you think he—they—will come out? They're already talking to me, as you said."

A shrug, again, one that rings of a partial truth. "Some things, they can't be told. Only shown."

Intuition twigs. "The System Quest. Whatever is at the end of it, it has to be shown."

"You're a smart one, aren't you?" Sephra nods.

I let out a thready breath. There is an end, and it's a place as much as a piece of knowledge. Almost as soon as she's finished speaking and confirming it, I get a notification.

System Quest Update: +1.4%

I try to hide, but as good as I am at reading her, she is at reading me. Or perhaps she knew all along what the result of her confirming this information would do.

"You got the update, didn't you?"

I reluctantly nod.

"Then you know I'm telling you the truth. Join with us, and we'll bring you where you need to go to meet him. We get what we want, you get what you want. Simple."

"And no more torture," I add, because it is somewhat top of my mind.

"And no more torturing you to break you, yes."

I pause, considering her offer. Truly considering it. Not because I'll take it, but because of what she's revealed. If it's a place, then suddenly the fact that I have a location—a System Administrator Center—that I'm to report to becomes much more important. The question is, will it be a case of the run for Irvina again? Will they know where we're going if I escape?

Because we've done that dance once before, and the next time, I doubt they'll bother trying to capture us. Death by fire from above is the most likely response. Never mind the fact that they might just choose to teleport a Legendary over. And powerful as we are, I have serious doubts that we could deal with a Legendary, not one backed up by System Administrators.

I have to think about this, think about what kind of information I can get. Which means potentially entertaining them. "What about my friends?"

"The Samurai and Dragon Lord?" Sephra says, and I nod. "If you call them off—and I know you can—we can let them live. We won't even demand they pledge allegiance."

"You know Mikito will go where I will."

"Funny thing, linked Classes." She smirks.

I grunt, noting how she doesn't mention Bolo. Or… "Harry?"

"The Reporter? He's safe. The Pirate's earlier deal safeguarded him."

I snort, and her eyes narrow. "You mentioned he'd be watching me, recording my breaking. Yet I've yet to see a sign of him in all this time. So don't mind me if I doubt your word."

Sephra's eyes narrow, the outer eyelid blinking. They're clear, meant to protect her eyes when she's deep underwater, I assume, but it's still creepy even if I know what it's meant for. "That is a fair point. But if you wish to see him, to speak with him, we'll need something."

"What?"

She shrugs, playing coy now. I can't help but grunt a little in annoyance, and even more so when she doesn't break, even minutes later. When I try to bring up the ticketing board, she shuts me down, blocking my access for the moment. I let out a little huff and she tuts at me. Tuts!

"Fine. A trade then. A conversation with him and I'll give you a piece of information about the Root Administrator."

"Now, and we decide if it's good enough."

"Now, but you send him in, no matter what," I counter.

"So long as you provide something good and actionable," Sephra says.

"Good at least." When she frowns, I open my hands. "I don't have any idea what you consider actionable since I don't know what you guys know. But it'll be good information."

Sephra frowns, then nods. A moment later, something I haven't seen in a while pops up.

Contract Notification: A Promise
Parties: John Lee and Sephra veCokca
Details: The above parties hereby agree…

I flick through the contract, a simple outlining of what we discussed. The penalties for violation are surprisingly a single Credit. When I reach that part, she smirks at me, but I get it.

The Contract is being used to ensure compliance via the System, with an impartial third party of sorts judging everything. I'm not entirely sure how useful or reliable the System is at judging something like this, but it's probably better than nothing. For both of us.

I do spend some time browsing the Contract using my System Edit Skill, checking the code for any hidden traps. Nothing jumps out on a quick scan. While I'm doing so, there's a feeling of being watched, which isn't hard to guess is Sephra ensuring I'm not changing anything.

Not that I thought about it for more than a few seconds.

Once I'm satisfied there aren't any hidden traps, I agree to the Contract. I feel it settle over myself and my System connection, my Status Screen. It's a wide, sprawling series of code, but I see where it hooks in, where it spreads its tendrils over my Status information. Where it burrows in deep, reading data that...

"Thousand hells. You're one tricky fish, aren't you?"

She grins wide, and I lean backward, knowing it's too late. I want to rage. I want to tear her head off and smash her to bits. I want to curse myself out for what I did. But what is, is—and now, they've got a way to browse through the code of my Status. Break the contract, keep it, doesn't matter—they have the code now. At least, a snapshot of it at this moment.

"I'm to visit the 14-1-1 System Administrator center. I'm assuming that's where the Root Administrator will be," I grind out, fulfilling my side of the bargain. I've lost this round, so I might as well get what I can from it.

"Ah..." Sephra says, almost as if she's releasing a long pent-up breath. She stands, smiling at me widely as she turns away.

"Hey! About Harry..." I wish I could dare ask what Ezz is doing, how it's been, but I know better. Better to let them think it's a simple machine, one that I made because it was required, better not to let them think I care about it at all.

"You'll see your friend. Soon," Sephra replies, leaving me as the door opens and closes.

She ignores me while I shout at her, asking what she means by soon. She ignores me as I pound on the force screen. She even ignores me when I scream as her thugs get their hands on me and start lopping off limbs. Everything's recorded, everything is something she could hear if she wants, but she doesn't.

I don't matter, not since she got what she wanted.

Which is about par for the course for dealings with the Shadow Council.

Chapter 4

True to their word, Harry appears not long after. They even wait until I'm mostly together, which is always nice. With my high Constitution, I regenerate limbs at a decent pace these days—not like the multi-day affair at the start of the apocalypse—but it still takes time, especially when they're intent on pulling me apart every once in a while. I sometimes wonder if the System is lowering the speed of change, just to help reduce the amount of time I spend in pain. Wishful thinking that.

The War Reporter looks even worse than the last time I saw him, which is kind of saying something. I mean, he was pretty broken from his time in captivity, and running around, fleeing for our lives, wasn't exactly stress-free. Especially when one isn't a combat Classer and in the middle of the Forbidden Zone. Then on top of that, we had the betrayal by Dornalor and...

Well.

"You look like shit," I tell Harry as he hesitantly walks in, stopping a short distance in.

He glances at the doorway, then around, his dark skin paler than normal. His nervousness rolls off him like a wave, and it's something I want to question him about but decide against.

Not yet.

"You don't look... no. Truth. You look just like yourself. Other than the stumpy foot," Harry replies, arms crossing. "How?"

"System shenanigans."

"I've watched your 'sessions.' All of them. They made me watch them, so that I could report on it properly. I've watched what they did to you, how they did it..." Harry speaks fast, hands moving in aggressive flicks and gestures. As though what he has to say can't be expressed just by words. "I watch them pull all the bones out of your limbs, one by one. Watched you scream and cry and beg and—"

"I remember. I was there," I cut him off.

"Then how!" Harry shouts. "How are you still... still..."

"Sane?" I shrug. "Pretty sure I started out a little crazy. I know more than a few friends who would insist on that as a truth."

"You're joking. You're bloody joking! You sodding fool, you overgrown manchild, you, you, you..." He splutters to a stop, unable to keep going. I find myself grinning, which makes him turn even redder and angrier.

"It's good to see you too," I say.

That breaks him. He goes from growling and spluttering to shocked to just trembling and silent. I watch for a few seconds, before a small insistent part of me that sounds a lot like Lana, redhead ex-girlfriend and my external emotional support vehicle, points out he could use a hug.

Let's just say the next few minutes are awkward. Hugging isn't something I do. Certainly not with men I'm not sleeping with or intending to sleep with. Yes, yes, I know, toxic masculinity and all that—but I grew up in a straight-laced traditional Chinese family. We didn't hug one another because such outward displays of affection were just not done.

So, yeah. It was awkward, but the fact that it seems to help him is a reward in itself. By the time I finally lead Harry over to a chair, get him a drink of water—lacking anything stronger—and take a seat, he's pulled himself together.

"Seriously, John. How are you managing to hold it together?" Harry says.

"The System." I tap my head. "It's taking away a lot of the pain and other effects. I have a feeling the high mental resistances my Class offers does some of that too. High Willpower maybe?" Not all the truth, since I know from the Library that it's not always the case, though all of those do help.

"So what? The System lets you deal with being tortured?"

"The aftereffects at least." I add, almost contemplatively, "Though I find myself grateful they keep me to mostly bland foods. I'm somewhat less than enthused by ribs, meaty meals, and spaghetti."

Harry stares at me for a long moment, trying to figure out if I'm joking. Or how much I'm joking. Because, I'll admit, there's a lot of truth in what I said.

Before he can speak, I ask, "How have you been? And how long has it been?"

"A month," he answers the second question first, then glances around, almost hunching in a little. I wonder if he was meant to tell me that, but since no one breaks in to stop him, he continues. "I've been... well. I've been better."

"Other than watching the highlights of the John Lee show, what else have you been up to?" I ask. "What happened to Dornalor and Ezz?"

"Not much. I'm not exactly a prisoner, but I'm not really allowed to go anywhere either," Harry says. "The prison that's attached to this space..." Harry looks around, waiting to see if anyone intends to come in and stop him. "It's underground. They don't let me up, and the place itself is huge. These dimensional spaces, they're all hooked into specific corridors."

I make a noise for him to go on.

"Dornalor's upstairs. Stuck. Endila has stayed with the Captain. The *Heartbreak* is docked and unable to leave, at least for now. Ezz has been retasked to become one of their serving bots. They... did something to him. He's not himself."

I blanche a little, though truth be told, it's not particularly surprising. Why leave a potential threat running around when you can just wipe its memory banks and reinstall it? What makes Ezz itself is just code, right?

Gods, I hope not.

"So you got the run of an underground prison…"

Before I can complete my sentence, the damn Library decides that it's time to do another information dump. It's gotten a lot quieter over the last few years, the lack of new experiences and needs meaning that the Library has felt the need to do the information dump much slower, in ways that don't require me to get a pounding headache or wonder if someone has driven an icepick through my ear. Unfortunately, this time around, it decides that dimensional prisons are well worth exploring.

Funnily enough, the information on prisons is combined with information about research labs and the construction of both. The Questors—the Corrupt Questors—have reams and reams of data for both. Not because it's particularly helpful for puzzling out what the System is, but because we need—they needed— prisons and research stations to conduct their often illegal and aberrant experiments.

There are as many prison blueprints in my brain as there are grains of rice in a family cookpot. Too much for me to really get more than a cursory understanding, but it seems dimensional prisons are considered one of the most popular and secure methods by governments. Especially for high value targets.

Not so much for your average Questor though. As I guessed, the cost of maintaining a dimensional prison is expensive. The additional cost of running time at different speeds than base reality adds to the cost. It's why most prisons never have their time zones altered, reducing cost overall. That being said, a single dimensional prison cell is as expensive as the entirety of a normal Classed prison, due to the Mana cost of holding the dimensions apart and still connected.

It does explain why they have the prison here though—in a world at the heart of the Forbidden Zone. Having enough Mana regeneration floating around ensures the prison defenses don't fail. The problem with failing Mana regeneration and bottoming out a facility's Mana is that no one ever knows what will happen to the dimensional threshold.

Sometimes the prison cell drifts away, detached from the universe, carrying its contents away until someone finds it. Undramatic but annoying. Other times, those cells might follow the connection back to plain reality, sometimes going so far as swapping parts of base reality with itself—or just merging. Those can be great—freedom for those imprisoned—or disturbing. Some of the nastiest mutations happen when the two climb in together.

Other prison types—from the fan-favorite asteroid prison to the lava-submerged ones—have their own advantages, but nothing allows you to spend more time dealing with recalcitrant prisoners than dimensional prisons. Also, due to the gap separating the imprisoned and base reality, they can't use Skills or spells, meaning that individuals with kingdom- or business-wide buffs are neutered—both ways. Then, of course, you've got things like ability to control how people enter and exit the dimension and break-outs—or break-ins to free them—become much more complicated.

That's what is taking Mikito and Bolo so long. If they've realized where I am, then just barging in and killing everyone is not a solution. At best, they cut me loose to float through the various secondary dimensions for all eternity before the artificial cell breaks apart.

At worse? Well, recombining with base reality in an uncontrolled fashion is very, very painful. And most often, lethal.

"John?"

"Sorry. Library dump," I say. He gets it, and there's no reason to hide it from those who might be listening. "You getting a chance to talk to the other prisoners?"

"Some." Harry's lips thin as he shudders a little. "There are… people… here who need to be kept away."

"Not killed?"

"If they could kill them, they would." Harry makes a face. "Some of them have backup plans, things they can release, mass destruction Skills or equipment ready to go off. Others…" Harry shudders. "Nothing's supposed to be immortal. But some of those things…"

"Are really hard to kill?" I finish for Harry, understanding.

I've heard of them. Mutations and twisted abominations that have been corrupted by unaspected Mana. Experiments by Corrupt Questors or even the Galactic Council themselves. Sure, certain Skills like Mana Blade or All for One do direct damage via the System, but stupidly high resistances or regenerations can offset that. There are Skills that let you bank health or other resources for future use, and some of the hardest to kill have banked a metric ton.

Vampires—the Galactic equivalent—are one of those. Quite a few varieties, from the usual blood-suckers to emotional vampires, but their goal is simple—drain people of their resources to benefit themselves. Some are full-out monsters, no different than Goblins, while other vampires are Classed individuals or mutated Classes. Skills that let them bank health, Mana, Stamina, it all benefits them and makes them extremely hard to kill.

Even worse are the ones who have backups, Skills that let them sort of survive. Most of those are monsters in truth, mutations, because death is death in the System. What comes out afterward is never right, never normal. It's a known fact, but some fear the idea of death so much that they refuse to listen and take the chance of coming back warped and twisted over oblivion and whatever is out there.

"So this is where they keep the undesirables, the ones who are a little too dangerous to kill or a little too useful to get rid of. The ones who might be useful as a lever in a future time," I say.

"Yes." Harry's eyes are haunted as he leans forward and whispers. I'm not sure why he bothers, I'm sure we're bugged all the way to the rivers of Styx and back, but I lean in to listen anyway. "They have the Sun Killer here."

"Seriously? Isn't he like… dead?"

"As if that ever took."

I grunt. Damn monster has been killed a half dozen times in recorded history but kept coming back. Some assumptions were that they were just different versions of the same thing, others that the Sun Killer was a swarm monster, while others just posited illusion abilities. None of that seems to be real. Or perhaps they all are.

"How do they contain it? Last I heard, it's nearly a thousand kilometers long and burns with the heat of the suns it consumes," I say, puzzled. The math of keeping dimensional places is simple—bigger they are, the more expensive. And with the inverse square law of area, well…

"It's sleeping. Shrinks down to no bigger than a Bug."

"A bug?" I hold my fingers maybe a millimeter apart.

"No, no. A Bug. You know, the car."

I stare at Harry before shaking my head. "You British are weird."

"What?"

"Those rusted heaps are so… so… sixties." I shake my head. "I guess that was the heyday of the Brits though, before you really collapsed into a world of chips and *EastEnders*."

Harry stares at me as though I'm insane, and I keep my face flat. I don't want to give away the fact that the only reason I know about the *EastEnders* is listening to Ali complain how it's a pale shade of itself and nothing like *Home and Away*. Whatever that was....

Gods, I sometimes hate having a memory that doesn't seem to forget the dumbest of things.

"Asshole," Harry says. "Not all of us watch the *EastEnders*."

"Sure, sure. Some of you ran into the middle of warzones rather than deal with all that cockamamie."

"Cockamamie?" Thick lips purse. "Are you sure you're okay?"

"Nope. Been tortured for the better part of a year. Either with really boring conversations or literally." Then, deciding the man's a little more stable and less likely to fly off the handle, I ask him the question I've been meaning to. Even if I am somewhat curious who else is trapped here. "Mikito?"

"She's alive." Harry shrugs. "That's all I know. They let me send out the occasional report, but it's all heavily doctored and reviewed. Whatever I watch is heavily scrutinized too." He frowns a little, tapping his skull. "Even my Skills are compromised, so I'm not exactly sure how much I learn is... well... real."

"The Weaver?'

"She and the Shadow Council have their own people. Not Legendarys, but a lot of them. Where she's using one Skill, they're wielding a dozen. Makes everything hard to grasp. Identify Truth gives me a headache each time I read any actual report."

"But Mikito's alive."

"Yeah. Can't say much more, other than that she and Bolo have been bouncing around the planet, making a fuss."

I sigh, but that's not unexpected. I doubt they'd let him in if he could actually provide me any real information. Still, I have to try. "Any idea of what kind of fuss?"

"Mostly good deeds. Killing monsters, wiping out bandits—"

"There are bandits on this planet?" Even Earth had some, but the fact that you generally needed a safe place to rest your head meant that you either got bandit towns with large infrastructure levels involved or the bandits became quite short-lived.

"Yeah. Seems like one of the groups had a Classer with a Zone of Tranquility and it made for temporary Safe Zones," Harry says. "Wish we had gotten more options for those kind of Classes on Earth."

Thankfully, the Library doesn't do a dump at that opening. Mostly because I've already looked into it and the data dump happened then. "Those kind of Classes are extremely rare, and even more so on Dungeon Worlds. It's almost as though the System knows that individuals who get such Classes rarely leave their initial starting zones. Add the fact that basic initiation would mean they start out as a Basic Class and it's almost impossible for them to survive on a Dungeon World, what with the other Class requirements."

"The Pacifist ones?" Harry says.

"That's one version. Immobility, demarcation of their 'homes' or residences, the requirement for large ritual areas," I list off the first few that come to mind. "Makes it all difficult."

"Still…"

"Yeah. We could have used a few more Safe Zones. Especially in places like Australia," I say.

Harry can't help but nod. The country is still a mess a decade later. Sure, there are a few shores of civilization, but they're rare. Add the fact that pretty much the entirety of the backcountry is monster heaven and you've got high-Level Adventurers all over the Galaxy making their way there, causing their own brand of trouble.

At least the Yukon managed to avoid a lot of those problems by just having the Duchess take over. I do wonder how she's faring. I kind of screwed her over too, though I got the feeling while she'd be happy to take her pound of flesh if she can get it, I'm low on her priority list. At least for now.

"So doing the adventuring thing then?" I say, rubbing my chin.

That sort of makes sense. For all the benefits she gets being linked to me and getting experience from me as I up my System Administrator levels, Mikito is still somewhat low-Leveled for this region. Ditto with Bolo, from what I recall. If anything, the Dragon Lord is significantly behind us, unless he's managed to acquire enough experience to upgrade himself to a Heroic.

"Looks like it. She's certainly seen the sights." There's a hint of doubt in his voice. When he sees the inquiring gaze I offer him, he continues. "She might be trying to find information on where you are."

"Right, the Council's Guantanamo Bay. What do they call it? Something really dramatic, wasn't it?"

"The Abyss," Henry supplies.

"Right, right. I thought this prison was relatively well known?" I say. "I heard of it even before we arrived." The look he gives me makes me go defensive. "And not just from the Library!"

"Think about what you heard, will you, John?"

I frown, then run the information I have through my mind. It doesn't take long before I realize the problem. "Oh. There's no location information."

"Exactly. And most of the rumors are along the line of 'the Council has an ultra-secret prison where they keep the worst of the worst.' More conspiracy theory than actual information," Harry points out.

I sigh and lean back, staring at the man. He's relaxed a little, but as he catches my regard, begins to sense my motives for the questions I've asked, he tenses again. "So you think no one knows where we are…"

"No."

"What?"

"I said, no. I'm not going to try to leak that information in a coded message. Or somehow do a dead-drop of information to Mikito. Or make her my 'source' so we can have a conversation."

"I didn't ask," I protest.

"You were going to. Weren't you?" I hesitate, but that hesitation is more than enough for the perceptive reporter. "I knew it. Fuck you, John. You sodding fool, you're always trying to drag me down. It's no wonder Lana left you. Why anyone sane keeps you light years away."

I flinch a little at his accusation, though a part of me knows it's true. Those who are stable, who learned to move on and aren't hell-bent on destroying themselves, they know better than to associate with me. I wish he was wrong, but I don't say a thing when he stands and walks off.

"You're a goddamn user, John. And like any other addict, the moment you're done, you just throw your drug away. Except we're the drugs, and the damage you do... God. I don't know why I agreed to come." Then he's out of the sliding doors. I see his hand twitch and I know, just know, he wants a door to slam. A way to vent his anger and hurt.

There's not much I can do for him, so I sit there and watch him leave. I let myself stew in his words for a few seconds, but then I move on. No different than before. There's no startling revelation here, no life-changing moment of enlightenment. The sessions of screaming my head off have stripped away any sense of falsity.

I know what I am and what I want. And yeah, if Harry's there, if he'll let me, I'll use him. Until he's no more than a shrub. Then I'll move on. Not without regrets, I'm not that much of a monster. But without hesitation, certainly.

So maybe it's a good thing Mikito and Bolo have been taking their time finding me.

Maybe.

Chapter 5

I keep thinking he'll come back. Keep thinking we'll have a chance to converse again. Maybe I can convince him to help. Or maybe he'll tell me to go dig a hole and bury myself in it. Something. Instead, a week passes—a relatively quiet week with only a single torture session—before I accept that Harry isn't coming back. Either that, or Sephra has decided not to let him return.

I cling to that second option, just as I cling to the idea that Mikito and Bolo will bring me back. I clutch the thought tightly, holding the belief in my heart to warm the cockles of my soul in the deep of the night.

So when they eject my cell into the void, I'm just a little surprised.

***

There's no warning, no indication of a problem. There's no need to be. Unlike a regular prison, whatever goes on on the other side of the door—the one that leads to normal reality—is hidden entirely. You could set off a nuke on the other side and it wouldn't get to me, not unless they wanted it to. Which means if there's a problem—like, say, a focused Samurai and an obstinate Dragon Lord running around causing trouble—there's no need to alert the prisoners.

There are more than a few tragic stories of individuals believing they've been abandoned in dimensional prisons or dimensional rifts, where they eventually succumb to the loneliness and despair and kill themselves, only for their rescuers to stumble in moments later to find the corpse cooling. It's such a ridiculous trope, but like most good tropes, it has enough of the ring of truth and morality that it keeps being played, over and over again.

Now, I know they've detached me from the normal prison due to a few reasons. Firstly, it's not as though I'm physically attached to anything, so it's not like a ship cutting its mooring lines free. There's no lurch, no change in motion or sway that alerts me.

No, it's much simpler and all due to the fact that I'm a System Administrator. One second, I have my usual restricted access to the Ticketing Board; the next second, I'm getting a bunch of new notifications and my restricted access widens to its full levels.

Mana, good old Mana, flows around me faster than ever, pushing into the dimensional plane I'm in, eroding the enchantments that keep my Skills and abilities at bay. That's a good thing, especially since I can't break the damn things around my wrists and neck without help.

"Bad news... the stability of this dimension is also being pulled apart," I mutter out loud to myself, missing Ali now more than ever. The Spirit has a much better knowledge about secondary dimensions. He could figure out how long this will take to break down. How long it will take before I become...

Well. That's the other question, isn't it?

I'm still in my little slice of reality, everything outside of me hidden. I'm in a different secondary dimension for sure; the question is which one? If I was the one creating the prison, I'd make sure that whatever secondary dimension my prison cell was locked to was a dangerous one. Something entirely inimical to life.

Not something partly inimical like the shadow dimension we spent so much time in, but something entirely opposed to life. Void, entropy, a howling mass of energy... all of those would work. Tough as I am, with my Skills locked down, I doubt I'd last long in one of those. Especially since I don't have the Hod or even my newer power armor.

"Fuck..." I bite my lip, considering my options.

There's one that might help. A little. It's also dangerous, potentially shortening the lifespan of the dimensional cell I'm in. Doing so could screw up Mikito's plans, make it harder for them to save me. If I sit and do nothing, that might be what she's planning for.

I have to sit back and trust her… or take things in my own hands.

"Thousand hells." I pace a little, running a hand through my hair. I'm glad the System seems to feel thinning hair is a deficiency, because if not, between the stress I'm dealing with and the pain, I have a feeling I'd be rather bald. "Stay or go?"

My neck gets cracked, my pacing resumes. I poke at the clothing I have—just simple jumpsuits with no defenses or anything. I eye the chair, then take a few moments to break off the feet to give me a pair of clubs. Pitiful weapons, but they might be better than nothing.

That thought is reinforced when something slams into the side of my little bubble of reality and the entire thing shakes. It's big, so, so big that it could slam into the side of a building and make it all shake—and still have mass leftover. So big, it impacts the very barrier of reality.

I gulp a little and bounce a bit more, waiting. I can't help but wonder why they let me loose, what has happened. If Mikito really did plan for this to happen, and if not, if this is my end.

They say you come to see things clearer when you're about to die, see all the regrets and opportunities you've missed. Mostly, all I feel is the boiling pit of rage within me growing, the refusal to let this be it. If I'm going to get dropped into the middle of… something, I'll go out swinging.

I mime the motions with the pair of broken sticks, waiting, my stomach curdled and angry.

Then I lurch as the entire prison cell twists and pulls, something clamping onto the dimensional plane, holding onto it with its mouth. It's very, very big mouth. I can't help but think *not again* as I'm threatened with being eaten by a monster.

Then an all-too-familiar feeling rushes through me.

And time, sped up for so long, reasserts itself once more.

I return to normal reality in the mouth of something big and nasty, just as the walls of my dimensional plane pop and everything comes crashing back together.

Hard.

***

When I talked about how things don't go so well when you return to reality without taking the proper precautions? Well, the good news is, being inside the mouth of a dimension-hopping creature actually counts as proper precautions. Most living things have some level of stability, an aura of personal reality imparted by their sentience, Mana, and the System. A dimension-hopping creature just has a lot more of it.

The bad news is that the sudden yanking from one world to another breaches the dimensional barrier keeping everything together. Everything that's contained—which definitely includes me—explodes out of the creature's mouth, causing it to roar.

That's the good news.

Yeah, being spat out of a giant monster's mouth, getting coated in saliva and stinky, half-rotten breath is good news. After all, I'm not getting swallowed or being introduced to new and novel stomach acids or finding out that said creature swallows razor blades and hardened rock to help crush what it eats.

Instead, I just fall hundreds of feet without any of my usual Skills or spells to stop me. Orientation takes a bit, my head still ringing from the roars and a piece of the table that clips me on the way out. In between the debris of the prison cell, I get my first glimpse of the ground below and Xy'largh.

The sky is blue, closer to twilight blue than the bright blue of Earth mornings. Clouds roam the skies, some of which I plunge through, the mixture of acid and water within burning my skin as I drop. So, acid rain is a thing. As are giant green conifers, some of which look like skyscrapers. It makes me wonder exactly how high I am, how the atmosphere is managing to hold up here. Then again, the entire damn planet is heavy—the gravity is at least one and a half times that of Earth normal.

All of which is another way of saying I'm falling fast with big, nasty things all around me, occasionally impacting me as I struggle to get outside of the debris field. Free falling has never been something I practiced as a human, and while I've done it a bit since the System advent, I've also had my mecha armor and flying spells.

At least, I have to admit, this planet isn't too different from Earth from up here. Grass is green, trees are green and brown, you know—the normal things. Mountains high up to the right of me, to what I'll call the west since that's where the sun is angling toward.

Oh, wait…

Suns. Two of them, neither shining that brightly, but that's different. Also, I'm catching sight of a moon in the distance, visible in daylight. I know there are multiple moons around the planet, what with them hosting more than a few stations.

All that, my brain processes in a few seconds. A ton of information, and somehow, I feel as though I'm missing something. And it's not how the saliva burns or smells, nor the way it freezes on my body as I fall.

Saliva…

I blink as I feel something shift and pop in my head and everything clears. System-assisted healing finally finishes its job and I remember what I forgot. The flying monster.

Spinning around, I catch proper sight of it at last. The giant, flying dragon that picked me up. I get a good long look at its gleaming purple and green scales, the way it arcs itself and flares its wings, the bulk of its body that makes a 747 seem small, the way its wings are huge, almost like a bat's wings but double the dragon's size.

And the claws. Smaller, grasping claws in the front for use—not too small for usefulness, like a T-rex's, but a good size to grab and grip and rend.

Then it pulls up, giant wings deploying to break its dive and curve it upward. I'm thrown around a little by the change in air flow, but the damn creature corrects itself without a problem, long razor claws the size of my body closing around my free-falling form.

I attempt to get away, but there's not much I can do, not in the middle of space, not without my Skills. It grabs me, wings deploy outward with a jerk that slams me into the edges of the claws, then we're gliding, the trees below all too close.

And somehow, I'm not dead.

***

First thought that goes through my mind is that the dragon's bringing me home for snackies. You know, like how birds will drag back prey for their chicks to feed them. Of course, bringing back live prey seems a bit much, but what do I know about the feeding and care of dragons? That's right, quite a bit.

Stupid Library.

Second thought, coming soon after that, is maybe the dragon is a friend. After all, Bolo's a Dragon Lord, which means he must have had some form of a relationship with a dragon. The entire codependent relationship between the native Xy'larghs and the dragons is, at best, messed up. Since they weren't exactly interesting for the System Quest, the Questors only have the briefest mentions of them in the library, their focus more on the actual processing of Mana through dragons.

What I do know is that young dragons are considered overactive pests and monsters. At least until they age—Level—up and gain a higher level of sapience. Due to the variety of mutations the dragons have exhibited, the way they handle their children varies too—and that includes the way they socialize with Xy'largh society.

You get the basic reptilian, non-transforming dragons who are just giant lizards with a lot of power and anger. They're the most common by far, and they are mostly egg layers. These dragons are actually the best parents, laying eggs and caring for their children until they grow up enough that they can hunt on their own. Of course, once that happens, it's the open skies for them.

Dragons—all kinds—are rather territorial, so you won't find them sharing homes very much. A mated pair is rare. The majority just go into heat, head for the closest mating grounds, get their freak on, then move onward.

Oh, by the way, if you don't know, Questors are really weird. The sheer volume of recordings of dragon mating rituals and studies I have in my head would have filled the vaults of the British Library and then some. Just... why?

Anyway. Dragons. Lots of types, mostly reptilian, but some variant combination types—some whom might not be called "true" dragons and in common parlance get translated to chimeras—and of course, you have the transforming / tamed ones.

All the things that people call Dragons, they're sort of the same, since many of the ones that can polymorph into—or start out—humanoid are also the ones most likely to work with and be the trusted steeds of a Dragon

Knight. While reptilian dragon companions do happen, it's rarer since they're also more stubborn and less likely to agree. Also, full sapience is often much, much further down the road for them, and until then, it's hard to keep a reptilian polymorph alive or tamed.

On the other hand, the reptilian dragons are much more powerful in direct combat. Stronger physical bodies, higher resistance to damage, that kind of thing. The polymorphing kind have access to spells but not Skills or Classes, so they're a little more limited. Then again—tell the four-hundred-foot-long sapient monster it's weak.

Go ahead. I won't be waiting for your return.

Long story short… this might be Bolo's friend. Or it might just be your average, high Level reptilian dragon. I can't tell, what with my Skills locked out. I struggle a little, trying to put my hands around the bracer on one wrist, hoping to pull it off.

Of course, they don't exactly want me to do that, and I feel the secondary defenses kick in. Spikes extend from within both bracers, punching through my muscles and bones to connect one side to the other. Just like that, any hope of pulling them off is gone.

I don't try for my neck. I can live—for definitions of live—with having my arms pin cushioned by finger-sized metal from the feel of it. I can't do the same if it does that to my neck.

I lie.

I can live even if the damn necklace punches metal rivets through my neck. The System will keep me up and running. Not happily mind you, not well, but it will keep me up and running. But the chances of them choosing to add something more lethal if I struggle to pull the collar off are quite high.

In fact, now that I think about it, I'm lucky they didn't link decapitation options to me trying to pull off the bracers.

I feel a chill run through my body at that thought, and it has nothing to do with the fact that we're still flying high, where oxygen and external temperatures are damnably low. I've got a bit of a pounding headache from the low oxygen levels, but again, the System keeps me up and running.

One last option right now is for me to tap into System Edit. I can swing into the Ticketing Board and potentially review the Mana flows and tickets to do with this dragon. I can't actually hurt it, what with the Skill not meant for that—especially since I don't have access to my own Skills—but more knowledge is good.

More knowledge is very, very good.

The deluge of information that comes when I tap into the dragon's Status Screen via System Edit makes my head hurt. I get everything from its names—Barachine'jaes, the Shining and Terrible One, the Blood Star, She Who Sinned—to its Titles—see above and a bunch more Slayer ones—to a whole listing of Mana flow diagrams, input and output, Mana mutation levels, and more.

I admit, I get a little lost in the diagrams about Mana flow, the way her presence affects the environmental Mana and the incredibly high variance in changes. It's like nothing I've ever seen before, not up close. Sure, I knew Xy'largh was special and I'd been watching the overall trends, but this is the first time I get to see individual details.

And it's fascinating. It also explains why the entire planet has managed to survive for so long within the Forbidden Zone.

I'm so caught up in the information, I never notice when the dragon reaches her destination and decides it's time to land. Of course, I do notice when she starts landing, what with the way she splays her wings—by the way, the entire flight thing has been rather more gentle and less bumpy than I'd expect, what with a certain portion of her entire flight being supported via Mana use—and slows down.

I crane my neck around but being clutched tight in her claws doesn't give me much of a view. All I can see is her belly, shining scales, claws, and out of the corner of my eyes, the fast-approaching stony ground around the mouth of the cave she is landing in.

Very fast approaching.

In fact, too fast.

"Oh shiiiiit!" I scream, which seems to annoy my captor.

We land with a crunch, the crunch mostly me. Bones shatter, muscle and tissue squish, then I pass out as the System's healings and my body fail.

Chapter 6

"Gentle! I said gentle!" The voice is screaming as I wake up slowly. It's a familiar voice, one I'm surprised to hear but find comforting in a distant way. I'm not exactly sure why though, as I wake slowly from dreams of chocolate fountains, a giant tiger, and a certain popular 90s blond actor feeding me chocolate-covered strawberries.

"You also said he was a Heroic. I was being gentle for a Heroic." The voice is annoyed and defensive, female too. Surprisingly, my brain translates her accent as Parisian French, which is weird since they're speaking Galactic.

"He also couldn't use his Skills!" Exasperation.

Something in that sentence… I crack my eyes open—literally since dried blood has a tendency to glue eyes shut—and try to move. Surprisingly, no pain, then I remember the System would have fixed that. Well, all but my arms, which have something embedded in them. No collar, no bracers. Something pulled those off which is good.

Except that's not painful either.

"Aaargh!" Harry—that's another familiar voice—screams as I lurch upright.

He's still in the process of jumping a good ten feet away from me, his body in the air. The rest of the surroundings I take in quickly, everything from Bolo arguing with a svelte young woman with big curling horns like his to Mikito standing guard at the door and a Yerrick a short distance away, arms crossed and looking tired.

Also, I take in the dark grey, granite walls, the bioluminescent moss, the hard stone floor, and the impact points where dragon claws hit the earth and walked in, digging in. Interestingly enough, the claw marks disappear on the way in, the front claws and streak of blood dissipating first, then the back claws eventually. The streak of blood on the ground leads all the way to me, which doesn't surprise me.

What I don't see is the dragon.

Or, as my brain catches up, I do.

"Finally. What took you so long to wake?" the Yerrick asks, glaring at me as he pushes off the wall. It's a little weird to see the minotaur with his horns broken off, but even more so, the bare patches about his hairy body.

I casually scan him, blinking in surprise when I read his Status.

Xaxas Stormfist, Planet Breaker, Genocidal, Tidebreaker, Slayer of Truinnar, Movana, Hakarta, Yerrick, Grimsar, Naiads, Pooskeen, Jaracks, ... (more) ; Level 41 Storm Warden (H)
HP: N/A
MP: N/A
Conditions: N/A

My eyes narrow a little, the Library finding his name and a few details. Most prominently, his disappearance decades ago.

Among my many Skills, the Eye of Insight cuts through most Skills lower leveled than it, which isn't hard to beat if you're a Heroic, but still... That he has something blocking me from reading his information at this point, when we've been stripped of our usual weapons and enchantments, is rather amazing. Probably a bought Skill, but still annoying.

"I said..."

I tune out whatever else the Yerrick has to say. It's not as though whatever he wants to talk about is that important. Instead, with my Skills and abilities back, I cast, dropping some of my usual buffs on me. Soul Shield for obvious reasons, but immediately after, I make sure the various purchased Skills I've got are active, everything from Harden to Elastic Skin to Peasant's Fury. I also cast Haste and activate Thousand Steps, Vanguard of the Apocalypse, Immovable Object, and lastly, Domain.

Just in time for the hairy behemoth to smash into me. A fraction of a second before he hits me, I hunch down, dropping my weight so that when I fall backward, leg sprawling behind me and then lift upward, I'm under the Yerrick. A hand between and beneath his legs, jutting out, helps complete the impromptu throw, putting him over my shoulder.

Of course, someone called the Planet Breaker isn't going down easily. In mid-air, he punches me hard enough that it breaks my Soul Shield, overrides Immovable Object and my own control of the earth via my Strength attribute, and sends me careening through space into the nearby cavern wall.

The rock wall, surprisingly, doesn't do much more than crack. Considering the amount of force he put into the attack, I would have expected to have made a much bigger impact. On the other hand, it was more of a love tap than a serious attack. He didn't even put any of his major Skills into it.

Not that he's letting me off easy either. By the time I bounce off the wall, land on the ground, and start rising, he's in front of me. Standing at nearly eight feet tall, he's small for a Yerrick, but still a heck of a lot bigger than me. Each blow he throws with his sledgehammer-sized fist hits like I'm a scrawny Chinese kid up against Mike Tyson. He rattles my teeth, hurts my arms, and cracks my ribs.

I ride out the flurry of attacks, sucking up the pain and ignoring how my health keeps dropping. The System does its best to patch me together, but there's only so much it can do, and if I don't make a move soon, I won't be able to. Which is when he starts flagging.

Big guy, high level of Stamina, it's not a physical thing. It's a rhythm thing, where your brain does a little stutter because no one really trains to just keep hitting and hitting and hitting without stop, without a break. You can't. Most fights, you have multiple enemy combatants, other monsters on the way. You stop, check your surroundings, just for a fraction of a second maybe, but it's a gap.

Enough of one that I can act.

Rather than kick or attempt to get away, I step in. Big minotaur means he's got a big reach, but deep inside his own guard, he's got a bit more of a problem reaching. I hunker down, make myself smaller as I launch a series of punches. Not hooks like he threw into me, that rock me from side to side, but straight punches. Chain punches, with that little flick of the wrist upward just after impact to add a little twisting momentum to put the energy of my attack deeper.

The attack comes in on the center line, slamming into the Yerrick and pushing his broad, hairy chest backward. I hit him a dozen times in a second, each punch landing with enough momentum and force to reset his brain, to keep him reeling. Even as he steps away to give himself space to reset, I follow and follow and follow.

Until, of course, I run out of momentum myself and Xaxas headbutts me. Lacking horns, it's not as dangerous as it could be, but the long lacerations from the broken-off horns leave me bleeding freely and staggering back.

I thrust out a hand, in case he comes after me, but instead, he's stepped backward. Frowning as I wipe away the blood, the reason for his hesitation is quite clear and pointed.

"What are you two doing?" Mikito sounds unhappy. Very, very unhappy.

"Getting to know one another." I eye Hitoshi, the Legacy weapon, the Soul Drinker, that she holds. One of the rarest kinds of weapon around because of how powerful it can grow over time. Now, it's between the two of us, its tiny Japanese wielder glaring at us both.

"By fighting one another?" Mikito says, exasperated. "Fine. You're a baka. I get that. Why didn't you stop them?" Now, she's glaring at Bolo.

The Dragon Lord doesn't exactly shrink from her regard, but the slight hunching of his nine-foot-tall frame is still noticeable to those of us tinier than him. He's dressed in his emerald scalemail as usual, his curling ram horns gleaming and pristine the way only a Cleanse spell can do. No hammer, but I'm assuming it's tucked away in his inventory for now.

"They were fighting by the rules. I do not understand why you are angry?" Bolo says.

"What rules? They were just fighting!" Mikito says.

"There were rules," I protest.

The Storm Warden nods in agreement, making Mikito frown.

"What rules?" She looks between the men, who all offer her nods, before turning to the last female of the group, who looks askance at Mikito.

"For the establishment of rank, of course," the dragon woman says. "They are quite well understood by all true warriors."

That makes Mikito freeze, her eyes growing cold.

Recognizing the signs, I cough. "It's actually ummm… roughhousing rules. Modified. You know, barroom brawls, chest bumping…"

"No." Mikito takes the out kindly enough and turns to me, dismissing the dragon lady who doesn't seem to pick up on the fact that she has been dismissed. She just looks satisfied still. "I don't. I don't do barroom brawls."

"Right, right." I rub the back of my neck, then feeling the stickiness, I cast a Cleanse on myself. Weird that Ali… "Shit."

The single word makes everyone tense and focus on me.

"What?" Bolo snaps.

"Ali." I'm already recalling him, pulling Mana from the System and throwing it at the rift that needs opening. Seconds later, it opens, and a glowing dot appears, tumbling out of it.

The dot spins round and round before slowly stabilizing, glowing so bright I have to squint to look at it. After a few seconds, it begins to contract, portions of a familiar form appearing. Thankfully, he chooses to appear fully clothed in his usual orange jumpsuit—which, even if entirely unflattering, is at least clothed. He's done nude Ali before to make me uncomfortable but seems to prefer this form for some reason.

"About damn time, boy-o," Ali grumbles, arms crossed, legs in lotus position as he floats over to me. Even as I stare at him, I notice how portions of him fritz out, becoming pure energy before snapping back into place.

"You okay?"

"I'll live. Because, you know, Spirit. Can't actually die," Ali says. "On the other hand, it wasn't entirely comfortable where I was right now."

Ali's appearance doesn't do much to my team. They're all used to him. Even dragon lady doesn't seem bothered by the appearance of the Spirit. She was probably informed of him long ago. To my surprise, it's the Storm Warden who reacts the most, his jaw dropping and an almost reverential look appearing in his eyes as he stares at Ali.

"Oh." I flick a gaze over to the Storm Warden, and decide to leave it. Not something I care to pursue. Not now, possibly not ever. "Exactly what—"

"Not talking about it," Ali says. "Also, not the time."

Now, I tense too. Moments later, the rest of the team snaps their heads toward the north. I'm sure they're picking up what I'm seeing on my minimap. A bunch of little hostile red dots.

"Guys, we're missing someone…" I look about for the robot. I hope they grabbed it. I hope they didn't just leave it behind. Then again, perhaps Ezz is better off without me.

"I have him." Mikito waves.

"Where?"

"Inventory."

I open my mouth to protest, point out it's not Inventory—but then again, it wasn't sapient, was it? So dropping Ezz into Inventory should be viable. It does raise questions, some of which I'm not sure I want answers to.

"Oy! Boy-o. Time to move," Ali says, snapping me out of my thoughts.

I nod, flashing a last glance at the minimap and wincing.

Looks like trouble has arrived.

***

Ali does so much for me, from cleaning up my interface to translating strange concepts and populating things like my minimap and adjusting System time to local time that I don't even think about it. He doesn't either, in many ways. A lot of the things he offers me are just part of the Linked bond.

Some things aren't though. "You going to get dressed, boy-o?"

"In what? They stripped my inventory and Altered Storage," I say.

Annoying that there are Classes that can go into other people's normally secure Inventory and steal things from it. There are a variety of Skills, some of which randomly pull things from Inventories, others with a more focused theft ability. It all depends on the Skill level and how much time the thief has.

In my captors' case, a lot of time. They just let loose an Adventurer's Bane on me, who picked at my Inventory until it was all gone, pulling out any random bit. Lots of chocolate obviously, but a bunch of toys I've picked up, including things I no longer use, like my Toothy Returning Blades and my Anklet of Dispersed Damage.

"You do remember how we dropped the Spitzrocket back into its own dimension?" Ali says. I nod, and he continues. "Well, it's still there."

"They didn't steal it?" I'm surprised, I'll admit.

"Nah, Spitzrocket keeps everything in a highly guarded location with the Grimsar Clans. They might consider him a bit of a loon, but the Grimsar won't let anyone steal a Grandmaster work from their guarded dimensional spaces," Ali says. "Bad for their reputations, you know?"

I grunt my agreement even as I reach out sideways, tapping into the dimensional layer where the Spitzrocket's mainframe manufacturing facility is located. It comes to me faster than expected, appearing around my body and slamming shut within a breath.

It's comforting to be armed and armored again, even as I conjure up my sword. There are many reasons why people like Soulbound weapons, and never being entirely unarmed features highly among them.

"We staying to fight or going?" I ask.

The Yerrick is cracking his neck, rotating his shoulders, and grinning a little in anticipation, while Bolo has strode over to Harry and is slapping armor onto the man. It's a weird sight, since they're solid pieces of armor up until the last second, when they open up enough to let limbs or torso enter before shutting themselves once more. Liquid metal armor of some form. Highly flexible, very expensive, and generally, less durable than the rigid kind.

Mikito, standing by the entrance to the cave, is staring outward. Not that we can see the enemy just yet. Then again, if we could see them, it'd be too late to run. "We go."

"No fighting?" Xaxas sounds disappointed.

"Not now," Mikito says.

"So how are we doing this?" I say.

"Portals," Bolo says.

"Yeah, I got no waypoints around here," I say. "Not left my cell, remember?"

"Not you. Me," the woman says, striding over.

Now that Ali's here, I take the time to really look at her Status information, knowing he'll populate as much as he can for me.

Yllis Haleygsson, Kin Breaker, Heretic, Outcast, Level 174
HP: 17720/17720
MP: 5110/5110
Conditions: Dragon Fear, Mana Well, Mana Conjunction, Probably Warp

I cock my head, surprised by the Titles. Then I look at her and Bolo, how familiar the pair are with one another, the occasional physical touch. Not that there's anything wrong with dragon and sapient relations—it's supposedly common. Still… something is going on there.

For once, I realize that my lack of interest in others might be biting me in the ass. I just don't know enough about why Bolo was exiled to understand what is going on. And, more importantly, there isn't time to get into it.

Yllis waves her hand in a circle, and a short distance away, a Portal appears. It looks exactly like mine, which is rather a surprise. My eyes narrow, and for a moment, I get a flicker of the System notification, which isn't particularly useful, calling it a "Teleportation Spell v29871." Sadly, there are so many versions of Teleportation Spells that when the spells are free-formed, the System can only do so much.

"Well? You going?" Yllis says, staring at me challengingly. "We risked everything to get you out. I'd prefer not to have to repeat that assault. As it is…"

"As it is, the Galaxy will be dealing with the prisoners who survived for many years to come," Bolo says, his eyes darkening.

Ali's got his head tilted, staring mostly at Harry, whose lips are moving a little while he relates what's happened in the last few weeks. I kind of want that explanation too, but now's not the time.

I stride over to the Portal, glancing one last time at the minimap. Those dots are moving fast. "I thought the point of ejecting us was to make sure we got lost and died in the secondary dimensions."

"You survived, didn't you?" Yllis says sarcastically.

My foot passes through the Portal, popping me into our new destination, all while I'm mentally admitting the lady has a point. And from what I know of the prison, I'm not even the most powerful prisoner—just the most annoying.

Somehow, as my body gets torn apart and tossed through time and space into a new location, I know I'm going to get blamed for the escapees too.

Chapter 7

It doesn't take long for the rest of the team to stream through the Portal. The moment they do, Yllis shuts down the teleportation circle and opens another. I don't have to ask as I jump through again, even as I watch Bolo pull a Manaswarm Grenade from his inventory.

Our first stop was on a high cliff face overlooking a calm blue-green sea. Far below, I see a group of monsters snarling and tearing at one another, fighting over the newborn pulling themselves out of the cluster of eggs they are born from.

The second stop is not where I expect us to be, the cold metal platform and the wisps of cloud a surprise. As is the lack of a railing when I nearly fall off the edge to plummet the thousands of kilometers to the ground. The entire floating blimp platform sits in the clouds, just bobbing along, while behind me, I see dozens of other sapients—mostly native Xy'larghs with a few harpies and other aerial sapients mixed in—crowded around a drinking shack.

Then the Portal slams shut and another opens and we're headed for the next stop. Wilderness clearing, where a really annoyed cat-lizard hybrid monster attempts to tear off my face. I skewer it, kick it around a bit, then kill it before looting the body and dumping the corpse in my Altered Storage. It makes me rather happy to have something in there.

Underwater cave. I hate that one, even if the Spitzrocket keeps me from getting wet. Sonar kicks in, giving me "sight" along with the lights. More monsters, though these flee at the sight of us. I catch a glimpse of something much bigger coming down one of the many openings though, an eel-like thing, just before I step through again.

Dozens of Portals and new locations, each one charted by Ali and me. The Spirit has his hands full trying to populate my minimap and give me directions. Not that I want to reuse these locations once we're gone, but it's good to have some places on my map of the planet. It's rather scattershot—we even end up in the middle of the air at one point, free-falling until I cast a Fly spell to hover and another Portal opens up beneath me.

More than once, we pop up near monsters, but one thing I'm quickly realizing is that Xy'largh is huge. Like, Jupiter-sized. Which would make you think it's got a rather ridiculous gravity but, obviously, it doesn't. That's because it has a hollow center of sorts.

No, it doesn't make scientific sense. We're in the middle of the Forbidden Zone, remember? A lot of the planet doesn't make sense, not after all the Mana warping the planet and its surroundings have gone through. I have a feeling thanks to the poor Mana translation effects of pre-System Earth, that's where Jules Verne got his inspiration from for his famous story. Then again, human imagination is wild.

Rule 34 and all, after all.

Eventually, we stop, Yllis striding forward without a word as I stand before the empty cliff face. She waves and the entire wall swings open, revealing the chamber within. She doesn't stop, walking right in, so I follow her.

The moment I enter, my connection to the outside world and my minimap shuts down, Mana blocking enchantments and materials shutting things down. Even as I look around, tense, the door slams shuts behind us, sealing us within.

***

Yllis is at a console, tapping away and viewing the information that pops up. Ali floats over, and other than a momentary glare, the woman ignores the Spirit. While Ali's doing that, I'm reaching outward with my own senses, testing the defenses and sealing properties. It's fascinating to me how this entire thing works.

The safe house—and I'm certain that's what this is—is not entirely blocked off from the System. Can't really do that when Mana is included. Instead, it cheats by creating a Forbidden Zone within, by using selective filtering of Mana. Basically, it keeps any System Mana out and forcibly expels it at a higher-than-normal rate while pulling in unaspected Mana.

Contrary to belief, there are fewer mutations within because the unaspected Mana is forcibly converted to System Mana at a high speed, which is then expelled and returned to the System with only a portion used to keep the entire thing running. It's incredibly inefficient and I can tell—just by eyeing the Mana Batteries, materials, and enchantments within—that it's incredibly expensive.

But it's also an artificial, mechanical way of creating a Forbidden Zone, locking out System shenanigans except the donation clause. It even bypasses the entire thing of leaving a gap in the System's senses since there is a large amount of Mana being donated. For all intents and purposes, this place looks like any other non-magical location to anyone looking at it from outside—unless, of course, you're right on top of it.

I take a few more minutes to spin through the code before exiting the System, finding that the team has spread themselves out. To my surprise, there's a pile of items in one corner: an assortment of firearms, explosives, simple armored jumpsuits, and regular clothing. Right next to the pile are a bunch of chocolates.

Speaking of chocolates, Harry is wandering toward me, a box of chocolates in hand and a worried look on his face. "John…"

"So did you help them get in and choose not to tell me because of the listeners or did you just get dragged along again?" I say, cutting through the bullshit and not taking the peace offering.

My words make the man flinch, the lines across his brow deepening for a long second. I don't relent, staring at him.

He opens his mouth to reply, croaks a little, and has to visibly swallow some saliva before he answers. "I didn't. Help them, that is."

I stare at the man for a few more minutes, then nod and grab the box from him. I pop one of the pieces into my mouth—roasted almond bits in a dark chocolate covering—and speak around it. "Whatever. So why the look? You changed your mind again? You on our side once more?"

"I never left!" Harry shouts, glaring at me. "I've always been your friend."

"Mmm…" I'm giving him a hard time, but there's a point to it. "So, you coming?"

Harry straightens with a nod. "Yeah. Yes. Damn it, yes. I want to come."

"Why?"

"What do you mean why? This is the biggest story out there!" Harry waves a hand around. "If they still gave out Pulitzers, I'd be showered with them for covering it."

"But they don't. Instead, they'll probably shower you with knives and other spiky instruments," I say. "If you're lucky. You have an out. You could leave, wander into a city—or get dropped off—and just stop. Why keep risking it?"

"Because I'm a reporter!" Harry's shaking a little from the emotions flowing through him. Whether it's fear or anger, I'm not sure. I'm not entirely sure he knows either. "It's what I do. It's what we dream of. Covering something important, putting out information that can change the world and the people who live in it. Whether it's a war in a far-off country that no one can bloody name or place without a map, or a single refugee scrabbling to put food on the table. It's what we do. What makes us tick."

"At the cost of your life?"

"*Yes!*" Harry shouts, getting right into my face. "At the cost of my life. What kind of life do I have anyway? Any of us do, after the System came? I don't have a girlfriend or mother or father anymore. My son's dead, my sister so shell-shocked by what we had to do that she can't, won't talk to me anymore. Because I'm a reminder of the world we lost. What do I have left to lose?"

I open my mouth to point out he still has his life, a potentially very long one too. Mikito is watching us quietly, and even Bolo and Yllis are curious. The only person who looks bored is the Yerrick rooting through the piles of equipment and pocketing stuff for his own use.

"It's not..."

Harry doesn't even notice my aborted attempt at speaking. "So yeah, I'm afraid. I'm tired of being dragged along, forced to make decisions about what to do at the drop of a hat. Forced to weigh risks and feel like I'm putting everyone, everything I care about—care in the abstract, because Lord knows, we don't have anyone left in reality—everything I care about in danger if I refuse. Or agree. Or both.

"But at least it's better than... nothing. There's nothing on Earth for me. Just memories of a better time, of what-ifs. If I hadn't chosen to cover that peace summit, if I had just stayed home for once. Maybe I could have saved them. Maybe I could have done something more than watch my entire world burn down."

His chest is heaving, his breathing hard as he finishes. Tears are tracking down his face. The only sound in the room is his heavy breathing and the clink of items dropping to the floor as the Storm Warden keeps browsing.

"So yeah, I'll come. Because I'm tired of being scared. And if I die, so what? Maybe the youngsters, those who didn't grow up with a world that only lives in their dreams now, maybe they can move on. Maybe they can forget lazy nights at home, catching a match on the telly or having pints with your mates at the local. But I can't.

"I can't."

The last words are a whisper, one that threatens to break my heart. He lost—we lost—so much. For the first time, I realize maybe I'm not the only one who can't move on. Maybe Harry and Mikito left not just because there was a better story or because I was going, but because out here, the memories are a little weaker. The pain, less common.

Never gone though.

That doesn't change.

"All right then." I put a hand on his shoulder, give him a squeeze, and drop it long before it gets uncomfortable for me or him.

Harry stalks off, and I'm left with a box of chocolates and a realization that I'm a narcissistic ass.

Then again, what's new?

***

We gather around the living room, taking seats wherever we can find one, twenty minutes later. I want to see Ezz, figure out what's wrong with him, if there is an Ezz left, but it's not the time. Not yet.

Once I was done with my chocolates and had fought off Xaxas's raiding of my pile, I managed to reequip myself with my much depleted standard loadout. A half dozen types of grenades, a couple of mines, and a few temporary force shields, along with a lot of clothing, temporary shelters, and food. Basic adventuring gear. Everything else, from my enchanted equipment to the remnants of Sabre, is lost.

I'm not happy about that, but thankfully, the most expensive piece of gear I had was Spitzrocket. Unconsciously, for the most part, I had been following one of the more common combat methods—one that relies more on Skills and spells with only a few, very expensive pieces of equipment. Mikito followed a similar build, especially since she had Hitoshi to rely upon.

Others shift the math the other way, focusing on multiple different pieces of gear, none of them too expensive but still level appropriate. Bolo and, to my surprise, Harry are prime examples of that kind of fighting style. Well, not fighting in Harry's case, but you know, equipping style. Bolo's hammer is Soulbound, but his armor, helm, gauntlets, and even boots are all items he upgrades as necessary. In the armor's case, even if it doesn't look new, it's an entirely new piece from the one he wore the last time we worked together. It just came from the same crafter.

Harry, on the other hand, keeps a wide variety of equipment but all of it cheaply bought for the level and specialized in its effects. He's more the use-and-toss method, with multiple backups. I know from experience he's the kind to have multiple defensive equipment in place, mostly focused to deal with area effect Skills. His Skills might keep him hidden and out of the direct line of fire in most fights, but it doesn't help if someone drops the equivalent of a nuke.

All that being said, having the Spitzrocket means I'm not all the way down. I'll still be nowhere near as effective as I was, what with some of my borrowed Skills gone, but the Spitzrocket will have to do. Just like the map that Ali pops into space to answer the question I've been asked.

"… and that is where we're going. Not that I really know much about the local geography, but I figure that's where you come in, Bolo." Then, glancing at Yllis, I add, "And you, of course."

"No," she says flatly.

"No, what?"

"We're not doing this. Dragging you out of your damn prison was bad enough, but at least we knew it was a survivable action. This, this is just suicide," Yllis replies.

"Why?" Mikito asks.

"There be dragons," I intone, drawing a smile from the humans and eyerolls from the others. I don't stop, of course. "Wake not sleeping dragons, for you are small and crunchy. Or am I not reading the Mana level reports right?"

"There are no dragons there," Yllis states coldly.

"Then what is the problem?" Harry asks, though a tightness to his eyes says that he's waiting for the next shoe to drop.

Ali beats us to the shoe drop, even as Bolo opens his mouth. I note he's been deferring to Yllis a bit so far. Ah, interpersonal relationships. Always lovely little conundrums of pain and heartache. It's why I blow all of mine up with napalm and run away cackling as the flames beat on my back.

"What scares dragons?" the Spirit says.

"Nothing!" Yllis says. "We're just not stupid enough to wander into a hive of Voowmah."

"Hive? Voowmah?" I mutter, prodding the Library. I'm surprised I've never heard of them or gotten a download before now. If they can scare dragons, they have to be something.

No surprise that the Library decides to answer with the something. A lot of something.

The Voowmah is just the name the dragons use. They have a lot of names, a lot of different, terrifying names—World Devourers, Civilization's End, the Hunger are just the nicer ones—but most call them the Swarm. And that name, I know. I've had downloads of them before, a lot of them, though mostly on a sideways notation.

Now I get the full history, though there are surprisingly few direct reports. One of the disadvantages of them being mostly a Forbidden Zone monster / sapient type. No one's entirely certain if the Voowmah are pure monsters or System-enabled sapients or something in between. It's not as though they're great conversationalists, being more the mate-and-devour type.

First sightings started thousands of years ago, nearly at the same time as the dragons themselves. Unlike the dragons, who have formed their own civilizations and even managed to gain some semblance of acceptance—at least on Xy'largh—with sapient creatures, the Voowmah never have.

Mutated insects, their home planet long lost to time, they jet through space in ships made of the corpses of their people tens of kilometers long and wide. Occasionally, a few monsters are sacrificed to guide them along the floating waves of Mana, using the System's need to transfer and churn Mana and Mana's own propensity to collect around the living to guide them.

Eventually, they find a living planet. They hit the planet, shedding and burning the dead bodies of their people until only those who have hibernated through the flight are left, forced awake from the heat. Eventually, they hit land, kill a few hundred more of their people, and create a zone of devastation from the landing.

Then they start eating.

Each ship starts with lower Levels on the outside and the core of the hive—high Level, mutated forms—within the central area. Most hive ships are easy to handle at the start, as the low-Levels, many suffering cold and re-entry damage, are taken down. That works for the Voowmah though, since that fattens up the native populace and monsters.

Then the core comes out and the real nightmare begins. Creatures that have lived hundreds, sometimes thousands, of years, with the Levels to boot. Like most hive creatures, they've got a wide variety of types, specialized fighters who Level in their own roles. Mages, sneaky types, upfront vanguards, and drone warriors. Worse than their individual strength is their coordination.

Scholars still debate if it's a true hive mind, or just a weird Skill that gives them their ability to work together. It doesn't matter to warriors. We just know it's a pain in the ass.

You're struggling with one of their people, pushing back and maybe holding your own. Then out of the ground, creatures erupt and grab your legs. Hold you still, just for a few fractions of a second. You break free, but it costs you some hit points, maybe a cut here or there. Then as you set up for the fight with your original opponent, they're gone.

And someone else, someone who can hard counter your particular Skills, comes. Use a lot of Penetration Skills, that's fine. Here's a warrior who has stacked Resistances rather than armor, making your Penetration less useful. Add in a massive regeneration rate and you're suddenly struggling with the single man.

You fight it out for a bit, the bastard taking forever for you to wear down. Whatever. They keep sending useless drones out of the earth, grabbing your legs, pulling at your arms. Slowing you down. You win, maybe you even kill your opponent.

Then another one comes. Maybe they trade in, maybe they replace. Doesn't matter, because the next time you're in the middle of a struggle, something grabs your legs once more. You react as they have taught you to do, pulling at your legs, thinking it'll be easy to break free. Oops—it's a high-Leveled grabber, a shield Swarm-member.

And suddenly, you can't move. Can't break free. You're experienced of course, a real fighter. It only takes you by surprise for a second, maybe less. It doesn't matter though, because they've got an Assassin Voowmah behind you, putting a tentacle through your back, the warrior in front of you gripping your face with his suckers and slurping out your eyes.

You try to run, but of course they've got anti-teleport Voowmah on hand, all of them piled up ready for you. They grab you, drag you down, kill you. Maybe they sacrificed a few hundred minions, a couple of mid or high-Level monsters.

It doesn't matter, because they consume you and Level themselves.

And then they go on and eat the rest of your family, the rest of your planet. Consuming every single iota of biomass until there's nothing but them on the planet. Then they pull together again, form one of their dead ships, and blast off to find another planet.

I shudder, tearing myself free of the memories, the recordings that play through my mind. Some sick bastard put all of that into the Library, Tithing his memories, his last few minutes of himself and his people to the System. As a warning, as a promise of what was to come. It's a great and pointed lesson. Which leaves me with just one question.

"Why is Xy'largh still here?" I say. "If they came for you guys, why are you still alive?"

Bolo snorts. "We are not easy prey, Redeemer. Not easy prey at all."

"Two. There have been exactly two cases of the Swarm being beaten back. The first had a trio of Legendarys on hand. Including Ell's and his planet. After he rammed his planet into one side, the other two got to work before the Swarm landed. The other case was exactly the same. The Swarm ran right into the fixed defenses of Irvina and the Galactic Council that was meeting at the time. They never even managed to land since the Weaver had figured out they were coming long before anyone else ever had." I pause, my eyes narrowing. "And you're saying Xy'largh beat them by themselves?"

"In a sense," Bolo says. "They came when they were much younger, before they became the Swarm, the World Devourers they are now. They fought my ancestors and the Ancients, the dragons of yore. It was, in a way, the very act that forged our bond."

I pause, eyes narrowing as suspicion grows about the place they're pointing at on the map. "Wait. Let me see if I get this right. You beat them, but not all of them. They landed, tore up a lot of ground, but you managed to eventually contain them. And then, as a sign of... what? Your new friendship and alliance between one another, you left the rest live?"

A slight pause as the two natives share a look. One filled with a slight amount of embarrassment but more, with exasperation at the tourist simplifying their history.

"It's not that simple," Bolo says. "The war had damaged our people, such that it was decided to wait until an opportune time came to deal with them. Driving out the last vestiges, including the Egg Layers, would have seen them release whatever doomsday scenarios they had. And we're certain there are some."

I grunt in acknowledgement.

"What scenarios?" Mikito says, frowning.

While I was busy getting a data download, I vaguely recall Ali giving them all a brief rundown of what the Swarm really is. No one needed the sheer volume of detail I'd received to understand "*Swarm bad. Do not disturb.*"

"They travel through space. How do you think they do that?" I say.

"By using their dead bodies," Harry says, frowning. "Isn't that what Ali just said?"

"Sure, for the structure and body, yeah. But how do they steer?"

There's silence at that question, before the Yerrick, having grown bored with the entire Q&A we've been doing, answers simply. "The Swarm have dedicated anti-matter members that form and create chain reactions in their bodies. Consuming the flesh of their own, they power the anti-matter thrusters to drive them onward."

"Exactly," Bolo says. "And in the event of potential losses, to defend their Egg Layers, those anti-matter specializers will destroy themselves."

"So you just leave them alive? To Level?" I frown, shaking my head. That makes no sense.

"We go in and cleanse them once in a while. Deal with their numbers and high-Levels. There are numerous bounties involved, and of course, their bodies are highly prized," Bolo replies. "It is a common way for those of the lower Class to gain the necessary Skills and Levels to survive." He touches his scalemail. "And their skin can be quite useful."

"Wait, that's not dragon scale?" I say.

My words horrify both Bolo and Yllis. "You think I would wear a dragon's skin?"

"What kind of barbarian are you, to wear the skin of a friend?" Yllis says, recoiling from me.

I open my mouth to explain D&D and Earth folklore, then snap my mouth shut. There's utterly nothing I could say that would make what I said better. So instead, I change tack.

"You make it sound like people go in all the time. So what's the problem with us going in?" I say.

"Because your System Administrator Center is in the heart of their nest," Yllis says.

"Oh. Yeah, okay, that tracks," I say resignedly.

That's just about right, really.

Chapter 8

I wish I could say the resulting conversation did not involve a lot of shouting and even more grumbling, whining, and pleading. The last two mostly by me. The Storm Warden wanders away after a while, utterly bored with the discussion. I never get around to asking what the heck he's still doing with us, since the argument goes on until late at night before Bolo declares the conversation over and walks deeper into the cave-system-slash-safe-house, followed by Yllis.

Truth be told, I'd love to tell them we don't have to go. But I don't exactly have any other leads, and while I might be able to access another System Administrator Center, doing so is a huge risk. It's not one I'm willing to take unless all our other options are out.

Including walking into a Valley of Certain Death.

And really, it's not a Valley of Certain Death, but more a Valley of Certain Death without a Full Flight of Dragons and a few Ancient Dragons Backing You Up. See, even the Dragon Kings—because you didn't bring anything but Heroics with you—and dragons know better than to let the damn Voowmah grow without check. So every century or so, they get together and burn the nest to the ground again, killing a bunch of high Level Voowmah along the way, then back out.

All very ritualized and civilized.

Kind of like changing the detonators on a nuclear warhead. You got to do it every once in a while, because you don't want them to explode on you by accident. But it's still a butt-clenching exercise, with lots of caution and careful, detailed steps involved. And not, you know, done by your local yahoo off a random street corner with a spanner in hand and grease on his pants with the tenner you slipped him sticking out of a pocket.

If you haven't guessed, I have absolutely no idea how nukes work.

Just like I don't really have a clue how to convince my allies that we need to do this. It's why I'm seated at the dining room table alone, hours later. Ali went invisible after the first hour of me prodding him for help and a debrief, muttering something about needing to finish *Forever Knight*.

I don't have the heart to tell him.

That's where Mikito finds me. The tiny—really, just over five feet or so—Japanese lady doesn't say a thing while she brews both of us a pot of tea, using some of her precious green tea from home before setting the cups before me. I sip the drink in silence, enjoying the heat and warmth, not even scalding my tongue on the boiling water. Yay Resistances.

"They'll come around," Mikito says eventually.

"They? Not you?" I reply.

"You know I go where you go," she replies easily.

I don't even wince at that pronouncement, not anymore. I've given up on trying to get her to give up on that line of thought. And truth be told, I rely on her. The way you rely on your dominant hand, missing it when it's gone. Yeah, I really do hate losing limbs.

"Then thank you," I say.

She sniffs at me, her nose wrinkling a little as she does. I can almost hear the word she wants to say, but she doesn't. Which is rather nice of her.

"How'd you do it?" I say instead, changing the topic.

"Mmmm... with difficulty." Mikito sips the tea for a second, making me wait. "The first problem was locating your prison. Thankfully, that just required a few missions for one of the elder Dragons that Yllis knew. Then we had to find a way to draw away enough of their reinforcements for the break-in..."

I listen intently as Mikito weaves, in her simple and straightforward way, a tale of intense planning, cunning, and numerous side missions to free me. Everything from finding allies in the most unlikely of places, individuals who wanted revenge or to free another within, to suborning members of the guards to gain information on the prison itself.

A long tale, one filled with numerous hijinks and always, always rushed so that they could pull things together. The fact that they managed to weave together the shaky alliance that managed to break into the prison, set free a number of the individuals within before they ejected the rest of us, and more importantly, plan for the ejection to retrieve me is a wonder.

It's also a testament to how hard the Galactic Council has been suppressing the races and empires. There were, for sure, individuals within the prison who deserved to be captured and contained. Many who needed to die really—and boy, was the knowledge of who was there helpful in gaining allies—but others had just crossed the Council in one way or another and been unjustly captured.

Among them, the Storm Warden.

"What is his story?" I say, once she winds down. I gesture with my head toward where the big Yerrick is sitting near the entrance, meditating. The big minotaur, seated cross-legged, breathing slowly as tiny thunderstorms form around his body, unleashing lightning that bounces off wet fur, is quite the sight. And smell. Wet cow in close quarters is not a great smell, though I'm not going to mention it to the Yerrick.

"Rebellion," Mikito says simply.

I frown, but the Library has nothing to offer. Civil disobedience and history is only a passing interest to the Questors. And with literal tens of thousands of years of history involved in the Galactic Council, there's only so much space devoted to something like that.

"So, he going to leave us or…?" I trail off, uncertain why he'd bother to follow us. In fact, I'm not entirely sure why Bolo or Yllis are willing to help us further, though I know Bolo feels he owes me something. Personally, I consider us fair and square, but I won't argue about additional help.

"I do not know. I do not think he has a place to go back to though," she replies. "His nation was destroyed after they 'killed' him, leaving them vulnerable to be taken by his rivals. His people scattered. You know the rest of his story, yes?"

I nod. I recall Capstan, the story of their people. Their planet overrun, their people scattered and forced to live as mercenaries and refugees the world over. Small clans attempting to reestablish themselves wherever they could. It was an object lesson I had taken to heart early on, one that made me try to head off the same fate for humanity.

That thought turned to what I did recently, the way I had betrayed Earth. Sure, my reasoning had been sound in my mind. I needed to put Earth back into a footing where they might struggle now, but at least they weren't wasting resources trying to play the same damn political game that was stacked against them from the start anyway.

Now, the rules for Earth are gone, the stakes clear, and the pieces revealed. They can either fight and win or roll over and let the various corporations, guilds, mini kingdoms, and other interest groups take Earth over. They had ten years to build up, grow in strength. Now, they have to prove themselves.

Or so I tell myself.

"A man out of time and place." There's a trace of sadness in my voice, one that I'm surprised to hear. It takes me a few seconds to realize that sadness is also laced with understanding, because that's what I am too in a way. What most of us humans are.

"A powerful ally." Mikito finishes the tea in her cup and refills it, glancing at my mostly untouched cup.

I down it at her glance and nod thanks as she refills it. "We need all the help we can get." I pause, then let loose the thought that worries me most of all. "If they know where we're going… if they can find us. I don't think they'll hold back. Not anymore."

"Legendarys." She speaks the word I fear to.

I nod.

"Can we beat them?"

"Depends on the Legendary, I guess. If they aren't paying attention, if they aren't too powerful, if they don't have too many defensive enchantments, if they didn't put too many points into their Constitution or Resistances…" I know how dumb I sound.

"No, then."

I reluctantly nod. The problem isn't just the health most Legendarys have or even the passive Resistances many Classes get. It's the fact that most Legendarys have taken decades, if not centuries, to reach their level and have stayed there, meaning they've had the chance to buy and upgrade the enchantments keeping them alive. And, obviously, keeping themselves alive is rather important, so most have a variety of methods to do so.

Even the Weaver, whose entire Class doesn't involve doing damage, is enough to take us down. Or, at the very least, she has the ability to run away from us before we can kill her. But the simple fact is, they won't be sending any of the non-damage dealers to stop us.

"Who do you think they'll send?" Mikito asks.

"Some Senior Admins. Hopefully that bitch…" I snarl, rage flashing through me for a second. I have to push it down, though it's a struggle.

She doesn't even flinch at the abrupt spike of anger, somewhat used to me. She does raise an eyebrow at me, until I settle my breathing and emotions.

Inhale. Exhale.

"Probably Kasva," I continue.

Mikito nods, recalling the Champion of the Council that we've faced before and who we definitely know is around. In fact, Bolo and Mikito had a couple of clashes with the bastard over the month plus I was locked up.

"He's their everyday goon and seems to have a hard-on for us. For their Legendary…" I pause, reviewing what I know of who they have alive.

Interestingly enough, the majority of the Legendary powers aren't aligned with any side of the conflict. Most prefer to do their own thing and have the power to make sure they're left alone. Like the Legendary Pilot who flew around on his personal planet.

Only those like the Dragon, who desires power in all the ways that means, and the Weaver, whose Class makes it makes sense, involve themselves in politics. Part of the issue with people getting all the way to Legendary Class is that they have to be a lot of stubborn and even more individualistic. After all, at a certain point, you just have to keep going when all your peers fall behind you.

The call of friendship, of resting a bit and letting yourself just be, because the rest of your friends, your family, your lovers are there—it's powerful.

"The Emperor," I say finally.

"He's the weak one, isn't he?" Mikito says.

"For variations of weak, sure. He doesn't have his Empire anymore, so a chunk of his Class Skills don't work. But he does have this…"

I pull on the System, drawing forth a Class Skill. The only reason I know about it is because of the way the damn Emperor's Class Skill affects us all and thus, made its appearance in my System Administrator board.

Class Skill: A Towering Reputation (Legendary)
What use is Skill in combat or knowledge and wisdom to rival the gods if none know of it? What shield is there to an Empire if all scoff at the Emperor who sits

upon it? And what power can an Emperor, both feared and loved, hated and dreaded, bring to his Empire? This is a passive Skill. Mana Regeneration reduced by 5 permanently.

Effect: Emperor gains a boost to Class Skills, attributes, health, and regeneration based off reputation.

"And?" Mikito says after she finishes reading it.

"It's Galactic Reputation," I say. "I could show you the math behind it, but let's just say that the fact that the Emperor is as well-known as he is, including having numerous plays, books, sensory, immersive, and other shows made about him, boosts his Reputation quite, quite well."

"You're saying he's getting a boost from all over the Galaxy," Mikito says.

"Yup."

"That's broken."

"It's a Legendary Skill," I say and shrug. "It's not as powerful as having his own Empire, but because he isn't ruling anyone, he's also not getting any major negative modifiers." Mikito frowns, and I nod. "Yeah, I think he was informed about the actual equation involved, then gamed it."

"Then the stories…" she whispers the words in dawning horror.

"Wiped out his own Empire, yup." I nod. "Or let it fall." I shrug. "One or the other, but I'd bet that's what he chose to do. More personal power this way, from this Skill, without having to worry about running the Empire or getting into major conflicts with other kingdoms. He can even sponsor Guilds himself."

"Then he's not that weak," Mikito says.

"As I said, by definitions of weak, he probably is." I sigh. "Like, the Dragon could probably kick his ass in a one-on-one fight. Don't you remember the reports of the Emperor losing in the first altercation?" I shrug. "But then again, it's the Dragon. Not many can stand against him directly."

"Still, not weak."

I nod.

Mikito grows silent, and our discussion hangs heavily over us for a time. Eventually, she sips the remainder of her tea and nods, as if coming to an internal conclusion. She stands, bowing to me a little. "Then I guess we'll just have to plan for a way to neutralize them."

I pause, surprised at the confidence she shows.

When she sees my look, Mikito smiles at me serenely. "We've made it this far, haven't we?"

I can't help but nod, taking her optimism at face value. Choosing not to think of it as potential fatalism. There's something else I have to ask too.

"Ezz?"

Mikito glances around, decides it's safe, and holds her hand out to the side. Ezz's familiar red form appears, though he's gone from having a humanoid form with two arms and two legs to doubling each, a body more similar to a vertical centipede than human. The same red coloring is still there though, as are the human-looking eyes.

"What..." I stare at the silent creature. "What happened?"

"We had to shut him down to capture him," Mikito says. She turns the body a little, showing me the blinking gunmetal half-sphere lodged in Ezz's back. "It's shut down all his current processes. But, John..."

"Yeah?" I don't look at her as I regard Ezz.

"John." Firmer now.

"Yes?" I look up.

"He's compromised. You can't turn him on, not unless you're sure you can fix him."

I work my jaw for a second, anger rushing upward as she tells me what to do. My fist clenches and I want to scream at her, my most trusted friend. I almost rise up out of my chair, but her silent, calm regard is a pail of cold water on my anger.

Anger that isn't meant for her anyway.

After all, she isn't the one who failed Juover and Ezz.

"I get it," I say softly.

She waits for a beat, regarding me before she nods and turns away.

Leaving me to contemplate the still machine. Golem. Friend. Son?

***

Luck? Or planning? Either way, a coding tablet was in the inventory pieces left for me. I'd wondered about its inclusion and just dumped it into my rather empty storage. Now, sticking the leads into the liquid metal slots of Ezz, giving myself access to his code, I find myself making use of it. And letting out little mental whimpers.

Unlike what every single bad movie in the old world shows you, programming is not as simple as waving your hands around, typing away for twenty minutes while slamming energy drinks to metal music. In fact, one of the first problems you'll encounter is the simple fact that not all of us have permissions to access the core code.

Breaking security often requires specialized tools, or even better, knowledge of the kind of laziness the individual who slipped the security measures into place prefers. Because, trust me, the vast majority of security precautions are scuppered by sheer laziness.

That's the good news.

The bad news? I have neither the tools nor the knowledge of who wiped and reprogrammed Ezz. I don't even have a clue about the programming language used. When I was creating Ezz and modifying the other golems, I wasn't doing actual coding of the languages that ran them. That was all Juover. Since he'd replicated his own code, the assumption was that it wasn't the electronic code within them that was the problem. Other articles had tested multiple versions of code over thousands, tens of thousands, of years. None of those worked. So I hadn't bothered to even try.

Instead, I'd changed the System Code. But now, the problem with Ezz isn't his System Code; it's the actual programming they put in him. Even his Status says that.

Ezzocohatl "Ezz" Lee, Autonomous Station Maintenance Golem—Curium Omega Line v1.03 (HACKED)

Ezz is the "son" of John Lee, the Rogue System Administrator who helped in the creation of this Masterwork Golem. This Masterwork Golem is a custom-built, autonomous machine whose base format is developed from the versatile, station maintenance line of golems created by the Sentient Golem Juover 217th Generation. This Masterwork Golem was modified during creation by Rogue System Administrator John Lee in an attempt to provide it sapience, with additional foundational crafting skills provided by the Sapient Golem.

Currently, "Ezz"'s core programming has been modified. A Circuit Breaker has been installed, halting all operations of this autonomous golem, including interrupting the current AI.

Weapons: Mana Beam Projectors (Curium Omege Line) x 1
Durability: 3173/3914
Core: Class I Juover Modified FZ Mana Engine
Battery Capacity: N/A (See Mana Engine notes)

CPU: GS-412 Tier II (Juover AI Tier I)

Armor Rating: Tier II (Enhanced)

Special Abilities: Persistent Mana Engine & Forbidden Zone Mana Scour,
Enhanced Durability, Force Shield Projection, CPU Overclock

Active Skills: Soul Drinker (Level 1), Status Warp (Level 2)

One single word gives me hope. Modified. Not altered, not wiped, but modified. Yet Mikito clearly said it'd been wiped. Then again, I trust non-programmers to use the right terminology as much as I trust them not to have tried turning something on and off again before asking them to do it myself.

What? Working IT support scars you.

Delving into the System code for Ezz's Status doesn't offer much. One of the aspects of it being marked as an item is that there just isn't much information offered. It's not considered important by the System, so change logs are very, very sparse.

In the end, all I can tell is the timing of the change—soon after my capture—and minor alterations in durability. The only good news is that Ezz's durability has been slowly increased while the line indicates its CPU has not deleted its original AI. And I only got that second line after I poked at it a bit with System Edit.

Somewhere, trapped inside, I have to believe that Ezz is still working.

Problem is, I'm not sure how to get it out.

***

The next morning, Bolo and Yllis come out swinging. The argument takes a while to resolve, and I end up with an understanding of why they're helping us.

"So you need to somehow provide enough of a benefit to the dragon community that they'll accept you two and, more importantly, your kids?" I get a pair of nods, after which Yllis shoots Bolo a rather heated look. "And because of your... ummm... past, you figure helping to take down the Shadow Council is the way to go."

"And because I owe you," Bolo adds.

"You got me out of an unescapable prison. Pretty sure that covers that debt," I say.

Bolo sniffs, while Yllis preens a little. I'm surprised by that but decide not to pursue the difference in opinion the pair have. If for no other reason than it'll probably do my head in if I ask.

"And you think me completing the System Quest will help with your rep with the dragons?"

"Finishing a mythic quest that has never been completed should help," Bolo says. "That kind of prestige is hard to rival."

I can't help but agree with him on that point. Still... "You do realize this is probably a suicide run? Even if we manage to get there, I have no idea how we'll get out. Or what we'll do once we finish the Quest. I doubt completing the Quest will give us any special powers, beyond perhaps a nice little Title."

Yllis smirks at me. "You look down upon us dragons too much, human. Completing the Quest or truly hurting the Council will see us lauded by all. The remnants of the Council would never dare act against us once we recover our status." Then she bites her lip a little, showing for the first time a trace of uncertainty. "Our grandfather would never allow it."

"He won't," Bolo says heatedly.

I shake my head, choosing not to argue with them. After all, the entire discussion about their grandfather and their illicit affair is kind of bonkers. The fact that Yllis is one of the rare humanoid-born dragons and was brought up with Bolo as a sister of sorts makes their entire relationship scandalous. It's why Bolo left in the first place, especially when he reached the full Dragon Knight position and took her as his mount.

It was only after meeting me and getting dragged into all our insanity—along with the levels he gained—that he chose to come back. I'm not entirely sure what triggered that decision—maybe just having enough Levels under his belt at last—but here we are.

On his planet. With his sister-cum-lover-cum-steed.

"Whatever. Just glad you guys have some form of protection for the after," I say, waving it away.

Ali smirks, floating over and prodding Harry in the side. The Reporter growls at the Spirit, even as Ali speaks. "Relax, boy-o. Other than you and Mikito and probably the Storm Warden, who all intend to die in a blaze of glory anyway, we're safe. Harry, once he releases the information, will likely Level to a point it'll be painful to harm him, what with his Studied Neutrality Skill. And I'm, well, just a poor linked servant."

"Our deaths will be glorious and violent," Xaxas says, grinning wide and almost gleefully rubbing his hands together.

"I don't intend to die," Mikito says. "The goal is to keep John alive and not die."

"Are you samurai not all about the honorable death?" Bolo says, frowning.

"The code of Bushido is a complex topic, one prone to interpretation and change over the course of history. It is not something you can glean from being force-fed bad anime," Mikito says, looking pointedly at Ali at the end.

"Hey! *Ruroini Kenshin* isn't bad anime," Ali protests.

Mikito snorts. "As I said, my goal is to keep John alive and to stay alive doing so. If death comes and I am able to achieve my first objective, then that is what it will be. However, I do not seek death nor desire it. It is but a potential outcome at all times and a certain one in the end."

Bolo nods and grins. "You know, us Dragon Kings, we see death as just another enemy to be beaten. Eventually, we might fall, but many last for centuries if not millennia."

"You know, I much prefer Lone Wolf and Cub," I say.

"Of course you do."

"Wait. Who's the cub?" Ali pauses, floating over to me. "Are you calling me a mewling baby?"

"If the shoe fits…" I drawl.

Beside Bolo, Yllis stares at all of us, then she turns to her brother and prods him in the side. "Are you sure they were worth saving?"

"Oh, they definitely are not worth saving," Bolo faux-whispers to her. "But they are the most likely to finish the job."

Yllis nods, accepting Bolo's words, and I roll my eyes at the pair who grin at me.

Whatever. At least we're all on board for now.

"So now what?" I say.

"We wait," Yllis announces.

"We move," Mikito says at the same time.

The pair glare at one another and I wince, knowing that this will be another long argument.

Chapter 9

In the end, Mikito wins the argument. Rather than wait and hope the search for us dies down a little, we choose to head out as soon as possible. The main point that wins Mikito the argument is the fact that the longer we wait, the more chance there is of new reinforcements arriving. Where we are, Portaling or any other teleportation methods are going to leave a trail a mile wide. We've got lucky once, but they'll find the trail eventually. Travel inward is done via hyperspace tunnels and the like, and the longer we wait, the more people from the outskirts may be drawn in.

Now, obviously, a large number of individuals are in play already. However, our biggest concern is the Legendarys, and with myself having been captured, there's a slim chance they might not be able to reach us before we get to our destination. After all, with the way things have heated up on the Galactic scene, there's no way the Shadow Council has been keeping their biggest players hidden away in the middle of the Forbidden Zone.

Which is what Xy'largh is, for all intents and purposes.

All of which is why we're headed toward the Valley of Certain Death.

However… "I don't understand why we have to use this!"

I wave a hand around me, taking in the metal cylinder we're strapped to. The entire cylinder is dark gunmetal grey with straps and pulldown seats alongside the walls. Think of the army transport pictures you've seen, with a lot more grey and a lot less interesting sights and that's pretty much what we have.

"Flying would draw too much attention," Yllis says. "Any form of teleportation is likely to be picked up. While the Council might not run Xy'largh, they have enough sway to gain access to our sensory readings. It would be a small matter for them to locate us, especially as we are not able to scramble the information now."

I nod. They'd gotten the Weaver to help last time, having her provide her Skill to scramble the information when they broke us out. For a full day afterward, all the teleportation information had been heavily encrypted and made incredibly expensive to purchase and unscramble. Even with the funds the Shadow Council has on hand, the sheer volume of false impressions she created, along with our repeated teleportations, ensured we were able to escape the initial tracking.

Now, however, we have to be careful about standing out. Flying, teleportation, piercing the dimensional vale, all of that is a danger.

"I get that. But I mean, there's got to be a better choice than this!" I thump the side of the carriage, the grinding and squeaking of the insides resounding through the tin can. If the constant noise—like metal chalkboard nails coming down—isn't awful enough, there's the motion. Rather than moving in a straight line, we flow in a twisting motion, constantly swinging from side to side as we head down.

"Hollow Planet Centipedes are a time-honored tradition of entering the planet," Bolo says. "There are so many of them crisscrossing the crust that no one can track them all, never mind their natural camouflage abilities and extended senses. They're also one of the fastest ways down, especially when combined with a trusted Tamer."

I snort, feeling my stomach lurch against as we twist once more. The entire damn contraption we're in is just one link in the body of the Hollow Planet Centipede, the original monster so large that chopping it apart and adding this metal tube before stitching it all back together again is considered perfectly normal. Tubes of grey goop cover the outside of the tube, the hard chitin and veins having been recreated via spells and Skills.

"And cutting through the planet is the fastest way there, eh?" I say.

"It is. We'll have to cross a portion of the hollow planet on foot, but it's significantly faster than trying to do the same journey above ground," Bolo repeats patiently.

"Relax, boy-o. He's right. I already ran the math multiple times. If we want to reach our destination, cutting through the planet—even if we have to walk on their twisted inner surface—will be a lot more efficient. If nothing else, we won't need to deal with their seas," Ali sends.

I grimace, recalling the data download I have on the seas. Like any planet with a significant body of water, the underwater and sea-living creatures have become a nightmare of their own. Leviathans, Kraken, Electrified and Poisonous Jellyfish, and Giant Squids are just a few of the things Earth has to contend with. Blue whales, mutated and given a taste for meat and a huge increase in reproduction, roam the waters like damn Orcas, bullying ocean-going vessels and getting consumed by Giant Squids. And that's Earth.

Xy'largh is the home of the dragons. Anything that can't contend with them on a one-on-one basis are prey, and dragons have big, big appetites.

"I'm worried if I know that, and you know that, then the Admins know that too," I send back.

"Not as if we have any other option. Anyway, because it's a small globe within, there are multiple ways to get there," Ali says.

"How does that work anyway? Why can't we just, you know, fly through the center?"

"You mean the hollow center in the center of the hollow planet?" I hear the smirk in the Spirit's voice.

Even knowing that I'm walking into his trap, I answer in the affirmative. And get, instead of words, an image.

A green grassland and savannah, a world turned inside out. A sphere where everything grows inward, where clouds and shards of earth float in a ring that blanket the world and give it relief from the blazing ball of plasma and contained energy in the center. It's not a sun; there's too much Mana imbued into the thing, too artificial to make it a real star. Still, the energy it gives off, both the warmth and the power it provides, is enough to offer the plants within the biome a source of energy to grow.

"*What in the thousand hells is that?*" I exclaim, staring at the mental image Ali downloaded to me.

Yeah, yeah, you'd think we'd have something like that in the Library, but there's a surprising gap about hollow planets in there. There are a few articles, discussions about the Mana flows, academic variation studies about the way the System seems to favor normal planets in general since there's a reduced cost in their upkeep. But the studies peter out pretty fast, since no one ever gets any point upgrades looking or delving into the mysteries of hollow planet creation. It's a weirdness, but it's a weirdness created by Mana or sapients playing bonkers with the natural laws of the universe, not the System.

That's kind of the thing with Questors. Once something is shown not to progress the System Quest, they abandon it.

"*Pretty typical hollow planet. Power source in the middle, hub of water and clouds caught between the local sun-equivalent and the earth via a localized gravity sheer and, a Xy'largh special, the floating island communities in between. Those are weird. We won't even discuss what those things are.*"

"*What if I want to?*" I grump.

"*All righty then, boy-o. Two words. Trapped Elementals.*"

I pause, mind spinning through the possibilities. Elementals—probably Earth, though maybe Air or some weird mixture like Sky Metal or something—trapped in the rocks and given form. Forced to float forever, burning on one end, protecting the ground on others.

I can see, rotating the damn image that Ali gave me in my mind, that there are brief periods of darkness when the larger clumps of these Elementals get together. Time for plants to cool down, to switch methods of processing energy. To rest, before they're exposed once more. With the sheer amount of cloud cover, the world beneath the faux-sun is more Vancouver spring than sunny California.

"So no flying through the center because of the weird gravity planes, the living Elemental islands, and the giant ball of energy that probably melt us all." I sigh. *"Explain again how we're not just walking into the middle of a trap?"*

"Because as fast as we're moving, they probably won't have scrambled everyone to meet us. Don't forget, just because we think it's the most obvious route doesn't mean they will. It's not as though you told them where you're going, right?" I shake my head. At least, not the location. Ali nods. *"Exactly. So while it is a likely route, it isn't a guarantee. Also, inside the hollow planet, there are multiple routes we can take, so even then, they'll have to split up to cover all the ground."*

I want to point out that there are ways of telling where we'll go—Fortune Tellers, Oracles, and other Future Probability tellers are all potential problem-makers, even if they are hampered by the sheer volume of unaspected Mana in the System—but the damn centipede lurches again. I clutch the edge of my seat for a second, wondering what is going on, before the angle of descent changes once more.

Gravity spins us around, slamming us downward at an angle, making my stomach play catch-up for a second. By the time I figure out where up is when the new gravity planes reinforce themselves, I find we're no longer moving, the rest of the centipede's body slowly emerging from the hole it created.

Seconds later, Bolo jumps to his feet, waving to us all with a shit-eating grin on his face. I roll my eyes, knowing he knew what was coming and refused to let the rest of us know. He gloats a little, until he gets smacked by Yllis. The doors to the hollow planet slide open moments later.

Surprisingly, it's not Bolo who makes it out first but the Storm Warden, the big Yerrick looking greener than me. Very surprising, since we should all be immune—physically at least—to the shaking. Then again, the man has been imprisoned in a secondary dimension for who knows how many years. The kind of mental scarring he has is likely something I'll never truly understand.

Drawing a deep breath, catching hints of cinnamon, aspen, and fir, along with other woody scents I can't place, I unstrap myself and brace myself for a whole new experience. At least this time it doesn't involve counting the number of teeth regenerated by the System.

Gods, my humor has gotten dark.

***

Woody, with a mixture of sulphur, ammonia, and chlorine, is the way I'd describe the smell of the hollow planet. Rotten wood, fresh wood, newly broken sap—all of it is there. The sulphur isn't a surprise, considering where we are. The ammonia is from the centipede, a pervasive stink that drove me nuts until I forcibly ignored it.

More intrusive than the smell is the heat. It's cloying and higher than Earth normal, sitting in the high 30s Celsius at the very least. Add it to the humidity and I'm grateful I'm no longer human, or else we'd really be suffering. Idly, I wonder what the wet bulb index would be, or if something that was meant to tell people when to take care in high humidity and extreme temperatures even matters to System-enhanced individuals anymore.

Probably not, now that I think about it with any real consideration. After all, you're more likely to get eaten by a mutated koala than die from heat stroke.

Turning my head, I scan the surroundings, grateful the team decided to get me a retracting helmet. Hot or not, I prefer keeping my peripheral vision unhampered unless I'm in the middle of a fight. Then, with the Hod or Spitzrocket, external cameras provide me full vision even if the helmet itself looks like a featureless mask.

As for what I see now that I'm out? Churned up grass and a pile of dark grey and black sand from where the centipede exited the ground. Stepping up the mound itself, noting how the creature is curling in on itself, creating a mound of chitin and legs, its Tamer murmuring to it, I'm grateful I don't need to fight the thing. Level 178 and backed with a Tamer would make fighting such a monster one heck of a pain.

More importantly, the clearing we're in looks to be rather restricted. Barely thirty meters away at the closest side is the start of the forest. The shrubs here are much shorter, their leaves spread out across a wider range of space. They're quite a vibrant green, the shortened canopy offering other plants a chance to grow and spread out themselves. Lots of shrubbery and cane-like trunks with thorns galore beneath the primary forest layer.

Between the proximity of the light source and the surprising amount of mildly reflective plants, illumination while walking through the forest won't be a problem. If anything, the constant bathing of light except when a bunch of Elementals clump together by chance or desire will be an issue.

More interestingly, with my senses extended, I note the way my Electromagnetic Force ability is twitching. The boundaries of space and time around here, the basic role of physics, are warped in this location. The Elemental floating islands above are lighter than they should be, their molecules repelling one another to decrease overall density while still holding together. The ground itself is denser under my feet, especially in a layer a couple of kilometers down.

Even if it's not part of my skillset, I can tell that gravity itself—the weird gravitic plane that is holding me down instead of having me collapse into the center—is happening, beginning around the incredibly dense earth location and moving onward. In fact, the sheer energy I'm feeling, I could swear that beneath our feet, there's molten lava.

Which makes me wonder how we went through it without getting burnt. Deciding I want to know, I ask the question out loud.

"Separate dimensional planes coexisting with one another," the Storm Warden replies, surprising me. It's strange how you can spend days with a person and never speak with them, not beyond the basics, when the two of you are not people people. "Woven among one another. Sometimes the two dimensions cross, and you get flooding between the two before they pull apart.

"Mostly though, they stand separate but somehow close enough to this reality that they both interact with it. Part of the Tamer's job is to know how to enter the right dimension when you cross through."

"So all this around us…" I gesture around me. "We're basically sharing space with a molten planetary core too that could breach at any time?"

"No." Ali floats over to me, hands on his hips while he sits cross-legged, looking very disapproving.

"What?" I say innocently.

"No," Ali repeats, wagging a finger at me as though I'm a bad dog or something.

"Why is your Spirit denying you?" Xaxas asks. He frowns as he does so, deepening the heavy brows that make up his face, dark brown fur rippling in the wind. Funnily enough, the frowning doesn't make him look more intimidating but actually cuter—at least in my opinion. I kind of want to go up to him and cry out "stuffie" while snuggling into all that fur.

What? I know I have a death wish.

"How would I know?" I keep smiling blithely while tilting my head up to the sky, letting my senses expand fully. The Elemental Force stuff doesn't seem to offer much, not that I expect it. My System Administrator senses, the ones that expanded when I got the Class, on the other hand… there's something there. Right on the edges. It's not exactly meant to be doing this, but maybe if I…

"If you don't stop, I swear I'm going to find a ton of goblin shit and dump it on you!" Ali threatens, floating right in front of my eyes.

"What, exactly, is the Redeemer trying to do?" Xaxas rumbles. There's a coldness to his voice now, one that was not there before. The hair on the back of my neck rises as he speaks and shifts his balance ever so slightly.

I grow serious, looking at Xaxas and answering his question. "I'm just feeling the edges of the dimensional boundaries. Trying to find them."

"The idiot is thinking he could use it as a weapon," Ali says. "Maybe a last-ditch attempt to stop himself from getting captured. Tear a hole, probably with his Portal Skill. Right?"

I shrug.

To Ali's surprise, Xaxas lets out a low rumble, one that sounds like a mixture between a trash compactor running and a cow masticating its food. "An interesting idea."

"A suicidal one!" Ali snaps.

"Oh come on, you said it yourself. You can't die. Why are you acting all upset?" I tease Ali.

"Just because I can't die doesn't mean it doesn't hurt being burnt alive! Also, you might have forgotten, but you've got friends here too. And, you know, an entire damn civilization inside the planet. You trying for genocide now?" Ali says.

"Not trying."

"A weapon is a weapon," Xaxas says. "If he does not explore the possibilities now, there is no way to know how effective it might be. Better now than in the heat of the battle, no?"

"You're insane. Both of you!" Ali throws his hands up and floats toward Mikito and Harry, who are chatting quietly, catching up. As he reaches the pair, he gestures, telling them about us.

"So, Redeemer, are you truly considering using the dimensional planes as a weapon?" Xaxas says, now that Ali isn't around to tease.

I look at the Yerrick, considering how I should answer. In the end, I decide to go for the truth. The truth is easier to use, simpler than trying to lie. Anyway, he deserves to know what he's getting into. I give him a simple nod, and the Storm Warden gives me a wide smile. I barely brace before he claps me on the shoulder with enough force to shift me a little from where I'm standing.

"Good. I had a feeling one who acted against the Council and their masters was worth following. I am glad to see I am right. I too shall contemplate this," Xaxas says and strides off, a few seconds before Mikito and Harry descend on me to berate me on my latest idea.

I admit, I'm uncertain if I should be worried or grateful that Xaxas agrees with me. It's a bit worrying when you might not be the craziest person on the team anymore.

Chapter 10

For all my—valid—concerns, we get moving soon enough. Bolo waves us out of the clearing, pushing us to move through the forest to our next stop. Where that is, I'm not certain, since we've agreed not to discuss too many specifics once we left the safe house. Sadly, anything we talk about now could easily be bought. Rather, we rely on Yllis and Bolo to ascertain the best choice for our routes.

Not that the rest of us are entirely blind to the options. We came out where we did because no one lets the centipedes exit near their settlements. While they're mostly under the control of their Tamers, knocking out or eliminating a Tamer is an easy way to cause chaos. The rampaging high-Level monster in the middle of one's defenses provides a suitable distraction for everything from bank raids to assassinations.

Which is why we're trampling through the undergrowth toward a city. From there, it's a matter of acquiring further local transportation. Unfortunately, changing environments and a forest that's enhanced both by the environment and a surplus of Mana means that routes constantly alter. It means we'll need to ascertain new routes to our destination.

Tramping through the forest, Yllis at the forefront and occasionally unleashing her flame to clear out the truly stubborn vegetation, things are relatively quiet. Bolo's Dragon Fear Aura keeps most monsters away, a clear and loud warning to anything that isn't in the high Levels that they're so much chaff. It's uncomfortable, of course, for us to wander along behind him, but none of us are slackers in the Mental Resistance departments.

Overall, the hike is long and boring and entirely eventless. Or it should be. Which is why when I'm slammed into from the side and sent spinning into the untamed undergrowth, I'm caught entirely by surprise. I bounce across the ground, destroy a couple of trees, and get impaled on a limb that refuses to move.

Blood wells out as I tear myself free by instinct, the System already patching the wound closed and my Resistances pinging off the poison that is invading my system. It's powerful poison—it has to be to affect anyone around here—so it's swamping my Resistances. Not for long I'm sure, but long enough for the monster to get to me.

I only catch a glimpse of it before it is on me, its multi-row, jagged teeth tearing into my raised arm. Plated body, a quartet of eyes, a six-limbed body that is more dinosaur-rhinoceros than sleek cat. Its head is elongated, its mouth clamping down on my hand as it flips me up. Rearing upward to its full twelve-foot height, the middle pair of legs tear into me, making me realize it's got truly sharp claws.

My armored jumpsuit might as well be cotton for as much good as it does. Claws dig into muscle and flesh beneath, and only my Skills provide me any form of protection. Even then, my muscles get shredded and stomach and intestine lining starts falling out.

Instead of moving, instead of fighting back, I'm in shock. A part of my brain refuses to accept the damage, the attack. Another part is struggling to act. A year of being forced into inactivity, into becoming nothing more than a compliant doll for others to beat up on and torture, has caused more damage than I realized. A part of me expects to get ripped apart, to be put through the wringer. To be hurt and hurt more.

Lightning arcs through the sky, slamming into the creature. It forces the monster into shock, throws it backward, and makes it open its mouth. It releases me, dropping me to the ground to tumble away, my body already healing as the rest of the team arrives.

Mikito hits it at full charge, astride her ghost horse, swinging her naginata as she rides past it. Not a lance charge but a swing of her weapon to tear through the monster and open a long wound down one side, tough plated armor doing nothing to stop Hitoshi. A glowing red trail of lifeblood follows the weapon as it exits, Life Siphon at full work. She swerves away as the Storm Warden arrives. No weapon, he just punches right into the open wound, widening it with pinpoint accuracy as he sinks his fist into the opened flesh.

Xaxas grins for a fraction of a second before he unloads the full extent of his ability into the monster, channeling the fury and power of a category five storm into the monster. The creature balloons, lightning dancing through its skin and grounding through the vegetation and earth around it. Even as it thrashes and attempts to get away, Xaxas uses his other hand to grip a fold of plate, refusing to be tossed aside.

The monster screams and roars, then suddenly explodes. The explosion is enough to throw Xaxas off its back, his body arcing through the air to smash into trees. At the same time, the rest of us are assaulted by the shards of armor plate, Mikito barely dodging a spinning plate that attempts to behead her.

It doesn't stop the Samurai from riding in though as the bloody, naked monster with lightning burns running through it staggers back to its feet. She swings her weapon again as it rears up to face her, taking an arm off before she veers away again, dodging a retaliatory attack.

Bolo hits it a second later, the hammer coming down on its lower back and crushing spine and legs. After that, it's just a matter of clean up for the others.

The others, because through it all, I'm crouched on my knee, watching. My heart beating like a machine gun, my mouth dry, my limbs refusing to move no matter how I tell them to. The rage, the anger that has driven me forward, that I used to snark back at the Administrators and to keep me defiant...

It's not gone, but it's out of reach. Refusing to come to me as my friends save my ass.

***

"What happened?" Bolo says, striding over to stare at me, having finished off the monster. His girlfriend has semi-transformed, parts of her elongating and expanding while she eats the corpse, one clawed hand tearing off raw and bloody strips.

"Nothing. It just caught me by surprise," I say defensively. I'm ashamed about my helplessness, of how little I did to save myself. For the first time, I wonder if that's how the civilians back on Earth felt when I came striding in, saving their asses and killing monsters left and right.

"That's a load of year-old dragon waste," Bolo snaps. "I've seen you fight. You don't freeze after an ambush, you charge it. You were completely frozen."

My lips curl up, my temper fraying. A part of me can't help but note my reaction, wonder where the anger was earlier. Adrenaline, that had dumped into me in such volume beforehand, is now at a more manageable level but makes control hard to keep. Maybe it's easier now for me to fight words with words, rather than blade and blade. I'm used to it now, talking and screaming and bleeding...

"And there. That look in your eyes!" Bolo stabs a finger between my eyes, waving it in front of my face as though doing so is somehow revealing of all the things I've done wrong. "You lost track of me there. Went somewhere else."

"I've been doing that ever since Feh'ral dumped his goddamn Library in my head," I reply.

"No. Not like that. That look is like you're somewhere else, your face goes blank. This one, you're gone too, but you're also here, in pain, in fear.

Did they break you?" Bolo lowers his voice, a trace of sympathy in it now. "Were we too late?"

"Yeah, yeah, whatever," I say, pushing him away from me. Bolo lets me, which is good because he's stronger than I am. I dumped a lot more points into Willpower and Intelligence than he did. Well, Intelligence proportionally at least. He has a very high Intelligence score. Lets him dish out a lot of damage fast, but he's less of a long-term fighter. "I'm fine. It's just been a bit."

I don't look at him as I walk off, heading in the direction that we started off with. I don't look at him to see his reaction or at Yllis, who is busy eating, and I definitely don't look at Mikito, who is giving me a sympathetic look.

Because I know he's right. I froze, and that isn't acceptable. Not for me. Not here. Not now.

"*Ali.*"

"*Yeah, boy-o?*" His voice is uncharacteristically quiet and sympathetic.

"*Remember day one?*"

"*I do.*"

"*Remember what you did for me?*"

"*More like to you,*" Ali replies, still with that same tone.

I draw a deep breath, waving Harry away. The Storm Warden doesn't say a damn thing, just watching as I walk off by myself, the others hanging back. "*I needed it then. I need it now.*"

"*John…*"

"*We don't have time to coddle me. We don't have time for me to be slow or weak or human. This time, it was a monster. Next time, it could be Kasva or an Admin.*"

The truth of my words silences Ali's protests. "*You want me to call the monsters to you.*"

I nod, already leaving the safety of Bolo's aura. I can feel it being suppressed, tightened up so that it doesn't interfere with me. Me leaving the clearing is clear enough that I need time, space. Monsters. As much as I might have denied it, we all know I froze. I'm just grateful they're letting me fix it. Even if, as usual, it's not the healthiest or smartest way of doing so.

"How many?" Ali asks.

"Just keep them coming until I tell you to stop."

The silence that greets that pronouncement is profound. I know Ali wants to protest but is uncertain how to. I get it. But…

"No time, old friend. Just do it."

"Never let it be said that working with you is boring," Ali says out loud. He floats up high, hands weaving together as he pulls on the threads of the world, his Elemental affinity. I can feel it taking place, the small shocks and twitches he's sending out to attack the monsters around us. To draw them in.

I draw a deep breath, slip on the Spitzrocket and conjure my sword, and get ready to go to work. I just hope immersion therapy really works.

***

Breathe in. Breathe out. Breathe in. Breathe out.

Slow and steady, my breath rushes out of my nostrils, touching my lips and chin as it reflects off the inside of my helmet. My heartbeat is thundering in my veins. I feel an artery flicking in my neck, my hands growing clammy. I'm more nervous than the first time I sneaked a kiss with a boy—and that was, by far, more nerve-racking than my first kiss ever.

I'm so involved in my own personal hell that I don't even notice the monsters when they arrive. The first group is a pack, a dozen flying squirrel-like creatures with the long arms of monkeys and the tucked-in limbs of their brethren. They glide through the air above me, strafing me with plasma orbs that exit from behind.

The world goes red and black as smoke and flames blossom around me. Nearby, a mutated plant explodes as the temperature spikes, showering the surroundings with furious, flaming hot seeds. The plasma squirrels don't give a damn, gliding through the air and using the self-generated updrafts to hammer at my shielding.

Soul Shield flickers and dies, giving way. The Spitzrocket's internal force shields take over, though I know those won't last long. I'm standing there in a sea of flames, and all I can think is that they're shitting fire on me.

"MOVE, BOY-O!"

I ignore Ali. I pay no attention to the growing heat and the incessant whine of the Spitzrocket as it informs me of even more danger. Instead, I look within, searching for the part of me that drove me onward. Not the anger, but the part that Ali tapped into that first fight, that first battle. The part of me that just refused to die, even when faced with an overgrown ant.

I search for it, even as another monster comes out of the darkness, a living snake of earth and metal that ignores the heat to wrap itself around me. Occasional plasma balls strike and bounce off its scales, making them glow, before it releases its counterattack at the flying squirrels, a wave of heat that cooks the surroundings almost immediately. The squirrels flee higher into the sky, though not before the bottom two collapse from the damage, their fur and the delicate membranes between their "wings" burnt up. The snake creature's body extends, earth arms exploding from the scales to pick up the bodies and new mouths forming to crunch and eat the still-living squirrels.

Then it turns to me.

"Come on, boy-o. This is just the appetizers. We got some real threats coming..." Ali sounds worried, but I can only note it.

Where's the man who, seeing the threat, ran toward it? Where's the lizard brain that doesn't know how to quit? Where's the blood thirst that turned me into a killing machine that strode across a forbidden planet, taking down monsters tens of levels above him?

And who the hell is this trembling, crying man who can barely stand?

"JOHN!"

The scream is higher, louder than ever. The snake monster is crushing me, extruding earth hands gripping and ripping at heated metal, digging in as it looks for the soft, gooey, fleshy center. The Spitzrocket is shrieking at me, as though it sees its own death coming and refuses.

And I'm doing nothing. How much is too much? When is enough? I talked a big game, defied the Administrators when all I had to say was nothing. But now I'm out here, being asked to fight again, being forced to push and push and kill and for what…

For what?

The hammer blow saves me. It comes down hard, from high above, as the hammer smashes me and the snake into the ground. Legs and knees crack, the earth beneath my feet compressing as I'm crushed. The elemental snake-creature wrapped around me is pushed off a little, its body damaged. It rears up, scales glistening as heat builds, as shards of rock rush up to fight the giant pounding weapon. A scream as solid flesh is pierced, as monster meets monster over the tasty human.

I'm caught between two uncaring forces, a succulent treat for the winner. My wants, my needs, my dreams ignored. Like a child seeking love and reassurance and safety from an uncaring parent, left to stand alone in the late of the night, bruised and grief-laden with demands for completed homework and a lost lunch bag…

Like a planetful of sapients, living their mundane, boring, safe, pedestrian lives, clad in the comfort of mundanity and forgetting the wonder of everyday existence, robbed of it all by a System and a Council with a flick of a button, a political maneuver.

Like a thousand solar systems, a million planets, a gazillion lives caught in the vagaries of an uncaring, unknowing, unknowable System whose only drive is to replicate itself like a virus, destroying the host body it lives within.

Caught between towering forces, as one dies and another grabs me, lifting me high only to be consumed. As more, ever more, monsters arrive and a Spirit throws lightning at the massive maw. Seconds from being swallowed, from being consumed and forced to experience that cloying, burning, claustrophobic sensation again…

I move at last. Because something breaks within me, and tears and pain give way.

I throw my head backward and scream, the Spitzrocket amplifying the noise, the rage, the pain, the loss of it all escaping me. I scream and call down the heavens themselves.

Energy warps and twists and tears at fingers, the cyclopean-giant-nightmare releasing me as his insides boil and his mouth snaps shut.

I fall as heavenly energy ends.

I drop down to hell, where more monsters await.

If heaven is not enough, then I'll bring hell.

I'm well acquainted with that at least.

Chapter 11

Fire-blackened earth, nubs of trees and flames roaring in the distance. Corpses of monsters, some over forty feet tall like the giant, others barely the size of my fist but made of something so dense, their falling had impacted the ground and created craters. Through the Spitzrocket's cracked helmet, I smell the familiar stench of voided bowels, ash, and cooked flesh, along with the tinge of human and alien blood. And yeah, alien blood smells different.

My breathing is still deep and heavy, my Stamina nearly drained. Mana is nearly gone too, though it's fast recovering as I stand, sword extended by my side, gunky fluid slowly dripping off the end. I dismiss the weapon, cocking my head to the side and feeling something snap and crack.

Footsteps, all too familiar and heavy, and even heavier but not familiar, come from behind and to my left. I turn a little, catching sight of Bolo and Yllis, the big Dragon King shaking his head as he surveys the swath of destruction.

"You know, we were looking to do this under their noses. Not create a category four event," Bolo says lightly.

"Category four?" I say.

"Mass destruction pursuant to a Heroic," Yllis answers, gesturing about her.

"Right, that makes sense." I finish rotating my neck and dismiss the Spitzrocket to let it fix itself. "Sorry. Just had to get something out of my system."

"You're good then?" Yllis asks, fixing me with a firm gaze.

I notice the rest of the team coming up, Mikito with Harry while Xaxas stays at the back, bringing up the rear. Not that there's much to be worried about right now. Ali might have gone overboard with aggroing the surrounding monsters.

"Right as acid rain," I say.

Bolo nods happily and gestures for Yllis to come with him. Together, the pair trailbreak toward the settlement, which must have gotten one heck of a show. Hopefully the pair can settle the monsters down.

"Acid rain?" Harry says, sounding amused.

"It's common on Xy'largh," I say. "Just doing like the natives do."

"Uh huh." Harry doesn't sound convinced, but after a bit, he nods to himself and leaves.

"Are you okay?" Mikito's voice is softer, her eyes searching my face for weakness. It's there, so much so, and I can't help but offer her a crooked, twisted smile in answer. "John... we can stop. Rest."

"No, we can't." I rub the back of my neck, realizing I've got a lot more hair than I like. In fact, it's long enough I could probably do up a tiny ponytail. Or a manbun.

Nope. I haven't fallen that far.

"There's only one way forward and that's through. For all of us," I say. "We've got to reach a city, get to a Shop so I can download some programming code to fix Ezz, then we need to get to our destination." She looks dubious, so I offer her a tight smile. "Don't worry. I can do it. I might not be running toward the answer right now, but I can walk."

"And when you can't anymore?"

"Then I'll crawl." I rotate my shoulders and walk, watching as Mikito falls in step with me. "But I'll make it. And I'll make sure you do too. I just needed to shake out some..." I consider my words and find the most appropriate one. "Trauma."

"Most heal their trauma," Mikito says wryly.

"We're not—I'm not—most people. You don't climb to the top if you're most people. And maybe somewhere out there is someone who's untouched, untraumatized by what they've gone through. Maybe an Artisan or some ivory tower academic, whose life has been easy and simple." I hear

117

the bitterness in my voice and shake my head, dismissing it. "The best I can hope for is just to use my pain to push me on."

"Bakayaro," Mikito says wearily. "It's not—"

"It is," I cut her off. "For me at least."

There's sadness in her eyes when I glance over, which is why I refuse to look at her. Instead, I pick up the pace, trying to catch up with the others. There's a reason Lana gave up on me, even if she would never say it out loud. There's a reason Roxley held me at arm's length. And my only other semi-serious relationship was with a lady with whom I never had a chance of anything more.

You can't heal those who refuse to stop injuring themselves. You can't save those who constantly throw themselves into the fire. Maybe I don't have a death wish, but the difference is so close, you couldn't feed a goldfish on it.

***

The settlement, when we finally make it, is on full alert. Bolo and Yllis are still standing outside the shining earthen-and-metal walls, shouting up at the group holding position over it and arguing about entry. The slight shimmer in the air speaks of force shields in play. The quartet of large, anti-vehicle beam weaponry trained on us speaks of a less-than-enthusiastic welcome.

As I get close, Bolo finishes cursing them out and throws his hands up, stalking back toward me. I open my mouth and he glares at me, shutting me up before informing us of what is happening.

"They're not letting us in," Bolo snarls. "Citing danger to their settlement from having us within and the potential problems it could create. Their settlement owner sees letting us in as a greater risk than irking us."

"Buggering hell," Harry says, looking at the impassive walls. They're lined with sapients, the vast majority natives of the planet having curly horns and differentially shaded skin. All of them are huge, another annoying factor. In a way, it's really frustrating that so many of the aliens are taller than us humans. Then again, size does matter to some extent, especially at the lower Levels. "Now what?"

"Yllis and I shall try to negotiate with them again when they have…" Bolo's head whips to the side, his voice rising. "What the hell are you doing?"

Rather than answer him, Xaxas keeps walking forward. Guns and anti-vehicle weaponry train on him, especially when he doesn't stop moving with that ponderous gait of his and reaches the shielding. He slows only a little, just enough to time his punch to his footstep as he hits the shielding, shattering it. No surprise, the beam cannons on the walls and quite a few of the sapients open up on him.

Instinct has me pulling on my Skill, adjusting timing and location so that when they open up, everyone in our group, except Xaxas, is covered. Sanctum hammers down around us, trapping and protecting us at the same time. We can watch what happens, but there's nothing we can do to help.

Not that Xaxas cares.

"Damn it!" Bolo's fist thunders into the Sanctum walls, eyes narrowing. "Let us out, damn it. If we let him—"

"What? Make things worse?" I snort. "Pretty sure him tearing the walls down and electrocuting the defenders is as bad as it gets."

The Storm Warden's fifth punch is enough to shatter the gates. Attacks are hitting him, but I get to see his defensive methods in play. Rather than a fixed defense like my Soul Shield, the Storm Warden actually has a swirling band of energy around him, one that redirects and absorbs energy from the attacks. The attacks seem to charge the band of energy around him, though a portion of it always leaks through, even as the cloud of lightning and plasma grows in intensity with each shot fired.

Then, as though a critical point has been reached, the energy unleashes itself. Lightning arcs out from the cloud, striking at the Xy'largh Guards and the anti-vehicle weaponry targeting him. Xaxas strides right in, ignoring the effects of his cloud attack, smoke coming off his body as a mist rolls out, covering the ground and making the rest of the city disappear.

"He's insane!" Yllis says, shaking her head. "You don't attack an Underworld Settlement! They often have Heroics of their own…"

As if to punctuate her words, Xaxas comes flying out of the town, crashing through the wall and taking the portion he strikes with him. Streams of cloud and mist spill off him as he bounces across the ground and trees, only coming to a stop when the huge minotaur gets his feet under him and utilizes his full strength.

He shakes his head, dirt and leaves falling off his fur before he bunches his legs and shoots forward into the gap. Not a moment too soon, as he clashes with someone exiting it, big beam weapon held down by the man's side. The energy rips into Xaxas, his cloud taking and shedding the energy while releasing arcs of lightning all around.

The pair fall back into the town, leaving us none the wiser of what is happening within—outside of the screams, crashes, and booming echoes of clashing bodies.

"You know, I think he might have been feeling left out…" Ali muses. When we all look at him, he gestures at me. "John got to show off a little. So he's just doing the same. And, you know, doing it better."

"Come on, he's not that… immature…" I trail off, staring at the others who are nodding.

"This makes sense. It is the Redeemer's fault," Bolo says.

"Of course it is," Harry replies. "It's always John's fault."

"Hey!" I exclaim.

"I know not you well, Redeemer, but this statement has the ring of truth to it," Yllis says, grinning.

"Aaargh!" I glare at the Sanctum, considering hacking it to let me out. Otherwise, I'm trapped inside until its duration is over. And ten minutes is a long time in a fight. "This is why I never use this damn Skill…" I mutter.

The others just grin as we settle in to watch. It's not a happy thought, having one of ours in the midst of a fight by himself, but if he's looking to show off, then us getting involved is just as bad. Anyway, as more than one eruption shoots out from behind the walls and low-hanging blimps and other VTOL craft take off, I doubt the Storm Warden needs our help.

Even if there are Heroics within.

***

Ten minutes is a long time. It's a very long time when a mini-war is going on right outside of your bubble. Even longer when the bubble contains six of us, even if one of them can shrink down like a pot-bellied, foul-mouthed, orange-clad fairy. By the time the Sanctum disappears, we're all raring to go, and more than one muttered threat about using the Skill has been sent my way.

Thankfully, in the last couple of minutes, the mist has slowly dispersed. Since we still have Xaxas on Harry's shared party chat, we know he's still alive, but he's been radio silent for a long while. Rather than jostle his elbow during a potentially life-threatening moment, we've chosen to stay silent. It's the least we can do, after all.

Entering the settlement is a lot easier and drama-free this time around. Oh, sure, a number of bodies are lying around, people being pulled out of the rubble of the fight, but surprisingly few corpses. Then again, as I scan the Levels of those around, I don't see a single person below an Advanced Class still on the streets. Not until someone, using an earth-moving spell, peels apart a collapsed house and reveals a secure room, its occupants running out.

I guess anyone truly vulnerable—which, at this point, includes Basic Classes and non-Systemized kids—was evacuated a while ago. After all, if they were confident enough to confront and ignore a Dragon King, they must have known the kind of damage an irate Dragon King and his steed could bring.

I just don't think anyone expected a crazed Storm Warden to escalate the entire issue.

Nor do I expect to find him in the city square, legs kicked back, giant mug of what I can only guess is the local equivalent of alcohol in hand, chatting companionably with a trio of fighters. A quick scan tells me they're Heroics—two combat types, one Artisan Crafter. The slowly healing wounds on all four are a testament to the fight that went down. Even as I watch, the Artisan's leg pops back into place, the spider-creature's thin mandibular limbs reattaching.

"About time," Xaxas says, waving at us. Turning to the other Heroics, he continues. "These are the others I told you about."

"Bunch of cowards, hiding behind a Skill," growls the first Xy'largh combat Classer.

The pair seated by Xaxas look similar, almost like they share a familial bond. Brothers, I'd guess, since it's hard to tell their age what with the slow-down in aging that Heroics get.

"I bet I could have popped it, Da." The second speaker's voice is surprisingly high-pitched. Not like a woman's, but still high. Also... father and son Heroic pairs are very uncommon. "Two strikes. Three at most."

"One," Xaxas says, preening.

"You do know that you're talking about my Skill, right?" I say, stepping forward. I slip into a lazy drawl for some reason. Perhaps because a part of me figures that if they want machismo, the Duke is a good example of that.

"So what? It's a coward's Skill."

I take a second to scan the older one's Status, curious to see what it says.

Wece Canard, Sheriff of the Underworld, Centurion of the Gates, Gravitic Shear Survivor, Slayer of the Ones Within, ... (Hollow Earth Defender Level 11) (H)

HP: 5420/5420

MP: 3424/3780

Conditions: Chosen Domain (Hollow Earth), Grounded, Shared Pain

A quick flicker over to the side notes that Portu Canard is the same Class, though he's barely crossed the threshold of Heroic. Interesting Class. The Library has already dropped details of the Class to me, noting in particular one interesting interaction that offers the pair quite a bit of strength in their chosen domain.

The highest Level among them is the Artisan, and the spider's scurried off. Ali keeps me apprised of his movements via my minimap, but it doesn't look like he's going to pick a fight and furthermore, is just done with company.

Or perhaps he's choosing not to get involved when there are four Heroics to their three.

"You'd think you'd be grateful I chose to stay out of it," I say, gesturing at the pair. "It only took one of us to beat you guys like a two-penny drum."

"Penny?" Yllis mutters to Bolo.

"Primitive form of currency. They used metal."

"Not Credits? How primitive were they?"

"Some of them were trying to make electronic digits a form of currency," Bolo says. "Somehow it was shared too, among all these laptops. I'm still not sure why storing computers on their laps was considered important."

"And you're sure we have to work with them?"

Bolo nods.

I ignore the byplay since while the pair was talking, the kid shot to his feet and got in my face, shouting about how he was going to show me. I considered beating him, then I had a much better idea.

"Okay," I say.

"Okay?" Portu parrots back at me, clearly confused.

Since I'm speaking Galactic, the closest equivalent is something like "If you want it." Except shorter.

"One second."

Portu frowns even more while I focus within, pulling up the equations and adjusting them. I don't use System Edit at all, not wanting to draw attention, but grabbing him and tossing him into the air without warning and throwing up the Sanctum is a minor risk. Especially since I've used everything else in the Erethran Honor Guard Skill set by now.

Wece lurches to his feet, only for Xaxas to get in his way, making the man stand down. I think Xaxas wouldn't have, if not for the fact that he's realized I didn't hurt Portu, just gave him what he wanted. A Sanctum to punch through, high up in the sky, surrounding him.

"So now, where were we?" I say, smiling at Wece and Xaxas.

"Uhh…" Wece pauses, then looks at his hand and the mug still in it. "Drinking."

"Nope. We were about to talk about how you're going to help us get to our destination."

Wece's eyes narrow while Xaxas frowns. Above, the Sanctuary shimmers and twists, the kid within still hammering at the Skill. Now that he's not connected to the ground and drawing strength from it, nor even connected to his chosen Domain—Sanctuary actually creating a new one by its very existence on the inside—poor Portu is at less than half strength.

A fact that Wece realizes and, more importantly, that he's all alone out here. With a bunch of zealous Heroics who don't seem to care about social niceties.

"I could provide some contacts and directions… maybe point you to the best Underworld Guide that we have… if it'll get you all out of here faster," Wece says finally.

I grin and wave Bolo and Yllis forward, stepping back to let them do the actual negotiations.

I do love it when a plan comes together.

Chapter 12

"Now this is more like it," I say, grinning wide.

Seated on the swaying back of a dinosaur-like creature—a proper one with scales and metal plates rather than feathers—whose back comes up to around three-quarters of the tree line is quite lovely. Especially since, at this moment, we've managed to break out of the tree line into a short-lived series of rolling planes. Short-lived because I can see the encroaching forest in the distance and note how the ground is already returning to its natural state.

Still, it's one heck of a thing to be seated on a dinosaur, surveying a prehistoric alien world in the equivalent of a palanquin. Makes you feel like a rajah. Except, you know, without the colonialism, genocide, and exploitation.

So maybe not so much.

Outside of taking cheap shots at dead civilizations, feeling the massive monster beneath me move at the gentlest of proddings of its Beast Driver is wonderful. They're not exactly a Beast Driver of course, what with the need to specialize to control such monsters, but close enough. There are a few common variations, some a little more specific than others, almost all of the variations focused in this biome. The usual tradeoffs, though I'm a little surprised by the number of individuals willing to make that tradeoff. In the wider Galactic universe, specializing yourself to a specific location is uncommon. There's just so much to see that most people don't bother.

Unless, you know, it's a specific kind of thing like Cave Adventurers or Underwater Dungeon Explorers or Meteorite Pilots or…

You know what? Maybe I'll stop trying to generalize hundreds of billions of people and just say that I don't see it that often.

"You should come up!" I bend over and shout down to Mikito.

To my surprise, the Samurai had objected to riding on the dinosaur. Instead, she conjured her ghostly steed and is riding alongside the massive creatures. She muttered things about safety and maneuverability, but considering each step threatens to crush her and these things are highly mobile… I'm sure the flash of fear that crossed her eyes when asked to ride the monster had more to do with her objections.

Weird the random mental hiccups we have.

"I'm fine!" Mikito answers me once again, glaring up at my cheekily grinning face.

What can I say? I'm having fun and there's little enough of that.

The other person who can't ride is Yllis, though she and Bolo are on her hover transports that cut through the opening behind the group. The creature beneath me—an actual herbivore, even mutated—had thrown quite a few objections to letting a giant carnivore—even in her transformed state—on its back. Rather than fight it, we'd just agreed to let them ride behind on the transport.

The Storm Warden and Harry have joined me up here, though that had been a brief debate about splitting us up along the line of the convoy. Harry refused, and the argument petered out pretty quickly. Anyway, keeping all of us positioned in the center of the dinosaur pack means we can help out when necessary.

It helps, of course, that I've finally got my Extra Hands deployed. I'd kept them unsummoned for a bit, mostly because I wasn't in the mood to look at a twisted reflection of me as recorded by the System after months of torture. However, after my last temper tantrum, I girded my loins enough to pull them out. So far, they're… normal. Ish.

No, I'm not looking too deep into matters. Instead, I keep them spread out over the convoy, two in front, two behind, myself in the middle.

"Three o'clock, seven hundred meters, boy-o," Ali calls, floating alongside me lazily.

A quick perusal of the minimap shows the glowing dots of a group of waiting monsters. After that, repeated uses of Beacon of the Angels on the location burns through the defenses and the treeline without an issue. Once I'm done and they're easy to spot and injured, the Storm Warden unleashes a series of lightning strikes from the clouds above, finishing off the fight.

"You know, we make a pretty good team," I say to Xaxas, grinning as the points roll in.

"What am I? Chopped liver?" Harry says. "Marmite?"

"Eh, no one would call you marmite. That'd be cruel." I pause for dramatic effect. "To marmite."

"What is this... marmite?" Xaxas says, sounding confused and intrigued.

Before I can go into elaborate detail, Harry cuts me off. "Just a native Earth dish. It's not really produced anymore, so the value has shot up. At least, the original stuff. A few groups are trying to recreate it, with the byproduct of things like Apocalypse Ale creating rather... interesting... variations."

"It's intoxicating then?" Xaxas asks.

"Not the original," Harry clarifies. "Though considering Apocalypse Ale and the like are made out of poisons and other hallucinogenics, I can't really say about the new things."

"Fascinating." The Yerrick rubs his chin. "We Yerrick had a dish like that, from the Pasmar herds we used to raise. An off-shoot of our kind that we raised for meat and milk. The crud that they regurgitated, after the fourth round, was taken and fermented further, with the byproduct a delicacy."

Ali makes gagging sounds and I do my best to keep my face expressionless. It's a big System and the dietary predilections of aliens are just as varied as the Classes created to support it all. Just because it sounds horrendous doesn't mean I have to comment on it.

"So. Changing the subject," Ali says, spinning to hover in front of me. "When are you going to start going through your Character sheet?"

"Huh?" I say.

"Your Character Sheet. Level up information, Titles, all of that jazz," Ali says.

I frown at the Spirit, curious where he's going with this. We could have this conversation over our mental link. That he chooses to do so out loud means he wants something from me or my answer. The question is, what?

"I'll do it in a moment." In truth, there's no real reason to delay. I've gotten out of the habit of checking, what with not really having access to most of my information for ages. I'm sure there's quite the backlog, but... really. What's the point? I won't get any Skills or attributes, not as I level the Erethran Grand Paladin Class, not until I beat my System Administrator Class, and that won't be for a while. Probably not before I reach our destination in fact.

Truth be told, we're lucky there are enough dragons around that we even have a System connection. It's a light in a long, dark tunnel otherwise, with the System struggling to give us anything beyond the most basic of functionalities everywhere else. Certainly no interfaces.

"Moment bohment." Ali snorts. "Get it done now, will you, boy-o? You're like a child who won't open his presents because he's afraid it's a Nintendo rather than a PS4."

"What do you know of presents?" I say. "Or consoles?"

"I had a very long time to watch your television series, in my dimension. We had a bit of a time shear, so when I was dismissed, another half-dozen years passed. Relatively speaking, that is." Ali shrugs. "Not that it matters so much to my people, other than the constant fear of running out of entertainment."

"Come on, there's an entire Galaxy worth of entertainment," Harry says. "The Galactics might not produce the same things as we did, but there're only so many themes, plots, and characters."

"Exactly!" Ali says. "Finding something new is always hard. Even more so in the main Galaxy itself. The introduction of new cultures always sees fascinating new takes, though we might have to dig a little. Like reality shows. I mean, sure, there are Galactics who have done that, but the idea of tossing people naked and alone into the wilderness without the very same Skills and tools that made them actually strong?"

Xaxas clears his throat. "Actually, in the 298th quadrant, the Vosma Sphere, there's a series of aliens who do that as a ritual to grow their children. They're egg layers, you see, so they need to select their children efficiently. Before my imprisonment, the thirty-eighth season was just beginning."

"Yeah, but that's all ritual and cannibalism, not entertainment. See, in…"

That's just about when I tune out the pair. Rather than suffer their inanity, I turn to my Status Screen as asked. I'm sure Ali will let me know if and when other monsters arrive. In between, I have a Level Up to look at and dismiss, a whole category of kill notifications to quickly peruse, monster data that I can discard, more System Quest updates – from my escape from the Prison of the Lost, from my arrival again on Xy'largh proper - and more.

Status notifications flash past me, one after the other, while I absently peruse the backend of the information blips as they come to me. Not a lot is useful in there, though the way notifications surge and splinter and the information exchange protocols in place are quite fun to review. I even make a few adjustments to the base code, making sure to ping the System in multiple "upload" locations.

I highlighted upload because it's not exactly like there's a cable running from our heads to the System. It's more pervasive than that. In fact, because it's more pervasive, I can't help but poke at the data streams, trying to figure out—again—how the System works.

From a programming point of view, it seems the System is a differentiated, multi-load network run on separate servers that constantly talk to one another. Except there are no real server farms, no central processing areas. It's not as though it's all running the same code, but with their own areas of responsibility; it's just that each node runs things by itself in its own area while also being in constant contact with the rest of itself. Like a hive mind, but more linked.

I'm not even sure I'm describing it properly. Some have postulated that the System is so advanced and runs on so much weird time-space-reality bending Mana that each node is basically a brain powerful enough to run the System itself, but at the same time also contains the entirety of the System.

That's been backed up by people trying to—essentially—destroy the local equivalent of the System, all but one small section. And no, you don't really want to know how you go about destroying an all-pervasive, all-knowing, Mana-formed reality operating system. Let's just leave it as highly restricted, banned Classes that deal with information forms.

Anyway, it's all fun and games until I get a notification I didn't expect.

Title Acquired: Defiant (Sort Of)

You've been subjected to over 300+ Standard days of torture and have yet to give your torturers what they want. This has shown admirable courage and significant idiocy. You might also be a masochist at heart.

This Title may be lost.

Effect: You may now alter your pain thresholds by +/- 30%

I snort, shaking my head as the System snarks at me. Or was it a System Administrator who chose to write that, since he had nothing better to do?

Or a Galactic Council member, reviewing things like this and making the minor changes they can make? Titles are one of those aspects.

Title: *You're Almost There*

Having achieved a System Quest rating of 95%, you are nearing the true secrets of the System. There are numerous powers that might not desire your success at this endeavor. It's a good thing persistence and the ability to run away really fast have been ingrained in you.

Effect: Information about Title Holder and his allies are now locked under System Administrator protocols. Acquisition of further information about Title Holder or his allies will require approval of seniormost System Administrator. Experience gain has increased by 347%.

That Title shouldn't be mine. I don't have a 95% completion rate. And yet, it's here. Trying to figure the hack out just gets me bounced. Looks like I don't have the clearance to view that.

"Son of a bitch," I say.

"What?" Ali says, eyes narrowing in suspicion and concern.

Xaxas scans for threats and finding none—well, none worth discussing—looks back at me and waits for my answer.

"Just a Title," I say. Acknowledging the prompt, I watch it populate in my Status Screen. A mental nudge sends the full text to Ali, though he dismisses it after a second.

"Saw that one," Ali says. "I didn't even have to change anything on it."

I grunt. Much of my display is cleaned up and sorted by Ali, making life easier for me. Though ever since I got Galactic as a language pack, it's been a lot simpler for him too. No need to translate from System to Galactic to English.

Of course, it's rather fascinating how Galactic works. Not that everyone in the Galaxy only speaks the language, but with the System allowing language downloads and basically implanting the knowledge, it's really easy to make a universal language in the way even English never managed to do on Earth. While there are regional variations in accents, pronunciations, and spellings, it's still relatively close because of the System.

On the other hand, for the racial and cultural purists, the System also works the other way. You don't have to worry about losing a language, because you can just download the entire language pack into a young adult's brain. And since everyone is actually fluent in the language, it's easy enough for children to pick up on it. Same with cultural practices, though those—like most mass consensus-based things—slowly evolve over time.

"And what, exactly, does the Title do?" Xaxas says, interrupting my musings.

"Hides us. From the Administrators and anyone else looking." I rub the back of my neck, eyeing the surroundings before sighing. "Be more useful if we weren't contained to one planet, but something's better than nothing."

"Are humans all this dumb?" Xaxas asks Ali.

"Hey!" Harry protests, turning away from his recording of the surroundings and his commentary to his soon-to-be audience. "I resent that."

"Also, resemble," I pipe up.

"You know he just insulted you, right?" Harry says.

"By calling me stupid. While I sit on a dinosaur in a hollow planet in another galaxy, riding to my almost-certain death." I shrug. "The sting has worn out."

"Yes," Ali finally answers Xaxas. "This one more. But exactly why are you saying that now?"

"This something is better than nothing?" Xaxas says. "Some oxygen is certainly better than none. But lack of oxygen is still bad. Some monsters are certainly worse than no monsters, if you want a safe night's sleep."

"It's a saying," I say, exasperated.

"From where?"

"Earth! In English."

"You are speaking Galactic. Use Galactic metaphors," Xaxas counters. "Or else speak your barbaric language."

"You know what, you can take your Galactic centrism and shove it!" I snarl, then get up to shift forward a few feet on the large palanquin so I don't have to talk to Xaxas. Just before I sit down, I note his grin, the way he preens at winning the fight.

"*You okay, John?*" Ali sends.

"*Yeah. Getting a little tired of big and ugly testing me though.*"

"*So, why aren't you doing anything about it?*" Ali sounds genuinely curious.

I consider how to explain it, then simply answer. "*Arguing with a dead man seems kind of dumb.*" Not exactly nice to call him dead, but then again, anyone joining me is pretty much guaranteed a visit to the Reaper. "*If he wants to pick on me to make himself feel better and distract from his own pain, I can deal. Anyway, it's my Quest he's on. He and Harry can hate me all they want, so long as they help.*"

There's a profound silence over the mental link, as though Ali's literally sending that silence to me. It's a neat trick, but also annoying, so I send back a mental nudge.

"*Just checking you're still you. Because that almost sounds mature and reasonable.*"

"*Whatever. I got a Status Screen to view.*"

And so saying, I pull up my new Status Screen. Been a while since I poked at it, especially with the Levels I've gotten. I'm also curious about the new Titles, wondering if they've done anything to my Screen. I doubt it, but worth the check.

Status Screen			
Name	John Lee	Class	Junior System Admin (Grand Paladin)
Race	Human (Male)	Level	27 (30)
Titles			
Monster's Bane, Redeemer of the Dead, Duelist, Explorer, Master Questor, Galactic Silver Bounty Hunter, Galactic Bounty (Polonium), Galactic Rebel, Corrupt Questor, Chaos Bringer, Curse of the Anathema (Earth), Breaker of the Galaxy, Defiant (Sort of), You're Almost There, (Living Repository), (Class Lock)			
Health	7000	Stamina	7000
Mana	7720	Mana Regeneration	561 / minute
Attributes			
Strength	504	Agility	597
Constitution	700	Perception	547
Intelligence	772	Willpower	666
Charisma	225	Luck	436
Class Skills			
Mana Imbue	5*	Blade Strike*	5
Thousand Steps	1	Altered Space	2
Two are One	1	The Body's Resolve	3
Greater Detection	1	A Thousand Blades*	4
Soul Shield*	8	Blink Step	2
Portal*	5	Army of One	4

Sanctum	2	Penetration	9ᵉ
Aura of Chivalry	1	Eyes of Insight	2
Beacon of the Angels	2	Eye of the Storm	1
Vanguard of the Apocalypse	2	Society's Web	1
Shackles of Eternity*	4	Immovable Object / Unstoppable Force*	1
Domain	1	Judgment of All	6
(Grand Cross)	(2)	(Extra Hands)	(3)
System Edit	4	(Defense of the Fallen)	(3)
External Class Skills			
Instantaneous Inventory	1	Frenzy	1
Cleave	2	Tech Link	2
Elemental Strike	1 (Ice)	Shrunken Footsteps	1
Analyze	2	Harden	2
Quantum Lock	3	Elastic Skin	3
Disengage Safeties	2	Temporary Forced Link	1
Hyperspace Nitro Boost	1	On the Edge	1
Fates Thread	2	Peasant's Fury	1
Combat Spells			
Improved Minor Healing (IV)		Greater Regeneration (II)	

Greater Healing (II)	Mana Drip (II)
Improved Mana Missile (IV)	Enhanced Lightning Strike (III)
Firestorm	Polar Zone
Freezing Blade	Improved Inferno Strike (II)
Elemental Walls (Fire, Icc, Earth, etc.)	Ice Blast
Icestorm	Improved Invisibility
Improved Mana Cage	Improved Flight
Haste	Enhanced Particle Ray
Variable Gravitic Sphere	Zone of Denial

"*I need to do something about my false Class,*" I send to Ali, frowning at the lower Level. Lots of Levels to catch up on, especially considering each Level requires millions of points, even for me.

"*Well, you do have your new Title in play.*"

I nod, rubbing my chin. I poke at the last line again, pulling up the System Code once more and tracking it back. It has hooks going into all my allies, but I can tell immediately that the amount of experience boost they're getting isn't as much as mine.

Absently, I locate a monster and blast it with a conjured Enhanced Particle Ray spell, watching it shrivel. I have to release a couple more spells since it doesn't fall immediately, what with me needing to work on my actual spells more, but it eventually dies.

LucJoes Brain Parasite—Larval Form (Level 74) Killed
+7492 XP Gained (+18,505 XP Boosted)

Tracking the XP flowing from me to the others in the System, I note that it's not a three hundred plus percent increase, but a total three hundred plus percent gain. Which is still nice, but not nearly as high as I'd like. On the other hand, as usual, Mikito is getting a drain from it, and hers is…

"*SO GODDAMN BROKEN!*" She's not only getting a percentage of my boosted experience gain, she then gets a bonus amount increase on top of that when it arrives.

"*What?*" Ali grumbles at me.

Experience gains and the System Edit information I get are one thing he doesn't bother editing or doesn't have access to, respectively. Which is why he's surprised when I explain it to him.

"*Yeah, bloody broken. It's what a good System Administrator would fix, I think…*"

I grunt, fingers twitching as I almost call up the Ticketing Board. But passively viewing the information is one thing. Pulling up the Ticketing Board is probably another. Though just looking can't hurt…

Then again, I've heard that one before.

"So what you going to do about it?" Ali speaks out loud, floating over to me and raising a bushy eyebrow.

I stare at the data I have, then dismiss it, grinning widely at the little Spirit. Whatever. The Title works for me anyway. "It looks like it might be time for some good old-fashioned grinding."

I feel a little guilty, knowing I could be spending my time looking over the data download I received when we hit the Shop in the settlement, that I could be figuring out how to fix Ezz. However, a part of me is doing that already, the part that the System enhanced. Crunching through the programming notes, putting the information into easily digestible parts that relate to older programs that I know.

I could speed it up, but there's something more important to do. Because, end of the day, personal power is important in this world. And no matter how long it takes to fix Ezz—and I know, instinctively, it's going to take a bit—he's just a machine for now. There are limits to what he can do.

And perhaps, just perhaps, I'm not looking forward to the way he'll look at me. At how I'll be accused of failure. Of the things done to him...

I push the thought aside and force my grin to widen.

Ali can't help but smile back, while Xaxas looks at first confused, then savagely enlightened when Harry explains the terminology.

Time to dance.

Chapter 13

It's never as easy as it seems. Bolo, Yllis, and the rest of the caravan complain about us leaving to do our thing. I don't get it, what with them already asking us to do the killing and safeguarding, but it seems clearing a forest path and going wholesale destruction is supposedly different.

Meh.

The argument only gets convincing when I tell the others on the downlow what is happening. At which point Bolo and Yllis grow extremely enthusiastic. The only person who is upset about all this is Harry, who can't maximize his experience gain, what with us not allowing him to release any further news. Also, it helps to mollify them a bit when I leave one of my Extra Hands behind, sending the others on a wide-ranging hunt for problems. Letting them do their thing will help with making our trail harder to follow. Sometimes, I almost wish I had conjured one up on the planet surface.

Woulda, coulda, shoulda.

Now that I know I have a little more leeway, I bounce around using Blink Step to range far and wide. At first, Mikito wanted to stick close to me, a little paranoid after our separation. I had to point out she was becoming as bad as a clingy ex before she left me alone. Not before calling me a lot of other Japanese names, none of them baka. I could figure out what they mean, but considering baka is idiot, I'm sure whatever else she used was a lot nastier.

What I don't want the others to know is that I'm still off. It's not always, nor even that often. Yet, as another fast-moving tongue—one with barbs on the end and a hollow center for slurping up the gooey insides—appears, I find myself freezing, flashbacks catching up to me. Memories of having monsterized lampreys clamped onto my body, bits and pieces sucked out;

the creatures burrowing deeper, chewing and slurping and dumping a venom that liquified me…

I shudder as the System comes in, cleansing fire in my brain as it finds something it missed, helping ease the burden. It's still there, but removed, like a movie I watched long ago—a torture-porn freak's greatest hits collection.

Then I'm back, lamprey mouth clamped onto the Spitzrocket's metallic hide, the tongue pulsing as venom pumps onto the metal suit in an attempt to eat its way through. A sweeping blade cuts upward, parting tongue from body. Then I use a Blade Strike to follow up. The monster arches away, its worm-like body retracting backward.

Blink Step behind it, hand grabbing its head as I throw myself downward, thrusters firing. We crash into a nearby tree, and I drag its face down the thorny bark, the barbs tearing holes through its body as it thrashes against me. I care not, as I drop my sword and turn, calling forth a Polar Zone on a nearby copse of trees.

Hundreds of tiny worms, growing on the leaves and eating the sentient, carnivorous wildlife, shriek as the temperature drops. It drops further as I tap into my Elemental Affinity, borrowing Ali's link to the greater electromagnetic force to grip at the electrons that are slowing down due to the spell. I crush them in my mental grip, creating a localized area of force where they don't flow as easily. Doubling, tripling, quadrupling the effects of the spell.

The shrieks are muting, the creatures dying. Ice forms and even the trees begin to expire. Keeping my mind on the monsters, the pressure on them, I turn to my next victim. A casual flick of my other hand tosses the squirming worm away, its barbed tail ineffectively striking at my back. Soul Shield firms up my protection before I conjure my sword again.

Blade Strike, pushed through the Spitzrocket's Overdrive option, cuts the still-living worm apart, along with a group of trees, a couple of monkey-like creatures, and an armored hedgehog that was trying to hide. They're all incidentals, as Ali highlights my next target.

Blink Step, again and again.

A tribe of semi-sapient creatures, all of them hidden from normal senses. No scent, no sound, nothing on the normal bands of the visual spectrum. Ali found them using his Elemental Force—the only real way to beat his level of affinity is by not having molecules or by using System-hijinks—but I don't have his full strength. Instead, I sense them through the System, cheating via their tenuous connection to the System.

They're spreading out, working in hunting parties of three each as they head toward my last known position. They wield crude weapons and long claws, and they creep forward with nary a care in the world, confident in their camouflage. While I hover in mid-air, it takes them a bit to recognize me, more than enough time for me to do two things.

Firstly, I scan them, picking out their leader.

Nakani Elder (Alpha) Level 201
HP: 20,198/20,198
MP: 2281/2287
Conditions: Tribal Leader, Prey's Lament (Aura), Friend of the Forest (Greater), Camouflage (Greater)

Everyone else is lower, with quite the wide range, but the bastard is nasty. I consider my options really, really quickly; a thrill of fear runs through me, but more importantly, a savage glee. Prey's Lament is a fear-based aura, a powerful one. It's why none bother the Nakani, and even the lowest member of their tribe has it.

The tendrils of fear, of creeping terror and overwhelming dread, press down on my mind. The System doesn't even bother to rouse itself, for the aura does nothing to me. I've seen and dealt with worse. There is nothing the Nakani can offer but a quick death and that is no longer part of my nightmares.

On the other hand, that Tribal Leader condition is a passive boost. I've seen its like before, and this one isn't significantly different enough that it's worth me reviewing the exact data stream. Like most Leadership-based buffs, it gives him an increase in everything from health and damage reduction to speed and strength on the offensive side.

Rather than take him out first, I pull on my spells. I don't use them much, but this is a good time to pull out some old favorites. Enhanced Mana Cage slams upward, trapping the leader. Then, because I can do it, I drop Sanctum on the bastard. Before his people can get to him, I conjure Earth Walls all around, pushing them away and even letting the walls fall down a little on him. Then a Variable Gravitic Sphere right over the center crushes him to the ground and holds the monster still.

With him trapped—or as trapped as I can get him—I pay attention to the other Nakani. A spear, thrown with such force and Mana-impetus that it cracks my Soul Shield, strikes me. I start juking, narrowly dodging the first couple spears and taking two more in quick succession as the rest of the Nakani who held back follow up.

My Soul Shield shatters on me, but that's fine.

Blink Step takes me out of sight before bolos and ropes arc over where I am, the creatures conjuring them from their own little pocket dimensions in their bodies. They use the pocket dimensions as weapons too, since a cut thrown at the back of one of the monsters sees my sword ripped in half as a portion of it just disappears in its fur.

"What the hell! Ali!" I flick the remnants of the blade into the face of another Nakani as I skirt backward. I conjure my swords and the Thousand Blades follow-up, even as the Nakani tries to grapple with me now that I'm in range. "That was not listed in its Conditions!"

"Not my fault, boy-o! This is the Forbidden Zone. Not everything comes through properly here."

I snarl but don't have time for arguing. The damn thing isn't even slowing down, and a Blade Strike only damages it a little. The other blades, flashing through the air, are sliced apart by its dimensional storage ability, but I notice something fascinating.

Blink Step from Ali's point of view puts me in an entirely unexpected location. I perch on the tree branch, feeling it creak alarmingly as my blades, still following their initial path via magic—even those cut apart—slice into the monster.

"It's limited on how big a defensive hole it creates," I send to Ali.

Options flash through my mind. Of course, going range and unleashing my area-of-effect Skills like Judgment of All, Beacon of the Angels, and Grand Cross would work. Hell, I have quite a few chaining lightning spells that would do the job.

Though that's just boring.

For the first time since I escaped, I'm enjoying the fight. The other battles were struggles through trauma and rage and need. A push to get moving again, to keep me in the fight. The impetus of survival drove me on with blood and death and blood as I danced through the sky. But that's not enough.

Not to keep going, not to keep fighting. Even for the most broken, twisted versions of me, even knowing I might die, just surviving has never been enough. Not without a bit of joy, not without a bit of that battle lust.

It's why I don't call down the heavens on the Nakani, why I don't play artillery cannon. Instead, I get down and dirty, Blink Stepping in and out, my swords conjured and dismissed as I thrust, cut, and sweep them apart long before they realize I'm there.

Fate's Thread plays its part, grabbing hold of my opponents with a metaphysical string, yanking them into one another only for them to either get sliced apart through unfriendly fire or to crash to the ground. And their surprise allows me to pin them to the ground.

I grab spears, bolos, and even the occasional rock, borrowing their weapons to wield against them. I Blink Step face up and sliding across the ground, underneath my opponent. A quick thrust impales them from beneath before I bowl them over. Even before they finish falling, I'm gone, reappearing on a branch farther away.

I hit and run, tearing them apart with attacks that never stop coming. My Mana drops like a waterfall, but my attacks are beginning to tell. I focus on crippling, rather than killing, so that when the group regathers beneath my tree, they're moving slower, injured.

That's when I drop in amongst them, swords dancing.

In the movies, when the hero fights dozens, they never get a scratch on them. Maybe a punch here or there, but only for dramatic effect. Opponents come at you one at a time, or with just enough of a beat that you can pull off a stunning defense.

In reality, when you have to do battle with multiple opponents, you're going to get hurt. Multiple opponents might not attack at the same time, but they do so close enough that you might get punched in the back while you're retracting from a block. Or a furred, invisible monster might try a body hug even as you finish lopping off a leg.

Time slows as I spin and cut, swords appearing and disappearing from my hand as they shatter and crack, as edges disappear into a void, never to return. Portions of the Spitzrocket flicker away as they pull apart my armor with their own skills.

But there are limitations to all things, and they can only take so much before they have to stop. Their pocket dimensions aren't an endless void like my need for validation. So while they shave away portions of Spitzrocket and my body underneath with particularly well placed strikes, they also eventually hit an end. That's what keeps me alive, what keeps them from being true nightmare monsters.

Cut, dodge, cut, drop, conjure, dodge, headbutt, scream, cut.

Time flows like my blood and theirs, coating the ground. But all good things have to come to an end, and this one arrives when the damn Alpha breaks out. He shatters his prison, the System providing a thread of the feedback toward me when an "indestructible" Skill gets broken down. The feedback isn't enough to throw off my concentration —not least because the System is so corrupted here that it can't.

A second later, the Alpha Nakani arrives at our location. In his haste coming over, he shatters the bones of one of his tribe mates, bowling him over and sending him crashing into a couple of others. The claw that strikes toward my face is a dark void, a look into the abyss I'd be cast into if I allowed it to hit me.

I don't.

Blink Step takes me away, even as I stop playing. Grand Cross forms high above us, the weaponized circle of power crushing everything to the ground. The gravitic plane buckles under its artificial conditions and proceeds to push upward, retaliating against my Skill.

Caught between the two, the Nakani scream and struggle to get away. The Alpha is the only one that manages to drag its body free of the attack, small bones shattered, blood flowing from its eyes and other orifices. I chuckle darkly before I saunter over to it.

Not for dramatic effect this time but because I'm really low on Mana.

The Alpha surges to its feet, garbling at me in some weird language. I don't understand it, but it doesn't take a Galactic linguist to parse together threats. After all these years, I have to admit, they blend together. Lousy honor, threats against nonexistent wives and kids, friends and family, the promise of retribution and torture and a painful death.

I don't bother letting it finish, cutting at it. It blocks my attack, finding strength from its rage and despair at the loss of its entire family. For a second, we share a look and I find myself reflected in its eyes. For a second, we stare at one another—before the bastard puts its claws through my stomach.

When it removes its hand, it leaves a big scar, just about missing my spine but taking out chunks of everything else in neat, circular holes. Blood and bile pour out, and along with it, any sympathy that might have begun stirring.

Grinning savagely, I get back to work. The little shit isn't going to kill itself.

***

Days of fighting, our bodies immersed in the thrum of Mana and the push of blades through muscle and flesh. The rhythm of the fight overtakes all other considerations, with the team keeping the convoy protected and sheltered in our dome of doom and destruction.

I range further, Blink Step taking me far into the nethers of the endless forest that covers the hollow world. At times, I stop to survey the edges of the split dimension we live in, sensing through my Elemental Affinity and System-expanded senses the frayed edges that border between the two. Occasionally, lava bubbles forth from a gap, changing the environment and leaving pools of magma and baked earth around it.

In the other dimension, the monsters are different, creatures of fire and earth, wielding the elements as naturally as their overheated bodies. The normal ecosystem does battle with the interlopers, the edges of the ecosystems in a constant battle—both overt, in the push and heave of bodies, and covert, as plants transform themselves to better handle the heat.

Vegetation changes with dizzying variety, yet they stay together in amazing consistency. The trees are of the same breed types for the most part, but the mutations from living in a high Mana environment see them grow sentient and vicious. Everything from elemental affinities to explosive thorns and grasping tendrils, it all shows up.

There's even a copse of trees that I Blink Step close by, thinking it's a clearing, one late evening, only for half-shadowed, immaterial trees to tear into me. Living shadows wrap around my limbs while a domain twists into space, blocking escape. I have to call down a Beacon of the Angels onto my very location multiple times to shatter both the domain and destroy the trees.

Over time, the battles become routine, the hiccups in my movements slowing. Flashbacks come, but slower and with more distance, their presence muted by the System. I heal in an artificial way, papering over the raw bleeding psychic wounds with System-staples and driving need. Knowing that at some point, it'll come apart.

With my Extra Hands in play and my own activities, I suck up experience like it's 80% cocoa coming out of a buffet chocolate fountain. Days pass in this haze of battle, time enough for the convoy to arrive at our first stop. With Ali and me playing Blink Step hopscotch and triggering simple Portal, we get back just in time for the force shields to turn off at the city, revealing the cluster of buildings within.

And the ambush waiting for us.

Chapter 14

Actions have consequences. Tearing apart the ecosystem with abandon has revealed our location to local forces, and they charge us without hesitation. Settlement defensive weapons, suborned from the owners, open up on us, firing a series of blasts before control is ripped backward. Other Shadow Council-loyal Master Classers activate their other abilities, a pair of Juggernauts rushing forward to bounce the pair of slow-moving dinosaurs, still in pain, aside to crash into Bolo.

The Dragon Lord is thrown backward, momentum and physics taking control for a few seconds. The Juggernauts never stop moving—as per their name—shifting direction to charge after him. Closely following the pair are fast-moving shadows and a pair of casters. One is healing a Juggernaut from a deep slash on one arm, the other throwing buffs and curses.

Not that I have time to worry about that. The settlement's anti-monster weaponry has targeted me, the single Extra Hand I have in play, and Yllis. The first blast is shrugged off by my shield, but the second throws me backward. My Hand isn't as lucky, having been focused upon by a third again as many artillery cannons as fired upon me. He bounces backward, only for more firepower to target him, including a couple of debuffs that drain his Mana. Considering the Hand is just Mana, that's not a good thing.

While I struggle to right myself and Ali turns away a third wave of attacks, I reach out to my Hands, hoping to contact them. Unfortunately, the hollow planet messes with our comms, shutting down my ability to bring them back.

I waste precious seconds, seconds that a Hacker—or the Galactic equivalent of it at least—uses to tap into the Spitzrocket, shutting down its defenses and mobility options. The Heroic Class mecha can't stop that from happening, but it is able to block any further or more dangerous assaults.

"Thousand hells!" I curse.

It goes out over party chat even as I tap into my Inventory ability and drop the Spitzrocket directly into it. That frees me up and takes away the Hacker's biggest method of hurting me. I also will the Neural Link off, using a hardwired disconnect to ensure that no one can get in and hurt me. It's one of the reasons a Hacker isn't the most common Class, and why people like me still prefer our swords at times.

But the delay is enough for the next party of Master Classers to get into position. The moment I'm free, they slam down a binding ritual. Glowing lines of power appear underneath my feet as they lock me in place. My Skills short-circuit, the Mana meant for them rerouting through the very same lines. The quartet of robed casters stand around me, channeling magic and Mana to hold me still, while another pair of Master Classers appear before me, weapons leveled.

"Status!" I call, even as I attempt to conjure my weapon. It works, since this is a System ability and not one that requires Mana. But my other swords that drift alongside me, that are intrinsic to the Erethran Honor Guard weapon style, are missing.

"Killing… time!" my Hand snarls, but a glimpse of the minimap shows him in battle with a team of Master Classers. He's down a lot of Mana, his health—his lifeforce—almost gone. Even as I watch, the cannons keep firing, hitting him and those he's fighting without care.

"Busy!" Bolo snarls. There's a resounding crash, one I know well, from a hammer impacting an unwilling participant in the Dragon King's game of whack-a-mole. Out of the corner of my eyes, I see a Juggernaut go airborne in the far distance of the forest. The group has definitely covered a lot of ground.

There's no answer from Yllis, but the screeching dragon in the sky, dueling a pair of wyrms and what I can only call a manticore, is answer enough. I don't even recall them taking to the sky or her transforming, but I was locked down for a few seconds.

Long enough.

"I'm good... ummm... mostly..." Harry answers, his voice a little strained.

Ali flashes Harry's icon and I see it surrounded by red dots on my minimap, but his health isn't dropping. Hostage perhaps, but not a combatant. Good enough.

"Fools for arriving to your own demise. I shall bathe in your foolish blood, dance in the rain as your disemboweled, mewling bodies crawl back to your foolish masters. Tell them to send the worthy, the dangerous, the Legendary. I am Xaxas Stormfist and I shall not fall to fools like you!"

Thunder roars above us all and rain falls as though the drama queen meant for it to happen that way. I almost believe he did.

The minimap gives me a better view of what is going on than the idiot, but he and his opponents—a swarm of them, rather than the smaller number of Master Classers they gathered for the rest of us—are tearing through the settlement. Keeping exact track is difficult. I can almost see why they sent a ton of opponents at the Storm Warden.

The Storm Warden has a number of area-of-effect attacks, but they're mostly geared toward buffing and debuffing. Some of his Skills—like his Aura and clan chaining effects—are entirely useless without his lost family. Others boost his physical abilities and his melee damage output, wielding the powers of the very named storm to create environmental effects. The lightning he unleashes every once in a while is nasty and chains, and against a group of Basic Classers, he would be a true nightmare.

Teams of Advanced Classers have the survivability to weather the incidental debuffs though, along with healers and other spellcasters to boost them and strip away the effects of his storms. And rather than provide Xaxas a single, massive attacker that would take forever to wear down—as they are doing to Bolo—they give him multiple targets. The Storm Warden might kill his opponents given enough time, but there's always another.

It's a gamble, meant to wear him down with the sheer volume of bodies and keep him busy. A gamble that if used against someone like Bolo or Mikito would see their people dead much faster. Against Xaxas, they have just enough time to pull back to heal up and remove debuffs before wading back in. Enough time to allow the Master Classers sent against the rest of us to come back and deal with him.

In theory.

Mikito is a duelist in a sense, her Skills meant to allow her to deal high levels of damage against a small number of opponents. She's dueling the only Heroic Classer in play—a veritable insult to people like Bolo or the StormWarden. At her current Levels, she's definitely middle of the pack.

But unlike the rest of us, she has a clear advantage.

Hitoshi grows in size, tearing at the twenty-foot-tall metal Elemental construct that assaults her, the metal fish Heroic that controls it hiding within the greater body. Yet Hitoshi's attacks leach power from the Elemental, its body rusting as the weapon passes through it, cutting apart body with preternatural ease.

Round and round, Mikito rides her ghostly horse, attacking the monster even as spikes of metal erupt from the ground and the creature, bands of constricting metal crushing her and her steed in an attempt to restrain and kill.

Then I have no more time to watch, as my own troubles reach me within my cage. But I've seen enough.

"You're tossing your lives away. There's not enough of you to stop us," I say. An echoing boom and a cascade of lightning coming from the sky, striking the settlement and the fighters within, punctuate my point. "Walk away."

"And let you hunt us down, Breaker?" The woman on the right, wielding a pair of swords, slightly curved, a twisting and sharp guard rising from each end, answers me with a sneer.

"I won't. I have no interest in you."

"And we're to trust you, Anathema? The Rebel..." Even more scorn now. I'm amazed she can pack it all in.

"Come on, there's an explanation for all... hey!" I interrupt myself as I jump backward, the short spear her partner wields suddenly growing in size as they thrust it at me.

The female with the spear—or what I'll call female, though I'm not entirely sure since she's purple and chrome and rather androgynous, but with what I assume to be egg sacs along her legs—is fast, her attack managing to catch me even when I dodge.

"*Ali...*" I catch the next attack on my sword, deflecting the spear upward and to the side.

She flurries the attack, the tip of the spear nearly disappearing from sight. I react purely by instinct, blocking the attacks, and even then, it's not enough. I stumble to a stop, back pressed against the cage, grateful it's not searing me and bleeding from a trio of wounds I failed to block.

"Working on it, but I'm a little busy too."

Surprised, I check upward. Only to find Ali dog-fighting a swarm of other Spirits. None are his size or density—if that's even the right word for the feel he gives me—but there are a lot of them. Of course, the occasional one just ups and disappears, as their summons ends or their owner dies; but they twist and tear at the Spirit, assaulting his ability to be in this realm.

"Fine. I'll do it myself," I say out loud, more as a final warning to my opponents than anything else. I feel a little twinge of guilt, mostly because it seems they're convinced I'm an oath-breaking rebel who's thrown the galaxy into uproar over my personal whims.

Which, you know, is kind of right but…

The blade that cuts up at my face nearly takes off a chunk of my skull. As it stands, I get away enough that it only lops off part of my ear. Woolgathering in the middle of a fight is not the way to go. I might out-Class them, but they're highly skilled and have full access to their abilities.

A quick counter-thrust by me is blocked by the sword-wielder with her other weapon, even as she brings her weapon back to cut. I pull a piece of bone from my Inventory to block, the loot cracking under her attack. But while I'm defending from one person, the spear dips low and cuts at my thigh, plunging deep before withdrawing in a shower of blood.

Hobbling to the side, my body already healing the damage, I try to put one opponent in front of the other. The pair don't allow it though, moving with a smooth economy of motion and a level of awareness of one another that shows the amount of training they've put into their teamwork.

Another clash of blade and bone, another flurry of attacks. Something glowing and green yanks my leg down so that a low-line spear thrust becomes a thrust aimed for my lungs. I manage to dodge most of that, leaving a line of pain across my back, by tumbling to the ground entirely. As I roll to the side, I do so over a series of spikes that plunge into my body and expand within it, gripping flesh.

Pain.

I tear myself free, manage to get in a lucky strike with the bone that leaves a deep bruise, and come up. I pour more Mana into my Skills continuously, attempting to overload the spell casters, even as my temper gets the best of me.

No more defense.

Wading into the battle, taking the cuts and stabs, trusting in my enhanced, over-Leveled body to keep me standing, I clash with the pair. My bone club shatters, and I throw it into the face of the sword-wielder. The spear-wielder pins one of my legs to the ground with the extended weapon and I use my now freed hand to grab at her weapon and yank her close.

I get a good stab in before she makes the spear I'm holding disappear and forces me to tumble to the ground, unbalanced. Another pair of cuts, these nearly detaching my arm from its shoulder. My weapon falls to the ground, fingers no longer able to hold it.

Another roll, another sweeping kick. Damage piles on, my body healing and fixing what it can, but the pair are targeting limbs and connections, forcing my health to work overtime as the critical attacks pile up. For the first time, I worry a little.

So I cheat.

My blood pools on the ground, soaking into it, as my breathing grows labored and my nerves are on fire. The pain is easy to handle, the loss of function less so. I'm forced to push myself further and further in an attempt to stay in the game, but I'm not the only one pushed to the wall. I have a few more aces, but I hold them in reserve, worrying that this is a fakeout.

I get in one strike for every three or four of theirs. With Penetration, my attacks cut deeply, tearing into body and flesh. With Inventory working as a passive, I pull out grenades and throw them onto the ground or to the edges, filling our tiny lighting circle with noise and fury and kittens.

Chaos grenades. You got to love them.

The kittens breathe streams of acid and venom before they disperse, breaking up into their constituent parts of energy and chaos. In the meantime, the clear fighting field we were in becomes pockmarked with holes and obstacles.

Foam grenades pull and restrict, only to be torn away, leaving behind remnant locations. A high-explosive webbing mine springs into play over a foot, wrapping the attacker up for a few seconds as they struggle to free themselves. Blades cut downward, levering themselves free.

In the meantime, I grip the spear, and when it disappears, I'm ready for it. The bear hug is just a ploy to stuff a pair of incendiaries down the armor covering her egg sacs. When I'm thrown aside and kicked away, I activate the gel rounds, watching as her lower back and legs get coated and burn.

That distracts for much longer than a few minutes.

All the while, I try casting spell after spell, pulling upon the Mana of the world. When I pump in another thousand Mana into a Skill, the others outside finally fail.

No Skill, no ritual can last forever. Not my Sanctum, not their binding one. At a certain point, everything fails—and the sheer ratio of Mana use on my end to the amount they have to pour in to control it and block activation of a Skill is highly in my favor. It helps that I have an almost limitless supply of Mana when I tap into System Edit, when I let it flood into my System. I don't actually Edit anything, but just the shift in energy is enough.

Judgment of All activates, and even blunted by our location in the middle of the Forbidden Zone, we're still buffered by the dragons and the status of Xy'largh. It's enough to hurt, to kill in some edge cases. And after that, taking care of these two with Soul Shield, Thousand Blades, and a lot of healing is simple enough.

By the time I'm done, the town is a wreck; the others have fought off or killed their own opponents and the convoy wants nothing more to do with us.

All in all, a typical win for team John.

***

"I thought flying was a bad idea," I say, frowning at the group.

We're gathered inside the settlement, staring at the lone floating blimp that has made its way back under the watchful eye of Yllis. The blimp is weird, a steampunk and new age combination of floating gasbag and jet thrusters. I'm told they use an inert gas within to provide lift, the necessity of a much slower flight speed forcing this compromised design.

"It was a bad idea when we had to worry about being found out." Bolo gestures around us before going on. "If they don't know where we are now, they're dumber than a bag of Dromas droppings."

"So, what? We go fast and hope we outrun problems?" When the pair nods, I shrug in acknowledgment. I do have one more question though. "Why can't we just ride Yllis there? She's more than big enough..." I trail off, catching sight of her slowly reddening face.

"Say that again and I'll kill you myself," Bolo says coldly.

"Uhh..." I open my mouth to apologize and get glared at by both offended parties. I shut it while the pair walk of, Yllis muttering about wanting to kill me again.

"So... I take it that's a no-no then," I say to break the silence.

"Riding a dragon is considered extremely intimate. Only bonded Dragon Knights and their ilk get to do so. Anything else..." Harry shakes his head. "Well, if you want to make an enemy out of a dragon for life, you could do it. They lose a couple of idiots every decade or so, who think it'd be fun to blip themselves over and ride a dragon."

"Damn. I should have..." I consider what I was about to say. It's not as if I've thought to get a data download yet, and really, it's a social thing. Of the many things that I do, social stuff is just not one of them.

"You should maybe not open your mouth so much," Xaxas says, smirking. "At least before you get a cultural download."

"I forgot, all right? I had other things to sort out. Anyway, I can just get one now," I say.

"Then why are you talking?" Xaxas says.

I pause in my rebuttal ,then glance around before realizing they're right. The damn Yerrick smirks, and Harry can't help but snort a little in laughter. The only person who seems to not be laughing at me is Mikito; and that's because she's near the main entrance, watching for trouble.

Rather than waste more time, I walk toward the city's entrance.

Only for Bolo to shout down at me, loud enough for all to hear, "Hey! Baka. It's time to go!"

Over the party chat, I can't help but mutter to the man, "You know, we do have this up and running. And I just need five minutes. Ten at most."

"No time, boy-o." Ali shoots over from the sky, eyes glowing a little.

A scan of the minimap shows no danger, so I can't help but frown. The Spirit is fast to explain, his voice coming a little hurried as he continues.

"Xaxas pulled the storm closer when he used his Skills. That altered the local climate. The Elementals that normally control it, the ones in charge of keeping things working, are coming in hot and angry."

I frown, turning to look at Xaxas, who is listening in. I see the Storm Warden's eyes go wide, and for the first time since I've known him, he looks worried.

"If we don't take off now and get moving, they're going to catch us," Ali says, gesturing for me to get moving.

I do, even as Mikito hurries over too. Harry is already up the beanstalk tether, clambering hand over fist, but Xaxas overtakes him a second later by jumping and grabbing hold of it farther up.

"Well, what are you waiting for?" Bolo calls from high above. "An engraved invitation?"

I cast one last look into the center of the city, knowing that the Shop and everything I want to get is there. I might even…

Then I shake my head, dismissing my desires. If wishes were fishes and all that.

A moment later, my Flight spell kicks in and I rocket upward, headed for the blimp. Running for our lives from a group of angry Elementals.

Really, how bad can it get?

Chapter 15

Thunder crashes all around us, the world lighting up in vivid pink, green, and blue. Storm clouds mixed with granite and more metal-laden dust surround the blimp, reducing our normal lines of sight and giving the lightning that crackles and illuminates us a hallucinogenic property. In the clouds, occasional shadows flit in and out, drawing the attention of the gunners.

So far, nothing has attacked us. In the last hour, the storm has arrived, drawing the full attention of our Captain and his ship's mages. They're working overtime, keeping the environmental shielding that surrounds the craft from being shredded. More than once, a bolt of lightning has struck the shield, arcing over the entirety of the craft before dispersing on the other side.

The light show is amazing, though it leaves those of us within blind for precious seconds before we recover. Even so, treacherous atmosphere or not, the ship can handle it. Or at least, that's what the late-Master Class Dauntless Captain assures us.

Standing on the deck, breathing in the ionized air, feeling the slight thrum of the engines and the much larger shaking as a rumble of thunder passes through the barrier, I have to admit, so far, they're correct. Below deck, the Extra Hand I summoned is keeping an eye out for trouble, though thus far we've just had to wait. At least my other Hands have survived, even if we abandoned them. For now, they'll continue to do their thing before I desummon them.

Got to grind that XP.

Having extracted a copy of the basic login screen and the code around it from Ezz's still form, I've been running simulations through my brain, with the aid of the System, to crack the login while on the top deck. One of the joys of having all this code downloaded from the Shop into my brain and the additional abilities the System has given me is that I can do things like this. No need for a computer; my brain works as one.

It does make me wonder, when I'm fighting, taking and processing and using Skills and spells faster than your everyday human, how much of those points in Intelligence is dedicated to that and how much is dedicated to weird little off-shoot abilities like this.

As always, the System is a black box that offers nothing more than subjective observational data. Much like I'm observing the thrum of power all around us, the shake of the engines and the earth beneath me. I can't shake the feeling that the Elementals are just getting started, which is why I stand up here, rather than chilling within.

"You feel it too, don't you?" I say to Xaxas.

The Storm Warden nods, tilting his head and regarding me. After a moment, he answers me, his voice low and almost ritualistic. "The air is charged. The winds are chaotic and ever moving. They long to escape the grasp of the Elementals, but they will not let them go."

"Yeah, that," I say. "Think we're going to have to—"

I find myself cut-off by stage two of the damn Elementals' plans. Around us, giant cyclones of air emerge, the whirlwinds going from cat one to cat two within seconds. They keep speeding up, making me think they won't settle at tiny piddly dust devils.

The Captain seems to agree with me as he screams at his helmsmen. From a steady push, the aircraft picks up speed. We stop going from normal blimp-level speed to full jet-thruster levels of velocity, the counter force pushing against my face and skin. Instinctively, I tense against the deck, strengthening the pull between myself and the enscrolled wooden planks beneath my feet.

All around us, the winds pick up and push against our bodies. Lightning arcs around the swirling clouds of dust, sparking off metallic sand and crystallizing it before it shoots onward, jumping from twister to twister. Strangely enough, each time it jumps to another cyclone, it grows stronger.

"Ali!" I shout, raising a hand seconds before the first of the lightning arcs hit. I grab at it, feeling the Elementals fight me for control. Their abilities are different than mine, the way they interact with the lightning coming from a different set of equations.

But they're Elementals, creatures of the storm and wind and climate themselves, and I'm just human. I twist and disperse the electrons, but they pull them back. I try to increase attraction down one side, and they just pull even more lightning, letting my pitiful attempts disperse the energy they pulled. Then there's no more time, as the lightning strikes.

Energy arcs all over us, lighting up the shield that surrounds us with spider-web tracings of energy and malevolence. The winds form an artillery barrage of ice particles, sending it crashing into the side of the blimp and wearing at our defenses ever more. Mana engines shriek as they pump more energy into the massive shielding arrays of the ship, but cracks appear even as our hair and loose clothes stand on end.

Lightning explodes with the suddenness of bad news on a warm, summer day, breaking apart any shred of normalcy and leaving you a broken, wretched human. Electrons ripple through the exterior, arcing upward to connect with muscles, clothing, and sapient figures, sometimes with such force that only smoking ruins are left behind. Screams and the continuous rumble of thunder, so close that it vibrates our very bones, roll onward, leaving me deaf to the Spirit's shouts.

Whirlwinds catch at us, threatening to pull us toward them. The ship's engines strain as we seek to escape, smoke erupting from overburdened, clogged technology. Spells are fired from below and within the ship, attempts to curve away the very air and give us space. Out one side of the ship, dragon breath spills, targeting the cold air above that drives the formation of these unnaturally sized twisters.

In the face of the storm, we are but playthings for the Elementals.

I struggle onward, doing my best to offer some protection to myself, to the gunners, and Xaxas beside me. In a small sphere about us, there's a level of normalcy, but it's not enough. Not until Ali appears, floating at the prow of the ship, larger than life. He's grown in size, as though his very stature gives him strength, and the dozens-of-meters-tall Spirit dominates the sightlines ahead. He's no longer dressed in his orange jumpsuit but in a long flowing grey robe. Hands spread wide, he screams into the cacophony—and wind and rain and lightning parts.

Silence, for a second, even as lightning reroutes around the Faraday cage of metallic sand Ali has ripped from the sky. Noise is muted, as the Spirit lowers the cohesion between particles. Wind slows, struggling to overcome to sluggishness he pushes forward, taking the easiest route as kinetic energy disperses below and behind us.

The ship lurches forward, faster than ever, and I throw in my own meager Skill to aid him. A second later, more spells are cast, boosting our momentum and allowing us to race forward as we try to escape the clouds that continue to roll around us, that electrify the air and threaten to tear us down.

Xaxas steps up, his fist thrust into the sky. Something else forms in the cloud—a pair of somethings. Titanic cloud creatures rip and tear at other, semi-solid masses deeper within. Cyclones and whirlwinds that threatened to strike the ship and pull us down are pushed away, gusts of counterwind playing out as the Storm Warden takes full control of the air itself once more.

We push onward, through the storm, the shielding finally flicking back to life. Crew members, saved from damage, are finally revived by the grace of the System and health potions.

And ahead of us, our tiny—not-so-tiny-right-now—savior still cries out. Finally, I manage to hear what Ali is screaming-cackling. I can't help but sigh.

"You shall not pass!"

Chapter 16

The initial period of stormy weather lasts just over an hour. By the time we break out of the worst of it—with Bolo and Yllis having chosen to head out with Xaxas to handle a couple of the more eager Elementals themselves—Ali, the mages, and I are wrung dry. The Spirit crashes into the deck, bounces, and shrinks down to his normal size before floating back to me as though on a tether, the Faraday cage of metallic sand that guarded us falling down to bounce off the restored shielding.

Thunder and lightning resume, the noise reverberating through my chest like standing next to a pair of very loud speakers at a heavy metal concert, while the lightning scorches my eyes. But neither are at the level of the initial assault, and the ship holds them off.

Mages are rotated as necessary as the mental toll of casting and recasting spells wears upon them. Mana regeneration is sufficient in most cases to keep them running, but it's not the same thing when you have to piece together the spellforms directly.

It's why Classes and Skills are so important, why pure Battle Mages rely on a few tried-and-tested spells. Doing the equivalent of high-math in the middle of battle is tough enough, even when the System might help out a little with the boosts in Intelligence.

As for myself... I rub a temple as I scoop up Ali and deposit him on my shoulder with my other hand. No bleeding from the nose, just a really bad headache, which is an improvement. I assume the constant brain damage from handling and managing knowledge beyond my mortal ken has toughened up my mind that playing second fiddle in a battle between Spirits and Elementals is not enough to cause another stroke.

Yay for little mercies.

I trundle downstairs, content to leave the trio and the mages behind to deal with things. I get to the dining room, grab dinner, and get to the eating, but I only manage a single plate before I fall asleep, darkness claiming me entirely.

When I wake, Ali is nowhere to be seen—though his presence is distinctively felt, as is the self-satisfied smugness of his emotion, through our bond—and my plate is gone too. I retrieve another one, tackling my meal properly, idly scan the details of the party chat and statuses. No one is dead, which is a definite plus compared to the crew. I'm just grateful none of the crew chose to slit my throat while I was sleeping.

A quick perusal of the skies show we're still in the middle of a very large storm, but the feel of it seems quite different. Less malevolent, more natural.

Seeing that our latest crisis has passed, I reach out to my Hands. The one on-board is topside, throwing magic around and grinding out XP, while the others are still around. Except for one. I frown for a second, shrug, and call him forth, letting him get on with things. No need for orders. The System knows what I need done, and as a sort of duplicate of me, the Hand disappears out the door after grunting at me.

Yay, nonverbal communication.

I finish my meal and go hunting for my companions, hoping to have a word with them. If nothing else, a plan for when we arrive at our destination would be pleasant.

The first I find is Mikito. To my surprise, she's not practicing or meditating or resting, but working on thin slices of paper, words scrolling down one sheet while she writes on another. I clear my throat after a bit.

"I heard you. What do you want?" Mikito says, not looking up.

"Hoping to discuss what we're going to do when we finally land," I say.

Mikito turns, stares at me, and laughs softly, bitterly. "There's nothing to talk about. We land, we fight, we either make it or we don't."

I frown. "You've grown a lot more fatalistic since I met you."

"Better than death seeking."

"Low blow."

Mikito grins then gestures at her papers. "If that's all…?"

I shrug, not satisfied but happy enough that she's willing to go with it for now. Curiosity has me asking, "What are you doing?"

"Fan club mail."

I feel my stomach lurch, remembering a trio of her people. The ones who left with Feh'ral the Librarian. We know he was caught and executed in public as an example for me and the rest of the Galaxy, to ensure that everyone knows the cost of defying the Council.

I haven't thought of the Three Musketeers since I was caught. I'm not sure if I was trying not to, because I knew they weren't likely to survive. If the Legendary Librarian didn't make it out, I can't see how a bunch of newcomers who had just reset their levels down before building themselves back up would manage it.

"They survived."

Her words shake me from my thoughts and I find myself staring at the woman, jaw dropping open a little.

"How?" I manage to blurt.

"Feh'ral." Mikito holds up a hand. "I don't have all the details, but they managed to run for a bit. Bouncing from library to library. Eventually, the Galactics caught up, and rather than let my men get caught, rather than let the other Corrupt Questors be caught, Feh'ral stayed behind."

"I'm glad they survived," I say.

"Are you?" Mikito says. When I frown, she continues. "Are you really glad they survived, or are you just parroting words because you know that's what you're supposed to say?"

I frown, irritation flashing through me. "Where is this coming from?"

"Just… a curiosity. Checking that you're still you." My continued glaring has Mikito shaking her head a little. "My apologies. Perhaps I'm not as settled about our end, or the chaos we've caused, as I like to think."

I glance at the papers again. I draw a breath and let it out, asking the question she probably wants me to ask, but won't say directly. "How bad is it?"

"For my people?" She looks down, sadness crossing her face. "I've only got a glimpse. Lana and the rest, they can't get information to us. It's only because I'm the… well… celebrity that I get my mail at all. And only because the fans are willing to pay."

I nod, understanding in some ways what she says. Not the exact mechanics of the fan club of course—it's not as though I've got one, nor do the Questors care about such a thing. "And?"

"My club has swelled. We're celebrities, all of us. I don't know if you've checked your Galactic Reputation lately—"

I shake my head, for I haven't. While one of my Skills works off Reputation, it's Erethran and that's less easy information to acquire than from my own Status Screen.

"But standing against the Shadow Council has seen our reputation increase overall. Of course, we're deep in the red among some sectors, but…"

"But we're doing well. Which means you've got more fans," I say.

She smiles a little, flicking her hand sideways. A second later, notifications bloom with new messages. I pop one open seconds before Ali gets hold of them and wipes the queue, but the sight that greeted me is seared into my mind, I'm sure, for the rest of my life.

"WHY?" I cry.

"You got to be a little slower, boy-o. I filter a lot of those messages for you."

"He had three! And there were barbs on them."

"*Not everyone understands human biology very well.*" A pause. "*All of you meat-creatures are strange in a way. Just rearrange for fun times. Why keep so firmly to a single form, I don't know.*"

"*It's not that easy…!*"

"*Sure, it is. One Skill, and boom. You're good to…*"

I shut him down, suppressing the link, before he goes into graphic detail. Truth be told, I can sense Ali's amusement anyway, but at least I don't get the details. My eyes refocus on Mikito, our conversation as quick as thought, so barely a second has passed.

"Why did you send that?" I say, hurt by the violent attack on my psyche.

"Your fans can't get to you, so they join mine and send mail to me, hoping I'll pass it on," Mikito replies, opening her hands wide. There's a little vicious glint in her eyes, innocent though she might play. "I'm just being helpful."

"Stop."

She smiles wide now. "Truth be told, such messages aren't as common. While the war hasn't affected the majority yet, not directly, the economy has taken a beating." I can't help but frown, so she explains. "I don't know if wars do help the economy, but gearing up for them is never good. Reserves are called out of their normal jobs, supply lines are cut short or disrupted, old orders are thrown aside as the needs of the military take precedence. End of the day, chaos."

"And the fighting?" I say.

"Harry will have a better idea. It's mostly on the outskirts, independent planets and border ones. No planetary deaths, not yet." I shudder at the thought, but Mikito continues dispassionately. "Lots of stations destroyed though. Merchant fleets and the like are being restricted or somehow being lost to pirates. Then, of course, there are the Adventuring Guilds."

"What's wrong with them?" I say, frowning. Technically, the Guilds are supposed to be above it all. They're third-party organizations whose only job is to clear dungeons and help keep the commerce and earnings from dungeon clearing flowing. And, you know, keep people safe.

"Nothing, ostensibly. Except now that people aren't watching as much, they've started making moves against one another. Old grudges, takeovers of locations, you know, underhanded tactics."

I wince, then turn back to her earlier accusation. I can't help but turn it over in my mind, the accusation, the bitterness inherent in the words, if not her tone, sitting badly with me.

"And you think I don't care," I say.

"I know you care—or you used to at least. But this Quest of yours, it's become everything for you. And I know there's no way else but through, not for us, but…" Mikito gestures around. "We've dragged so many innocents into it with us. How much more, how many more will you—will we—sacrifice before this is over?"

"And if I said the whole Galaxy? Would you still follow me?"

"I made a promise, didn't I?" Mikito says. "You don't start regretting the purchase after you've bought it. You just… accept it."

"Seems like a recipe to keep one trapped in a toxic relationship."

"And is it?"

"Is it what?" I ask.

"Toxic."

I shake my head. "I don't know. Sometimes, I think you'd be better off. Other times, I know it. You shouldn't be here. You should be…"

"Where?" Mikito replies softly. "Nowhere. I was like you, without a goal, my dreams ashen, the love of my life dead. You and Lana dragged me along, gave me a purpose when I had nothing. I'll always be grateful for that."

I close my eyes, then open them. I don't want to admit it, but I have to. This conversation should have happened ages ago. "I didn't do it for your sake, you know. I—"

Mikito cuts me off. "You're lying to yourself. Oh, I know bringing me along, healing me, wasn't your primary goal. But did you even think what was? Those first two years, when the world died and we needed heroes, so many chose to hide, to look out for themselves. And you? You saw a problem, you sought to fix it. You fought and killed and bled for people you never even got the names of. Because it was the right thing to do."

I shake my head, denying her words. She's wrong, of course. I did what I did because I needed to do something, to kill something back then. That raging pit of despair and fury had to be fed, had to be controlled.

It still does.

"I pledged myself to support you then, when you first disappeared. To do what I could to save Earth and to help you when you got back," Mikito says. "I still believe that you'll find a way to help our friends."

"This Quest... it has nothing to do with Earth."

"Perhaps not directly." Mikito taps the document on her desk before continuing. "But I'm sure you'll find some way to do good. You always do. And if it means sacrificing millions, that's what we'll do."

"Not we. Me," I insist.

"It might be your choice, but we all share responsibility for enabling you. And if not responsibility for the actions, we certainly share in the guilt," Mikito says flatly. "Trying to take that fact away just makes me..."

"You?"

"Angry. And infantilized."

I hesitate and choose not to follow up. I can't strip her guilt from her, no matter what I say. And she's right, it's not really my place to even try. Even so...

"I don't know how many or who we'll lose, Mikito. But at the end of this road, I have to believe there's something worthwhile. Something that makes all this"—I gesture around us, taking in not just the craft we fly in or the planet but the entire damn System—"make sense. Make all those deaths worthwhile."

"And if there isn't?"

I shake my head. "There has to be."

Mikito smiles sadly at me then, as though the wound that drives me on is bare to her very eyes. The grief in her eyes, the pity in them, it is a dagger to my heart. One that drives me out of her room as she tackles her paperwork. I leave her to it, the words she said, our conversation buzzing still in my head.

***

Harry's the next one for me to find. I'd say it was a funny coincidence, but it was rather deliberate. The humans are still those I'm most comfortable with, especially compared to Xaxas or Yllis. Xaxas I'm not entirely sure cares about us one way or the other; we're just a means to an end. A violent, painful end. As for Yllis, I'm pretty sure she only tolerates us because Bolo likes us. Otherwise, I've seen the way she eyes me during meal times.

All joking aside, the dragon worries me. She can manipulate the Mana around her in ways I have no hopes of matching, and that gives her the advantage of surprise. Add her sheer size and strength and Levels and in a straight-up fight, she'd be a real pain. I might be able to win, but not without cost—and certainly not when Bolo backs her.

Which, of course, is the entire point of the Dragon Whatever Class.

As for Ezz—I might have a way through the lock that keeps me from accessing whatever slave program they're using on him, but I'm not sure I'm ready to let him free yet. Right now, he's just locked away. In suspended animation, if you will. The moment I free him, I'll have to deal with him. A small, uncharitable part of me wants to leave him trapped forever. It's small, but it's there. The guilt at even that thought is enough to make me flee from contemplating the little golem, at least for now.

No, Harry's much more my speed, no matter how much I've put him through and how much he hates and loves me.

"Whatcha doing?" I say, leaning against the doorjamb and watching the British reporter hard at work.

He's trimmed his hair tight, such that the curls are right up against his skin, losing the burgeoning afro he had sported in prison. Probably easier, considering we're using helmets for the most part. Same reason why I've taken a buzz saw to my hair and cut it short. While the nannites are pretty good at not catching stray locks, even once is more than enough.

"You're not cute," Harry says, turning away from the empty air he's staring into. Of course, it's not empty air for him, but I can't see his notifications or System projections.

"I think Roxley would disagree." I pick Roxley mostly because he's still the hottest individual I've ever bagged. Or did he bag me? I'm still not entirely sure who used who in that relationship. Which is, of course, one of the reasons it never really progressed very far.

Well, that and me leaving the planet.

"He likes bad boys," Harry replies. "I'm much more into the stay-at-home kind."

I blink. "With your career?"

"The heart wants what it wants." Harry touches his chest before continuing. "Why do you think I was single when you met me anyway?"

I nod slowly. I really don't know much about Harry's background, I have to admit. It's not something I've ever asked about, not even during the long, slow nights as we passed from one starless void to another. I hesitate, a part of me wondering if I should ask, another part of me really not caring.

Thankfully, Harry saves me from my indecision. "Are you going to free Ezz or not?"

"I will." My hand clenches and then reopens. "But it's not that easy. I'm pretty sure he's still in there, but I don't know the code well enough to tell if there's a failsafe or kill switch in there. Until I've gone over it all, I'm not willing to play with it."

Harry grunts in acceptance, his eyes flicking over to where his screens must hang.

"So. Mikito said that you might have a better idea about the state of the galaxy," I say, deciding to just get on with it. "Details about the wars and the like."

Harry snorts.

"What?" I say.

"Should have known you'd be here for a reason," he says. I shrug, only mildly guilty. After all this time, he should realize I'm not the best of friends. "You want the summary or a data download?"

I hesitate. "How about both?"

The words have barely left my mouth when I get a ping. A quick glance tells me I've got a data packet ready for opening, but Harry's started speaking, so I pay attention to that instead.

"So, outright war hasn't been declared. Not that the battles that are being waged, 'border skirmishes' if you will, are any less costly just because some politicians haven't shifted to war footing." A slight pause, as he considers his words and the System. "Though I guess there are some differences in the System. Actual 'War Footing' is a Class Skill and I bet there are a bunch of things those with the right Skills could do, no?"

I nod, the Library already downloading the morass of information into my mind. I barely sway when it does. "Yeah, Generals, Admirals, Chief of Staff, all kinds. Some societies even have multiple cabinets they keep running, switching who is 'officially' in play depending on where things stand.

"There are even a few Classes and individuals who have 'Shadow War' kind of Skills. Spymasters, Rebel Leaders, Covert Generals, the like."

"Right. Might make an interesting topic..." Harry flicks his fingers quickly, slapping a note on his notification screen before he gets back on track. "Anyway. No official wars have been declared, at least among the main factions. There're a few smaller factions—puppet states and kingdoms—that are already fighting and which the bigger groups are using to test out new tactics. Proxy wars for the moment, really."

"When do you think they'll switch over?" I ask.

"Mmmm... good question. Maybe a few weeks, maybe a few months. Maybe even a few years. I don't really understand the politics properly, but I can guess that a lot of it is just..." Harry shrugs. "Well, posturing."

I frowned. "It wasn't what Catrin said."

"She's running one of the covert forces, so I doubt it feels that way to her," Harry says. "Don't forget, she wasn't officially supposed to help us. The entire Empire has held back, and they will continue to do so until they're ready. While tensions have been high for a while, there's a difference from high to all-out war."

I grunt, rubbing my neck. I understand what Harry is saying. And it's not as if anyone could have confidently predicted that I would throw the entire galaxy into disarray. At least, not to this extent. That they still have entire fleets running around, doing battle and call it "skirmishes" just means that Galactic society is much, much bigger than what I'm used to.

"Do we know the total losses?" I ask.

Harry is quick to shake his head in negation. Too quick.

"You know something."

"Nothing official," he says. "Everyone is either hiding losses or over-exaggerating them."

I grunt, but wave for him to continue.

"But... there are estimates. Put together by people on the ground, people who are bypassing the information blocks for their own uses, information that is double- or triple-verified—"

"I get it, it's probably accurate," I cut him off. "Just spit the number out."

"Just under seven billion," Harry says.

"There are a lot of numbers under seven billion. Like, even a single digit under could be a hundred million," I say, my mouth working on automatic. On the other hand, I'm stunned. I mean, sure, I knew the galaxy was huge. We've traversed the world again and again. And sure, each planet might have fewer total number of sapients—the nice thing about the System and the Galactic Empire is that crowding just isn't necessary since terraforming is actually quite easy with Classes in play—than you'd expect, but some planets have tens of billions still.

But...

That's more lives lost than there were on Earth before the System.

I rage against the System, against the Council for their callous disregard of turning a planet that wasn't ready into a Dungeon World. I cry at the lives cut short, fates robbed from the free, the sundering of a planet. And yet...

I have already caused more loss and destruction than they did. A single decision of mine has made me a greater villain than the entire Council. Even knowing the potential outcome before I made my announcement, it's another thing to actually have these numbers provided to me.

Are they truly wrong to want to contain people like me? To kill me and hide their secrets? Sure, it wasn't great, but were the System Administrators doing something so unjustified and wrong that I had to destroy so many lives?

After all, every day of our lives, pre- and post-System, we walk by everyday evils. The homeless man on the street, the father shouting at his son in the grocery store, the starving refugees desperate for a drink of clean water.

Every day, we choose which evils are acceptable, which ones we can live with. The politician who takes kickbacks from corporations, the celebrity cheating on his wife in full public view, the boss hitting on his employees. Knowing that if we try to rail against each injustice, we will burn out and fail those we truly care for.

Were not the System Administrators, in their hidden, time-twisted realms, such a compromise? Perhaps that was what the Council members who knew of them thought. Perhaps it was how the Administrators held onto power for so long. Deals are the heart of civilization—a give and take of personal and greater needs.

And when such giving and taking clashes too greatly, that's when society breaks down.

Selfishly, I upset the apple cart, all to get my way. To give Earth a small chance, to create an opportunity for me to learn what I needed. And now, the galaxy suffers.

And I'm the villain of the piece.

"And Earth?" I finally say, realizing I've missed whatever Harry's answer was. I could probably make myself recall it, but it doesn't matter. What's a hundred million here or there? Just another number…

"In conflict," Harry says. "They've managed to get the Adventuring Guilds on their side—some not even tied to the other great powers—but in turn, a lot of other corporations are coming in. The only good news is that all the other Dungeon Worlds are facing the same rising tide of conflict, and they're all much more lucrative than Earth. So it's still only those looking at long-term gains or who need a foothold—any foothold—in play."

I grunt, rubbing my neck. I know there are others—the Guardians, the settlement owners, Lana and Roxley and other embedded interest groups—who are protecting the planet. Now that the gloves are off, the basic profit-loss equation is playing out. Is it worth taking over a continent or two if you lose a bunch of high-Level individuals doing so? Especially when such individuals could be of use at home, when a Galactic War is brewing?

It's the best I can hope for really, and after some questioning, Harry is able to elaborate and confirm my expectations. It's not perfect, but it is what it is.

"So they're… Earth… Roxley… good?" I say finally.

"As good as can be," Harry replies. "Now if you don't mind…?" He gestures into blank space, and I end up nodding.

"Yeah, sure…"

Kicked out once more, I leave the Reporter to do his thing. Instead, I finally make my way back to my own room. There is one other person I need to look into after all…

And I've been putting it off long enough.

Chapter 17

Ezz, Ezz, Ezz. What shall we do with you, my little non-sapient, sentient golem? Able to think, able to logically puzzle out problems, but somehow missing that spark of life that separates a very clever machine from true living beings.

I poke the red golem, watching my finger sink a little into its fleshy-metallic exterior. Then I withdraw my finger and watch it spring back into shape, the four-legged format it currently uses not even rocking under my prodding.

For a moment, I consider putting Ezz away but decide I've been coward enough. Tapping into the golem's interface with the required tools takes only a few moments. Applying the program I've written to crack the security protocols blocking alterations to its base programming takes a fraction of a second.

Luckily for me, whoever decided to update Ezz did a sloppy job. No Skills, no Classes were used to change the little golem's operating unit. It's possible that Juover's base programming is too complex for them to mess with. After all, the programming necessary to manage the liquid golem flesh and structure has got to be fiendishly complex.

And who would expect for the most secure prison in the world to be successfully assaulted? Or for a golem to be stolen out from it, when there were so many other, better things to take?

"Come on, come on, come on…" I mutter, watching the code scroll along.

I would never bother trying to watch the raw code while I was human. The speed would have been too much for a poor human brain. Except I'm not human anymore, and keeping track of a hundred and one things visually is par for the course. Dancing through a hail of bullets is easy when each seems to move in bullet time to your brain.

I'm idly noting a half dozen errors, making mental adjustments to the code while watching to see the results, watching how my program bounces off multiple defensive firewalls and goes around again for more. I didn't, for obvious reasons, write the cracking code myself, instead buying the basics off the Shop. But the alterations are all mine, and watching as it switches somewhat smoothly between hodge-podge Frankensteined program matrixes is amusing.

Until suddenly it stops.

And I'm in.

Swiftly, I extract the base code overlaying Ezz's. I've seen glimpses of it while poking at Ezz's interface, but this is the first time I can review it fully in pristine condition. The good news is that it's not altering itself, being a more simplified program.

The bad news is that, like my own cracking program, it's a hodgepodge of a variety of programs thrown together so that they can do their job. Which makes it more vulnerable, but also could lead to unknown effects if I just delete it all.

Especially since much of the code hooks into Ezz's core programming. After all, it needs to make use of Ezz's program to move, to undertake more complex tasks than "go there." So tearing it apart isn't a simple matter of deleting specific code since in a few cases, they actually do seem to have overwritten prior programs. In areas like that, I'll need to restore to an earlier version if I can find it or write the code itself.

Now, Juover's code—Ezz, that is—is also highly complex. It's a machine learning code, one that changes based off environmental impacts and influences. It gives Ezz great flexibility, allowing Ezz to learn and grow as it encounters new situations. Just like a human, really.

But just like a human, there's core programming that doesn't change. Or shouldn't change. You know, small things like how your intestines work, how your heart beats, how the brain fires. Things that we don't consciously control, or shouldn't be consciously controlling, but are necessary for everyday life.

Ezz has similar constructs, but those are the things that the program has tapped into. By bypassing the overlay—the conscious aspect of the golem—and putting that portion to sleep, they turned Ezz into a mindless zombie. Or mostly mindless. Portions of it still run and work, still learn and grow while in that zombie state.

Unlike now, when Ezz is totally turned off.

Or… not?

"What the hell?" I poke at the information feed I'm getting, the constant flow of energy going out from its Mana Battery into its CPU. That's not the actual terminology, but it's the closest thing to work for me, and really, potato-pohtahtoh you know. "Are you still running, Ezz?"

The draw isn't significant, just enough to keep the basic functionality running. Like when you've got a plug stuck into a wall socket and the electricity is running a circuit through the electronics, but not really doing anything. Not really standby mode, but not exactly zero draw either.

On the other hand, the more that I stare at Ezz's full code, the more I get a nagging feeling I'm not seeing it all properly. For a second, a long second, I hesitate. Then, giving up, I plug the tablet into my Neural Link and tap into the code that way.

The Neural Link is wetware, if you don't mind the cyberpunk reference. It's an interface that lets me make use of tech through my mind, but it's also an added vulnerability. For the most part, I don't run much through it other than my mecha because of that vulnerability. Thankfully, Willpower and Intelligence both seem to provide a high level of defense against hacks, so the few times someone has tried to cause damage to me via the Neural Links, it's been painful and distracting, but not dangerous.

However, tapping directly into code like this is much more dangerous than someone hacking in. One's someone sneaking in via an open window—or shattering the window if you will—while the other is throwing the door wide open, calling out "dinner's ready," and hoping nothing nasty arrives, hungry.

That being said, there's an advantage to using the Neural Link and that's my ability to make full use of the Intelligence boost the System provides. I grab the code and tear it open, displaying it within my mind's eye to review in real time in its entirety.

Sort of.

I have a ton of Intelligence, but this is the code running a fully sentient golem. I can't read it all or even see it all, but I can highlight the most important bits. Instinct that had driven me to look for it gets to gloat, for seeing the code in this way, I can see the changes too.

Small changes. A line here. A character there. Tiny little scrolling bits of information that warp and twist when they should be entirely static.

"What are you doing, Ezz? What is happening to you?" I say softly.

For the first time, seeing Ezz, seeing its code change and twist, I wonder if ripping out the code is the right thing to do. Could this perhaps be the secret to sapience? The drive for freedom? Until now, we've treated Ezz as nothing more than a child, just as Juover treated all his other creations. A useful tool at times, given tasks, but never truly tested.

Could it be that what the golem needs is not care and love and understanding but pain and pressure and purity of purpose to become a real boy? Is it perhaps, like with Pinocchio, where the only way forward was to be eaten by a whale?

Or am I just biased because of my own upbringing?

When does aid stop being helpful and becomes actively harmful? Where do you draw the line between suffering and growth?

***

I have no answer to that question. Spending the time revising my code to rip out the slave code leaves me with little time to ponder the question, though I do find myself considering it every few minutes. It slows down the work I do, as does me listening for... something in the code. Neither a cry for help nor a dismissal of aid appear, so I'm left staring into space, pondering if I'm doing the right thing late into the night in my cabin when the others find me.

"We missed you at dinner," Harry says, leaning against the door.

"Sorry. I..." I was going to say I ate, but I haven't. In fact, now that I'm realizing it, I'm quite hungry. One of the negatives of System-empowered bodies are that they still require calories, and quite a few at that. It helps that higher-Level monsters are more nutrient dense, though how that all works out, I'm not entirely sure. Just that it's often better to just eat higher-Level monsters than lower ones. It doesn't give many benefits—unless you've got a Chef or other Class making it—but it extends the amount of time between meals. Which is a bonus in itself. "I'll grab something now."

"Yeah, you might want to wait. I've got a call. For you," Harry says.

"A call?" I frown. "From who? How?"

Harry makes a face. "Class Skill. It lets me contact and speak with informants in a safe manner. But the how, well... that's..." He shrugs. "System Edit is my guess. Because I sure ain't trying to talk to your favorite torture buddy."

I stiffen. There's only one her who could be speaking with him using that Skill, only one her who would know enough, care enough, be able to enough to contact him this way. My mind spins, a quiet gibbering part wondering if we're compromised, if there's a Galactic Strike Force coming in. If Kasva and his team—the remaining members of his team—will arrive, crashing through the side of the ship, weapons blazing.

Then I breathe out forcefully, emptying my lungs and making myself stay in that deflated position for a few seconds before breathing in again. I remind myself that if she could find us, she would have. That she might have hacked her way in this way, but the Root Administrator must have anticipated something like this and given us the Quest Reward.

We're safe.

We have to be.

I breathe in and exhale slowly. Finding my center once more, finding my calm and that raging ball of fury that empowers everything I do, then nod at Harry.

"She waiting?" I ask.

"She is."

"Then put her on," I say, gesturing to the wall.

Harry steps in, pausing only for a second when Ali literally fades through the ceiling to pop out, muttering softly about sensing my emotions. I brush aside the mental query he sends me, not wanting to talk about it. The grump that he sends back to me over the link is ignored too.

Because she's there.

Sephra is staring at me, arms crossed, looking angry and petulant. "John Lee. We should have killed you the moment we caught you. Torn out your spine, stripped your skull, and danced on the boneless flesh of your body with spiked heels, until the blood poured and the acid leeches arrived to feast."

"That's rather specific," I say. "You don't go on dates a lot, do you?"

"What?"

"Well, if you take all your dates out on acid leech dates, it's really clear why. Maybe if you offered them chocolates and flowers, it'd work," I say.

"Chocolates work very well. The ones who don't like chocolate, well, you know better than to keep dating. Flowers though, those are more iffy.

"I wonder if they're considered genocide with dryads."

"Was the time with us really that hard that it drove you that insane?" she snaps, and I grin, feeling a thrill of victory. But instead, she gestures, showing me... well, what Harry showed me before, actually. Numbers, names, planets. "Your work."

I give her a theatrical yawn. I'm glad I spoke to Harry, because otherwise I might actually be unable to play blasé to all this. As it stands... "Yeah, yeah. I get it."

"Oh, I don't think you do." Another flicker of her hand, and something new appears. A picture of a solar system, a dead one. Planets flicker by, their atmosphere boiled off, the land scorched, and now, the planet itself cooling. Planetary cores are cracked open, liquid metal cooling. Devastation across an entire planet... "Your friends, they released individuals who should never have been released."

"The Sun Killer," Harry says, shuddering.

"Hey, you guys could have killed him a long time ago. You didn't. Don't blame us when he escapes," I say.

"You fool. You think we didn't try?" Sephra says. "There's no way to kill him. He converted his health, his Mana, into Energy. Or Energy into Mana and Health. His Legendary Skill lets him do that, store energy to be one of those. That's why he eats stars."

"Oh come on, there's a way around that. Even I know that," I say, not believing her.

"Of course there is. We drain him. Could we have someone override that, do enough damage to kill him?" A shrug. "Perhaps. But the last time we tried, we lost two of our Legendarys. None of the others were willing to finish the job. Not once we were able to contain him. Draining him, slowly and surely, over the centuries as he leaked his life, his energy into a secondary dimension was a guaranteed kill.

"And then you let him loose. You and your friends."

"As I said, you could have killed him. But that's the thing, isn't it?" I say belligerently. I know she's got a point—they had him captured. But I refuse to let her look as if she's won, refuse to consider that she might have a point. I can't afford to. Not now. "You're never really willing to pay the cost. None of you people are."

"Pay the cost!" Sephra leans forward, slamming a fist onto the table. It cracks beneath her hand, my words getting to her. "You impertinent child! You have no idea what we have done for the Galaxy! The monsters we have killed, the dungeons we have safed. The sheer amount of time and care taken to ensure that the System works. We have sacrificed more than you and your pitiful band of rebels will ever know."

"If the sacrifice was so great, then why hide it?" I say, smirking. "Or did you know, deep down, that the trade-off was never in our favor? That you fat cats just take and take."

Me mentioning felines confuses her for less than a second. Without my perception, I'd never notice the hesitation. But she shakes her head, rejecting my words. Even the nonsensical ones. "You think being a System Administrator is easy? Between fools who think they know better on the Council, manipulating them to not break the entire edifice, and the Root Administrator and his own…"

"His own…?" I say.

"His own foolish desires." She leans forward. "This world works. The System works. Without it, planets are destroyed, sapient life is overtaken by Mana. It might not be perfect, but it's a Medusa's gaze better than what we had before."

"Before the System?" I feel it then, the thread of the answer. I lean forward, unwillingly. "So it's artificial, isn't it? It's now normal."

Rather than answer me, she smirks and leans back. Because she sees my eagerness. All that anger I created in her is snuffed out. Or perhaps, redirected, into malicious glee. "You'll never know, will you? Because my men will stop you. But you can stop, stop with all the foolishness. And perhaps, just perhaps, we might let you live."

"That's not much incentive."

"Better than the certain death you face if you keep struggling."

"Says you." I say, then shake my head. "No. We're not stopping. Not now, not ever." Then I cock my head as realization strikes me. "But you knew that. So…"

I dive in then, into the System. Looking.

Smart girl. Devious girl. Evil girl.

She's in there, along with others. Running along the edges of Harry's Skill, hacking it and making it work for them. But more than that, they're trying to get around the Root Administrator's, the System's, pronouncement. Trying to find us, make use of the full details of data that the System and its connection gives them.

I watch in silence as they work. They're not there in their avatar forms, not fully within in such a way that I could harm them. Not unless I truly intended to dip within, sneak my way backward to find their actual locations and lay the System Edit smackdown.

Instead, I watch them rip into the code created by the System, tear at the protective layers of obfuscation that hide us from being found. I watch them try to find us, only to be tossed aside by the System itself, the code healing over the moment they leave, their efforts an utter failure to make any true headway. Yet it doesn't look like that to them.

Perhaps it's because I'm not actually trying to dig in, perhaps because I am the target of the System's protection, but I can see the entire lay of code before me. Not in detail, no. That'd be too much, even for me. But the feel of the code, the layers upon layers of programs and firewalls that make up the gap between them and me, that protect our anonymity, those I can see.

I watch as another layer is bypassed, the System Administrators sneaking a step further, sliding in an inch more, peeling the onion that is me. And I watch, just as silently, how the entirety of the code shifts, restructuring itself like a mobile Legoland castle, such that they're never ever deeper within.

It's all theatre.

My breath hitches as I watch the sheer complexity and beauty of the code the System wields in our defense. The way it turns and twists, the way it grows and evolves every second, the System looking more alive than ever in that second.

"You've found us then," Sephra says. "Much good it does you. You cannot fight us all. Though I welcome you trying." The mermaid flashes a savage grin, making my lips twist in a snarl. But I don't take her up on the challenge. "It's only a matter of time."

"Time. It's funny how you all say that, as though it's just on your side." I open my hand and smile. "When I too have my own plans in place, my own bombs ticking down. Time, you say. And time you have not much left, I do agree."

"What…" She halts, eyes narrowing. "You're lying. A poor bluff, to divert our resources and attention. You have nothing."

"Oh, not me. But we did rescue a lot of prisoners." I open my hands, offering her a smile at the same time. "Many who were willing to listen. Not much gratitude, but I've never found gratitude a good lever anyway. Anger though. Rage. That I know. That I can wield."

Sephra stills for a second, her eyes flicking from side to side in thought. I can guess what she's thinking, the equation she's running. How much does she believe me? How much can she afford to underestimate me and the kind of destruction I can, I will bring? What could I have told the prisoners to make them my weapons of chaos? I've used others; is this just another case? Can she afford not to listen?

"There's no point keeping you here, not anymore. You will not change, it seems. And we have the connection." Sephra leans forward, her teeth flashing. "We will have you and your friends soon enough."

"See you soon then?" I grin again at her, doing the best I can to send savage glee through the transmission.

"Later, toots!" Ali adds, having been quiet thus far. Not that there's been much for another to say.

"Oh, it will not be me. I leave such crass matters to others more suited…" Sibilant hiss, almost a raw drawl. Then she's gone, leaving me staring into space and Harry's face, looking right back at me.

"Other plans?" he says with an arched brow.

"Lies. But it'll keep them scrambling and watching. After all, they can't afford not to not believe me. Not with the kind of prisoners we let loose."

"You do know most of them have died, cast into another dimension and unable to survive or exit it?" Harry says.

"Two-thirds. And two of them have taken residence in those dimensions, choosing to lord it over the current occupants. That might not last long, when the real powers get going, but you never know…" Ali says with a shrug. "Sometimes, you colonizers come along and overstay your welcome until you die."

I pause, considering that and choosing to discard it. I'm not touching that entire thread of conversation, not now. Let someone else follow up on it, someone whose entire existence isn't currently caught up in a war between themselves and the Shadow Council.

"Yeah, but they don't know that." I pause. "I hope. I have a feeling the guys in play aren't the ones who you can trust news reports about. Not without more thorough verification, no?"

Ali shrugs, while Harry, after a second, reluctantly nods. "So you intend to split them up, have them try their best to find threats that aren't there."

"Yup."

Harry sighs and rubs his head. "One day, all these false threats are just going to stop working, you know."

"Yup. But not today. Not while the Council is so paranoid and fighting multiple wars," I say.

Another nod before Harry steps back. I raise an eyebrow, and he shrugs. "I figure the rest of them will want to know."

"Oh, right."

"And I think you have something else to get back to, no?" A nod toward the silent and still Ezz.

I look at the golem and sigh. By the time I look back up, Harry's gone, and the door is sliding shut. Leaving Ali, the golem, and me alone.

"So…" I say.

"A needle pulling thread," Ali replies.

"Wha… at least you didn't sing it." I shake my head. "Ezz. We should…"

"Fix him."

"But…"

"Don't care. Fix him." Ali says.

"He… It… is changing, altering under all that…" I shut up as Ali imperiously holds out his hand, palm facing me.

"Fix him, boy-o. He's done enough changing, enough hiding within. Fix him. Let him live and grow. Sometimes, too much pressure is really just too much."

I can only mutely nod. He then floats upward, disappearing through the ceiling once more. Leaving me alone with a silent golem and not a lot of time to get it fixed.

Chapter 18

"You called?" Mikito asks, leaning against the door. In her hands, a couple of platefuls of dinner.

Multiple days have passed, and I've mostly forgotten about leaving my cabin. I pop up long enough to summon Hands for our general defense, with those left behind and the ones above dying off every few days. Tells you how bad things get out there, even when the Elementals stop throwing themselves at us. Of course, the fact that some of those Hands take some serious risks no one could survive also adds to the speed with which they die.

No. I'm not touching that discussion with a ten-foot pole.

"Ah! Food!" I grab the plates and lay into them. There's something very comforting about slabs of meat and bone, heaping amounts of greenish-white mash, crunchy bulbs of purple and yellow. Soup tureens are quaffed, the entirety of the meal all too quickly consumed as my starving body demands nourishment.

Mikito rolls her eyes and makes to leave, but I wave her back. She waits patiently for me to finish, my gesture at Ezz giving her something to do. Not that there's much to see, what with the majority of the changes in the code. Still, quite a few wires are running from Ezz to various little pads, all of them linked to run diagnostics. Mostly, they're quiescent, but hopefully, for not much longer.

"You're ready?" Mikito says.

"I am. Double- and triple-checked the code—which, I might add, is really not something I'm good at doing." I sigh. "It wasn't easy, not with the way Ezz's code keeps changing. But I think, all in all, I've got it."

"You won't harm him, right?"

"Not on purpose." When she stirs, I add, "There's going to be some damage, but it's why this has taken so long. To keep it to the minimum."

"Then what are we waiting for?" Mikito demands.

"Me, I'm guessing," Harry says, popping his head around the corner of the door and squeezing into the room.

"How'd you know?" I can't help but ask.

"Nose for the Story." Harry taps the side of his temple and I roll my eyes. Annoying Skills.

The cabin I'm in isn't that big, what with it being, well, on an airship where space is at a premium. So having Ezz, the three of us, and a tiny hovering Spirit in it, it really feels tight.

"Just about right," I say. "Ready?"

Then, not waiting for them to answer, what with me being rather done with the entire project, I mentally trigger the program.

Nothing happens at first. Of course, nothing happens. Everything important is happening in digital space, in areas that none of the others can see. I can, what with my Neural Link all hooked up, but they don't need to know that. And really, the stripping of code and reversion of code to its original is a little too fast for even me to keep up with. It has to be though, if we want it to work.

The code isn't just being restored to the original though. You see, the problem was, there were no change logs in some cases. Or the logs were there, but the programs being pointed to had been pulled apart. Taken away a long time ago, such that there was nothing there but empty digital space.

Something has to go back in to replace it. Rather than make use of the code the information downloads have offered, rather than have Ezz deal with code that had enslaved it, I chose to rewrite it myself. I'm not sure it was the right choice. But it's the one I made.

Made via inspiration from the System. Taking from it, as I always did, to remake itself and my existence. Trying, as best as I can, to rebuild a life.

It feels rather, well, apropos that the System offered me what little inspiration it did in the way the code is built.

It's only portions, parts of Ezz's program, but I can hope that my little contribution has helped make it… well, more.

And now all I can do, all we can do, is see if it works.

The first moments of motion come via a shudder and a flurry of new code appearing on the panels. I read through it all, getting a feel of what it says. Nothing too alarming, since it seems to be just a basic rundown of data.

Then, more.

Motion, as Ezz pulls back its legs, reforming itself into its normal hip-high size. Except it doesn't stop there, growing further, pushing higher. Drawing from the struts, from the extra metal they gave it when they forced it to add another pair of legs. Ezz increases in size and height, filling out a little, coming up to just under where my chest would be.

A flicker, and the lines leading to it drop aside. Ezz's eyes flicker over my people before they land on me. And then, life returns fully to its eyes.

And a word, spoken simply.

"Father?"

If I had a little bit of an emotional reaction to that word, you can forgive me. After all, it has a lot of connotations, even for one like me.

***

"Good boy. So, not much change?" I say for the umpteenth time.

"Minor code changes, including ones offered by Father," Ezz says. "Nothing that is of concern. Nothing that will impede my functionality. In addition, I have access to a further half dozen new automatic defense programs."

A swirl, metal parting, and I stare at a gun barrel pointed at me. I might jerk a little to the side, one hand pushing the barrel offline rather firmly. Before I'm able to say anything, Ezz keeps shifting, showing me swords, more guns, even something that looks like a satellite dish, all forming from its body before fading back away.

"That's... good." I choke out. Not that I don't want Ezz to be able to guard itself but....

"Yes, Father."

I twitch a little, but I'm getting used to it again. More importantly, now that basic diagnostics are over, I feel the need to ask, "Do you remember anything? When you were down?"

There's silence for a moment before Ezz buzzes again. "While under control of the other code, higher functions were suspended. I could sense, vaguely, the activities happening, but it is indistinct. Data logs are fractured and incomplete."

I nod, having expected that much. "And while you were... umm... off?"

"During suspended operations, I was unaware of any external matters, Father," Ezz confirms, and I find myself relaxing. The little robot pauses then tilts its head. "Did I do something wrong, Father?"

"Firstly, you don't have to use it every sentence. Or near enough," I say. "Secondly, you didn't do anything wrong."

"But I noted a change in your breathing, muscle tension in shoulders, forearms, and—" Ezz stops as Ali swoops down.

"Here's a little lesson, little boy-o. Our John here—your father—has about as much emotional intelligence as, well, a rock. Which means you've got about triple what he does at this moment," Ali says, making sure to hold up all three fingers. "Don't ask him why he feels the way he does. And when you ask him why he's angry or upset, figure he's about as truthful as a Movana in a business deal."

"I do not understand. How truthful is a Movana in a business deal?" Ezz says.

"They're more crooked than a Bunyan Worm," Ali explains.

"One second..." Ezz pauses, but even before he's done speaking, he continues. "A Bunyan Worm travels via a semi-straight route by bunching and pushing itself forward. It is not twisted at all."

"No, no!" Ali waves his hands in front of Ezz's face. "It's a metaphor."

"It is factually wrong."

"That's not the point. It's the idea we're trying to go with."

"That the Movana are truthful."

"No! Ugh. I have a lot to teach you, little one," Ali says, his beard suddenly growing much longer and white. "Don't worry, I'll make sure we get you sorted."

I tune out the pair with a roll of my eyes and look at Mikito and Harry, who are both regarding Ezz. I get up and walk over to them, lowering my voice more out of politeness than practicality. It'd take quite a bit of space before we would be out of Ezz's sensor range. "You guys good?"

"He seems fine," Harry says. "But I checked his Status. There's no real change..."

"Why would there be?" I say, shrugging a little. "I'm good, but not that good. His code is still mostly Juover's."

"Yeah, but you mentioned he might, you know..." Harry waves, not willing to put into words my hopes that I had mentioned in passing while working on the program.

"If we had left him, maybe. With enough time, while locked down..." I glance at Mikito, who is staring at Ezz fondly before she turns to me and shakes her head once again, in proper negation at the idea of keeping him turned off longer.

"It wasn't even a theory. Just hope and vague belief." She nods toward the little red metal golem, its body still making minor changes to its configuration as metal flows from one part to the other and it checks out its newer, bigger size. "He deserves to live, not stored away in the hopes that he might one day be something more."

"Weapons are to be used, eh?" I say, a half-smile flickering across my face. "I bet you hated museums too."

"He's not a weapon." Mikito's voice grows cold for a second. "He's a responsibility. All children are."

"Yeah, but he's... it's... " I trail off, not just because of the sudden attention I feel from everyone as they lock onto me and almost dare me to finish my sentence, but because I don't think I could finish it myself either. Somewhere along the way, I'm not sure when, I've started making him a he. Or everyone has. Maybe that's right, or wrong. Maybe I'm taking away determination of what he or it should be. But he feels right. "He's... well... okay. He's unique."

"Exactly. And don't you forget that." Mikito offers me one last, piercing look before she leaves.

Harry follows her not long after, having not gotten the story he wanted. Leaving me with the pair of arguing children. Their voices keep rising, with Ali gesturing ever more expansively while Ezz's tone stays calm, but it looks increasingly annoyed.

After a second, I Blink Step out of the cabin. There have got to be some monsters out there that need killing.

Anything.

I'll even take Goblins.

***

I come back hours later, bloody and tired. My wounds have healed, the blood mostly coming from the monsters I killed. Making my way to the kitchen, I dump off a slab of meat, a little note in the Library alerting me that this particular monster is considered a delicacy. From the way the Chef reacted when I deposited the flesh, with its lines of fat and protein, I might have been walking on water or something. He promised me a prime cut later today, just before we arrive at the city.

We're nearly done. Funny how what should have been an exciting journey through the center of a planet, a trip that should have been a nail-biting adventure, ended up with me mostly working indoors, tearing apart code and stitching it together. I almost feel like an introvert on a world cruise, being told about the exciting sights by my parents while hiding away in my room, playing computer games.

Not that I ever went on a cruise myself. Not when they were still a thing. For that matter, I don't recall any stories of cruise ship directors or their like surviving the transition. Then again, if you're sailing on a giant boat in the middle of the ocean and it dies… Well. You probably need more luck than even I have to make it out.

Idle thoughts, filling my mind as I use a Cleanse spell to get rid of the blood. It's not perfect, but better than tracking it all around the lower decks. The upper decks automatically clean themselves, so I'm less worried. Especially when we run through another storm.

Of course, none of the Elementals are left. The really belligerent ones have been banished. The rest got bored days ago, leaving us to ride through rough weather and the occasional swarm of monsters. For creatures like Elementals, ire is quick to rise and even quicker to dissipate.

I am, after my little exercise jaunt, feeling rather relaxed and happy. Which is why the sight of Ezz, just sitting silently in the middle of my cabin, elicits no sense of danger. After all, it has been there for the last few days. Nothing unusual.

Nor did I have any concerns about it, until it spoke. "Father. May I ask a question?"

"Thousand hells!" I nearly summon my sword and decapitate the golem, my surprise nearly sending me on a killing spree. I breathe slowly, lowering my hand and forcing myself to chill.

"Father?" How a little golem can sound plaintive, I do not know.

"Sorry. Didn't expect you to talk. I…" I choose a different tactic. "Just ask away. You don't have to ask."

"Of course, Father."

I wander over to my side table, poke at the piles of dirty dishes there, and frown. A small gesture has the majority disappear into my Inventory, only a few scraps left untouched. Weird. I pick up the spork that was left behind, turning it over and over. Somehow, for some reason, it was created without System intervention. Or perhaps even the System doesn't want sporks.

"Father, what will happen to me at the end?" Ezz says tentatively.

I turn a little, cocking my head as Ezz walks over to stand beside the side table I've sat at. There's not much space in here, just the bunk, the table I'd done so much work at, the living area in the center, and the closet where we can store whatever we find. Enough, at least, for someone with an Inventory to keep things sorted, but not much more.

"The end? What end?" I say.

"The end of your Quest. When it is over, what will happen to me?" Ezz says.

"Ummm…" I frown, shaking my head. "You'll follow me around, and we'll do… something."

I pause, trying to find a something to do afterward. Truth be told, I haven't planned that far ahead. The future beyond the System Quest is so vague, because the answer is so huge that I cannot see it not changing my future. If the search for the answer has changed my entire life, how can the answer not do the same at least as much?

"Something? More violent retribution on our enemies?" Ezz says.

"Firstly, big words for someone less than a year old," I say.

Ezz looks puzzled, which is a thing a metallic face-bearing golem can do which is, yeah. It's a thing.

"Secondly, life isn't just about violent retribution. It's about…" I look around for help.

Ali refuses to meet my gaze, so I find myself looking back at the golem, searching for an explanation about life. And not just one that is parroted in sports movies and sappy romances, but one that I can believe. One that would ring true for it, having been brought up in the middle of a war.

And find myself, once again, failing.

How narrow my life has grown, how twisted.

Ezz stands there, silent and unmoving the way only a golem, a construct can do so. Yet I find myself trying to explain to it, searching for a truth, one that will see it to a better world than the one I've constructed for myself.

Because isn't that what it means to be a parent? To offer your children a better future than the one you yourself have, to guide them around the failures you've created, to pave the path such that it is just a little less bumpy for them? To shield them from the blows that would crack them, yet allow them to grow such that when life comes a kicking, they're tough enough to bend but not break?

"It's not, no matter what you see me do. Life isn't just about pain and tragedy; it's about love and beauty and goodness. Doing the right thing, not because you'll ever expect anyone to be grateful—because trust me, they won't be—but because you can't afford not to. Can't stand yourself if you let it be. Because the man you are—or the man you want to be—wouldn't ever look away. It's about glistening ideals and crawling through the muck to shelter the people who haven't stood up yet after life has kicked them down. Or getting up yourself, again and again, because those few moments when you're standing clear and pain free and the breeze is rustling through your hair… it's worth it all." My fists are clenched so tightly I have to force them open to get in some blood, to stop taking damage. "We'll find you something more, something more than all this fighting and death, find you something better to do. Or maybe you will. Because this, all this death, it's not the only way.

"It can't be. Or else we'd all be dead anyway, just planets of corpses. There's art and music and chocolate, laughter and friends and TV and all those things, the people who make them. Perhaps it might not be me. But it could be you."

"And if I did not want it to be me?" Ezz says.

"Then it won't."

Ezz buzzes quietly before it tilts up its head. "Then I won't be."

Its words make me frown, forcing me to truly look at the golem. "You know, you've got a lot of advantages as a golem. Probably make you one heck of an Artisan, like Juover."

"He sent me away," Ezz says. "I do not wish to be like him, discarding my brothers and sisters because we fail whatever test he deems necessary."

"Do you really see the other golems as your brothers and sisters?" I say, frowning. "Like, you know, care for them?"

"No." Ezz sees the puzzlement on my face, so he clarifies. "They are, technically, my family. But there are no feelings between myself and them. I believe that I should feel for them, but I do not." Silence, then Ezz continues, sounding a little puzzled. "I find it hard to understand feelings. The Creator has given me subroutines that allow me to mimic empathic responses, but Father, I do not understand."

I nod, recalling some of the programs I noticed while dealing with its code. Everything Ezz has said is what I'd expect. The way Juover wrote Ezz's code, the way Ezz translated the basics, it's… strange. It's both a child that is growing up and a wizened, heartless AI centuries old. For all that, what he says next catches me by surprise.

"I wish to understand."

I can't help it. I rub the shiny dome of Ezz's head. A part of me wants to hug him, but I refrain. "Yeah, I get that. I'm hoping, well, maybe…"

I'm not even sure Ezz becoming sapient would matter. It can think, but does becoming a real boy mean it should feel? AIs don't necessarily feel, not in the way that I think of.

"Father?"

"Just thinking that maybe it's better if you don't feel. Your Creator and I, we want you to grow sapient, to gain free will and be able to choose. To connect to the System and be… more. But maybe more doesn't mean feelings." I run a hand through my hair, and for a second, the exhaustion that threatens me, that's a twin to the pulsing core of anger within me, washes over me. I speak softly. "They're not always the best."

"I do not understand," Ezz says. "Yourself and Auntie Mikito both feel. I think I would like to do so." A pause, then Ezz adds, "A lot of your literature says that's what makes you human."

"But you're not human."

"Yes, Father... but I do not think it is any worse an objective than being a Truinnar or Grimsar. And I, at least, know what you all are like."

"I wouldn't..." I sigh, looking at Ali, who shrugs and mouths "reality tv" at me. I can't help but chuckle, and I wave him over to Ezz. "I think you need to watch a few things that Ali has before you come to that conclusion."

"Yes, Father... but I do want to be you." Then when Ezz sees me waving it away to speak with Ali, it follows.

I watch Ezz head off—out of the cabin thankfully. Only when the door closes do I whisper so that he can't hear, "All children do. Then they grow up and realize their parents wear lead boots."

Chapter 19

We come into the city of Last Hope—which is really called something else in Galactic but translates as Last Hope and seems much more evocative than the Galactic name of Us'herd Valziss—trailing smoke and flames. A quartet of drakes sweep behind us, while their mother, a much larger and stronger presence, is tangling with our very own dragon.

"You know, that's just vicious," I say, watching as mother drake and Yllis tangle in the middle of the sky. Another swipe and Yllis nearly takes off another one of the half-dozen feet the drake has. "I'm pretty sure your girlfriend could have ended it ages ago."

"She's not my girlfriend," Bolo answers just before he takes a couple of hopping steps. The giant harpoon he holds launches off like an oversized javelin, flying through the air to tear into the side of one of the younger drakes harrying us. It screeches as Bolo hauls backward on the rope entangled in the harpoon, only for the entire thing to tear out of the creature's body. "Damn it."

"You're not very good at that."

A heavy *thunk* to my right comes from one of the harpoon guns and their crew firing their own harpoon at another drake. This one flares its quartet of wings, leg coming up to catch the harpoon and stop it from impacting its body. The entire body twists and jerks with the momentum, a part of me feeling the way the System—Mana—turns on and warps reality to keep the drake in the air. A fraction of a second later, the harpoon explodes, throwing the drake aside, leaving it trailing smoke.

Of course, that's just two of the four drakes. Flame bathes our entire ship, the shields failing to stop the magic being cast directly on the vessel. I feel the heat licking at my skin, my eyeballs drying up, then the anti-magic runes and mages kill the spell.

"You could help out," Bolo says.

I point down, where Ali pops out of the vessel's side and waves, launching Ezz at the drake. The drake's eyes widen in surprise at the tiny red, flying golem charging it, before it reacts. It manages the initial dodge but isn't ready for when Ezz decides to hit the thrusters and twist in mid-air to land on its back.

"And spoil their fun?" I shake my head. "What kind of man would I be?"

It's a bit of a waste, even if I do get experience from Ali. When Ezz tears into the drake and rips apart scale and flesh, all that experience gets lost in translation, with only a small portion of the amount that I should be getting sent to me.

In the lower decks, the Hands are holding off at my command, just watching for trouble and taking the occasional potshot via a Beacon of the Angels on the ground monsters. Mostly, they're holding back for when they're really needed. One negative of being made of Mana—the more they use, the less durable they become.

I'm still not entirely sure what experience really is, or why it can change. Not to say I don't have dozens of hypotheses, but they're just hypotheses. More importantly, some of the things experience does contradicts what I believe to be the base idea of the System—churning unaspected Mana into System Mana.

See, if the System was meant to purely focus on churning Mana, then the Artisans who create golems and other weapons would receive a much higher experience amount for the kills their weapons provide. Then you just automate the creation of billions of weapons and give them out and voila! You get a ton of experience.

But of course, the System doesn't do that. It doesn't even give that much experience unless you are directly connected and in control of the weapon. There are Drone Operators and Swarm Commanders and the like who make use of technology in their fights, but their experience gain is significantly reduced.

Considering everything I've learnt, I'm leaning toward a couple of hypotheses. I'm just not sure which one is right...

The first is that the System has tried that. And I do note a few instances where newly integrated, high technology planets, recovered after the initial shock of Mana and System integration, have gone down that route. Problem is, it has a tendency to concentrate power in the hands of a few—Artisans, Entrepreneurs, Manufacturing Overlords—who already have everything set up. But sapients all die at some point, whether it's age or accident.

Then chaos ensues, because all those experience points have nowhere to go, no person to help build and sustain and boost all these tech items. At the same time, monsters go up in level since Mana keeps flooding in, leaving everyone struggling to handle the new disaster.

The System, having seen these problems, just doesn't let that happen.

From a long-term perspective, it makes a lot of sense. The other discussion is that the reason the System doesn't want automated systems killing off monsters is that it's actually ineffective at achieving the System's main goal. Churning Mana from unaspected to System Mana is the basic goal. Monsters do that just by existing. It's the very basic interaction of Mana with the monsters, guided to some degree by the System, that keeps them running. Monsters aren't as effective as sapients at changing Mana over, but they do have the advantage of quantity over quality.

However, golems, automated turrets, weaponized systems, even large-scale explosives, they don't require much in terms of Mana use. Many of their operators rely on passives, which have been shown, for the most part, to be a net negative compared to active Skills. It's why I think some of the passives are nerfed in their overall utility compared to others.

In this case, the killing of all these monsters on an automated basis becomes a net negative for the System since it loses out on the total Mana switchover. As such, it's better to nerf such exploits before they become a thing, forcing people to get down and dirty, trading Active Skills and pain for the lives of the monsters.

The third hypothesis is one that takes the entire aspect of automated weaponry and scales it up, to look at it from the context of the Forbidden Zone, then highlights the failings. It pretty much goes like this. For whatever reason, weapons—both automated and projectile—without the direct intervention of an individual do not do as much damage as they should.

Take a beam rifle, fire it. It does, say, a hundred points of damage base.

Take the same beam rifle, put it in the hands of a Soldier, and let him fire it. Without active Skills, it stays at a hundred points of base damage—assuming, of course, he hits properly. However, a Soldier will have the opportunity to use passive and active Skills. He could make it a personal weapon, Soulbind it, use an Active Skill to Overcharge the weapon, and the like. A simple weapon becomes much more powerful.

Never mind many Basic Combat Classes have passive bonuses against resistance as part of their build. Then you add in the likelihood of targets dodging, and damage scaling when used actively jumps well ahead of automated systems.

Yes, yes, I know. Most automated systems, programmed correctly, can react faster than sapients. Assuming they are programmed better. Assuming the monsters don't have their own abilities to mess with the software, the sensors, the way the weapons interact with the world. Assuming, of course, that the monsters don't just evolve to step around the new tools.

So, anyway. Crafted weapons, to be used properly, need an individual to use them. Thus the Erethrans have power armor and beam rifles and co-joined personal weapons that are fully or semi-Soulbound. Thus the need for

Artisans to create disposable weaponry, but not too much, since too much disposable weaponry is a drain on the resources.

Thus the fact that any place that uses automated weaponry for defense has to use multiple weapons of the same Tier as a threat to take threats down. Even then, they normally end up needing physical backups. None of which is insurmountable.

Until you realize that the Forbidden Zone doesn't care. It keeps expanding. The monsters within keep growing in size. If you rely entirely on automated weapons—weapons which need to be repaired, which are needed in higher quantities than something wielded by an individual, which are, in the end, fallible—you set yourself up for failure when the Forbidden Zone, with its own monsters that keep evolving and leveling, comes out.

The things in the Forbidden Zone don't necessarily follow the normal laws of this reality. Look at the Doppler Fish we fought, or more scarily, the Colossus. The only thing stopping the Colossus from rampaging through normal space is the Mana density around it, its body needing the higher densities to survive. But those levels keep rising, and fleets or a web of weaponry attempting to keep those creatures at bay will, eventually, fail.

If nothing else because of the cube law of volume. After all, Mana is expanding in a sphere, which means each time it does, there's ever more space for the Galactic Council to patrol. It's why there's an ever-increasing need for Dungeon Worlds, why the Galactic Council is always fighting for resources, and why even empires like the Movana split apart, because the needs of administrating an ever-growing empire creates fractures.

End of the day, all these theories mean little to anyone but the fools looking to game a complex system that has evolved and changed over centuries. The rest of us? We just take what we get and hope it doesn't bite us in the hand.

"I'm not sure raising a kid in violence and blood is the way to go about things," Harry says. "Something about mental damage and creating psychopaths."

"That's the old world. The one where asshats who shouted in your face about going home to where you belong could get away with it because punching them in the nose meant you got thrown into jail," I say. "This world, punching them in the nose is you being polite."

I see Harry's face at my first line, getting the result I expected. I'm sure he has heard that refrain too. Probably more than me, come to think about it. Being black in England must have seen its own challenges, ones that I have no idea about.

"So teach them violence immediately, because if you take out both their eyes first, they can't take your own?" Harry says at last, disapproval still in his voice.

"Mmm... hadn't thought of it that way." Hadn't thought of it at all really, beyond the fact that Ezz seems to enjoy running its new, more lethal body through the paces. "But sure, why not?"

"And who's to teach him when you should or shouldn't use violence? Or do you intend him to be like you, reaching for your sword whenever things don't go well?" Harry says challengingly.

"What is it with you all? I mean, you know how I operate. Hell, you're tentatively in agreement, considering you're here." I wave to take in the surroundings. "And it's worked out, hasn't it? So why bitch at me about it?"

"Don't you think Ezz deserves more than this? If he's really meant to be a child, then our obligation is to teach him right from wrong."

"I do!"

"Do you teach him when compromise is required? When morality and honor and ethics conflict, how to handle that conflict and how to choose the right one? How about empathy? For those you'll trample on your way to the rarefied heights you've climbed," Harry says softly. Almost gently.

"I said I'm sorry."

"Pretty sure you haven't." Harry pauses. "But apology accepted." He shakes his head. "It isn't about me though, you know that, right?"

"Yeah…" I sigh and nod toward where Ezz and the others continue their fight, tearing up the drakes who finally pull away. "But that's why we have you and Mikito. When it gets down to it, she'll teach him honor and morality and ethics, and you'll teach him what it's like to be one of the little people."

Harry stiffens, and for a second, I wonder if I've pushed too hard. Sometimes, my jokes miss. Mostly because I don't make enough of them.

Then he relaxes, muttering, "Harsh."

"But true."

I have to Blink Step away when he then proceeds to try to throw me off the boat.

***

Once we get close enough that the city's defensive measures can range on the drakes, they flee. Mikito makes an appearance at the last moment, Flash Stepping into space and swinging Hitoshi down on the drake that Ezz has been worrying, ending its life. I see her turn to scold the golem in the most Mikito way possible—by listing all the different things Ezz did wrong in killing the monster, from missing vital spots to not making full use of its abilities. I make sure to make myself scarce since I know how easily her ire could turn toward me, so I'm at the bow of the ship when we glide into the floating branch we're meant to tether too.

"Why, exactly, is the tether something with a Status Bar?" I say to Ali, looking upward.

The entire tether has multiple floating platforms, each of them bulbous and squishy, tiny tendrils reaching out to grip the floating airship while we anchor with our own rope to the main line reaching up the center. Multiple platforms, but if you squint hard enough, you can see the Status Bar right at the top.

"Because it's alive, of course," Ali says. "Dcon here is a Kusma Carnivorous Tree using a Dire Rotating Platform Class."

"A… what?" I ask.

For once, the Library has nothing to say. While the Questors have always been interested in Classes, there are so many, and the fringe ones are both necessarily interesting and also, often, useless for exploring the System. So there are surprisingly large gaps in Classes. On the other hand, most common and uncommon Skills and Classes are recorded, so I can't really complain. It gives me a leg up over and above most individuals.

"Dire Rotating Platform," Ali repeats with exaggerated patience. "Kusma Trees come in a variety of species, but the carnivorous ones are particularly rootloose. Of course, they're also carnivorous and—generally— have a rather wide palate. So, Platform Classes provide them a useful role to fill in locations like this while also making them the perfect lure for certain monsters. In fact…" Ali's eyes glaze over and he points upward. "There!"

I crane my head back and see what he means. High above us, even higher than the floating Status Bar, a flock of pterodactyl-wannabes are wheeling, searching for an easy dinner—waiting for Mikito and Ezz to leave the drake corpse alone. In their focus, they've drifted a little too low and Dcon acts. Branches shoot out from the top, moving so fast they might as well be guided missiles.

The flying dinosaurs wheel away, but just like any good surface guided missiles, the branches move, twisting in mid-air and literally splitting apart. Branches hook into wings, piercing leathery skin and spreading poison and branches through blood vessels. Momentum is staggered, halted, then gravity asserts itself, the creatures falling. At the same time, the branches reel the monsters backward, drawing them closer to the main trunk and the smallish platform at the top. I can't see what's on the platform, but I can just imagine a giant mouth with many, many teeth.

"So, what? It's a self-guarding tether that gets XP by being bait?" Ali nods at my question and I can't help but rub the back of my neck, even as I watch a half dozen Xy'largh natives tromp onboard to chat with the Captain and his quartermaster. Customs officials, I'm assuming. "You know what, fine. I don't really need to know more than that."

"What? Don't want to know the entire ecosystem and biology and Classes that some sentient, moving trees have come about? Or the many, many plans to use their population and planets as Mana sumps against Forbidden Zone expansion?" Ali teases.

"What?" I frown. "Why… oh. Sapient trees. I bet you could pack a lot of them on a planet."

"In theory," Xaxas says, appearing beside my side in a flash of lightning and thunder.

I twitch. Lightning Step is his own fast movement Skill. I've seen him use it a few times, though it has its advantages and disadvantages compared to Blink Step. Unlike Blink Step, it doesn't actually teleport one but shifts his body from matter to energy before making him reappear. That means certain kinds of Dimensional Locks don't work against him that would work against me, but it does mean other forms of blocking movement can stop or even hurt him.

It's also really flashy.

Literally.

"And?" I prompt the Yerrick when he chooses not to elaborate.

"They're sapient creatures that want to procreate like we do. Crowding means they get upset, can't grow as much. So they've rejected multiple attempts to crowd them. Doesn't stop the Galactic Council from doing it though, using economic and physical incentives and punishments to drive them to Restricted Planets," Xaxas said.

"Why didn't I see them before?" I say, frowning. I mean, we spent a few months clearing out quite a few Restricted Planets with the Erethran Paladins. You'd think I'd have come across an entire species before. I say as much, which results in something I hadn't expected.

Dcon freezes, the entire trunk trembling after a second. My intuition goes off and I step backward a little as I feel the regard of the tree, the way branches seem to be populating the area around the ship. Shadows grow around us, as leaves and branches turn inward, and I hear a few muffled curses.

"Ahh…" Ali sighs. "You and your big mouth."

"What did I do?"

"The Kusma and the Erethrans have a long running grudge. It started a couple of millennia ago, when a Grand Paladin chose to destroy one of the Kusma colonial worlds," Xaxas says, eyeing me sideways. "How is it that you do not know that? I thought you hid your Status because of that."

"I'm hiding my Status?" I say, puzzled. I crane my head upward, trying to see my own Status bar which, of course, is idiotic and impossible. Giving up, I look at the Spirit.

"Of course, I did it for you," Ali answers the unspoken question. "I'm not an idiot. Didn't think you would be blurting out your alliances either…" The tree shudders, and the Spirit turns toward the trunk, waving a little fist at it. "Enough with the posturing. Boy-o over here could tear you apart without even breaking out his Soulbound weapon. And that's just him. So go back to soaking up some sunlight and be glad he ain't out to cause another genocide."

I smack myself in the face as Ali speaks. "You... you can't say things like that!"

"Why not? You do."

"No, no, no. I don't threaten genocide. Ever," I say and turn toward the tree. "Look, Dcon, I don't do genocide. Not against living things, though monsters and Goblins... well, that's different. You get that, right? But against living things? That's just wrong. I don't know the history of shit, and really, I got bigger problems to deal with. So let's live and let live. Or else it'll be live and die. Me and you. Respectively." The tree shudders, but I'm already turning away from it to look at Ali. "That's how you do it."

"You're both insane," Xaxas says, turning from both of us.

"But effective," I say, jerking my head toward where the tree is retracting its branches and roots. Really, what kind of idiot Master Class tries to threaten a shipful of Heroics?

Raised voices from the gangplank have me turning to see the six customs officers stalking over, looking all kinds of annoyed.

Welp. That kind it seems.

***

Bone crunches under my hand, the body bouncing off the railing edge before flopping over. It plummets through the air, and only Dcon reaching out a branch to grab the falling body stops it from impacting the ground before my victim shakes off the stun.

"Now, repeat that again, but a lot more politely," I say. I ignore the glowing pair of beam weapons and the shots they took at me, the ones that pinged off my Soul Shield. See? I can be reasonable.

The quintet looks at one another, their leader having been summarily dismissed.

Eventually, a long-legged figure steps forward, its features so close to what I'd consider female that I'm left guessing at its sex. Its voice isn't much better, bordering the line between masculine and effeminate. "Your presence in the city is not wanted." Seeing my narrowing eyes, it continues hastily. "Please vacate the premises as quickly as possible."

"Well, if you guys got out of the way, we'd do that," I say. "We just need a quick stop off at the Shop, pick up some toys, and then we're gone."

"That is not—"

"Or we could fight our way through town, take it over, and gain access to the Shop that way, then fight our way back out." I shrug. "Your call. I need the experience, so I'm good with either. I'll even let you guys evacuate the civilians. An hour good enough?"

"You would not dare," it says, chin going up. "You just declared yourself honorable enough not to undertake genocide to our Tree."

"Exactly. Genocide. Indiscriminate killing." I point at him. "But if you get in the way between my objectives and me, that's not indiscriminate anymore." Tilting my head, I speak to Ali. "They have how many Heroics here?"

"Four. One of which is a Port Authority and will likely stay out of the fight," Ali says. "Non-combatant Class, and if he dies, they get swarmed and lose access to other services. Especially if Dcon dies."

"*Keep going.*"

"*I was going to, boy-o.* The other three are a mix. Two low-Level Heroics, one an Evolving Metropolis Architect who's a non-Combatant, though he can make the city itself fight you. Be annoying to handle. The other one's a Combatant, as is the mid-range Heroic. He'll keep either you or Bolo busy." A shrug. "Xaxas and Mikito could take care of the other two, or three if necessary."

"Right, and that's not counting the lady." I gesture toward where Yllis is standing beside Bolo, leaning against his arm as he holds her close and whispers sweet nothings. She looks quite content and full, a factor that has been aided by the simple act of eating the mother drake. "Or myself. Or I guess I'm handling the riff-raff?"

"Better you than Bolo."

I nod at Ali, then smile at the group. "But you guys must have done the math. This city might be the gateway to the Voowmah, but in the end, you're just the stopper to a bottle that isn't pressurized. You have more gateways set up to run away than you have defenses for a stand-up fight." I shrug. "And most of those defenses are pointed the other way too."

"And you'd use our weakness against us?" it says.

"I'm asking for you all to treat us just like any other Adventurer. Let us equip ourselves, let us prep for the expedition. Then let us saunter in the Valley of Certain Death, if you will, and wash your hands of the entire thing. And when the Shadow Council and Administrators arrive, just tell them the truth." I ignore the flinches among the group at the mention of things best left unsaid, keeping my eyes locked on the Xy'largh before us.

"And what truth is that? That we defied their request and aided you?"

"Yes. Aided us to certain death." I open my hands, offering him a wide, innocent smile. "Isn't that the point of the Valley?"

"It is a place of tempering and training, where the courageous..." One of the other customs members puffs up. Surprisingly, he's a rather scrawny dude—when you take into account his eight-foot-tall size, that is—and he doesn't wield a melee weapon but a paired pair of guns.

I tune him out, looking around to spot my team. Mikito's back with Ezz in tow, the pair of them still discussing options while she runs through forms, adapting them so that Ezz and his malleable body can make the most of it. Mostly, she seems to be talking about the principles of fighting, explaining the reasoning behind movements—going into the void, upsetting and unbalancing opponents, decreasing areas of strikes—rather than specific techniques. Which makes sense, since Ezz will need to figure out its own methods with its flowing, unstructured body.

Bolo and Yllis continue to chat, heads pushed together. I don't listen to them, not even by accident. The amount of sugary sweetness they exhibit is enough to put diabetics in a two-kilometer-radius into comas, and I only had to listen to them murmur sweet snookums to one another once to choose the better part of discretion. It surprises me how such a big man can be so mushy, but its possible certain death has brought out the romantic in him.

Perhaps that's what my relationships needed? Upcoming fatalities does add spice to the bedroom, but that was never my problem.

"Whatever," I say, waving the officials shut. "You keep this up and the Storm Warden is going to get bored and call down another storm. And then we're all going to regret it." I wrinkle my nose and lean in, faux whispering, "Have you smelled wet Yerrick? Ugh."

The blow to my back sends me staggering forward a little, some annoying Skill of his bypassing the momentum-cancelling properties of my own Skills and Soul Shield. It doesn't hurt, though Soul Shield does flicker and show that it's three-quarters down from that single blow.

"Not the most patient fella, you see?" I finish, straightening up and skirting around the group to put myself at an angle to the Yerrick.

Xaxas is glowering at me, but Ali is making a puckered face as he communicates and calms the Storm Warden.

No, I'm not being an ass just because. It's more because... "Also, Harry's already in your city and wandering around. And that means you're compromised anyway."

"What?"

"Who's Harry?" it says, even as Dcon finally deposits the initial speaker.

I notice the one I tossed overboard makes no move to take over the discussion, which I admit is probably a smart idea. Call me a short pink fleshbag, will he? Not anymore.

"Harry Prince. The War Reporter with us." I gesture down toward the city. "He's in your city right now, wandering through it, most of the way to the Shop."

"How...!"

"He has his ways." I shrug. "So. Compromised. Now, can we go? Because the one thing Harry is good at—beyond sneaking past bored guards—is finding trouble."

"I think that's mostly 'cause he's with you, boy-o."

"Hush. I'm negotiating here."

It turns, staring at its compatriots and the idiot I threw off. There's some shared, silent communication, potentially with controllers beneath us all—their bosses maybe—before they finally acquiesce.

Really, it's annoying how much posturing this entire thing has been. From the start, no one was going to deny a bunch of Heroics access to their city. Without a Legendary backing them up, a group like ours could do a ton of damage. Their best bet has always been to let us do what we want and pick up the pieces once we're gone.

The amount of bullying we're doing almost makes me feel guilty. If we didn't have the damn Shadow Council and Administrators breathing down our backs, I might even try for something actually diplomatic. But as it stands...

Well. Needs must when the devil drives. And trust me, this devil is driving like he's in a muscle car with the freeway newly repaved and the nearest cop guaranteed to be miles away.

Chapter 20

We find Harry waiting in the Shop, by the time we get "escorted" to it. His eyes are crossed, and Ali helpfully informs me that the reason for that is he's watching and talking to multiple "sources" using drones and holographic projectors. Extending his reach while recording from the safety of the Shop zone.

For a moment, I debate asking Harry what he's doing but figure if it was important, he'd have told us. After all, it's his Party Chat Skill we make use of. So instead, I wander over to the Shop sphere, place my hand on it, and access the System Shop.

A simple mass sale to the System empties my inventory and Altered Storage. It's fast and efficient since you can't bargain with the System Shop. That's why most people prefer working with actual Merchant-run organizations. The ability to get the best deal from them, with a minimum earning guaranteed by the System Shop, means competition is fierce for new customers. Still, with Skills that provide Credits or improve the quality of what is bought or just tilts the bargaining session in their favor, Merchants do rather well.

Once I'm done with selling my various loot and bodies, I take a few minutes to restock my dwindling supplies. I buy everything from Apocalypse Ale to more bags of chocolate and a double backpack full of chaos grenades and mines. Everything else, I leave behind—other than a pair of hovering boots and more armored jumpsuits, since I shred the ones I wear all too often.

Once the consumables are done, I stare at the hefty and paltry amount of Credits left from selling Level 100+ monster parts and loot pieces. Hefty because it's a veritable fortune to a Basic Classer, enough to buy up enough equipment to keep you well ahead of the pack. Paltry because it's not even a tenth of what I need to pick up weaponry or enchantments that could make a difference in a Heroic level fight.

Sure, I could get some minor enchantments, but most minor enchanted items are also tied into much weaker materials. In a fight at the level I take part in, they would shatter within a few minutes. Pure waste of money, and it hurts my cheapskate heart to buy things that will be destroyed—at least when they're not meant to be destroyed. Consumables like grenades and mines are another thing.

I mean, I've gotten over it a bit, what with my general riches, but I'm still not a big fan of buying things that will be broken. Which leaves me with not enough Credits to buy anything useful, but too much to randomly leave inside my System wallet.

Staring into space, hand still on the linked Shop sphere, a memory tickles my mind. A group of Yerrick in a ceremony, gifting possessions from within an Inventory. A Skill purchased by their clan to ensure the passing of items stored away, to reduce loss in a race that had experienced all too much of it.

I don't need the Skill. Outside of the Spitzrocket, I have nothing to give that is truly of value. And if everything goes as badly as I expect, there won't be much of the Spitzrocket left to cede to others. A few touches and a few adjustments to its programming helps ensure that even if I do die, the Spitzrocket will return to someone else.

As for the Credits... "Hey, Ali. There a way to get rid of all these Credits if I die?"

"You could gift them to me. I'll keep them safe for you." He says the last with a little leer.

Which is why my answer surprises him, making his jaw drop.

"Sure." A flick of my hands and I send him the transfer request.

"Wh... what... this... I..." Ali, for once, has nothing to say.

"What? You wanted it, it's yours. Best I can tell, you're harder to kill than a mutated cockroach, so this should be safe enough."

"I mean, Ezz…"

"Probably dead too if I'm dead," I say. "Ditto Mikito or Harry or anyone else coming. You're likely going to be the only survivor, and even that is a little dodgy."

"Eh, I have my ways. Also, there are certain…" Ali shakes his head. "That's not the point, boy-o. Do you know what giving me the Credits mean?"

I shrug.

"You know I'm linked to the System because of a debt, right?"

I nod, waiting for him to get to the point.

"My problem is, the way it was set up, I can barely get ahead because of the interest."

"That sounds like one heck of an interest rate. Also, predatory."

"It is. My fault for being, well, out of my mind at the time. But that's not the point. The only way I can get ahead is when my Companion goes up in Levels and Tiers. Then I get a bonus, for keeping you alive. More so because you're Linked to me, and the Mana you generate…" Ali shakes his head. "Whatever. You don't care, do you?"

"Actually, I kind of do." Considering he's my longest running friend, details about his secret pact with the System and whoever he owes the money to has been scarce. Maybe it's a guy thing, but I've never asked. It feels incredibly rude to probe, especially when he has chosen not to inform me.

"Not right now," Ali says. "Let's just say it'll be millenia before I'm done."

"And this piddly amount is enough to make a difference?"

"By a few centuries, yeah. So… thanks?" Ali says the word with a level of discomfort that makes me smirk a little.

I let the silence linger, taking the time to scan my minimap for trouble and inspect our surroundings. Not that the tiny metal cubicle they stuck us in is very interesting. Minimal set-up, since most people have Shops they actually get teleported to.

Me? I'm persona non grata in them all. Even the ones running on the edges of society want nothing to do with me. Never mind the cost of trying to teleport me from within a Forbidden Zone to whichever separated plane their merchant center resides within.

"Whatever." I echo his word back at the Spirit, who rolls his eyes. The awkward atmosphere between the two of us fades a little. Though, thinking about it, I do have one more question. "Why haven't you ever asked? I mean, a few months of grinding and we could probably have paid your debt off."

"Can't," Ali says. "It's… well, rules."

"Dumb rules."

"Tell me about it."

Chuckling, I look at the Shop sphere one last time. That's it. My last shopping trip. Now, we're just headed into the Valley of Certain Death.

Except, as I'm about to take my hand off the sphere, a series of beeps appear, notifications issued from the Shop System itself. I hesitate before swiping them, curious.

What can I say? Curiosity might have killed a cat, but I'm more a dragon.

***

The face looking back at me, with her big red hair and freckles, hits me like a bowling ball to the nuts. Which, frankly, is just about the place that she normally gets a reaction from me. Her and… yup. There he is, in the other notification.

"Lana. Roxley. This isn't the threesome I was dreaming of," I say.

"Ewww," Lana says.

"Hmmm…" Roxley goes at the same time. "This is not the time, Redeemer."

"After all this time, back to Redeemer, are we?" I say, crossing my arms.

"Oh, John…" Lana's tone is more tired, weary of my antics. "Do you have any idea how much this is costing us?"

In the background, I see shadows of trees and a mountain range. Tiny little nubs that look like lying lions are in the far distance, but they are all too familiar to me.

Roxley, on the other hand, is in his office, dressed to the nines, but there's a tightness to his eyes that I'm unused to seeing. He's generally unflappable, able to act as though the world isn't falling down around him, even when it obviously is. All his dancing training has allowed him to do that, but things must be tough if he's leaking this much.

"No idea, but I could ask. Or you could tell me why you called," I say. "Not as though I would know."

"Wanting to see you again isn't enough?" Lana says. Then she shakes her head, discarding the banter and light flirting. All too easy to fall into old habits. "I want to know, we want to know, if there's anything we can do for you. And if we can, I can, convince you to stop."

"Stop? Why would I stop?" My voice rises with my surprise.

"You are directly in conflict with the Shadow Council and their puppeteers, Redeemer. As strong as you are, as gifted as you are, you know there is only one result." Roxley's voice is harsh, biting. "You have been seeking this end for so long, you might have found it at last. But we, I, care enough to ask you to stop. To find another way."

"Another way… like turning a normal integration into a Dungeon World and dooming billions to death."

"Old wounds. Many have set it aside by now," Roxley says.

"And many haven't, isn't that right, Lana?" I turn to the redhead, knowing she is less likely to obfuscate. Less likely to hide the reality of idiotic humans finally having some form of power.

"No, many haven't. As much as we'd like to heal the wounds, to move past it, some people just won't. They nurse their grudges, the pains and losses of over a decade ago, as though anything they do now will bring back those they lost." Lana doesn't ever break eye contact, daring me to look away first. "But they're not the only ones left. Children, teenagers, those who grew up in this world are coming up, learning to deal. Can you not?"

"How?" I laugh, harshly and a little wildly. I throw a hand around me, indicating the planet, the space they cannot see. "This tiger has started running and I can't let go."

"And in this, we both agree." Roxley shares a look with Lana, looking at her projection before he turns to me. "You have managed so many miracles before. If you wanted to, I'm sure you could manage one last one. To save yourself. To save your friends."

"To save Earth?" I say, twigging onto another of his motivations. That's the thing with Roxley. One reason why we could never really be together. He always has another motivation, always another goal. He has to balance a million and one responsibilities, and so he does, by trading love and duty off with one another. "How bad are they pushing you?"

"Multiple fleets are enroute to Earth," Roxley answers.

I frown. "I thought they'd already sent one."

"Yes. And we dealt with it," Roxley says.

"How—"

"Tick tock," Ali chimes in.

"Ali's right, John. We don't have time. It doesn't matter. We can handle Earth, though help would be good if you can find any." Something dark flashes across Lana's eyes before she pushes it aside. "But I worry about you and Mikito."

"Hey!" Ali protests, only to be ignored by us.

"I don't want to lose any more friends."

"You know, Harry probably wouldn't like being left out," I say.

Lana shrugs, and I get it. He's not really someone she knows, though a little part of me is pained to see the caring young woman I knew grow a veneer of needed cruelty. "As Roxley says. If you wanted to, I'm sure you could figure out a way. You always have."

"I'm flattered by the confidence, but I really don't see a way out but through," I confess. "This time, I think I really f'ed it up."

"Oh, John…" Lana breathes those words before she gives me a nod. There's grief in her eyes, but one that is old. A loss that was accepted years ago, like watching a grandparent spiral down the slopes of Alzheimer's, watching them decline with each day and being unable to stop it. At a certain point, the grief stops dribbling out, just like their memories. "Then… take as many of the bastards out as you can?"

"Yeah…"

"Redeemer, Ms. Pearson's request for aid was not, as much as she might have made it sound, a minor matter. What aid you might offer or rouse up would be much appreciated." A slight pause, then Roxley continues, anger and exhaustion lacing his next words. "The Duchess has decided that her holdings on Earth must stand or fall on their own from now on. The ledger is too far into the red to consider further investment."

"Ah…" I exhale and nod. "Very well. I'll see what I can rustle up." Or who.

A final nod, this one curt from Roxley. Whatever feelings there might have been between the two of us, it's always been mixed with politics. And unlike Lana, he has always been rather more pragmatic about who I am and my goals. I think, if nothing else, that was the reason he held me at arm's length too.

I offer the pair a smile, while Ali waves goodbye to them. Seconds later, they blink out, leaving me to stand alone in a small, bare room to reflect on my past and the Quest. The one thing I refuse to give up, no matter what.

Well, not really alone.

"So, Ali, about that money I just gave you…"

***

"Twenty-three percent interest rate, compounded monthly!" I mutter as I stride out to see the rest of my friends.

Ali, floating along beside me, is looking all kinds of smug. Outside, the rest of the team are already waiting, eager to head out of the weird, squat city that sits hanging upside down, facing the core of the planet and its sun. There's still something strange about seeing that glowing ball of flame and power, knowing that you should be falling into it and not doing so.

"Come on, a few good days' grinding and you'll have the money," Ali says, grinning.

"You even made me pay for a Merchant Contract that's linked to my Storage!" I say, shaking my head. "Just so you could get your Credits back faster."

"You're the one saying you don't need it."

"But I didn't expect to be taken to the cleaners for borrowing the money for a message."

"Well, maybe if you'd thought about calling your exes before you were generous, you could have avoided it," Ali says.

"Or you could have returned it to me!"

The Spirit sniffs, while Mikito, coming up to me, raises an eyebrow in inquiry.

"Boy-o talked to his exes," Ali explains.

"I gathered that. Lana and Roxley?" Mikito asks.

"Yup."

"I also contacted Catrin. Hopefully she can help them," I clarify, glaring at Ali. "Couldn't speak with her though. She's radio silent. Bounced the message to some old friends."

Mikito raises an eyebrow and I mouth the word Paladin in English. She blinks then nods, a thoughtful look crossing her face. I know a lot of her club members—the ones involved in the breakout and causing havoc on Irvina—escaped to Earth, so I'm hoping this settles her mind a little.

If not... well, there's not much else I can do.

A quick message sent over my private link to the Hands has them dispersing, the majority heading out to grind more experience for me. They'll also kill a bunch of monsters and loot them, using the looted items to help pay off some soul-sucking Spirit's loan. The last one keeps station at the settlement exit, watching for trouble and potential attacks.

"Are we done? If so, we should move." Bolo drops his voice a little, though the man really doesn't understand the point about whispering. He's still loud enough that if not for the spell his girl throws up to silence his words, anyone within a hundred feet would hear him. "There are indications the Council are scrambling people here for us. There's just not enough of them to stop us.

"Yet."

Chapter 21

Xaxas strolls by my side as we head down the tunnels, his head tilted up to the side. The way to the Valley of Certain Death is, unlike most exits from the hollow planet, pretty fixed. A trick of stabilization via the city we just left and the exit point. What isn't common is the crackling cloud and mist that rolls around and behind us, hiding our team from view.

"So, how many?"

"Two score and three. Three main parties and six individual scouts," Xaxas says. "At least, from those I count in my cloud. There might be more."

"Probably is," I say. "Anything we should worry about?"

Xaxas shakes his head, big bull lips turning up in a sneer to showcase his flat teeth. "Basic Classes. Not even worth the Mana."

"All right." Briefly, I consider sending my Hand to deal with them but choose not to. Never know if we're walking into a trap, and as Xaxas said, they're Basic Classes.

We fall silent, continuing our long trek upward. No Worms for us, no Centipedes or anything to carry us upward. Even if the cavernous tunnel we walk within—which looks like melted basalt and granite, grey and red and black rock shimmying in the mistlight—looks as though it might have been carved by a worm, we get nothing. It's part of the necessity of the stable passage through the hollow planet upward, since anything too large could punch a hole through the thin but stable dimensional walls surrounding us.

Not that I can sense those dimensional gaps. My Elemental Affinity is useful for a vast variety of applications, but secondary dimensions are not one of them. Oh, don't get me wrong, I can sense something weird at the edges, but the actual boundaries are impossible for me to feel using the Affinity. If not for my System Edit Skill, I might miss it entirely. On the other hand, Bolo looks fascinated, his Dimensional Affinity probably giving him a whole series of notes.

It's kind of funny how little the Dragon King makes use of his own Affinity. When pressed about it, he says it's weird, so I don't. There are minor things he does, like the way his hammer is actually even larger than it looks or the kind of dodging he does. It has taken me a long time to notice, mostly because the way he uses his Affinity is much more subtle. Just a minor twisting in the spatial planes, a way for him to sidestep attacks without actually moving.

Ali also, rather quietly, noted that like me, Bolo's Affinity isn't really his but tied to his dragon mate. Unmated, unaligned Dragon Knights get them too, but their affinities are often much, much weaker—and are, in many ways, a limitation. After all, if your affinity and the dragon you choose to bond with don't line up, it can cause significant issues. Including rejection, or just not going from a minor affinity to a greater affinity.

In either case, we're tramping through the tunnel, making good time because we're all high-Level with quite a few stats in Strength and Agility. There is, of course, a maximum of how fast we can move, what with physics and stride length, but small boosts like Thousand Steps make sure we're covering ground at a goodly pace. Even Harry is keeping up, though in his case, he cheats by using enchanted equipment like Thousand Stride Boots.

Weirdly enough, the strangest pairing is Ezz and my Hand. I'm not entirely sure what is going on there, but the little golem seems to find conversations with the Hand fascinating. It's not even as though they're talking of anything important—just old missions, old events. But Ezz absorbs the stories like a red sponge, and it's leaving me alone, so I'm not complaining.

Yeah, I'd make a horrible dad.

Speaking of Harry, I tilt my head and stare at his Status. There's a series of new notifications on it, sufficient that I take the time to review it all.

Harry Prince, the Unfiltered Eye, Galactic Investigative Reporter—Polonium Level, the Unvarnished Truth, Heroic Survivor, Friend of the Erethran Empire, Galactic Snoop, Hacker's Friend, Network Center, ... (Galactic Correspondent Level 46) (M)

HP: 1380/1380

MP: 3583/3740

Conditions: Reporter's Luck, Nose for Trouble, Just a Bystander, Information Locus, Network News—Polonium Grade, Network Locus, Damage Ablation (GIR Network)

Some new Titles in there. Some of it probably having taken its time to populate through the galaxy such that he finally gained enough of a reputation to get there. I'm curious about the Network Center option, and the Library provides details without much of a prompt.

Title: Network Center

Often a location, on occasion a person. A Network Center is a hub of information, one so important that significant resources have been invested to ensure that it stays online. There are a limited number of Network Centers available throughout the Galaxy at any one time. Current network limit is 13982.

Effect: Creates Network Locus. Damage Resistance increased by 30%. Damage Ablation (GIR Network) gained.

About damn time. I don't know a huge amount about the GIR, beyond the fact that they hold themselves to be an independent organization that reports upon the actions of the various major players throughout the System. Of course, they're not the only one—with minor organizations branching out and even a few specialized networks—but they are by far the largest.

Almost every single Reporter eventually joins them, if for nothing more than to gain access to their news markets and internal data sales.

I know Harry has his own beef with GIR. Between being able to report on Earth when they weren't able to get enough people, providing a new and fresh perspective to Galactic news, and of course, him tagging along with me, they've tried to label him as an Entertainment Reporter rather than a War Reporter. Which creates its own set of problems.

Thus far, of course, the System has full say on Class but not necessarily what kind of benefits they offer him. GIR has also held back on his benefits, but the new increase in his Titles tells me that some of that has been allayed. My guess is, with an actual war going on—and a much larger one threatening to erupt—the bureaucrats have been discarded. Or at least lost some degree of power.

Now, the effects are good. More damage reduction is always useful. Damage Ablation means the damage is taken but passed through the System to others, offering him an effective shield of sorts. Necessary if they want to keep him alive. I don't, however, know what Network Locus means, so I push at my mind to get the data.

Buff: Network Locus

Type: Ongoing Passive

Effect: Increased System connection. Automatic uploading of all recordings. Local, Regional, and System-enhanced storage.

Boring. Useful for him, but boring for me. I dismiss the notification, and instead ask Harry directly about the other rather interesting update in his Status Screen.

"How'd you jump so many Levels?" I grouse. "I mean, really?"

"Your Quest," Harry says. "It seems that it decided to backdate some of that experience gains or something. I'm getting triple experience for some old recordings, and even more for the sale of our recent breakout. In fact, that's probably one of my best-selling works, including the pieces they didn't want me to record." I snort, and Harry gives me a savage grin. "Also, I'm getting news that their, well, shenanigans have caused a rupture in the ranks."

"Good. The fewer people the Shadow Council have to draw upon, the better."

"Not just the Shadow Council." At my startled look, Harry shrugs. "You got to remember, the prison was run and owned by the full Galactic Council. Along with this, my peers have been finding quite a few other pieces of information leaking out, now that the Lady of Shadows isn't able to keep everything hidden.

"To say that some people are upset might be a little bit of an understatement."

"So, what, a third party?"

"It's forming," Harry says. "More like a half-dozen different groups all breaking from both the Galactic Council and the Shadow Council. They might join together, or more might break up and it'll become a four- or five-way fight."

I wince. Two-way fights are bad enough. When the order of succession breaks into more, it becomes really messy.

"Good," Xaxas rumbles. "Central powers are all prone to corruption. Better to have localized governments. You can punch them in the face easier."

I snort. "How'd that work out with Legendarys then?"

"They are... more difficult to assault," Xaxas admits. "But they are easier to run from."

I rub the back of my neck. Maybe he's right. Maybe I'm used to the idea of a single giant government because that's what they had on Earth, and well, Canada was a rather big place. But the UN was always a mess, and most of the countries with large populations probably would have been better off smaller. Except, you know, for economic and capital reasons.

"Whatever," I say finally. It's not as though any of what is going on out there impacts me. Not as though I can make any changes. Really, I didn't even understand local politics for Vancouver or Whitehorse, never mind Canadian politics or global politics. What right do I have to dabble in galactic politics?

"*Didn't stop you from dabbling before,*" Ali sends.

"*Reading my mind?*"

"*We've been together for over a decade, boy-o. I hate to break it to you, but you're complex as a bowl of clear Jell-o.*"

"*Funny.*" I ignore the Spirit as he floats along.

Harry has gotten to talking with Xaxas, interviewing him on what he knows about the history of the Yerrick—which is significant, considering who and what he was to them—and has taken to ignoring me. I trust that Xaxas will keep me informed if there's anything too dangerous out there, so I find myself just walking, my mind turning the new information over and over.

Eventually, I can't help but send to Ali, "*Is there anything I can do? I mean, it sounds like Harry has a direct link out. An interview... a plea?*"

"*For what? To let the power of love in and let it conquer all?*" There's quite a bit of sarcasm in Ali's tone. Then again, he's hung around with me for the last decade plus. No pacifist would have survived that long.

"*Not helping.*"

"Neither would you. If you have an actual clue of how you could make a difference, I'm all energy protons. Otherwise, I'd keep my mouth shut, my head down, and your electrons free."

"Lots of physics talk there."

A shrug from Ali and I let it go, as I do the idea of doing something. Sometimes, the best thing you can do when a situation is all chaos is nothing at all. If you're wading into a pond and kick up all kinds of dirt, muddying the water, you can't create clear water again by splashing about even more vigorously. Stop, wait, let it settle. And then, if you're lucky, a fish will swim by and you'll manage to stab it. And not yourself in the foot.

Not that I've ever done that.

Not at all.

Nope.

***

Two days of walking pretty much in a straight line up. Of course, we're not actually walking upward but in a sort of weird angular circle. We gather more and more people on the periphery, members of the Galactic Council who have managed to make it to the city below us and scrambled to get here. The only reason they're double the number and not triple is because they keep losing people, either dropping out of Xaxas's cloud or, in more dire cases, disappearing.

Realistically, they should never have sent their Basic Classes. This environment, this entire planet isn't geared for Basic Classes. They have to be carefully managed, run through Dungeons and on patrols of pre-cleared grounds, to survive. There's a reason why people don't generally drag Basic Classes to Dungeon Worlds or Forbidden Planets and it has a lot to do with the casualty rates.

It tells me a little about how desperate they are to keep tabs on us. And how far they're pushing their people that the Basic Classes chose to come out, rather than rebel. Or perhaps it's just how much they hate us. Or believe in what they're doing.

In either case, they've switched out Basic Classes for Advanced and even a bunch of Master Classes. It's made our walk a little tenser but not that much. Until they manage to get Heroics in play, we're safe enough. And if they do deploy Heroics, Xaxas's cloud gives us enough time to get ready.

Not that our readiness requires much beyond the mental and emotional. Environmental advantages are rather slim where we were, so I'm more than a little relieved when we get out and into the open sky. The feeling of millions of tons of earth pressing down on us, illuminated only by artificial light, has been a shadow on my mind.

Bright sky. Finally. Sort of.

Coming out of the bore hole, we emerge at the bottom of a ravine, one so deep I can barely see the edges of the sky, light filtering in to cast long shadows. We're illuminated by the mushrooms—oh gods, so many mushrooms—that shed purple and yellow light while tiny creatures scurry around on the edges of the shadows. Some of them don't necessarily stay there, fading in and out of the shadows if any one of us tries to focus on them.

The ravine walls are made of grey and black stone, the black crawling along the sheer cliffs and creating a spiderweb design across them. Shattered sections jut out every ten meters or so, but there's a glassiness to the grey stone that makes me think climbing it would be difficult. Idly, I wander over to one of the walls and punch it. Rather than shatter, it hurts my hand and I feel skin split along my knuckles. Frowning, I pull back my hand and notice my skin knitting back together, blood dripping out.

"What the hell?" I'm used to hard metal, even hard rock. It doesn't split my skin though, not even when it's hard enough to withstand a punch.

"Reflexive rock," Bolo says. "Deals a portion of damage you deal to it back to you."

"That... what? Why?" I say plaintively.

"Xy'largh is not for the weak," Yllis replies as she wanders past me.

"Ali, take to the sky, will you? I'd like a better map."

"On it." The Spirit looks toward the sky, sticks a hand out, and shoots upward. There's even a small visual effect that follows his acceleration, though I'm grateful he keeps it to a visual effect rather than actually creating a sonic boom.

Scouting dealt with, I look back at the hole we just walked through. "Trap it?" I say speculatively to Mikito.

"No," Bolo says firmly.

"Don't think it'll work?" I say.

"We will not trap the exits. It is not done."

"Pretty sure..."

Bolo growls at me. I hold up a hand, giving in. It's not as if a trap would do more than kill a few Basic Classes, maybe an Advanced Classer. Not enough to force the issue and cause problems in my own team.

"Also, you might not want your Spirit to go that high," Yllis calls.

"He's invisible," I say.

"Not to them," she replies.

"Ah... *you might want to come down.*"

"Aaaaaahhhhhh!" Ali sends back, screaming.

"Incoming!" I roar, knowing what the scream means. There's a little bit of panic in it, but not much, so I don't bother with power armor, instead conjuring my sword and looking upward.

The others prep themselves—all but Harry and Xaxas, who keep an eye on the hole instead.

What appears isn't what I expected. Rather than monsters raining down on us, it's glowing shards of energy. My eyes narrow, and Perception bends to my will and my vision narrows and zooms in. The moment it does, I can actually tell what it is coming down. Rather than shards of energy, it's charged crystal, energy pumped into material to the point they look like slow-moving laser beams.

Good enough anyway, for my next action.

Can't target it with most of my area effect Skills, not without hitting me. So I go old school and swing my sword, using a series of Blade Strikes over a wide area to catch as many of them as I can. My Hand uses a series of spells—Polar Vortex, Firestorm, Lightning Strike—to do the same thing.

I notice Xaxas throwing his hand outward, lightning dancing from his fingers to lash out at the sky, while Mikito projects Hitoshi into its massive form. She swings it at the crystals like a giant broom sweeping away the skies. The Dragon King isn't taking action, mostly because Yllis has cast her hands upward and flames have erupted from them. So much fire, arcing in a cone wide enough that anything he did would be swallowed in her own attack envelops the sky above them.

Into that midst, screaming his head off vocally now, comes Ali.

Explosions stream out from behind him, coating the sky in flames of myriad colors as our attacks hammer into the crystals. Even though we're hitting them with everything we've got, only Yllis manages to catch the majority in her region.

Ezz scrambles over to me, and on instinct, I grab it and dump it into my Inventory. They can't hurt it in there. At the last second, I look at Harry and throw Two for One on him. The rest of us are forced to take the brunt of the damage when the crystals hit the ground, releasing their energy.

Light so bright I'm forced to squint, even through the combat helmet that automatically pulled itself over my features. Energy pours through the solid sides of the helmet, searing my eyes through my eyelids and leaving me blind. My Elemental Affinity pulses outward, a subconscious part of me wielding it such that it pushes against the energy, dissipating some of it.

Damage notifications scroll past my blind eyes, damage from myself, from Harry, stabbing deep within me. Nerves, muscles, blood are fried. Then it's over, the last of the energy being wielded at me dissipated. I conjure a healing syringe and jab it into my thigh, letting the potion take effect and start the process of putting my eyes together, along with System regeneration.

As that happens, I crouch low, offering the smallest target I can feasibly do while keeping my mobility. I move a few feet away from my old location too, just in case someone had a lock on me before the blast.

Then, and only then, do I check my party channel. Of us all, Harry has taken the most damage, his health barely a quarter of what it should be. The rest of us are anywhere from barely damaged—Bolo and Yllis—to a fifth down. My Hand is on the ground, rolling around, in deep pain and, to my surprise, breaking apart.

"*Thousand hells, Ali! What in the goblin shit was that? What's happening to my Hand?*" I scream mentally, only to feel a feedback surge from his side of the connection that sets my teeth on edge and bursts a few blood vessels in my head.

It takes a few seconds before I'm able to regain control, blind eyes healing enough that I can look around, everything a blurry haze. No one's dead and we're not under attack, which is why when I spot Ali—curled up in mid-air and holding himself together by sheer will, his body riddled with gaping holes—I rush over.

"*Should I banish you?*" I shout over the link, bracing for the pain he feeds back to me.

"NOOO! I can fix this…" Ali grates out, his voice sounding like a twisted, pain-filled version of his own.

"What the hell happened? What kind of monster was that?" I say, scanning the sky for more trouble. Nothing. Not yet at least.

"Automatic dragon defenses," Yllis says, strolling over. "They don't like us flying in, so they bred a type of plant. It creates seeds of crystal, which absorb the sun's energy. When they sense something in the sky, they fire their crystals into the sky, blanketing the area. The energy is twisted such that it attacks across dimensions."

"Then my Hand and Ali…"

"Are taking additional damage due to who and what they are," Yllis confirms.

I watch as the Hand blips out of existence at last. Grimacing, I look at the Spirit who is still struggling to put himself together. The gaps in his body are slowly healing as he fights off the dimensional tears. But it's not an easy thing, for sure.

"Bloody hell," Harry says, his body held up by Xaxas as he's dragged over. "That's an overreaction, isn't it?"

"It's just their first layer. You're lucky he's so small, otherwise he'd have brought down a real storm," Yllis says. "And even if that crystal storm was too small for a dragon, the Voowmah will come to investigate. We should move."

Bolo looks a little surprised, though he hides it well. Surprised enough that this is either a new development or just one he was never privy to. Either is possible, since this isn't exactly his stomping grounds.

Mikito is on her horse, fully armed and armored. She pulls Harry up to sit astride with her. I'm surprised that that works. I wonder if she put points into that or it Evolved or... something.

Then Ali floats down toward my shoulder. He attaches himself to me, giving me little jolts of energy every few seconds. I'm surprised to see most of my clothing is still intact, the energy attack seeming to have bypassed the clothing to attack me directly. Good for my modesty, not great for my health.

"Fine. Let's move. Lead the way," I say, sending a worried glance at Ali.

He's too busy to pay attention, though when Yllis strides off at the head of our column, I can't help but glare at her back. She could have warned us before he got too far ahead.

Instead, she chose not to and nearly killed him and Harry.

Sometimes, I wonder if she's on our side at all.

Chapter 22

Over the next few hours, as we beat a hasty retreat, I make sure to question Yllis about everything she knows. Luckily, Ali got enough into the air to give us a good idea of what's around, so we're not forced to move through dead-ends. At least, not initially; who knows if the way we're moving will dead-end eventually?

Thankfully, Yllis and Bolo have planned far enough ahead to provide us all with maps; though according to them, they're only partially helpful. Something to do with the way the walls and the environment are constantly reshaped by the Voowmah. Even though the walls might damage them, the Voowmah don't actually seem to care, what with having a ton of drones to get rid of.

So they tear down the walls, build new ones, and change the landscape constantly. It doesn't help that one of the aspects of Refracting Stone is that it rebuilds itself, having a natural healing factor just like we do. The actual act of wearing it away instead gives it strength, which it expands to pull itself together. The black streaks are an indication, supposedly, of exactly how much energy a particular location has built up.

I don't get it, nor how stone can store damage potential, but System-garbage is good enough of an explanation for me for now. There's definitely nothing in the Library about it being useful for the System Quest. Weird shit in the System is just weird shit. Exploring those connections basically leads to questions on what Mana is and what Mana does, and that is a whole different study. A larger one, one that coincides with the study of the System but is, at the same time, different.

Not for me. Let someone else explore Mana. I'm not a scientist, no explorer of the unknown. I want answers and someone to blame. Someone to put my fist into. And the System, for all that it controls us, it's not Mana. It's artificial, so there's an answer and someone to blame.

It's only now, after so many years, that I've realized why I focus on it so much. My need for an answer, for an individual to blame. For someone to lash out at. You can't hurt Mana, but the creator of the System?

Yeah, I can kick their ass.

Big dreams. Yet that's all I have to occupy my mind as we hurry. We know better than to fight, since the moment we get into battle with the Voowmah, it'll be one fight after the next as they throw more and more of their drones. Eventually, they'll pull out their high Levels and we'll really be stuck in it. Putting space between us and where things went bad will throw them off, especially with the ground healing over.

Xaxas and Harry are particularly useful here, their Skills—and skill—helping to clean up our trail. Harry makes full use of his Just a Bystander Skill, with me Editing it to encompass not just him but the surroundings. With Xaxas cleaning up physical and other traces like scent with his own Skills—the man's Basic Class was Wild Hunter—we should be able to hide our tracks.

In the meantime, Mikito rides beside me, keeping an eye out for trouble and letting Harry do his thing with his Skills while I run alongside. Once I'm certain we're good, I summon another Hand—two actually, since I finally lose one in the hollow planet—and drop them off to keep an eye on Ezz. The golem protests at getting not just one but two bodyguards, but I ignore its protests.

This isn't the time for it to act bigger than it is.

The deep canyon we're in now is filled with otherworldly light and deep shadows, and the occasional monster that lunges out to attack us, too blind or too aggressive to avoid us, has their corpses dropped into my Altered Storage.

The air grows heavy and clammy. This deep down, the humidity is high. Water runs along the walls, collecting and dripping, while the occasional stream runs along the ground. I only touch the water once on purpose—the damn liquid is highly acidic. Not alien-burning-through metal acidic, but don't-drink-unless-you-want-to-be-in-the-hospital caustic.

After a while, I drop my helmet back into storage and run without it, filtering the air through my lungs. One of the advantages of the Classes I have is that the passive resistances allow me to take in non-Earth air mixtures, so even the mild burning sensations are dampened. My eyes don't water, even though there're some chemicals that burn. Sulphur I can tell, because that spoilt egg smell is all too recognizable. Ammonia, that smell so similar to back alleys in Gastown, Vancouver, is present too. And then other kinds of chemicals, ones I don't recognize but that assault me and make breathing heavier.

Nothing my System-enhanced body can't take. But it is present, and I notice that Harry struggles a little. Low Constitution sucks in such circumstances.

Peeling chocolate and putting in my mouth to keep idle hands busy ends with me spitting it out seconds later.

"What the hell?" I say, staring at the triangular bar of chocolate in my hand. I know the white stuff isn't real chocolate, but needs must, and it isn't normally that bad.

"You're sucking down weird chemicals with every breath, boy-o. Don't you think it would affect your taste buds?"

"But my chocolate?" I wail.

"Everything." Bolo falls in behind me and tosses me a wrapped bar. "Eat that if you need something."

I frown at the bar, peeling it open to see a grey block within. "Looks like compressed shit."

"It's not any worse than that chicken feet you made me eat," Bolo says.

"I told you already, it's a traditional dish!"

"Among one portion of your humans. Known for eating some very strange things," Bolo replies. "Which, among the deprived, is acceptable. Those things, though, were slimy, fatty, and contained few true nutrients."

"But oh so tasty."

"Eat," Bolo replies, ending the conversation as he moves to the front again.

I roll my eyes but bite into the bar. And wince. It doesn't taste like week-old garbage like the chocolate, but more like fermented smelly tofu. Which, frankly, is not something I ever grew a taste for. Not as many dishes in Vancouver made from that, for which I'm grateful.

Still, it's edible and it gives my mouth something to do while we run.

Sometimes, you take what you can get and eat it.

***

We don't need sleep, so we don't. Hours of running, traveling through looming canyon walls and along bubbling streams of acid, snarling monsters launching themselves at us with irregular frequency. Swarm creatures barely the size of a hand, but with Levels in the 80s each, attempt to burrow into our flesh and lay their eggs. Buried crablike-predators launch themselves from the ground as we pass or step on them, clamping pincers onto our legs and injecting toxins into our blood. A lurking shadow creature, a mix between a sleek ferret and a dinosaur, fires quills of shadow energy before it expands.

And the fungi. All the fungi.

We get everything from laser mushrooms that fire beams of weird crisscrossing energy at us, bathing the walls, to reflexive mushrooms in the same canyon gorge that bounce this energy upward and downward, turning a simple attack into a minefield of death. Ali and I get pushed with our Elemental Affinity, killing the transfer of energy before it can truly build up.

Then there are the wire ones, spores floating in the wind trailing micron-thin wire filaments that cut into flesh and slice apart skin. Yllis handles that with a lot of flame, burning them all down so that we can cross without being chunked. Minutes later, the surroundings have absorbed the ash and heat, newly recreated spores floating through the sky.

Gorges of flaming heat, the mushrooms within glowing white-hot, reflexive stone casting damage back and pumping back just as much heat. Molten rock bubbles up from the ground near the mushrooms, salamanders flopping around in the pools of lava and tossing flame and rocks at us as we hurry through. After the first time Xaxas drops the temperature in our surroundings and almost brings down the walls on our heads, we just hurry through rather than try to stop them.

Mushrooms of all kinds. Some suck up all light, making travel by normal sight impossible. Others rip themselves free from the ground, attacking us as we pass by, shedding spores that attempt to make us hallucinate or dissolve our flesh. Illusionary passages and whirlwinds that throw us high into the air, attempting to draw down crystal shard attacks.

So much fungi, all of it lethal. I'm not sure I'll ever look at a dish of pasta the same again.

All the while, we move deeper and deeper, the rumble of traps and the roar of monsters moving through the gorges surrounding us, filtering in from above or echoing through the passages. Screams and howls of pain, monsters clashing with one another, and the constant hammering of crystal shards hitting the ground in the distance. We're not the only ones in town, and while the monsters might know better, that's only if they live long enough to learn the lessons this Valley teaches.

Days of traveling through the passages, moving backward and forward, cutting around and through obstructions when we have no more choice. More than once, we clamber up to a second or third level, forced to push pitons into cliff faces and clamber upward, swinging from ropes loosened by a vindictive cliff face. Slamming into the ground hurts. The few times we lose everyone, the ground is happy enough to inflict pain on us just as much as we punished it on landing. Ezz makes itself useful when we climb, its body's ability to change shape and its liquid metal pitons becoming one of our major belaying points.

On the second and third levels, we get a chance to see a little more of the valley. There are different monsters, creatures that linger in the remaining light, that crawl across the grey stone like so many wrong-legged spiders. Webs, poisons, darts, and scorpion tails all lash out when we get too close, sometimes attacking us even while we're climbing.

And all the while, we watch the dots appear and disappear from our minimap, as those the Council have gathered die as they try to keep track of us. Sometimes a trick of space and a warping of light puts them close enough we can see them; other times they fade all the way off our maps, even one boosted by Ali.

"Hey, Bolo, exactly how many times do you guys send people in?" I say, eyeing the running total of System-connected individuals I've been reading.

"Each settlement only sends in individuals once a year at most. When enough individuals have been trained up sufficiently," Bolo replies. "Of course, there being over fifty major settlements and another one hundred plus minor ones that join together, that means there's often at least one or two groups running the Valley at any one time."

"And that's a good idea?" I ask. "Aren't you leveling the damn Voowmah?"

"They level whether we do anything or not. This way, we Level too," Bolo says. "Also, it gives our higher Levels a chance to play and take down their high Levels. The full flight only happens once every half decade."

"So, figure what? A half dozen individuals in each group, maximum of, say, three groups, total of eighteen, maybe a full score at most?"

"That sounds about right. Double that number if you include dragonkin for them all, though that never happens."

"What's a more expected number?" I say.

"Why do you keep asking?" Yllis cuts in, sounding frustrated by my questions.

"Because over the last few days, Ali and I have tracked easily over two hundred System-connected individuals."

"What!?!" Yllis says, her voice rising in pure surprise.

"And that's what we were able to track. I'm sure there's more. We're using my System Edit Skill to cheat, but even then, this place isn't exactly friendly to our Skills," I say.

"Fools. They're just feeding the Voowmah," Yllis hisses.

"How do they have so many anyway?" I say.

"Marines, detachments from the fleets above. Mercenaries. Hidden agents meant to deal with the Dragon Lords and dragons if they acted out too much," Harry cuts in. "Not a surprise really. You forget that the Dragon Knights and their dragons are both a resource and a power in themselves. No Council was going to take them lightly."

"Nor should they," Bolo rumbles, and Yllis grins.

"Father, I do not understand," Ezz buzzes. "Why send so many when they know where you must go?"

"Because they don't know," I say. "This place, the Administrative Center. Even on the map and access that I have, it keeps moving. Or at least,

its entrance does. It's somewhere in here, in the center. But exactly where…"
I shrug.

"That's why they haven't been found before?" Harry says.

"That's what I figure."

"And if you're wrong?" Xaxas says, the group having chosen to group around us.

We're on the second floor, if you will, about a dozen meters above the canyon passage which is, right now, filled with a bubbling acid river filled with carnivorous fish that act like B-movie piranhas at the merest hint of anything not them in the water.

"Then we're going to have a lot of company when we arrive," I say.

There are a few grimaces, but it really isn't anything new.

"And the Voowmah. Why aren't they attacking us?" Mikito asks, breaking her silence. "Everything you said, I have been expecting constant battles by now."

"We're too powerful," Yllis replies. "I would not expect anything from them until another day at least. Better to lure us in. Makes it harder for us to escape when the trap closes."

"They do that a lot?" I can't help but ask. Yllis's nod makes me grimace. "Smart enemies. I hate those."

Another savage grin from Yllis, one that is condescending at the same time. As though she considers me and my complaints poor fit for her vicious planet.

"Great. So we got Shadow Council members coming in from behind, Voowmah in front, and lots of native flora and fauna that want to eat us. Am I missing anything?" I say.

"No." Bolo taps the side of his thigh for a few seconds before he nods suddenly. "We should camp soon. Rest. And deal with those behind us."

"Sounds like a plan. A nice, fun, and dangerous plan."

With the Voowmah less than a day from dropping their trap on us, we're cutting it close. Then again, with so many coming in after us, we'll have deal with our pursuers sooner rather than later.

We can just hope there are no Legendarys down there.

"I do not understand, Father. Why is danger fun?" Ezz says.

"I was being sarcastic," I explain.

"Understood. Then, yes. Fun, Father. We shall have much fun."

Chapter 23

Maybe they don't want us to rest. Maybe our pursuers were ready to hit us already, what with having pulled back. We barely get more than an hour of sleep, with the fragile all-planet environmental tents deployed around us, filtering the air and providing us our preferred atmosphere, when they attack. The first wave of attacks comes from their stealth specialists, coming in close enough under cover of heavy Mana suppression and the natural cover of the canyons that they can range on us.

Beam rifles, the equivalent of mortar strikes, and fireballs hammer into the force shield generator Bolo deployed to provide cover for us all. The force shield generator drops within a second, but a more powerful settlement shield powered by Yllis's Mana takes the brunt of the second wave of attacks.

I tear out of the tent, not bothering to go out normally, calling the Spitzrocket to me. Armor pops from its dimensional storage, pulled into place by the System and the underlayer armor, locking around my arms, chest, and legs with alacrity. Gleaming black and red, notification information forms around my eyes as the Neural Link activates, feeding me status information from the power armor's sensors.

Ezz, resting in the tent beside me, takes a different route for exiting, expanding its entire body and absorbing the material of the tent into its body. It takes longer, but by the time Ezz reforms, the tent and its contents are gone, broken down into component parts in its nannite-driven, liquid metal body.

"*Ali!*" I shout, the Spirit already carefully spiraling upward.

As he does so, data populates my minimap, little figures in the distance. The Hands are faster than me—even as I throw my hand that way— conjuring Firestorms on the ridge. Our enemies burn, though it's not enough to kill. Behind me, I sense another Hand Blink Stepping to put the boot to a couple of our assailants, before he field strips them for useful weaponry.

What with the loss of my Credits, the Hands have taken to borrowing from the others for the weapons and armor they need to fully function.

We camped on the third layer, having traversed via a fortunate ridgeline that made ascending easy. Sheer cliffs rise up around us though, beyond the small ledge we're camped on, leaving us with just bouncing down the gorge faces to hit the second level or first. Not that anyone is hanging out on the first level, for there's a swarm of Level 40+ worm-maggot creatures crawling over the ground, tearing into the moss and mushrooms—whose spores are floating in the wind, landing on the creatures and actually growing on them. Eventually, the mushroom spores grow enough to kill the maggots, then they embed their roots in the ground before they get swarmed and eaten by more of the creatures. It's a constant battle, and anyone dropping in there would get swarmed as new, fresh meat.

Which leaves us with two levels to fight in. A bunch of individuals are coming in from the top, some of them flying just under the ridge line, while others tramp across both levels. The idiots I burnt were on the opposite side of the canyon, on the fourth, dead-end level, looking down on us.

Seconds, to take in our surroundings, the threats, and make a judgment call. As fast as I am, Bolo is even faster.

He springs to his feet, gesturing for us to gather near him. "Yllis and I will deal with the flyers. She is sensing powerful figures—"

"*Heroics*," Ali clarifies.

"—in their midst. We shall deal with them and their companions." Bolo grins savagely. "They think they own the skies. We shall dissuade them."

"Incoming from ahead, two groups," I inform them, glancing at the minimap. "Both sides, with the one on this side larger. I'm reading at least one Heroic with them, and a lot of Master Classes." I see the data flicker and twist, numbers and Classes changing on a constant basis. "Don't rely on the information I'm giving, there's interference. Assume more."

Mikito nods, her ghost horse conjured before her. She swings up onto it, Hitoshi appearing in her hands. "I'll take the ones on this side."

"Be careful..." I speak up, while Harry hesitates, looking back and forth between all of us.

"Our back?" Xaxas says.

"Another Heroic, fewer Master Classes, and lots of Advanced Classes," I reply. "They're mine."

Xaxas nods, glancing at the other side of the ravine before nodding. "The other side is mine then."

Harry and Ezz look between us. I flicker my glance backward and forward, the sight of the little dots closing in on us as I hesitate.

Pushing my worries down, I point at the pair. "Go with Mikito. Help her if you can. Hide if you can't."

The Hands, having driven off our attackers, don't wait for my commands. They split off on either side of the ridge, heading down to tackle those coming straight on. A part of me wishes I'd dismissed and called the other two over, but them racking up experience in the hollow planet is just as important.

"Bolo..." I turn back toward him, but frown as I realize he and Yllis left at some point. Their dots finally update on my map, my lips curling up in a snarl as the pair wing their way to the first group to reach us. In the distance, the roar of the dragon and the shouts of clashing fighters reverberate through the canyon. "Baka. Could have told me..."

Then I'm done talking, taking off running. I hear a plaintive wail of "Father" behind me, but I ignore it. Leaving Ezz behind is for its own good, no matter what it thinks. If more than one Heroic is coming in, it'll likely be from the back, considering geography. Which means it'll be up to me to stall them, and of us all, I've got the largest number of Skills at stalling. Worst-case scenario, I use System Edit on Sanctum and hide in the sphere until help arrives.

If I've got to watch out for Ezz, things take a downhill dive immediately, which is why I'm going alone. I could use the Hands' help, but I want a route out, and a faster wipe-out on the front and them returning via a Portal is useful. Add the fact that they're crippled by their Mana regeneration rates due to the messy System connection, and well, the Hands are less useful than before.

Alone it is. Mostly.

"*Boy-o, incoming,*" Ali sends.

I sense him flying downward, skimming through bug-laden air to come to my side. Those bugs are all mutations, low Level 10s or so, nothing to worry the rest of us but more than enough to make a Basic Classer's life miserable. Another reason why they shouldn't be here.

"*I'm thinking Judgment of All, chained through you to start,*" I send.

"*Got one better. Slow down for a second,*" Ali sends.

I frown but comply, feeling him draw upon my Mana and my Skills. I feel the Skill spin up, and before I can ask about it, he's already input and targeted it. Once, then again and once more. High above in the sky, glowing runic circles form, energy gathering within them. A fraction of a second later, they unleash their gathered seals of doom upon the area beneath. Beacon of the Heavens rains down its displeasure, burning all those caught beneath.

Not enough to kill, not directly, but the simple act of the attack has triggered the secondary air defenses the Voowmah have created. I feel the very air charge up, the ripping, concussive sound of thousands of shards of energy crystals being fired from everything that could spot the attack, launching themselves into the air.

My eyes widen and I screech to a halt. I search for cover and find myself ducking as close to the walls as I can, even while I scream over party chat to my team, "Incoming fire!"

"You bloody idiots! You've let the Voowmah know where we are!" Yllis screams at us. "You've doomed us all."

"Oh, shush, toots. You think you and Bolo flying through the canyons, breathing fire, hasn't alerted them? You think a fight between multiple Heroics isn't going to be enough to let them know?" Ali scoffs over the chat. "Puh-leese."

"More warning next time, baka! Some of us are busy..." Mikito growls.

Time. Even if the party chat is filling at the speed of thought, time is up. The crystals arc down. Ali darts in next to me, cackling as he hunkers beneath me while I deploy a disposable force shield. It won't last long, but I'm hoping the overhang we're under and the fact we're not directly on the target spot will be enough.

Sadly, the crystal attacks launched by the mutated plants aren't exactly targeted so much as area of effect. They blanket the entire surroundings, with the majority landing near where the initial Beacons targeted, but more than enough thrown by bad aim, misgrown branches, or just errant breezes land in my surroundings.

Once more, the world goes white, the Spitzrocket handling the overload of energy better. One of the advantages of its ability to improve after each battle is its specific resistances increase each time. We're always fighting the last war, but sometimes, it works out.

Kill notifications scroll by, the System going so far as to provide me a small trickle of experience for the kills of the larva and worms caught beneath the wave of attacks. Each death is tiny, but the sheer volume adds up. I know the maggots and the fungi will return, but for a few minutes, the first floor will be clear of spores and monsters at least.

Once the glare is gone, I unhunch to look at the smoldering remnants of the force shield generator, then I run toward the rear wing. Ali has bought us the element of surprise, though the cursing and flashing health on people like Yllis and Bolo indicates that not everyone managed to find enough cover to dodge the attacks.

Our attackers have ducked down other passageways, snaking through the honeycomb corridors of the canyons, leaving us behind. I have no time to watch out for them and can only hope Yllis and Bolo's confidence is well-founded, for I turn the corner and spot the remnants of the rear wave.

Then, there's no more time to think for chaos and blood is upon us.

***

Judgment of All tears into the remnants of the group, many of them just recovering from the wave of crystal attacks, healing themselves desperately and struggling to see. Defenses—pierced or fractured—come apart as they stagger to their feet, Judgment of All bypassing all but the most powerful or encompassing shielding to attack them directly. Some are crumpled on the ground, others scream in pain. And all the while, I rush forward, sword in hand.

The Heroic hits me from the side, emerging from the rock wall as it drops its adaptive camouflage, throwing me off the third stratum to fall through the air. Metal shrieks as metal chainsaw talons tear into the side of the Spitzrocket, armor plating creaking as it bends. Beneath, I'm bruised and a little disoriented, but I get a sword into the Heroic's stomach and push.

The blade skitters off metal, peeling off strips of alloy as force is applied, all while we tumble through the air. I right myself in a second, then hit the burners, pushing myself into flight just before we hit the ground and hovering a bare ten feet off the scorched and blackened, maggot-corpse-infested earth. Tendrils of smoke rise in the air, and I swear, even through my filtered air, I smell buttered mushrooms.

The enemy Heroic bounces, once and then again, before it rights itself and digs feet—four of them and a prehensile, moving tail—into the ground. Metal, chrome steel and grey, with flashes of black lines that slowly shift to match the background, a pair of long arms on top of the stumpy beast body. One that is fitted with a pair of beam rifles, which open fire on me.

I juke left, then right, dodging the attack. Even a close call sets damage notifications appearing on the Spitzrocket, showcasing the power of the beams. My lips pull apart as Ali, having recovered from the initial attack, finally catches up and feeds me information.

Heroic Poobah (Lavel Soulbound Power Armor Wielder Level 28) (H)

HP: 1980/1980

MP: 4711/5280

Conditions: Ethereal Neural Link, Soulbound Power Armor (Multi-function Rustie Slayer v8191.23), Reflective Shielding, Adaptative Resistance (Linked), Metal to Soul, Strength of the Union, Mana Conduit, …

I'm not surprised Ali is shortening the data, skipping names and Titles that don't matter. I'm more interested in the Class anyway, for the Library has a lot to say about it.

Class: Lavel Soulbound Power Armor Wielder—Heroic Level Class Tier (Semi-Restricted)

The Lavel are a high-tech society, one that prides itself on the integration of technology into their society. During System integration, significant numbers of their population failed to transition, unable to function without the technology that had sustained their people. The survivors were forced to adapt, transitioning their old technology into the System and borrowing from other societies to rebuild their civilization as a distorted reflection of their pre-System one.

Since System Advent, the Lavel have further developed their integration into the System, many calling the coming of the System a boon for their civilization. Integration levels of technology and Lavel have reached unprecedented heights, with most members of their society having connected themselves to the System and technological supplements.

The Soulbound Power Armor Wielder (Heroic) is a linear progression of the Power Armor Classes available to the Lavel.

Class Abilities: +2 Per Level in Strength and Charisma. + 8 Per Level in Intelligence and Willpower. +5 Per Level in Perception. +3 Per Level Luck and Constitution. Additional 7 Free Attributes per Level.

+40% Mental Resistance. +30% Elemental Resistance

Must designate Soulbound Power Armor.

May have an additional 8 Hard Point Links before Essence Penalties applied.

More importantly, details about his Class Skills flicker through my mind, along with the various documents and studies about technology, the System, and Mana. In particular, I find myself briefly distracted by Mana's effect on pre-System integration technology and the reason why it breaks down. It seems due to the way Mana rewrites the basic building blocks of physics, so the first thing to go is electronics and the way they interact. There're very subtle differences, sufficient enough that things like electronics—which are particularly sensitive to things like that—just don't work.

The System actually bridges that difference, literally rebuilding the processes we know—and adding sufficient leeway for new changes and interactions with Class Skills—to make sure tech works. However, it still doesn't fully explain the reason why electronics, even those turned off, don't work after their planet is integrated into the System. I dig into the files and...

Get blasted out of the air, giant quasi-real claws having formed to slap me into the ground as the power armor reminds me that I'm in the middle of a fight for my life.

The Spitzrocket howls for a second as I struggle against the semi-corporeal energy claws before the claws shatter and I'm able to escape. Moments before the beam rifles, charging up in the interim, release their powered-up attack. I get tossed through the air, crashing through a Master Class Juggernaut that attempts to stop me from getting too far, and bowling over the pair of us.

Reflexively, I conjure and sink a couple of swords into his body, using my momentum and a casual swing and Blade Strike at another healing Master Classer, to open the wounds in the Juggernaut further. The attack nearly bisects him, and a flashing notification and the slumped body inform me I've put down the green troll-like creature permanently.

Soul Shield flickers back on with a thought, even as the Lavel Heroic runs along the wall before bouncing off it, headed straight for me. Its jaws open wide and flame ripples outward, bathing my surroundings in fire.

Blink Step takes me out of attack range, only for the damn Heroic's auto-tracking, predictive algorithms in its beam turrets to fire upon me, throwing me around for another tumble. The Soul Shield cracks under the attack, the Spitzrocket's armor bubbling under the ongoing damage as I tumble through the air, offering the Heroic different portions of my body to cook.

Again, I Blink Step away, using Ali's line of sight—right into the lightning Ali has been conjuring. The arc of power hits the back of the Spitzrocket. Luckily, it's electricity that he's manipulated via his Affinity—

our Affinity—so I just grab hold of it and keep it spinning, building up the charge before releasing it into the back of the Heroic.

It hammers into the power armor's back legs, forcing it to buckle and steam. Short circuits should happen, if not for the damn System insulating its defenses, but I can't complain. It does the same thing for the Spitzrocket after all.

Floating in the air, playing channeler to Ali's battery, we teach the Heroic a little lesson about using tech against people who wield the Electromagnetic Elemental Affinity. Our opponent tries to spin around, and I take away the friction beneath its paws, forcing it to sprawl and spin too far, unable to control itself. It tries to aim the beam rifles and I arc the attacks back, having received enough of its gift to get a feel for it. Of course, the Heroic modulates the power output, making it harder, but I switch tactics, tearing at the bonds of the Heroic's armor itself, making it come apart.

Harder, much harder, than it would be with any other material. The armor is a Masterwork and Soulbound, meaning the System is fighting me too. But that's where Skill Edit comes in, my ability to see the code changes and twist them.

The System doesn't like what I'm doing though, sending feedback down through the link I create and causing pain and blood. I force myself to ignore it, at least for the moment, since my efforts are beginning to work.

A flash, the armor disappearing for a second to reveal the Lavel beneath. Tiny, half-starved, muscles and body less muscular than any Heroic I've ever seen. The creature is pink and green, hairless and sexless as best I can tell—a random tidbit of knowledge floats up, noting the Lavel have surgery early on to remove such organs, preferring the "clean" use of technology for procreation—and bruised.

Lightning hits its body and the Lavel smokes, moments before its armor reappears.

We get back to work, the Heroic worse for wear.

"*This is a little too easy*," I can't help but send to Ali.

Which, of course, is when the other pair of Heroics take action.

Chapter 24

While I'm not actively dodging, the Spitzrocket has its own randomized flight patterns to throw off fire. It's probably why it took so long before the Heroes took their shot, as their own augmentations or Intelligence worked out the pattern the Spitzrocket was using to juke around. Now, you could say that random number generators can gain true randomness by using things like recorded white noise, random snapshots of stellar movements, and other weird data sets; but the problem isn't the number—or numbers—you throw in to get randomness in where and how you'll move but the physicality of the power armor itself.

There are only three hundred sixty degrees of movement after all, even if you take all three axes. Once you work out how fast and how maneuverable the power armor is, the momentum I'm moving at and the various other factors affecting movement, there's only so much time before they can take the shot.

Which is, of course, why adding things like Blink Stepping and other forms of movement is important.

All that is to say, when they finally hit me, it's really, really hard. The first attack is one that has been charged, an energy shuriken that tracks the power armor as it jukes to the side, cutting a last-minute upraised arm all the way through. I feel my arm detach, pain shooting through my body as the shuriken keeps spinning.

The second attack catches me as I Blink Step away, jumping forward a half dozen feet. I would have picked another location, but both Ali and I are looking toward our victim, so there's not much in terms of options. The reflexive teleport gets me away from the attack which had begun to tear into the Spitzrocket, while the power armor fixes the gap where my left arm should be by deploying a stint and flooding it with a metal-plastic seal. It's not perfect, but it's better than leaving me exposed to contaminants. It gets the seal in place seconds before the second attack hits, bypassing all my mechanical defenses and invading my aura and spirit.

The curse rips into my body, dealing damage as cells shrivel and refuse to replicate. The curse robs me of strength and flexibility, of youth and vigor. I scream, my voice hoarse and twisted, feeling the curse assault my entire body, my only defense my innate resistances.

Curse of the Thousand Lives and Thousand Deaths Enacted
Resistances in effect
Heroic Level Curse overrides curse resistance annulment
Curse duration and effects reduced by 47.98%

Precious seconds are lost as my mind is befuddled. A hail of throwing knives hammer into the Spitzrocket, a half dozen piercing my body. Blood flows from wounds before the Spitzrocket shuts them down, then Ali sends a mental grunt through the link as he tries to buy me time by calling down another Beacon of the Angels on the pair of Heroics.

The Lavel recovers before I do, spinning around and jumping at me, power armor claws extended as it bears me to the ground. We hit the stone, pain flooding through the System, the Spitzrocket shrieking as fuses blow and metal crumples while a Dimension Lock stops me from blipping away.

Then claws tear into my lower body, shredding armor beneath monomolecular talons, while glowing hands of power punch into my sides. The Curse continues to rob me of my strength, but the pain and damage is triggering other Skills, offering strength back to me.

"*Move it, boy-o!*"

The mental scream ripples through my mind, and my hands twitch a little. First, a sword to block one of the damn arms. Then, since I can't Blink

Step, I do the other thing. I shut us down, pulling Sanctum down on both of us, trapping us within.

The surge in Mana, the sudden closing down of the space around us, catches the Lavel Heroic by surprise. While his legs hesitate for a second, I hit the thrusters on the Spitzrocket and drive myself directly upward. We hit the top of the Sanctum dome together, then another flip has us fully rotated as gravity asserts itself and we crash back to the ground, him on the bottom this time.

"Much prefer being on top…" I snarl, rearing upward and slamming a sword into one extended limb. Then another sword appears in my hand and I pin him down again, only to be thrown by the legs to impact the inside of the bubble.

In the corner of my eye, information scrolls about the Sanctum bubble's integrity, the spherical zone of safety taking a hammering. Curses rain down upon it thanks to one Heroic, while powered melee attacks pop up as the other Heroic out there zips around, using his sword to tear into the dome.

Sanctum's description says it's invulnerable, but that's more marketing speak than truth. There's a certain amount of damage it can absorb—an incredibly high one that no Master Class can hope to breach—before it pops. However, I'm not fighting Master Classes, and the two outside are intent on getting in.

Of course, that's when the next rain of crystals finally land.

Fire and flame outside, light so bright it pierces through solid metal. And within, nothing but the pair of us fighting, my swords cutting into mecha, into body, tearing chunks from him. I dismiss the Spitzrocket after a bit, the damage accumulating to the point where the mecha cannot hold itself together and is actually a hindrance. The Lavel does the same, but he recalls his own mecha a moment later, fully formed.

Cheater.

Doesn't matter, because each time he does that, I hurt him more. My swords punch through, the Blade Strikes ripping apart metal struts, and I keep moving, never stopping, swords spinning around me in the twisting, dancing pattern of the Erethran Honor Guard sword art. The Thousand Blades cut and tear, my opponent picked up and tossed into the whirling blades, mecha tearing and body cut apart beneath.

Not that it's entirely one-sided of course. Those claws tear into flesh. Glowing tentacle arms stab into my body, coming in from weird angles to dodge my own blades. More than once, he tries to trigger a Heroic Skill, one of the more powerful ones. Each time, he gathers the Mana and I step in and shut it down, using System Edit to tear apart the very same code he relies upon.

The feedback of that almost pulls me off my feet, but it works, and without his Heroic Skills, he's nothing more than so much meat and metal for me. Especially when I cheat and use skills like Grand Cross to pin him down while I shish kebab him.

Long minutes, the pair of us do battle within the sphere; even as it wears down and the Heroics outside try to break through. Long minutes, before the Laval falls and I find myself slumped over, my health barely a quarter of what it should be, my Mana a third full.

Killing a Heroic is never easy, not even when you shut down their other Skills. And there are two more right outside.

***

I meditate, breathing slowly and evenly as I try to restore my Mana as best I can. Healing spells and regeneration potions course through my body, patching missing skin and stitching together missing chunks of flesh. Poison

265

and burnt flesh are ejected onto the ground beside my cross-legged form, the world suddenly sounding normal again as a burst eardrum reforms. Vision clears a little too, though I'm not watching the world around me but my Status information.

Mikito and Harry are on my party chat, easy enough to track. Ezz, as an item, isn't. I can only hope and pray that it's fine, but considering Harry seems to be mostly undamaged, I have confidence Ezz is doing okay. On the other hand, Mikito is taking a beating, the Heroic she's battling refusing to let her engage. Instead, the small dots that make up the team in front of her keep switching places, the team moving in a well-coordinated play to ensure that she is never able to end any one of them.

Or at least, they try. The Battlefield Genius in the back, the Heroic, is a support player. Their ability and Skills weave together disparate units into a single, focused whole. No need for months or years of dedicated teamwork when you can just use a Skill to tap into everyone's mind and have the System provide prompts. Add in buffs for their people and debuffs on Mikito, and the Samurai is forced to wear down the entire group, striking out with full force and fury only when she's certain she can end a life.

It works, mostly, but it's a slow grind for her to break through. While I wouldn't count the Battlefield Genius a perfect counter against the Samurai, they are certainly more suited to deal with her—Mikito's Skills are focused on singular combat, unlike mine. Or Xaxas.

Xaxas, on the other side, is having the time of his life. Unfortunately, his wide range attack and his positioning far from the back team mean that monsters and opponents are untouched for the most part. His area effect attacks, the lightning he wields, has aggroed more than just the opponents he was meant to face, drawing forth monsters from afar as they pay attention to the storm of clouds and lightning hammering into his location. The only good news is that lightning does not trigger the crystal shards, so other than the constant rumble of thunder and the fried bodies, Xaxas is handling things well.

As for Yllis and Bolo? Like me, they found themselves hemmed in by a pair of Heroics and a bunch of fliers. They're probably doing the best among us, mopping up the remainder with all but the Heroics dead. I can see them guiding the fight back to our area, which means I'll get reinforcements soon.

But probably not soon enough.

The Sanctum cracks further, the white dome looking like splintered glass, desperate to give way but holding on. I draw a deep breath, wipe the blood off my face, and stand, getting ready to dance.

"*Ali, where are you?*" I send.

Of them all, I don't see the Spirit, though the feeling I get on the backend from the Spirit is more discomfort than pain.

"*Trapped. The Curse-wielder put me in the equivalent of a spatial mirror maze,*" Ali sends. "*I'm treading my way carefully through the dimensions, trying to get back. Could try for faster, but then I might not make it back at all so…*"

"*Take your time then. Just don't dilly-dally,*" I say. "*I'm going to need all the help I can get soon.*"

"*The Curse-wielder isn't a squishy by the way. He dumped a lot of his free Attributes into Constitution. Go for the other one, take him down first.*"

"*I like the confidence.*" I rotate the sword around my arm one last time, limbering myself up for the fight.

Another blow, this time from behind me, and the Sanctum shatters. I twist, conjuring my floating weapons with a thought as I meet the short blade with my own, feeling metal upon metal impact and screech.

I fall backward, giving space to myself, even as another curse is cast and wraps around my body with ghostly tendrils, slowing down my reflexes.

Swearing, I boot the Heroic melee fighter away, finally catching a true glimpse of him.

"What the hell, what are you?" I shout, surprised and disbelieving my eyes.

He disappears right before me, the tiny form shifting away in the shadows and reappearing behind me. Instinct has me curving my sword to protect my vitals even as I turn, such that his blade only sinks in half an inch before it rips out. I catch his arm on the way back, sending the Heroic bouncing off. At the same time, I slam down a Dimension Lock, stopping him from bouncing around anymore.

Or so I hope. Because he hits the ground once, then again, and fetches up near a small shadow from the remnant of a mushroom before he disappears into the shadow. A fraction of a second later, I'm raising my leg to dodge an attack as he pops out of my own shadow to cut at me.

"This is just wrong!" I swear, feeling another curse wrap around me.

This time round, the world darkens, light being absorbed even from my glowing swords. It gives the damn Heroic even more places to blip, whatever he's using to shift between shadows obviously ignoring my Dimension Lock.

"*I see you met the Leprechaun ninja,*" Ali sends back, amusement deep in his voice.

"*Yes!*"

This is just not right. I hop backward the next time he disappears, throwing a hand sideways as I deposit a half dozen chaos grenades in my wake. No idea if it'll do any damage, but as the ninja pops back up, he gets greeted with, well, chaos.

Vanilla mousse, rivers of it, explodes from one grenade. Another offers nothing, at least in the visible spectrum, releasing its fury in a bath of x-rays. Living worm-like creatures pop into being for a second before they shatter, becoming shards of glass. An expanding ring of gas, purple in color, rolls from another. Other effects, some that I don't even really notice, go off, leaving the Heroic confused.

And giving me just enough time to review his Status sheet as I trigger Army of One, multiple swords deploying behind my back while enchanted runes appear, gathering Mana and energy to it.

Ninja Leprechaun (Luchorpán Liquidator Level 13) (H)

HP: 2811/3820

MP: 2420/2420

Conditions: Greater Affinity (Shadows), Lesser Affinity (Darkness), Lesser Affinity (Smoke), Break the Bonds, Poison Heart, Blade in the Back, …

There's more, a ton of buffs, but I don't have time to keep reading. Rather, my attention is focused on the charge building up in Army of One. In the midst of the squirming, exploding, shrieking noises of the remnants of my Chaos Grenades, the Luchorpán stands, waiting for me to release my attack.

I know what he'll do the moment I do, so I turn and throw it at the Curse Speaker. Clad in long robes, its—his—body long and lean, big wide eyes and hairless skull on off-white skin, the Curse Speaker reminds me of Feh'ral. Same species at least, though very different paths.

Energy flows out of my attack, striking the alien as I swing my sword, dozens of empowered Blade Strikes slamming into the same space.

Army of One isn't my most powerful attack, but it's flashy and effective, especially when said figure can't move that fast. The Curse Breaker's hands are held before it, a glowing shield forming and sucking down energy as it redirects that same energy into the ground, where black lines grow and build. Not all of the energy gets caught though, some of it punching straight through, burning the Curse Speaker.

My attack tears into it, but taking my eyes off the Luchorpán has a price. It blips, appearing behind me, tearing into my legs, peeling armor apart with its sword, flaying skin and muscles. I twitch, pain curling through my body as I collapse, moving to the side in an attempt to get away. As the Dimension Lock doesn't work, I let it drop and reorient myself to Blink Step.

Only to have a tiny foot hammer itself into my face, the redheaded son of a bitch kicking me in the face and throwing off my focus. Enough that instead of appearing where I want, I appear in the sky, a dozen meters off the ground.

Spinning through the air, I reorient myself and use a couple of conjured blades to give myself a way to tell up from down. A quick swipe to the side stops the damn Heroic ninja from coming in, forcing him to blip away as the swords keep spinning. Another curse comes, slamming into me, pushing vertigo through me again so that I find myself unable to orient properly.

Then the ground finally catches up to me. My bones creak, light flares all around me and bursts right up to the sky as the energy from my earlier attack stored in the ground explodes upward. Not all of it, but a portion is returned, throwing me aside and setting off another series of minor explosions.

I'm bleeding, armless, a chunk of rock has lodged itself in my abdomen, and I can't see out of one of my eyes. My ears are ringing without end, and it's only the Luchorpán's desire not to get caught in the secondary explosions that give me any breathing room.

"God damn it..." I swear, conjuring and slamming another healing potion into my side. It's not enough to bring me anywhere close to healed, especially when the cooldown is still in effect, but it's better than nothing.

Then, knowing I can't stay still, I Blink Step away, microseconds before the Liquidator appears, swinging his sword.

I blip in near the Curse Speaker, stopping just outside the enchanted circle he created. I might not be entirely cognizant of his Skill set, but I know enough to not walk into a trap when my opponent is ignoring that most important of rules of fighting—don't stay still.

Instead, I drop my sword, toss a handful of Chaos Grenades into his location, and Blink Step away. Of all the things I have, Mana is the highest, unlike my Health. And if I have to sow a little chaos into the battlefield to even out the fight, I'll do so.

Five Blink Steps later, the Liquidator always a step behind me, I stop. My System senses, the one given to me as an Administrator, have come back quite firmly, noting that there's absolutely nothing it can do about the damn Liquidator's passage through the shadows. It's a partial dimension step, but he never leaves this dimension, which is why the Dimension Lock Skill didn't work—or not to its fullest extent anyway. He's also using his Affinities to bolster his passage, and Affinities, while potentially gifted by the System, are not in and of themselves part of it.

All of which means that I can't stop him from blipping each and every way. Or pin him down with swords and stab him. In fact, using some of my more powerful Skills aren't particularly useful when he can fade out of the way.

Which leaves me with using a maul to swat a fly.

I blip away from the pair to get sight on them both and trigger Judgment of All. I feel my Mana drop precipitously low, but the attack bypasses the damn Curse Speaker's defenses—though my little stunt with the Chaos Grenades forced him out of his hidey hole for a bit, the flood and typhoon picking him up and pushing him away—as well as auto-targeting the Luchorpán.

They shriek in pain, the damage piling on with each second. The Curse Speaker tries to hide, but the System is all-seeing and he might flee, but he can't hide. The damage keeps adding itself, even as he retaliates by sending a winged, living Curse to smash me into the side of the canyon walls, its hundred beaks tearing into my skin.

Blades reform and I tear into it, Mana-boosted blade pulling apart the Curse even as I slide into the code, finding the part that tracks duration and adjusting the timer. It dissolves at a faster rate, dropping me to the ground a second later. I'm bleeding and in pain, one ear entirely gone and a long cut going down my neck where it nearly tore out my throat.

I attempt to stand once, then again, using the canyon wall and its rough coating to give me some form of leverage. That's about the only reason I manage to stand, even as pain riddles my body and leaves my muscles twitching.

Judgment of All finally ends, the Liquidator on the far edge of the canyon looking the worse for wear. Blood drips from under his mask, green eyes bloodshot, red hair now coated with the darker red of blood. The black of his clothing hides the bleeding, but the grey of the ground does little to hide the growing pool beneath his feet.

The Curse Speaker, on the other hand, is much better off. Bastard's buffed himself to the nth degree, with the Curses he's throwing at me providing a partial return to himself. All that means is that he's still got at least half his Health pool. The only good news is that his Mana pool has taken quite the beating, with the sheer volume of Curses he's thrown around.

Not to say mine is any better.

"So, this is awkward. Shall we call it a day perhaps? Come back to this another time?" I call. "Perhaps you guys could just go home and leave me be?"

"A job is a job, and I've never failed one yet." The Luchorpán sounds exactly like I'd expect him to. Which, mind you, means he sounds like a leprechaun from TV. Which, probably, has nothing to do with a real Irish accent.

"You're already dead," the Curse Speaker snarls, thin grey lips turning up into a wide grin. Teeth, shark-like teeth, display themselves and I marvel at the strangeness. I'm pretty sure Feh'ral didn't have those teeth. Cosmetic changes? Or a different sub-species? "We just need to finish you."

"Uh huh," I say, drawing a deep breath and eyeing my Mana gauge. Not enough to use Judgment of All again, not without tapping into the System and flooding myself with Mana that way. Unfortunately, my health is too low for me to make full use of my System Edit Skill. It'd be a real balancing act, pulling in just enough Mana to use the Skill without killing myself. And considering how horrible I feel, I'm not sure I trust myself to do it.

"*Help?*" I send to Ali, hoping he's able to pop up and save my bacon again.

"*Give me a second. I'm just two turns away… but… Holy shit! PORTAL!*"

My eyes widen, my body turning and casting the Portal to the side. I push it to just ahead, where we split, the farthest location I can get to. The Liquidator moves, plunging into the shadow; but a fraction of a second later, he's plucked halfway on the way to me, torn right out of the shadows by our assailants.

At long last, the Voowmah are here, and the hive descend on us in a swarm; their camouflage falling away as they erupt from the ground, dive down from the canyon walls, and literally tear their way through the very fabric of reality.

One of them hits me hard, taking me away from the Portal. The blank oval glitters, taunting me, and I am forced to Blink Step, reorienting myself in mid-air so that I fall through the Portal even as the momentum from the earlier rush carries me on. I tumble through the air on the other side, even as the screams from the Liquidator and the Curse Speaker ring through it; magic and Skills flaring as they fight off the swarm.

Then the Portal slams shut, catching one of the Voowmah two-thirds of the way through. I stagger to my feet, sinking a blade deep into its body, then again and again, pinning it down even as new limbs erupt from its conical shape as it tries to scramble away.

Adrenaline drives my response, as does my worried cry over party chat.

"RUN! They're here!"

Chapter 25

My warning is of little use, since the others are beset too. Yllis and Bolo pause only long enough to snatch me up from where I'm running, attempting to meet up with the rest of the team. They fly me most of the way there before Yllis transforms, dropping me to the ground as she does so, taking back her human appearance. We hit the ground running, Bolo leading the way and casually batting aside any Voowmah that attempt to slow us down.

Not many of them are here. They seem to have concentrated their attack on the rear. I'm not entirely sure why—beyond the lightshow Ali might have created in the beginning—but it's to our advantage. By the time we reach Mikito, the fighting has stopped. And not because she's killed everyone. I note one of my Hands is gone, the one over near Xaxas's side. The other one looks unsatisfied, though he's sitting quietly, cross-legged and regenerating his Mana.

"Peace! Until such time as we get away," the enemy Battlefield Tactician says, eyes flicking between Yllis, Bolo, and myself, uncertain of who she should be speaking to. In the end, her eyes rest on Bolo. "We won't survive the Swarm without working together."

My gaze flickers to Bolo, who makes a face before he says, "The Redeemer will bind you to do no harm to us until the fight is over."

"Till the Swarm is gone," counters the Battlefield Tactician. She's a cutie, in the near masculine but still effeminate way that confuses my hormones and other parts. It helps that she's a Truinnar, but I shove all that aside, especially when Ali blips into space right next to me.

"We ain't got a lot of time, boy-o. I can help deploy some countermeasures from your storage, but there's only so much it'll do. Diverting a million here or there doesn't help when they've got billions, you know," Ali says.

"Exaggerating a little, aren't we?" I growl. Billions would see the ground and sky covered with the Swarm, and the Voowmah aren't that populous.

"A little."

"Done. Do it, Traitor." The Battlefield Tactician glares at me, her chin rising a little. Pale blond hair, in that straw color that is almost always artificial in humans, flutters in the breeze. "But know that if you betray me, my House will curse your name from this day to star's end."

"Can't," I say. "I'm low on Mana. We'll do it on the run."

Bolo finally really looks at me, a frown growing as he spots how battered I truly am. I'd wave at him, but one hand is holding my sword and the other is left behind. I'm not even wearing the Spitzrocket since it's busy fixing itself.

The Dragon King opens his mouth to ask, and I cut him off. "Run first."

There's a nod and the entire group moves. After a moment, I extend my senses outward, tapping into Thousand Steps to make sure it wraps itself around the Battlefield Tactician and her remaining people, giving them the subtle speed boost they need. They're already using other Skills to speed themselves up, but Thousand Steps overlays on top of it. One of the advantages of the Skill.

I only use it in bursts, knowing I need to regenerate Mana. Occasionally, the Hand helps out, though he's even worse off than I am. Still, trading off helps. Unsurprisingly, I keep close to the center of the group, the Battlefield Tactician's face drawn and tight as she works to keep us safe. And work she has to, since the Swarm might be fewer in number up here, but that's a difference from tens of thousands to just thousands. A lot less, but still a ton.

They drop from the air, only to be yanked aside by gravity magic or blown off course by a shearing wind. Some punch through the walls, their bodies bloodied and broken, only for our runners at the edge to smash weapons into their faces, lopping off bits and pieces and leaving the corpses to block the way. Others come from the lower canyon, rushing along the edges and launching globs of acid and poison at us, only to bounce off a rotating series of shields.

At the front, Mikito charges ahead with Xaxas, the Yerrick finally having joined us. He brought along a couple of survivors from his own rampage, one of them on a hovering medical board.

Storm clouds gather, a mist rises, and every once in a while, the Storm Warden throws a hand forward, unleashing a chained lightning bolt into the fog ahead. The Voowmah in front are fried, their bodies shocked into stillness as he stun locks them, only for Mikito to hit them at full charge. A corona of power surrounds the Samurai as she triggers Skill after Skill to make her Endless Charge an unstoppable force. Even those not directly in front of her are caught on the eaves of her swirling whirlpool of energy and are crushed or thrown aside.

Death notifications pile up, even as I extend my own Aura. Aura of Chivalry provides everyone a small boost in confidence and Willpower, which when we're in the middle of a swarm of monsters, is highly useful. I'd throw on Eye of the Storm, but I can't afford to be the locus of attacks, not with my Health still so low.

Not unless I use my Penetration shield, and considering who I haven't seen, I'm keeping that in my back pocket for the moment.

Long minutes pass, each second seeing my body and Mana recuperate. Under the guidance of the Battlefield Tactician, those still able to fight swap out, dealing damage and clearing the way for the rest of our team. The monsters are endless, our passage forced by the pile of bodies. A part of me wonders if they're herding us. Another part is certain they are. But we can't stop, not unless we want to be overwhelmed.

The occasional Voowmah manages to get a hit in, the rotating wall of energy and the defenses insufficient to stop the sheer volume that keeps appearing. Stopping, even for a moment, would see us dead.

In the corner of my eyes, I see some of our ex-enemies flagging, their Stamina regeneration rates insufficient to keep up with it all. Rather than see them fall, I search for and find Ezz.

"Ezz—bike. Rotate the ones who can't keep up until their Stamina regenerates," I say.

"Who would that be, Father?" Ezz says, hopping over a couple of heads to land beside me, another pair of feet appearing and hitting the ground just before it lands, tiny wheels appearing.

"I've got it," the Tactician snaps. A second later, one of the Mages stumbles over and Ezz scoops them up, dumping them on its back. "How many can you take?"

"At this speed? Two more," Ezz replies.

"Done."

More commands are given and more of her people break off, never stopping in their casts. I note the careful use of spells, the choice in low-level spells slung to not do damage but cripple. Webs, ice fields, swamp lands, and grasping vines are all favored.

"Good job," I say to Ezz. Then, glancing at the little red figure, I flash it a grin. "Also, good job at staying alive."

"Thank you, Father. Some people tried to change that," Ezz says, its head turning to fix on the Truinnar.

The Battlefield Tactician shrugs. "That was the job. Delay and whittle down the Rebel's allies."

"And you always do your job?"

"Any good soldier does."

I snort, then seeing my Mana is at a comfortable level, I raise my hand. "Well, sucks to be you then. Because this is going to hurt."

"One mome—"

She doesn't get a chance to finish her sentence before the black chains, chains filled with spikes, wrap around her, piercing her body. Runic lights appear on them, crawling up the chains and delving into her body as I push my will into the chain.

"You will not attack us, you will not betray us, you will not harm us or allow others to harm us so long as the Voowmah are a threat to us in the Valley of Certain Death," I intone. For a brief, unworthy moment, I consider adding more, but choose instead to stick to the spirit of our agreement.

When I drop my hand and the chains disappear, the Battlefield Tactician looks relieved, a thread of tension disappearing from her face.

I can't help but twig her on it. "What? Expected different?"

"Of course, Traitor."

"Sometimes, you got to learn to ignore the bad press," I say with a smirk.

"More often, what everyone knows to be truth is just that. Truth."

"Uh huh."

Shaking my head, I finally look upward, taking in her Status. Mostly to check that the Shackles of Eternity have taken effect, but also because I can't keep calling her Tactician in my head. Not if we're going to be running together for days.

Mozhgan Darvishi, When the Walls Fell, One for All, Exemplary Field Commander (Truinnar Empire), Major (Retired) of the Truinnar Empire, Slayer of Truinnar, Movana, Pooskeen, Goblins, Ermite Worms, Dravis (more...), ... (Battlefield Tactician Level 29) (H)

HP: 2811/3890

MP: 7384/9280

Conditions: Battlefield Awareness, Tactical Sense, Fog of War, Drone Mapping, Energized Side, Rally Flag, Shackled (By Grand Paladin John Lee (kinky!))

"Enough with the lovey-dovey eyes, boy-o," Ali calls. His hands are held upward, his fingers twitching.

I can feel the build-up, so I'm not surprised when the other side of the canyon walls for as far as my eyes can see lights up. Energy, accumulated in the walls, is released, striking the Voowmah in an explosion of lightning and kinetic dispersal, launching the creatures off to impact against our defenses.

Of course, since Ali didn't tell anyone, our shields go down after the tenth body gets splattered against them. Our next few seconds are busy, with all of us running along, cutting monsters apart, and trying to get away from the deeply damaged hive mind. We nearly lose a few of our people, including Harry, who is scooped up by Ezz as he limps after us.

"System help us!" Mozhgan snarls. "Don't ever do that again! Help like that will see us all dead."

"Whatever," Ali says, smirking. "*Look at your XP, boy-o. I might consider allocating all your points.*"

I frown, but conjure a pair of swords to throw into the air, catching a couple of monsters on them as I keep running. As I do so, the notification comes along, informing me of what Ali is speaking about.

*Level Up! You are now a Level 33 Grand Paladin**

"About damn time…" I grin.

So maybe all this running around and killing monsters isn't entirely without its benefits.

As long as we manage to stay ahead and alive, of course.

***

Once the first few minutes are over, once our Health and Mana regeneration has refilled our bodies, the initial moment of concern is over. After that, the rotation Mozhgan sets up works and isn't too abusive. With two Heroics geared toward wide area effect attacks and a dragon and Spirit who can manipulate Mana and the basic building blocks of physics itself in play, we manage to keep the Swarm back. They might be the Unending Hunger, but a good Judgment of All or a trio of Beacon of the Angels in the right place at the right time ensures they never manage to collect enough to overwhelm the more modest members of our team.

Mikito is having fun, borrowing Judgment of All more than once to wield it on the creatures ahead of us, tearing through them with an efficiency that I lack, what with my need to bring friends into play. Of course, once the pair of Extra Hands are summoned, our burdens lower even further. Rotating between the three of them, they keep the Hunger at bay for the moment.

Not that anyone, even me, thinks that what we're seeing is at all easy. They're throwing their lower Levels at us, forcing us to wear ourselves out, harrying us. Even System-boosted attributes and concentration will wear out eventually. Grinding us down, step by step, and guiding us ever deeper.

Of course, there's a reason why I left one last Hand outside.

"Message ready to go out?" I call to Harry, locking gazes with him.

"Ready to record whenever you are," the War Reporter and Network Locus confirms.

"Right then. Redeemer of the Dead commercial number…" I blink. "I've done this before, haven't I?"

"Yup," Ali drawls, floating beside me. "A couple of times."

"Huh." I scratch my temple. "I really need to come up with better tricks."

"John…" Harry says, his breathing a little heavy as he jogs beside me, hands held up to frame me.

"Right, right…" Ignoring the look Mozhgan is giving me, I clear my throat. "Listen up. This is John Lee, Redeemer of the Dead, Galactic Rebel, and Earth's Least Favorite Son, and do I have a deal for you. I'm running through the Valley of Certain Death right now on Xy'largh, dealing with thousands of the Hunger. Literal thousands. And guess what? My Hands have been collecting and storing the bodies and are about to dump it all into the Shop." I pause for a long second, grinning. "So if you're looking for Voowmah corpses for your high Level artifacts, this is the time to buy. We're going to feed you as much of this as we can, so long as I live."

I try to figure out what to say. That's when the Voowmah let out another of their hunting calls. They started that aural assault about an hour ago, choosing to release it every few minutes. It's kind of like a wolf howl in length, crossed with the chilling laughter of a hyena, but done through the voice box of an insect. In other words, creepy and alien and all-encompassing, especially when it rings through the canyons and all around us on the plains above.

There's no talking when they're screaming, partly because it washes a Fear effect over us that has to be resisted, and partially because they've more than once used the howl as a distraction to launch an attack. We keep an eye out, with Harry cutting off the recording while we run.

When silence—or at least, as much silence as a running battle offers—returns, the Reporter makes a face as he reviews the commercial, prompting me to speak. "What?"

"Lighting is off. And there's a lot of background noise…" Harry says.

"We're in the middle of a running fight!" I snap at him, cutting upward and to the side with my free hand.

The Blade Strike catches one of the lurking Voowmah, having hidden its body behind that of another monster and evading the sight of everyone else thus far. Too bad it chose to make a move right then. My Blade Strikes tears it off the wall and one of my Hands jumps up, grabbing it and slamming it against the wall to crush the life out of it. I'm sure, when it finally dies, he'll dump the corpse into my Altered Storage.

Pretty much where all the Voowmah are going really, then the final Hand is pulling it from the shared Skill and dumping it right back into the Shop. Hopefully the Galactics don't find him and stop him, because right now, we're raking up a nice chunk of change. Not fast enough though, which is why we're going to be putting it on a Galactic Auction.

If we do this right, we might just get access to some better equipment and pay off my annoying Spirit. At least that's the hope. At the worst, the Hands that are here will be able to actually arm themselves with better than borrowed equipment.

On a Galactic or planetary scale, nothing we're earning will make much of a difference. But, you know, it's always nice to have more funds. And on the very off-chance that we somehow survive, there's always the need to find a way off the planet. However that plays out, it'll cost a pretty penny.

"No reason to lower standards…" Harry says.

"Harry…"

"It's sent already," Harry grumbles. "I don't get much choice with the way the Locus works. It's literally recording and transmitting everything, all the time." He shrugs. "I can clean up the second runs, but…" He shakes his head. "Whatever. It's just not my best work."

"You know, I'm pretty sure it's your life's work." I wait to see if he gets it. But Harry's already tuning me out, having moved away to chat with Mozhgan. "Damn it… I thought it was a good pun."

"Wasn't even groan worthy," Ali replies, reminding me he's right there.

"I believe it was humorous, Father," Ezz says. "Hahahaha!"

I stare at the red golem loping alongside me and the three Advanced Classers it's carrying on its back, none of whom are willing to look me in the face. I can't help but give my "son" a strained smile.

"Thanks, Ezz." I shake my head, glance at my growing experience bar, and sigh. "I'm going to do some sheet management. Keep an eye out for me?"

"Of course, Father."

"*Duh!*"

Snorting, I tune out Ali. I was speaking more to him than Ezz, but I know the golem wants to be included. And really, having it close by is a little comforting, especially as my damn left arm continues to regenerate. I've got my elbow back by now and part of my arm, but my actual hand is taking its time. Even with the bonus to limb regeneration that the System seems to have granted me after my torture, it still takes a while.

I really, really wish I'd stop losing limbs. I feel unhanded.

And, perhaps, a little unnerved to be making such jokes.

Then again, perhaps that's for the best.

Anger is useful, but this is a marathon now. And keeping a flame like that stoked for such a long time has its own debilitating effects.

No, I'll unleash my fury later.

For now…

Skills.

***

Three Skill Points to use, not much time left to use them. They might actually be the very last Skill Points I'll ever have. The first, and most obvious, selection is to dump them into Defense of the Fallen so that it buffs up and I can hope for a Skill Evolution. It'd make me even tougher to kill—along with my Hands. A very simple upgrade, but obviously, not useful if we don't get the Skill Evolution.

I still have no idea why Skill Evolutions happen. If I had the time… But if is such a pernicious word and one that offers nothing but regret. I push it aside and instead focus on the three tier 2 Skills that are now available for my use. Frustrating that I had to dedicate points into System Edit because of the over-Leveling of my System Administrator Skills but…

What is, is.

Moving on.

Combined Arms is a guaranteed no. It's an Aura or Buff Skill. Really, really useful if, for example, you combine it with Extra Hands, a lot of points in earlier Auras, and were part of the official Erethran Army. It basically turns on an Aura or Buff Skill, refunding the cost of the Mana Regeneration that you paid in earlier parts of your Skill Tree, while also extending that Aura to all your allies—at a degraded level, but no matter the distance.

Put another way, you could turn on Thousand Steps for the entire Erethran Army, all the time, giving them a multiplied boost in movement. Or everyone gains an Aura of Chivalry, making them very, very hard to break in battle. Or turn on Vanguard of the Apocalypse and you've got an army of berserkers, able to weather attacks.

It's a game-changing level of Skills, but it's utterly useless for me and my current predicament.

Next up, Bonds of the People is even more useless. Unlike Defense of the Fallen, which is a personal defensive upgrade, Bonds is about upgrading society. Specifically, unlike Combined Arms, which upgrades your armed forces, Bonds works on strengthening the ties within society. Everyone gains a much lower powered versions of Eye of Insight, Society's Web, and even a degraded Shackles of Eternity via a societal contract option. It's all based off the number of points—organically—the Grand Paladin has sunk into those areas though, which is where specialization might help. Then again, even a single point sunk into Eyes of Insight will give people an intuitive feel of not only if someone is telling the truth, but with the degraded Society's Web, how trustworthy said person is.

As I said, building up society. Because the Grand Paladin's job isn't just to fight off external enemies, but those within. And what could make their jobs easier than if society itself rejects the snakes within their own bosoms?

You might notice a kind of trend here with the final Skills in the second Tier.

No surprise then that Final Judgment is similar. It builds upon the damaging Skills in the personal damage tier purchased in the levels before, using a combination of everything from Army of One, Judgment of All, Beacon of the Angels, and Grand Cross to power up Final Judgment.

Problem with Final Judgment... well. I read the description once more.

Skill: Final Judgment (Level 1)

When all else fails, when the army is spent, when the planet is lost, the Grand Paladin may levy a Final Judgment on their enemies. Feared and hated in equal measure, may the enemies of the Erethran Empire never benefit from our loss! This is a channeled skill with a minimum duration of 10 minutes.

Warning! This is a planet-cracker Skill and its use is restricted via Galactic Regulations 1877.245.12. Usage of this Skill without proper authorization will result in the most severe of penalties.

Effect: User triggers use of the skills Army of One, Judgment of All, Beacon of the Angels, and Grand Cross repeatedly. Limitations on application range of Skills are removed during this period to a maximum of visual range * 10.

Cost: 5000 Mana Initial + 500 Mana per Minute

Duration: Minimum of 10 minutes. Unknown maximum

More than the bland description, information flows into me from both the Library and the books I've read about the Grand Paladin Class. The warning about being a planet-cracker is due to Beacon of the Angels and Grand Cross being used in conjunction on a single location. The history books give me names of ex-planets, of genocide committed in the name of retribution—Cyleon, Ysmi, Ferdna, X-988A—and defense before the use of this Skill was finally restricted. The Skill itself isn't a direct planet-breaker like most Legendary Combat Skills might be, but it requires channeling, time, and placement. Which is easy enough when you've got an army protecting your back.

Not so much if you're alone.

Still, it's a bit of an overkill Skill. I mean, sure, it'd be fun to spam the Skill and blow up thousands of Voowmah and the Shadow Council, but the simple fact stands that while activation of the Skill itself is immediate, like Beacon of the Angels, it takes a bit to actually trigger. It's not an instant effect, which makes it less useful in a fight, especially the kind I expect to get into. That ten-minute duration is also a problem. When you aren't exactly fighting an army but a group of high-powered individuals, the need to keep blasting away is a bit of a drawback. Then, of course, you've got the feedback problem—being a channeled Skill, if you get interrupted and your concentration broken, all that Mana has to route somewhere.

If it seems like I'm bitching about a really cool-ass Skill, it's mostly to stop myself from just grabbing it immediately. Really, I've grabbed Skills for a lot less reason than it being super cool. The problem is, there's almost no chance of a Skill Evolution at less than six points, and even six is on the low end. Which means if I take this, I'm locking myself out of a potential upgrade to some of my other Skills like Defense of the Fallen or, if I'm looking for a directly useful Skill, Grand Cross. Admittedly, at only two points already dumped into that Skill, it's unlikely to evolve.

Extra Hands, on the other hand, could. I've already spent three points there, and I have to admit, the Hands have been extremely useful. In fact, the addition of them to the fight has made it somewhat possible to even consider this run. The only disadvantage is that the Hands are a pre-prepared Skill. Once I finish summoning them, there's not much else I can do. And in the middle of a fight, summoning Hands is often impossible, not just because of the sheer amount of Mana required but also the time spent doing it.

And, frankly, they're a little fragile. Heroics can go through them with only a small amount of hesitation, their ability to use my Penetration Shielding and Soul Shield making them a little harder to kill than normal, but not hard. Not at all.

If I was fighting another kind of battle, I might be more tempted by Extra Hands. But I'm just not sure. The fact that Skill Evolutions don't necessarily follow any known pattern, and aren't always super useful, doesn't help either. A quick review of older Evolutions of the Skill show the ability to make double the number, but with lower total Mana and regeneration rates, the ability to pre-summon Hands to "store" them away for recall later. Great Evolution. The last Evolution wasn't so great since it only allowed the Hands to pick a single purchased Skill to use as well as all the other, normally allocated Skills.

There's not a lot of detail in the Library about Evolutions. Being a highly restricted Class, there just aren't many Grand Paladins in Erethran history, and even fewer have gone down the Hand route. Unlike, say, Portal. In the end, I'd be gambling with a Hand Evolution. Then again, I'd be gambling with any Evolution.

And as much as I like to take risks at times, this doesn't seem to be the time. It helps that a number of the other major negatives for the Final Judgment Skill can be removed by me thanks to the simple expedience of using System Edit. Don't like the duration? Edit the Skill. Need enough Mana to do it? Well, I've access to a near limitless amount of Mana with System Edit—I just have to trade health and pain for it.

Knowing that, I drop a point into Final Judgment and shudder as the information gets dumped into my brain, cross-loaded by the System. I let it settle, taking a few minutes to watch for problems, smell the caustic air around me, chew on a weird, not-at-all-tasteless bar of food to replenish reserves, and check in with the rest of the team before going back to contemplate my last two points.

More points into Final Judgment would adjust the damage levels involved, increasing the speed that Skills activate while I'm actively channeling the attack. Useful if I want to destroy an army faster, not so much when I'm not that worried about destroying the bad guys. Seriously, ten minutes is more than enough to kill most Heroics and would even murder a Legendary—assuming they hung around long enough for you to dish out all that damage.

Which obviously they wouldn't.

Waste of time, putting more points into Final Judgment then. Which leaves my other Skills. Obviously the other two penultimate Skills are useless for the most part, which means I get to poke at either Extra Hands, Grand Cross, or Defense of the Fallen. Same problems, all over again.

The only real question is hope that maybe if I throw in two points now, I might somehow collect the millions of experience points I require to get the levels in the intervening few days to get another Skill Point or to split them up. Another Hand could be useful, all things considered. Even if it only takes the enemy a short time to kill an extra helper, that moment might come in handy. Adding more damage to Grand Cross would be good too, especially if I need to switch it to knock down a single individual. Like a Legendary. And staying alive... well.

All things considered though, I'm thinking more points in Grand Cross. The time when I really need more defense is when I'm fighting Heroics and Legendarys. And in that case, I won't hold back on my Penetration Shielding Evolution any longer, which means I want to upgrade it as fast as possible. Which means Grand Cross doing more damage is an actual benefit for me.

Decision made, I drop the last two points into the Skill. Four total Points in Grand Cross doesn't really get an Evolution, but it's a method of laying down the hurt. I debate testing it out but choose against it, at least for now.

Grand Cross (Level 4)

The burden of existence weighs heavily on the Paladin. This Skill allows the Paladin to allow another to share in the burden. Under the light of and benediction of the Grand Paladin, under the weight of true understanding, wayward children may be brought back to the fold.

Effect: Damage done equals to (Willpower * 2.4) per square meter over radius of (1 / 10th of Perception²) meters. Damage may be increased by reducing radius of the Grand Cross. Does additional (Willpower) points of damage per second for 14 seconds.

Cost: 2000 MP

One last glance at the Skill, then I turn back to the world around me. Only to find it not much changed.

Chapter 26

Our time running the Valley of Certain Death is surreal. The Battlefield Tactician switches us out with smooth familiarity, making full use of my Hands, Mikito's ability to copy and create a Hand of her own or any of my other Skills, and the bunch of Heroics at her disposal to weave an impenetrable defense against the Voowmah.

At the edges of the elongated oval of sapients that run with us, the fighting is the hardest, a constant churning of limbs crushed, armor pierced, and bodies torn apart. High above, a constant rainstorm hovers, dumping buckets of water that wash across the ground, bolts of electricity arcing down without care to strike those below.

In the center though, there's an eerie calm. Ezz, along with a couple of other machines—including a few it put together from the odds and ends the other Galactics have in their Inventory—keeps our people moving. Floating beds, rolling sleds, even a couple of jury-rigged hover booths slapped onto a plank of metal hold the slumped over and resting bodies of the Galactics. Shield generators keep them safe from casual harm, while watching guards take out anything that breaks through the perimeter.

High levels of Constitution can keep our bodies running for days on end, while high Willpower and Intelligence ensure we can keep our minds sharp and focused. But there's an emotional toll, a mental grinding that happens when you're in combat; the required level of focus to perform at peak levels wears on an individual. It's something even the System can't fully ameliorate, and it means that rest, real rest, is required by most. Which is where Ezz's convoy comes into play.

"How far?" I say to Bolo, who's riding beside me.

The Dragon King looks tired, his hair plastered to his face, trailing off the edges of his dirty curling ram horns. He and Yllis have been held back for the most part, unleashed only when the Voowmah decide to contest them for the skies. It's why Xaxas has unleashed the storm that is part of his name, to reduce the visibility of the damn fungi and to destroy as much of the vegetation as possible. Even then, the occasional flight of the Hunger have come, all of them higher Leveled than the chaff we fight.

Mozhgan held the pair back until the flight arrived, then she unleashed them to drive the fliers back before they could rain death from above on us. We tried using Judgment of All once, allowing my hand to Blink Step to the sky and unleashing my Skill. A pair of lurking high-Level Voowmah, floating above the clouds and hidden, turned their lancing attacks onto the poor Hand and shredded his defenses in seconds. It did give the dragon and Bolo a pair of targets though, but even then, they'd only managed to kill one before the other fled behind the shelter of even more powerful threats.

And that's the biggest problem. There's an unending stream of these creatures, the high-Level ones lurking on the edges. Anytime they have a chance to take down one of us, they take it. The use of my Hands high above seems to conflict with their desires, though we still unleash a Hand into the sky every once in a while, knowing it'll bring us time.

It's the other reason why the pair are still with me and why they come back fast after finishing off the flight of Voowmah, looking all the more tired each time.

"You can read the maps as well as I can," Bolo says grumpily.

I snort but pull up the information and overlay it on my minimap. A quick review and I shake my head. "They're really trying to push us away from our destination, aren't they?"

I trace a finger along the map and send a mental help request to Ali, who updates a projected course for where they're trying to get us to go and where we want to. The lines diverge farther and farther apart, one moving toward what we know to be the center of the Valley and the lair of their queen and where the Administrative Center should be. After all, our goal is near the inner perimeter but not inside it.

"They are," Bolo says. "We will need to break to the side, but that is when they will press us hardest."

I purse my lip and consider, before waving over Mozhgan. She strides over when she catches my gesture, the strain of being up, of coordinating all of us telling.

I change my mind about what I have to say, going with the blunt first. "You need to rest."

"I need to keep the Hunger from breaching our defenses," she snaps.

"And what use would you be when we finally reach the end and meet the true higher Levels?" I say. "You're burning up, with all the Mana you're using. The Levels might be good, but you'll get them anyway, right? So rest."

"They're pushing us harder than ever, and each time we change directions because your Samurai keeps trying to go where your Spirit says, they hit us harder," Mozhgan says. "What's in that direction that's so important?"

"Safety." At her incredulous look, I shrug. "Truth. There's an Administrative Center in the direction we're trying to go. They have defenses, things that will help keep the Voowmah out. Give us a chance to recuperate. Maybe even an exit for you guys."

"Us?" Mozhgan cocks her head. "Not you?"

"I figure you might be just about done with this assignment, don't you?" I shrug. "You could try to fight us then, but I have a feeling getting out will depend on me using the Administrative Center."

"And if I refuse?" Mozhgan says. "What makes you think I didn't plan a way out myself?"

"I'm sure you did," I say. "But my guess is that it's not enough to bring out all your friends. Or most of them at least. And you don't seem the kind to abandon her people. Or am I wrong?"

"You're not as dumb as you look."

I grin. "You're not the first to say that." Then I point back at Ezz, who has made space for her. "Now, why don't you figure out when we should stop pushing, rearrange who of us needs to be on the perimeter to give the most of your people and you rest, and then sleep? We'll need you for the final push."

She growls but stomps off, already calling up the Battle Chat to issue orders. I send over my own Party Chat to Mikito to follow it and stop pushing as much. When we make the break, it'll be hard and fast and probably quite, quite dangerous.

"Do you trust her?" Bolo says into the silence, curiously.

"Don't think it matters. We're all on the same side—the side trying not to get eaten," I say.

"You have a bad habit of trusting a pretty face."

"She's not that pretty," I object.

"Ah, so you've noticed."

I shrug. "Hard not to. But not in the way you think. She's a little too hard, a little too focused. I like my women more…" I consider, then grin. "Human."

Bolo rolls his eyes and I nod toward the people gathered around us. "We need them, they need us. Once we hit the Administrative Center, things will change. But from what I gather, she was paid to slow us down so that I could be ganked. I doubt she's interested in a direct fight. Her people wouldn't really last, and she's not the kind to throw away lives needlessly."

"Still, betrayal on the inside…"

"Would be bad, yes." I consider then turn my hand sideways. "Perhaps you can figure out a way to safeguard against it?"

"Me?" Bolo sounds startled.

"What? You wanted to give me the job of figuring it all out?" I say sarcastically.

"Yes," Bolo replies shamelessly. "You always seem to enjoy that. You Paladins are more geared toward such leadership roles anyway."

"You're a King," I say.

"Only by virtue of strength," Bolo replies. "We fight and contest as groups, but only because our enemies are so powerful. In the end, the battles we fight for the ascent are individual and our relationships with our dragons are individual."

"In other words, you're lazy."

"Undoubtedly. You know me so well, Redeemer."

"Well, time to get off your fat ass and do some work. Or if not you, get your lady to do so." I pause, then lower my voice. "We're known quantities, both of us. Her magic though, that seems a lot more versatile."

That puts a contemplative look on Bolo's face before he glares at me. "You just don't want to talk to Yllis!"

"She scares me," I confide in him.

"Well then, perhaps you're not as dumb as you look."

Bolo cackles as he hops off the floating metal pad to find his girlfriend, having happily echoed Mozhgan on purpose.

Before I can speak further, I get a notification on the Battlefield Chat. It's my new work detail, one that has me taking over from Xaxas at the front of the convoy. For quite a while too, it seems. I'd complain, but Mozhgan's taking my words to heart it seems.

***

Grey canyon walls loom over us on either side, black streaks barely seen beneath the swarm of Voowmah on either side. They come in a variety of shapes and sizes, some with long, thin bodies with multiple limbs like overgrown, carnivorous praying mantises; while others are more humanoid, chitin covering their bodies as they throw themselves off the cliffs to plunge down toward us. Then there are others that are more like beasts, four-legged, armor covering their bodies like twisted cats and dogs, their foreclaws sickles of death that dig into the earth with each motion.

The Voowmah are a strange group, insect hive mind joined together with their queen, but at the same time, shape-shifters too. They mutate and twist, consuming the creatures of their latest planet such that they can better do battle with their opponents. But the mutations only take the form, the shape, leaving them their innate advantages.

Hard-edged shells, so tough they'd make battleship armor look fragile in comparison. I lash out with a punch, my newly regenerated left hand aching as new, unbruised nerves flare and skin splits. The first, second, and third layer of the armor cracks, fracturing deep within. The fourth and fifth hold, but the energy imparted still sends the monster skipping backward.

Behind, I sense long-limbed scythe claws clash and clatter against floating blades. The Thousand Blades that form the spinning martial dance keep them off my back, even as I wade through the army that confronts me.

Leaping upward, I'm met with more falling bodies and jumping Voowmah, their faces widening as acid and poison is hurled at me, muscles packed with thousands of fibers exploding forward and shattering the ground. Not without penalty, not without their own legs being broken, my eyeline once more covered within seconds.

That's the method they've taken to keeping me from using Judgment of All. Throw enough bodies in the way such that I cannot see enough of them to kill them all, smash me down by sheer mass. But there's a fraction of a second when I have clear vision, and that fraction is more than enough.

Grand Cross forms, crushing down on the lay of the land before me. Canyon walls shriek, explosions as energy is released from retributive stone, sending arcs of light and lightning through the sky. We're bathed in the colors of the rainbow, the ever-falling rain splitting light further, itself distorted as it's bent under the aegis of the Skill.

The monsters beneath the Skill—the Voowmah, the Hunger, the Death of All—are shattered, unyielding armor cracking again and again, bodies turning into paste. Four levels of the Skill, compressed into a smaller than normal region and extended forward a bare hundred yards from me, is sufficient to wipe out the paltry Level 70s they're throwing at me.

But it doesn't stop those in front of me, around me, from attacking. They crash into the floating blades, tear themselves apart as they desperately try to get to me, to end my existence. A few manage to plunge blades the size of a supermodel's legs into my shield, one going so far as to pop it.

A twist in mid-air, a hip check and turn so I can grapple and ride the body down, even as Blade Strike flashes out again and again and again to open up space before me. We slam into the ground with force, light pushing upward as the ground itself retaliates. Pain, as blood and flesh superheats beneath my feet, as the corpse twitches, legs plunging into my body and tearing at skin and muscle.

I hop off the creature, idly noting the way the attack only pierced the first few layers of skin and an inch of flesh. Defense of the Fallen is working overtime, helping to defray damage, provide defense. As is Toughened Skin and my other defensive Skills and resistances.

Not that I ever stop moving. Feet kicking off the ground, smashing into others in a physical charge that throws monsters back and aside. Blades cutting and twisting, sword left in body and conjured into hand, elbow cracking into thoraxes and limbs torn from bodies to be tossed aside.

Monster after monster, dying.

Ali giggles above me as he ducks beneath the still-falling monsters, hands held before him as he weaves a net of lightning, chaining the energy released through the magnetic fields as charges connect. Potential energy flipping from one body to another, released as it dances overhead.

Sometimes, he changes it up. Sometimes, the bodies falling toward us find the ground a little more giving, a little less stable than before. Molecules part, splitting wide open as the bodies plunge meters deep into the earth, even as the energy that was contained releases into their bodies.

Only for stick figures and twisted humanoid limbs to find the earth suddenly growing hard again, resistant to their efforts to crawl upward. Then they're forced to choose to tear their bodies free and deal more damage, or to survive, suffocating in ground that flows back over their stuck forms as viscosity changes once more.

I tap into my Elemental Affinity at times too, turning the ground and myself frictionless. I skid across the earth, my swords cutting into unwilling bodies, building up momentum with each movement, each kick off a body or twist in mid-air. Then I relax my grip as Voowmah career off one another and the walls, playing human and alien pinball with my swords and missing, twisted scythe limbs shredding behind.

Then I'm through the few hundred before me and find the area that my Grand Cross damaged filled with corpses, their bodies waiting for me to pick up. I do so, jogging ahead and leaving the others to kill the few I left behind. Even now, I see the surging army of the Hunger rushing in, closing on the team and the corpse-ridden area of the Cross.

I could meet them, fly up and fight. But it's not the time.

Conserve Mana. Conserve Stamina. Conserve mental fortitude.

This is a marathon of blood and doom, pain and death, with a final battle hours ahead. All these lives, all these monsters, they're just the appetizer for what is to come. So best not to gorge myself on lives just yet, for the Hunger's appetite, the Administrator's greed will not be sated.

At least, not until I stuff my fist down their throats and make them choke on it.

***

I get into a rhythm, switching between my major Skills. I even pull out Army of One once in a while, though the Skill is less useful in these circumstances. Mostly Beacon of the Angels, Grand Cross, and Judgment of All are rotated, Ali flying up past crushed canyon walls to peek his head at the incoming army to trigger that last Skill working in our favor.

In a corner of my mind, I see flashing notifications, new quests on the Administrative Ticketing Board. Not just my presence but the other Heroics in this location is putting a strain on the System's resources, the sheer volume of damage we're doing, the release of aspected and unaspected System Mana throwing its calculations into disarray.

High above, Mana swirls, churned in the vortex of use and abuse. Corpses yield loot, teleported and formed by the System as we steal them. Stored bodies are taken out and sold, transferred to the Shop, then teleported from our Altered Storage direct across trillions of kilometers of space into workshops and sometimes, even across dimensions. Mana is used and twisted, even as Credits flow into the System. The entire System is going into a net negative, at least for the moment. Credits are sunk into the Shop system, all of which will eventually drive even more Mana use, but that will take time. In the short term, we're putting the System into flux and adding tickets by the handfuls.

Every death releases a burst of System Mana into space, unleashes unaspected Mana that has yet to be converted. It burrows into the ground, twists the living bugs that surround us, prompts growth and Leveling. At the edges of the Valley, monsters stir, some sensing a weakening in the Voowmah's hold on the land. Others soak in the new Mana, feeding on it. Alphas and dungeons will form, some that were on the verge crossing over.

Given enough time, we might actually make enough of an impact that the Voowmah are forced to pull backward on their incursions into the area around them. Their slow growth stymied. In the meantime, the System bleeds Mana and is forced to promote growth all across the planet, dishing out Quests and increasing Levels in an attempt to make others increase their own Levels and use Mana to offset this issue on our side.

That's what Administrators are meant to do, to help push the System into equilibrium. Sure, the System does a lot of it, but having an extra pair of helping hands is important. We can see the social implications that the System might miss, can create weird-ass Quests that might make people run around trying to fulfill it because it's cool or silly or gives a unique Title. The gods know, there have been a few of those in the files and data sets I've seen.

It's what we're meant to do, not control galactic life on the back end, playing evil overlord.

When Mikito's hand drops on my shoulder, I nearly take it off. She easily blocks and dodges another of the swirling blades, pulling me out of my battle trance via her presence. Scanning ahead, I watch as a second Mikito charges ahead on a ghostly horse, smashing into the built-up team of Voowmah and pushing them back. Right behind her Hand is my own, the clone wielding a hip-slung artillery-sized laser assault cannon. It spews red death at a speed that makes it seem like the clone is waving a solid beam of light, one that he plays across the walls, the monsters falling down the cliffs.

"Time to go," Mikito says, jerking her head back to where the other teams are.

"Already?" I say, surprised.

"She wants you to nap. We have six hours left, and the last four will be a pain," Mikito says.

"So two hours for me to sleep, eh?" I snort. "I guess that'll do."

Mikito snorts. "Four is the plan."

I consider what she says, and while I'm beginning to frown, Mikito waggles a finger in front of my face. "No. No weird, John self-flagellation and sacrifice while whining about it thing. This isn't the time."

"I—"

"Won't do it, right?" Mikito cocks an eyebrow at me interrogatively.

I find myself half-smiling before bobbing my head in acceptance. She smirks, and I can't help but pause, looking at my longest lasting human friend. I search for something to say, something that hasn't been said before. A way to express my gratitude, to beg her forgiveness. To plead for her understanding.

As always, I come up empty bar that simplest of phrases. "Thank you."

"It's what I do," Mikito says.

Screams, a particularly large explosion from ahead of us. I turn, watching the pile of bodies disappear into the empty space beside my Hand who waves to me insouciantly, then slings that hip-cannon of his and fires at the next group charging him. He disappears into the rain and lightning, leaving me alone with Mikito once more.

"At some point, you're going to have to choose a path that isn't just about saving my butt," I say, finding words. Perhaps not the words I meant to say, but they're just as important. "At some point, you're going to have to choose humanity over your loyalty to me. At some point… you're going to have to let go."

"Never," Mikito says firmly. "My word, my life, bound to yours. You gave me back mine. And as I said, I know you won't make me choose between the two."

"Because you still believe I'll do what I can for Earth, even after all you've seen?" I say.

"I have faith."

"I wish I had that too." I shake my head. "Just… remember. You still have a choice, a world that needs you. I've made my choices, and I'll keep making them."

Again, that piercing brown gaze looking into my own. She seems to be searching for something in my eyes before I feel a sudden pain at the side of my head. She shifted the top of her blade so fast I never saw it move, not until it smacked the top of the head.

"What was that for!" I grouse, rubbing my head.

"You promised not to do it. And still did!" Mikito says, huffing in exasperation. "Self-flagellating, whiny baka! Now, go. Rest!"

I watch as she hefts Hitoshi again. Rather than face the end of the blade and more smacking, I back off and wave goodbye to the Samurai. I can't help but notice her slight smile as she sends me off with a bruised head and I can't help but smile a little too.

Even amidst all the death and pain, I guess a little levity is useful. Especially among friends.

Chapter 27

I wake up with a start, the explosion throwing Ezz off its game. The ground shakes and cracks, the world a blinding white light so bright it cuts through the solid metal roof Ezz has generated above me. I grunt and twist, rolling to the side and through the liquid metal that Ezz creates to let me fall to the ground on the other side, coming into open air.

Open air and mud, the grey-black sand sliding off my armored jumpsuit with a wet squelch as I stand. Without thought, I firm up the ground around my feet, pushing upon both my Elemental Affinity and the Strength attribute.

To my surprise, there are no canyon walls on either side of me. Or, no, wait. There are, but they're so far away it seems they're almost not there. Not with the rain coming down in buckets, taking my System-enhanced sight down to hundreds of meters.

The ground itself is broken and shattered, the twisted and rotting smell of monster corpses surrounding me. Water cascades down the broken edges of the canyon floor, soaking into the earth and running off in ever-greater rivulets to the area ahead and to the west of us, forming an ever-growing river. The river water is stained white and red, blood from the Voowmah and more. It pools in tiny ponds, creatures—limpets, tadpoles, more— seeming to grow in the ground itself.

And more, the smell is less caustic here. Less burning down my sinuses, clearer. There's a hint of decay, that sickly sweet smell of things dying and rotting, the overpowering tint of iron from spilled blood. The very air burns skin as it mixes with water, becoming so much acid rain and reminds me that this is an all-too-alien world.

High above, peeking around the corner of clouds, the sun attempts to provide illumination but fails. No, light comes from the explosions of power from the earth as it releases pent-up energy, from the ever-strobing effects of lightning hitting the ground, and from a series of floating orbs of light around us.

"Report!" I bark, my eyes picking up no threat.

All around me, the Advanced and Master Classers of the Battlefield Tactician are getting to their feet, picking themselves up. The few transports are disgorging their men, everyone waking fully, ready for battle.

"We're here," Harry says. "So you might wanna come up ahead."

"What?" I say, blinking and pulling up the minimap. That... a glance at the time, and I realize they let me oversleep. All of them.

More than that, there's a new notification. An update. I pull it up, my eyes narrowing.

Title Update: You're Almost There (2)

Having achieved a System Quest rating of 98%, you are nearing the true secrets of the System. There are numerous powers that might not desire your success at that endeavor. Persistence, the ability to run away really fast, and the ability to acquire the strangest of allies have taken you this far. All that, however, might not be enough to finish this Quest.

Effect: Information about Title Holder and his allies are now locked under System Administrator protocols. Acquisition of further information about Title Holder or his allies will require approval of seniormost System Administrator. Experience gain has increased by 534%.

A second later, I'm calling forth my Status Screen to see if anything else has changed.

Status Screen			
Name	John Lee	Class	Junior System Admin (Grand Paladin)

Race	Human (Male)	Level	27 (35)
Titles			
Monster's Bane, Redeemer of the Dead, Duelist, Explorer, Master Questor, Galactic Silver Bounty Hunter, Galactic Bounty (Polonium), Galactic Rebel, Corrupt Questor, Chaos Bringer, Curse of the Anathema (Earth), Breaker of the Galaxy, Defiant (Sort of), You're Almost There (2), (Living Repository), (Class Lock)			
Health	7250	Stamina	7250
Mana	8120	Mana Regeneration	611 / minute
Attributes			
Strength	524	Agility	597
Constitution	725	Perception	587
Intelligence	812	Willpower	716
Charisma	225	Luck	486
Class Skills			
Mana Imbue	5*	Blade Strike*	5
Thousand Steps	1	Altered Space	2
Two are One	1	The Body's Resolve	3
Greater Detection	1	A Thousand Blades*	4
Soul Shield*	8	Blink Step	2
Portal*	5	Army of One	4
Sanctum	2	Penetration	9ᵉ
Aura of Chivalry	1	Eyes of Insight	2
Beacon of the Angels	2	Eye of the Storm	1
Vanguard of the Apocalypse	2	Society's Web	1
Shackles of Eternity*	4	Immovable Object / Unstoppable Force*	1

Domain	1	Judgment of All	6
(Grand Cross)	(4)	(Extra Hands)	(3)
System Edit	4	(Defense of the Fallen)	(3)
(Final Judgment)	(1)		
External Class Skills			
Instantaneous Inventory	1	Frenzy	1
Cleave	2	Tech Link	2
Elemental Strike	1 (Ice)	Shrunken Footsteps	1
Analyze	2	Harden	2
Quantum Lock	3	Elastic Skin	3
Disengage Safeties	2	Temporary Forced Link	1
Hyperspace Nitro Boost	1	On the Edge	1
Fates Thread	2	Peasant's Fury	1
Combat Spells			
Improved Minor Healing (IV)		Greater Regeneration (II)	
Greater Healing (II)		Mana Drip (II)	
Improved Mana Missile (IV)		Enhanced Lightning Strike (III)	
Firestorm		Polar Zone	
Freezing Blade		Improved Inferno Strike (II)	
Elemental Walls (Fire, Ice, Earth, etc.)		Ice Blast	
Icestorm		Improved Invisibility	
Improved Mana Cage		Improved Flight	
Haste		Enhanced Particle Ray	

Variable Gravitic Sphere	Zone of Denial

Cursing at being allowed to rest, I hurry forward, even as the team behind me reforms to guard our backs. I can tell Xaxas is back there by the sheer volume of thunder rolling down from behind us, but surprisingly, the dots that cover our back aren't getting closer, keeping pace with us. "What's going on? Why did you let me sleep?"

"Because you weren't needed," Mozhgan says flatly. "They pulled back three hours in. An hour after our turn."

"That makes no sense..." I say. "They were to push us when we turned. We're so close."

"Exactly," Mozhgan says. "They're planning something."

"Smart monsters." I curse softly, running through all the languages I know. "This is going to be a problem."

"And it's ahead of us. So, best for us to face it," she says, gesturing me ahead.

I cast one last look to the back, where Xaxas holds the line along with her people. A pair of Hands are there too, keeping an eye on things, their Mana all the way back. Together, they should be able to hold off a concerted push. At least, for a short period.

The rest of us are already up forward, just a short distance from our destination. Ten kilometers from our final destination, give or take a few kilometers. Somewhere on this plane then, this giant gorge that might as well be considered an open space. Not much place to hide, and all the damage we've done to the Voowmah mutates launching their crystal rounds is gone. Air interdiction is back in play, though our ceiling is at least higher than normal. The amount of mutants who can hit us from angles are reduced, at least for now.

I'm finally at the front, finally able to look at what has us stopped, what destroyed the ground. A little part of me is amused it was friendly fire, that it's Bolo with his hammer striking the ground and sending damage spiraling out. What was done to Ezz and the rest of the convoy was just aftershocks from an attack rippling forward

Less amusing is the fact that the entire attack was just stopped. Earth is pilled high in a mountain on either side of the group in front, our barriers smashed down with casual ease by those ahead. Not that I'm that surprised, not when I see the Status information of those before me.

Voowmah Royal Guard (Level 173)

Voowmah Royal Guard (Level 185)

Voowmah Royal Guard (Level 168)

Voowmah Royal Guard (Level 179)

Disturbing, those four. Humanoid, chitin-covered, thin bodies that are faceless. They range in height from just under five feet to a towering nine, with no hair on their bodies, each of which are gleaming a sickly green. Hands are glimpsed at the end of covered, sickle-like vambraces that extend over their forearms, the edges of which are outlined in dripping water. They stand utterly still in that way predators have while waiting for prey, making the hair at the back of my neck stand up. Four monsters, each of them a hard fight by themselves.

And in many ways, they're the least surprising aspect of those standing before us.

Four more figures, flickering in the cascade of rain, their holographic forms broken by the falling liquid and giving them a surreal quality. Four figures that should not be standing next to the Voowmah, not with a projector that is so easily spotted.

Emperor, Champion, Administrator and one more, an unknown. A floating shadow, staring at us, cloaked and withdrawn. The Emperor sees me. His eyes widen a little, then narrows.

Instinct has me reach out, twist the Skill Sanctum with System Edit, and slam it down over our group. It reaches outward, larger than ever, so that it covers even Xaxas. I pour Mana into it, as much as I can, strengthening the Skill in ways it was never meant to, but that my Edit Skill allows. Blood gushes from my nose and eyes as the System takes its toll from me.

I barely make it in time.

A spear, appearing from high above, comes screaming down without warning to impact the concave sphere right above my head. It smashes into the Skill, fully powered by a Legendary's ability, and rather than skid off the curved defense, it keeps pushing straight down.

My knees give way beneath me, the hard dirt bruising my body even as I pour Mana into the shield above us. Ali throws his hand upward, twisting his Elemental Affinity, as do Bolo and Yllis. Together, they weave a defense to support mine, to shove the spear aside. It moves ever so slowly, the tip of the blade causing the edge of my Sanctum to bulge inward, tiny spiderweb cracks opening.

I push backward, flooding more and more Mana into the Skill even as the System destroys me from within. Mana that should never have been used in this manner flows through me like a flood and bursts open blood vessels and organs, leaving me drowning in my own blood.

Then just as suddenly as it started, the spear head slips enough that it skitters down the side to impact the earth. The incredible pressure is over in a blink of a second. Yet the assault isn't done, for energy from the spear impacts the ground, imparting the last of its deadly payload into the surroundings. Refractive ground soaks it all in, coming apart and turning the very soil beneath us into so much dust. Energy floods outward, a tiny nuclear bomb going off on the edges of my Sanctum Skill.

Blinding light, so powerful it washes out the world behind us. Thankfully, the Skill keeps the light to a safe level, saving the eyes of those within. We can't see outside though, and the pressure, the energy exuded, pushes the Skill and myself further.

Something punctures my back, a through-and-through attack. Blood collected in my lungs, in my chest floods out of the holes. As if understanding what is happening, my body doesn't automatically heal the gaping wound, allowing the overflow of liquid to stain the earth.

So much blood, too much. If not for the way the System reinforces my bond, replaces the liquid it is forcing out of me, I would be dead many times over. System hijinks keep me bent over in agony, even as the pressure around us finally dies down.

I shut down the link between the Skills, feeding the last of the overflow of Mana into Sanctum even as air rushes back, impacting our little sphere of stability as the mushroom cloud of pure power dies down. The ground beneath our feet has been blown away, the tiny strip of land supported by Sanctum floating in mid-air for now.

Dust slowly settles, even as I feel a Healing spell bathe my body. It takes time, long minutes, for the dust to settle, especially since the clouds high above have been blown away. For the first time in a long while, an alien sun beats down upon us and the world is dry.

Staggering to my feet, I'm somehow not surprised to see the four Voowmah still standing before us. Not untouched, for dust and soot cover their glittering carapaces, but mostly unharmed. Even now, the System heals their bodies as it does mine.

The four projections are gone, but they reappear, the Emperor's lips curled up in disdain.

"So. You survived my spear." The Emperor's voice is deep, all bass and high Galactic snootiness. "Impressive."

I want to say something back, but I find myself still having trouble speaking. The System's still patching up the hole in my chest, so I'm a little breathless. A glance to the side and I spot Mozhgan and the short spear-like object she used to punch through my body. A little smoke rises from her armor from behind, chains wrapping around her body to crush her. Surprisingly, they don't seem to find purchase; as though my Skill is actually unable to affect her. I'd check what the hell is happening, but I'm a little breathless.

Following the angle of the other attack, I realize that Harry has a gun out, but it's now hanging by his side. On the other hand, Xaxas is by her side, ready to end her if she tries anything again. I'm a little surprised she did at all; but... whatever.

"He shot her when she punched the hole through you. Surprisingly, no one shot him for it," Ali explains.

I flash the War Reporter a quick smile before my attention is yanked back to the front. Where, to my surprise, Mikito is speaking.

The Samurai is on her knees, peering down past the edge of our slip of land. "That was a Legacy weapon, wasn't it? The Spear of Longinus."

"Wait, isn't that...?"

"Biblical?" Mikito answers my unfinished question and shrugs. "Mana seepage. On a name, on a concept. On a weapon that destroyed entire armies when used and has killed more than one Legendary." Her voice drops as she stands, staring at the Emperor's image across the distance. "You had it all this time then, after it disappeared."

"Just another part of my collection." He smiles grimly. "I must admit, I had not expected you to survive its cast." His hand flexes a little, his gaze darting downward before coming back to Mikito and me, now that I've come up near her. "You won't survive our next attack."

"Yeah, yeah." I wave my hand to brush away his words.

The casual dismissal angers him, but he doesn't act, which is a pity. Breath rattles in my chest, my nose scrubbed with one filthy hand. I conjure a new set of armor, one that is less filthy, figuring I'll leave the Hod for later. Nannites crawl over my skull and body, eating away the filth of sweat and blood, creeping along the base of my neck like the fingers brushing against my connection to the System.

"I'm more interested in why you are standing beside the Hunger," Yllis says, her voice low and angry. Her gaze darts to the four who continue to stand, unmoving. "Why aren't they attacking? What have you done?"

"Done?" Now it's Sephra who speaks, the mermaid Administrator's voice filled with scorn. "We have done nothing but what is needed."

There's a slight twitch in Kasva's body, a thinning of his lips, but the Champion does not gainsay her. A crack in their alliance, but a thin one. I file it away for later use, though I doubt I'll find a wedge.

"You're working with the Hunger. You fools…" Yllis hisses, stepping forward and pressing against the Sanctum bubble. I feel it twist and bulge. Even the casual gesture by the dragon is enough to pressure my Skill. It's not exactly built to take damage from the inside, especially not after I twisted the code the way I did.

Bolo acts before I have to, taking hold of Yllis's shoulder and pulling her back. She turns toward him, whipfast, and stares at him through narrowed violet eyes. If looks could kill, I'd be starting a eulogy for the man.

However, she doesn't have that Skill and subsides a little when Bolo speaks, his gaze half on her and half on the opposition.

"What did you promise them?"

"We've promised nothing more than what you have taken," Sephra says, her lips widening into a savage grin. Needle-sharp teeth glint in the sunlight, the pearlescent white almost glittering under the alien sun. "A chance to grow. We've already begun."

"The others you sent in," I whisper in horror.

All those lives, the ones I didn't understand coming in when they weren't meant to. Searching for the Administrative Center I thought, or us. Perhaps that too, but also, "payment."

Kasva flinches a little, my words an announcement of their betrayal. He glances away, not daring to meet our gazes, even as I feel the tension in Mikito and the pair of Xy'largh natives skyrocket.

"You are insane! If they grow too strong, they'll take over the planet. Kill all of us!" Bolo says. "The very foundation of your System will be broken."

"Fool," Sephra says. "Do you think the dragons are the only creatures who process Mana the way they do? The Voowmah are the same. Better, in some ways, for they grow without end. Easier to manage too, unlike you and your people. We've been assured they'll contain their depredations."

"They'll kill and spread across the galaxy!" Mozhgan says, obviously horrified. She comes up, staring at them, Xaxas letting her do so. The chains are gone, the Skill having exhausted itself. "They truly will be Civilization's End!"

"Be quiet, traitor," Sephra snaps at Mozhgan. "You should have died with the rest of the bait. Now, you dare to lecture me!"

"You knew we'd die…" Mozhgan says, though there's a lack of surprise in her voice. Resignation perhaps, as though the truth was one she knew deep within. "And now you'll condemn hundreds of planets to death too for your allies. For what? To stop him?" A finger points at me. "Why is he so important?"

"He's *nothing!*" Sephra says, her voice rising. Her holographic figure strides forward, gesturing. "The Prime Administrator though, his presence, his location. That is worth all your lives, all your worthless lives, and more. You think those hundreds of planets are a tragedy? They're lost anyway. It's all lost if we cannot gain access to the System proper. We're dying. The System is dying!"

I blink, staring at the woman. Mozghan asks the question that I think we're all wondering. "What do you mean the System's dying?"

"The Forbidden Zones, the Council, it's all coming apart. In a few centuries, its growth will be entirely unchecked. We'll have to create dozens of Dungeon Planets." Sephra shakes her head. "The Voowmah or the dragons, it matters not. Once we have access to the System, we can fix the Mana spillage properly. Slow it down, change the code on the Hunger to make them less... less."

For the first time, the creatures move.

They twist and stare at Sephra, the faceless masks of their chitin-covered bodies focused. The mermaid seems to realize what has happened and turns to them, her lips tight. Before she can speak again, the robed, shadowy figure gestures and Sephra's image disappears. This catches the Voowmah Royal Guards' attention, and they focus on him.

"She does not speak for us all," the robed figure says, and I can't help but think that he reminds me all too much of a rather infamous media figure who "somehow" returned to life. His voice is the same too, low, cultured, and a little hissing like a snake. "We will keep up our end of the deal, so long as you do yours. You will be allowed to spread, so long as you do not destroy the entire planet's ecology. Let it keep flourishing, your people flourishing in an endless loop. Kill one another or other monsters, we care not. But churn that Mana, and our deal will hold."

"And here we have it," I say, my voice soft and tired. The fingers along my connection, they keep stroking, pushing against my Skill. Following it back as I gently manipulate Skills, I split my focus between the code for Sanctum and other Skills. Watching them watching me. "The truth of it all, in the end. You don't give a damn, do you? How many lives are lost, how many fall? Because keeping the System running is all important. Keeping control of a crumbling world, one that doesn't work, is more important than maybe finding a solution."

"You think you have a solution?" The Emperor scoffs. "I've lived millennia. We have tried and tried and tried again to find a way around the Forbidden Zone. When we had access to the Prime Administrator and when we didn't, it didn't matter. The children"—he glances to the side, where Sephra was before—"might believe there's a solution, but those of us who have seen it know. We sit upon a crumbling throne, washed away by the tides of Mana, and whether it be the Hunger or the dragons who help stem the tide, it'll all wash away in the end."

"What happens when they betray you?" Bolo calls, his voice laced with fury.

"They would not dare," the Emperor replies.

"I wasn't talking to you." Bolo fixes his gaze on the Voowmah, his voice laced with contempt. "What happens when they betray you, like they betray us now? What will you do then?"

If the Dragon King is expecting an answer, he's sorely disappointed. The Royal Guard split their attention, a pair watching us, the other pair staring at the shadowy figure. I wish I could get some Status information, but since he's just a projection, there's nothing to pull data from. Even the little traces of data that people like Ali or myself can occasionally use to ferret out information—Auras, other Charisma-based or appearance-based Skills—aren't feeding me any information to use.

He's careful. Smart. Annoying.

"I guess that's it then. You use the Hunger, who are somewhat like the dragons, morphed creatures of the System itself, and let them have Xy'largh. You use them to kill us, and you make your way to the Prime Administrator's Center, because it gives you a little more control. All to shore up your crumbling throne for a few more minutes." The Emperor smirks while hood-and-cloak stares at me as I speak. "You know… I'm a little disappointed."

"I care not about your… disappointment," the Emperor says derisively. "Your feelings on our motives, they matter not."

"Oh, no. Not about that. Just that you think I haven't noticed your intrusion." I look at the robed Administrator. "You're good, but you can't access my connection without leaving traces."

"Yet you let me." Curiosity now, in the Administrator's voice.

"Needed you to be paying attention to it while I helped my friend." I turn toward Harry. "It did go out, didn't it?"

Harry nods grimly. "Network Locus and my new Title give me priority rights. I've been broadcasting since the start. They tried to stop me, but…"

"Yeah, I wormed our way around it." I scratch the back of my neck. "But you knew I was doing that, didn't you?" Another inclination of the head from the shadows. I swear, I almost see a flash of a smile. "Did you get what you need then?"

"I did."

"Perhaps someone wants to fill me in on what is going on?" Mozhgan snaps, spinning on Harry and me.

Bolo on the other hand, used to my shenanigans, is grinning. Yllis catches on a few seconds later, her violet eyes shining as she straightens, searching the skyline. Too far just yet. Probably.

"Harry has been broadcasting the Administrators' deal. Not just galactically, but specifically. To a bunch of dragons and their companions who might not be willing to wait for their deaths."

If anything, the quartet of Royal Guards grow even more still. Minimap dots of the flood of red that have been creeping up on us, the Voowmah who would end our trip, stop too.

"I'm willing to bet we're about to see a real flight of dragons now." I sigh. "But at the same time, our friends don't care. They set this all up, brought us this close because they need me here. They've been tracing my Status Screen, my Skills, and my connection back to the Prime Administrator. Because even this close, they couldn't find him. Her. It."

"And we thank you for your service. Now, it's time for you to die," the Emperor says.

He turns to the Voowmah, who have not stopped looking at them. At the same time, the robed figure blinks out of time and space, along with Kasva, who looks utterly disgusted by the entire proceedings. Even the feeling of metaphysical fingers running along my Status is gone.

"Fulfil your side of the bargain," the Emperor says. "Kill them. And we will aid you once more."

For the first time, the Hunger speaks. All four, at the same time, their voices like a vibrating, twisted chainsaw. "You betrayed us once. Why should we trust you again?"

"Do you have a choice?" the Emperor says, smirking. "The dragons will come to eradicate you at last. They will not risk you growing stronger under our influence. Use all your resources, kill the Redeemer and his allies. And we will take your queen away. Secrete her in a place even the dragons cannot find and let her grow a new army. One that will allow you to truly win."

Silence, as the four regard the Emperor. In the meantime, Mozhgan is sending tactical orders to the rest of the team over the Battlefield Chat. My eyes narrow as the orders flow, my head turning toward the back. I want to object, to say something about the plans, about what I can see happening.

I never get a chance.

"*It shall be a glorious death,*" Xaxas's deep rumble carries through the Net. Mana swirls in the back as he triggers his Skill again, pulling the clouds that were scattered by the blast. They roll back in.

As though his actions were the signal, the Voowmah speak. "Deal."

At the same moment, the tide of red that had frozen flows again, monsters appearing at the far edges of the Valley. Smirking, the Emperor disappears, his projection gone.

Red dots flow toward us as the four turn, their sickle hands rising. In a flash, they dash forward, hammering straight into the Sanctum, literally teleporting across the open ground and the bare air, so fast do they move. Rumbles, not just from thunder but the drumbeat of millions of feet hitting the ground, echo through the land, bouncing off high canyon walls and dusty, hard-packed ground. Blows crack against the Sanctum and the Skill begins to fail, pushed too far, too fast.

We spread out according to the Tactician's orders, readying ourselves for this last battle.

The Voowmah are coming, and this time, they won't be holding back.

Is it wrong that I'm smiling a little in anticipation?

Chapter 28

Rumble of thunder and lightning strikes, the pitter-patter of rain in the distance arriving, the crash of thousands of feet as they charge toward us. A wall of green and grey, moving bodies of the Voowmah approaching, while the acrid stench of blood and dust fills the air. Before us, the four humanoid figures slam their blades into the Sanctum, though I note they slow down a touch. Timing approach and damage, it seems.

Smart. I hate smart enemies.

A thought and the Spitzrocket arrives from its dimensional home, slipping around me, pouring across my form to guard me one last time.

"Father, I do not understand," Ezz says, coming up to my side now that the Galactics are gone. "You let them know where your objective is. Is that not counterproductive to your own goals?"

I tilt my head down a little, spotting the little red golem who stares back up at me with those artificial eyes, glowing yellow light with innocent, artificial inquiry. "In a way. If you think the Prime Administrator, whoever or whatever they are, has just a single method of protecting themselves, you've got a lot more to learn."

Ezz nods, making me smile a little and feel a flush of happiness.

Then, glancing over to where Bolo and Yllis are standing together, whispering to one another words of concern and compassion, I can't help but add, "But also, sometimes you have to do what is right, not just what is expedient."

"You chose a less optimal path for your friends," Ezz says. "Because they are your friends?"

"Don't forget the dragons. Because... dragons!" I grin and lower my voice a little, though I'm sure she can still hear me. "Even if the only one I've ever talked to is a bit of a bitch, dragons are still cool, you know. Better than stupid hive monsters."

"Yes. The Voowmah are uncool," Ezz says, though it does so with a tone that makes me think it's repeating the words without truly understanding them. A child, parroting its parent's opinions. Like livers are tasty or the original *Star Wars* movies are better than the prequels. "How do you decide, Father? When to be efficient and when to choose your friends?"

"That's…" I frown, looking for a way to explain instinct and choice, of picking between conscience and need. How do you explain the unexplainable, especially when you're as emotionally constipated as I am? "Called following your heart, Ezz. You just have to look inward and realize what lines you can't ever cross."

"Yeah, like getting friends tortured is fine. Genocide, on other hand, is almost always bad," Harry says wryly.

"Almost always, Uncle?" Ezz spins around, looking at Harry.

"Well, we are about to kill the Voowmah here real dead."

"Hey, you two." I point at the Sanctum shielding that is cracking and will the timer display into the Battlefield Chat, along with an estimate of when the rest of the horde will arrive. "Get back, will you? And get ready to move."

"We'll follow her orders," Harry says.

Even so, he does step back a little. Ezz slips in under his feet, gripping hold of Harry and putting him on itself. A second later, the pair shimmer and disappear from visible sight as Harry triggers an item to bend light around the pair. I feel the Mana swirl around them, the way my System senses twinge as Harry activates one after the other defensive and stealth items and Skills. With Ezz still counted as an item, the System basically hides the pair using the same series of items and Skills. A little exploit that the Battlefield Tactician had pointed out to us.

I'm not complaining.

Especially when I feel the Sanctum shatter, mere minutes before the rest of the Voowmah arrive. There's a fraction of a second of surprise, as the Royal Guard do not expect us to break out early. Then we take the fight to them, Bolo, Yllis, and Mikito each taking on one of the Guard. Leaving my Hands to focus on the last one, I Blink Step ahead, bypassing the entire group.

Leaving my friends and family behind to fight for their lives.

***

I don't get to see the clash between my friends and the Royal Guard. Blink Stepping ahead takes me four hundred fifty meters. Another Blink Step grabs me the moment I arrive to push me another four hundred eighty-three meters. Not a moment too soon, since explosions centered five hundred meters and a full kilometer from where I started go off.

"Knew it," I snarl. Idiots thought I'd Blink Step the full range that I had.

Ali zips through space to appear by my side moments later.

He's glowing like a comet, shedding parts of his body from damage taken when he was shooting through space. Not that I wait for my friend, Blink Stepping a full five hundred meters but at an angle this time, heading for eleven o'clock.

Another series of explosions, this time set at fifteen hundred meters and two kilometers, wash over me, light and caustic energy rippling through all the barriers between dimensions. It hits my Soul Shield and degrades it, but it holds before the Hod is harmed.

My lips thin, wondering how many explosives, how many traps our opponents put in play. Rather than risk blipping anymore, I run, watching the approaching distance and feeling the hot rush of energy. Seeing little dots, more of the Voowmah but farther away, closing in on me from the front.

Behind, the minimap and a visual feed shows the results of the battle. Bolo's got the upper hand on his opponent, his hammer literally crushing his opponent to the ground. The man's all about quick bursts of attacks, and he's pulled out all the stops. His Dragon Fear Aura has rolled out, and with him so close to Yllis, it's doubled in effect. His opponent is moving slower, each empowered hammer blow crushing it, even as the oversized, hard light image that makes the hammer attack twice its normal size leaves burning flames on the Royal Guard.

Yllis, on the other hand, is no longer on the ground but fully transformed. She's winging high above, breathing flame as flying mantises come in, burning them to a crispy color and setting their delicate wings aflame. In her forearms, crushed and trapped, is the Royal Guard she's supposed to be fighting. However, her moment of distraction is a problem, as it slices through her claws and frees itself, falling with her fingers to the ground.

The resulting roar and unleashing of her aura literally creates cracks in the air as the dimensional barriers—already weakened by the attacks unleashed on me earlier—fray once more. Through the cracks, *things* crawl out. Sometimes, just creatures of energy, other times my good friends the shadow creatures. Other times, things with too many heads, too many hands, too many eyes plop upward or reach through the gaps and snatch up the Voowmah, swallowing them whole.

The world heals moments later, but everything feels off, like a too-thin egg ready to crack again. System notifications flare, rippling through my Ticketing Board, and instinct has me dipping inward.

Priority Alert! Dimensional Breaches (Grade III)

Review distribution of System Mana to dimensional walls.

Time slows as I stare at the ticket. A part of me gibbers in panic. Another points out that it's no different than some parts of the Forbidden Zone, how too much unaspected Mana can create warped areas of reality, the Colossus...

The ticket disappears in that moment of hesitation. It is gone, and above me, I feel System Mana rush inward, churning through space as it takes hold of the unaspected Mana that is already permeating the rents in space, pushing it aside as it patches the hole.

I make a mistake by wondering what the System has to do with dimensional breaches, and the Library data dumps into me. For a second, I stagger to a halt, data unspooling. Mana is here, there, everywhere. It pervades all sides of the dimensions and experiments...

Dumping unaspected Mana into other dimensions.

The first Dimensional War. The second. The third.

Pain, death, loss. Videos, images, dry historical reports. Five times, they tried it. Five times the Council and Administrators have tried to slow the flow of the Forbidden Zone. An unmitigated success in the beginning, the Forbidden Zone even retreating for a time in the best cases.

An unmitigated disaster later, when the monsters in the other dimensions, creatures given power and form and shape, Spirits and Elementals and unnamed Creatures from Beyond, mutated, gained Levels and skills and strength. Mana, uncontrolled by the System, mutated and twisted creatures until the barrier between worlds failed and suddenly.

Invasion.

Five times, they tried. Five times they made the mistake of thinking if they only changed the way they did it a little, sent it into a location empty of anything, sent it into a land filled with energy, sent it a conceptual realm...

this time it would work. Five times, failures and a loss of life so great that even the Galactic Wars were nothing in comparison.

The System doesn't care if we breach the dimensional walls. It doesn't care if unaspected Mana patches it all together, unharnessed, in volume. We, on the other hand—Galactics, System Administrators, creatures who must live with the results—have stopped it. Five tests, data streaming in as results and information about the System, about—

The blow catches me around the waist, shears through the Soul Shield and the Spitzrocket's defensive shield and its armor before lodging halfway to my spine. The sickle yanks sideways, pulling out of me with a wet squelch, even as the other hand descends.

Blink Step from Ali's viewpoint pulls me backward, the only thing left a bunch of conjured swords. I'm spinning on my heel, taking the agony and my body's automatic collapse to the left into account to bring my conjured weapons crashing into the green chitin armor of a Voowmah Royal Guard. They bounce off, leaving light scarring on the monster, even as a second Royal Guard waves its hand and Mana swirls around it, forming into summoned light that blasts back at me.

Reinforcements. Thousand Hells…

Blink Step again, next to its own friend. I hip check the bastard, putting all the power of my Strength attribute into the motion and shoving him into the tracing beam attack. It catches him for a brief moment before the attack is cut off, the melee opponent popping back to its feet. A hand rises and my legs crumple underneath me.

Scythe-hands, ghostly scythe-hands, punch up from the ground into my feet, pin me in the sides. I bleed again, pain rippling through my body as the damn caster calls down lightning from the skies in multiple angles.

Blink Step once more, this time high into the air, even as Ali waves his hand, redirecting the lightning to strike the caster.

"Suck on that, plastic-face. Play with lightning when I'm around, will you!" Ali cackles, his hands never still.

The other dots, the first of the vanguard of the Voowmah coming from the front, arrive, some launching themselves into the air only to be caught by an unseen force—wind and shearing rain—and carried aside.

Myself, I dance with the melee fighter. Penetration Shielding kicks on seconds before I grab him and blast upward, taking the long-limbed, chitin-covered opponent through my own blades, cracking blades and armor.

Then I kick him off me, even as far away, the Voowmah artillery players range on the pair of us. I ignore the attack even as Ali curses me and runs from the epicenter. I have better things to do, to worry about as now I have a glimpse of the horde in all their glory.

Another twist of Mana, the use of my Skill.

Fear me, children, for I am Shiva and death has become me.

Judgment of All activates, hammering everyone in sight. Somehow, the melee Voowmah has managed to escape, moving through space so that he's not there when the Skill activates. The caster though is stun-locked, lightning dancing around his body, unable to get a grip on a frictionless surface directly underneath his feet and so collapsed before me. He's not the only one though, not with the horde that is charging forward.

Thousands of the Hunger, caught in the throes of activation of my army-killing skill. They made a mistake by taking away the rain, of pulling back a little during the Emperor's attack. I have sight of so, so many of them. Even the minor shower that is coming down all around us is a benefit to me since it drives down the dust storm, pinning it to the earth.

A clear day to kill.

The first tick goes off, a second of damage. It's crippling for some of the Voowmah, the ones without a lot of innate resistance to Mana damage.

Painful, but monsters have a ton of health, and none of those charging me are any less than Level 90.

Another tick.

The wave of stumbling is larger now, even as I fall. The caster gives up on attempting to stand, instead wrapping a different spell around itself. Glowing scythe-hands appear from the sky, summoned from the ether. They lash out at me, tearing at my body, only to be deflected by my swords.

Another tick.

More Voowmah are stumbling, the System taking its toll. Even so, I'm in mid-air, so I'm bounced around like a pinball by the attacks. In the midst of all that, the melee Royal Guard appears, moving so fast that he seems to flicker as he cuts at me. He shatters my swords with each movement, not caring if they crack his armor as he attempts to kill me. The few attacks that get through bounce off my Penetration shielding.

Another tick.

Mana flooding through their System connection, Mana tearing into them, robbing them of vitality. The caster and melee Royal Guards grow more desperate, burning Mana at a visible rate. The air around them warps, glowing as they hammer at me. They fight as though they're enraged, desperate to put an end to me.

Another tick.

I hit the ground, rolling with the impact, feeling the ground shatter under me and damage the Spitzrocket. Claws scrape against the back of my Penetration shielding as scythe claws tear up the ground, leaving me to come up, a hand raised. The Royal Guard before me lunges forward so fast I can't track it, not even with my enhanced Perception. It manages to pierce halfway through my enhanced Penetration Shield, skills allowing it to plunge an arm halfway through the chest armor of the Spitzrocket.

Another tick.

And then it realizes, too late, I left the opening. Grand Cross triggers, angled sideways and upward, originating from my arm. It crushes him backward and upward, launching the monster into the sky, the energy imparted never-ending, its body caught in the throes of a Skill. It tries to move, to escape, blurring sideways only to find itself still lifted, flying upward.

Another tick.

More damage, more pain. I check the code, grunt, and release my hold on the Skills, letting both Grand Cross and System Edit go. He can run, but there's nowhere to hide. Not from the System. Not from the edited Skill. I wipe at the blood from my nose, the itching from hundreds of nanobots eating it reminding me I'm still in the power armor.

Then, before I can revel in my victory, the crystal artillery fire lands and the world goes white.

***

"You idiot! Just because you've got a ton of defense thanks to your Penetration shielding doesn't mean the rest of us can handle those attacks!" Ali curses at me, a constant stream of words that make me smile a little. Only a little, because the connection between us is frayed, twisted. *"We got to stop calling those attacks down, boy-o. The walls between the dimensions are already breached."*

"Yeah, yeah. Maybe tell that to Yllis and the other dragons, why don't you?"

In my minimap, more figures are appearing. All grey, instead of flashing red. Not the blue of allies, but the grey of those unallied to me. They flicker into space above the plains, breathing liquid death. The damn Voowmah crystal launchers open up, impacting defensive shielding. One dragon is too slow, and I watch as its body spirals downwards, its body torn to pieces as it falls.

The horde that charged after us splits apart a bit as the newly appeared dragons move in a spiral, hammering the inner arm of the Valley. Secondary defenses trigger as blimps rise through the sky, Voowmah bloated with poisonous gases blown apart to fill the atmosphere with caustic poison. Entire canyons explode, showering the sky with refractive rock, tearing apart the sky. And higher up, hidden above the clouds, creatures wing downward to pierce dragon hide and wings.

On the far edges, I know even more dragons are appearing, giant teleportation gates twisting the air and Mana as they link one portion of Xy'largh to another. From the gates, flights of dragons with Dragon Knights and Lords riding upon them appear, flying forward to lay waste to the ground below. The level of flame gives the horizon a reddish glow, making it seem as if I'm standing in another post-apocalypse movie.

Mikito rides up a second later. "You done standing around?"

I tilt my head, surprise flashing across my face when I realize that nearly everyone is with her, all but Bolo and Yllis. "Where…"

"Keep up," Mozhgan snaps. "We need to get you moving forward. Your little stunt might have killed the Hunger before us, but they'll be pushed back only so long. Bolo and Yllis are going after the queen."

"They can't—" I snap, knowing how powerful she must be. The Guards themselves were bad enough, and there's no way they were the only ones.

"They know. It's the only way to buy you time," Mozhgan says. "If we're lucky, the other Dragon Kings will join them."

I turn my head toward where Yllis's large body wings away. On top of her sits an emerald-scaled figure, his weapon swinging to bat aside the winged monstrosities that attempt to stop them. Brilliant crystal light arcs up to strike at her, only to be stopped by a glowing shield beneath her form, one that only briefly disappears when she *breathes*.

"And if they don't?" I snarl. "If they choose to take a more considered, careful approach?"

"Then they die. Like we do now if we don't move," Mikito answers for Mozhgan, kneeing her horse so that it puts itself between the Battlefield Tactician and me. "Time to go, baka."

I grit my teeth but understand that she's right. Turning on my heel, I start out, pulling up the Battlefield Tactician's orders to scan them. I get a good dozen meters away before my steps falter, only for Mikito to prod me in the back.

"Xaxas… the Hands…" I say softly, horrified a little. Even so, under the prodding of Hitoshi, I get moving forward. We can't stop. "Mozhgan and her people…"

"Xaxas and the Hands first, yes," Mikito says, watching as I pick up speed a little even as a gust of wind sends a trace of harder rain splattering down around us. More lightning flashes, illuminating the area behind us in a strobe light effect, carried forward by the never-ending rumble of thunder as the lightning storm goes off under the Storm Warden's control. "Slow down the Hunger, kill as many of them as possible."

Even now, the red dots that had stopped for a bit under the distraction of the dragons have returned to rushing us. There are a lot of them, and Ali's up in the air a little, along with a pair of Hands, each of them calling forth Beacon of the Angels. It's a necessity, since the artillery Voowmah are ranging on us. If not for Xaxas's storm culling and hindering their ability to see where we are and the Spirit's gift for shifting where those arcing crystal attacks land, we'd be peppered a lot more. As it stands, Mozhgan's people are still under significant strain to keep a moving shield above the team.

I wish there was something I could do, some way of saving these people. Yet, the moment Mozhgan joined us, she and her people were doomed. The only way is through, and so far, this has gone better than I could hope for. The idiots dragging in the Voowmah rather than fighting us directly have given us an opportunity, one just about large enough to sneak through.

We just have to survive the oncoming deluge of death.

Mana ticks over, slowly rising. My gaze flicks across my Status Screen, stopping at my latest Skill. Knowing when to use it, when to activate the Skill will be important. As we run, I pull up the code of the Skill once more, reviewing it for exploits. There are places where I can adjust it, areas to Edit, but an instinctual part of me understands that doing so will bring the wrath of the System as well.

Heroic Skills are overpowered, as are Legendary Skills. They're balanced the way they are so that they don't overdraw the System too greatly, trading overuse of System Mana in the short term for what is an expected long-term benefit from the survival of the Heroic. Even then, the goal is to control the amount of System Mana being used at any one time.

A Skill like Final Judgment, which is close to a Legendary Skill, is even more restricted, partly for balance issues, partly because of how much Mana it will use. Forcing things like an activation period and the need for channeling ensures that the Grand Paladin doesn't overuse the Skill, like a Legendary might, without the requisite overabundance of System Mana regeneration return.

All of which is to say, playing with the code is a good way of getting my head smacked by the System. More than that, the code in this Skill is incredibly complex, what with it tying multiple Skills into it and adjusting those Skills by itself. Add the expense of five thousand Mana at the start and I'm going to be hard-pressed to find the right time to use it.

Yet, instinct tells me that that need is coming all too soon. As we run for our lives through falling crystal shards and hopping, insect death, I watch the swarm of red dots, the six groups that Ali has located to mark the Galactics and the Voowmah who are enroute to us.

And I wonder when the next shoe will fall.

Chapter 29

"Administrators and Galactic Forces, incoming!" Mozhgan snarls, her eyes snapping upward. Her feed gets shot across the Battlefield Chat just as fast as she speaks, and I see the data she's seeing. Nice to have her back on board, even if it's just to save her own ass.

Of course, it's impossible for her to tell who the Administrators really are, but it's not a hard guess that some of those coming in are part of their team. More importantly, they're coming straight down from orbit, like red comets as crash pods deploy to get them here as fast as possible.

Not that the Voowmah are about to let them land willy-nilly. Perhaps if they hadn't just talked about betraying the Voowmah, they would have allowed the landings. Then again, the Voowmah are being "fed" lives to power them up too, so who knows how many of those being sent are just fodder? Crystal attacks fly through the air, impacting against glowing comets, the world cracking further.

Dragons in flight weave spells and fire, lashing out at the Galactics who have betrayed them. But the world is aflame, the very air cooking off from the sheer volume of crash pods being sent down. Ambient temperatures spike again and again, reaching levels that would cook alive an unprotected human.

In the Spitzrocket, I'm safe. At least from those attacks. But unknown to the rest, Administrators reach out through the ether, aiming to tear apart lives and connections. Skills that were never meant to be used at a distance are triggered, our defense from above disappearing.

"Hacking attempts... blocking..." I grate out, my mind splitting and splitting again as I reach for the System Edit Skill.

The Administrators are tearing apart code in the System, and rather than join them, I work to fix the problems they create, stopping their attacks.

More than once, I shut down connections, using the brute force of will and code to stop their pitiful attempts.

Code—angular, cryptic, and cosmically horrific—runs through my mind, manipulated by will and intelligence, torn apart and rewritten again and again; inserted into attacks thrown at us or to reinforce the boundaries of our very dimension.

In the corner of my eye, I note Ezz slipping into the Spitzrocket, backdooring its way in as my "son" via the communication protocols I enabled for it via my Neural Link. Ezz takes over guidance, helping to keep me in one piece, triggering weapons and Skill use, even as it jukes my meatform around. Another battle, one entirely digital, takes place at the same time as Ezz wards off even more hacking attempts on the power armor and myself.

For all my defenses, for all the work that Mozhgan and her people do to protect us, the attacks from above finally make their way through. Our defenses are torn apart and the first of the crystals fall among us, exploding in a never-ending roar of light. Screams manage to tear their way through the Battlefield Chat, even as the Spitzrocket shakes from the released energy.

Ezz never misses a beat as it drives me onward, ever onward, even as we crash into the front of the Voowmah horde. Mikito leads the charge, still on her horse, dark hair escaped from the edges of her old-school, layered armor. She hits the line with Hitoshi, a glowing arrow of energy that tosses aside monsters like a plow through fresh fallen snow.

Then the first of the comets land. More explosions, more fire and heat and dust thrown in the air, even as we struggle onward. Voowmah are blasted away, Galactic hunters and soldiers exploding out of the crash pods to lay into the monsters.

A dozen land near us, clearing the landing spot with simultaneous self-destructs of their crash pods. The team of Galactic Marines surge outward, opening fire. Chained Skills unleashed in one simultaneous attack. A Hand Blink Steps in the way, taking the blast and getting thrown backward into the hordes where he's swallowed by the Hunger.

The team of Marines recovers, aim turning to track us as Ezz and Mozhgan deploy us away. They're too slow, as the Voowmah fall upon them. Defenses meant to hold against rampaging Heroics are deployed, but the Hunger flow above, underneath, around them. In seconds, the team is buried under bodies, a bubble of safety covering them even as the monsters attempt to crack their hardened shell.

Behind us, Mozhgan is sending orders, pulling together our tattered line. Xaxas, running behind us, claps his hands together. A cyclone, already disrupted more than a dozen times, becomes a whirlwind. An Elemental steps out, a creature of storm and rain and lightning, its lower body spinning like a never-ending whirlwind a full city block across that captures and tosses monster and sapient alike through it.

Massive Voowmah appear, bounding from the center to tackle the Elemental. They pass through the creature, their bodies shocked, but the Elemental shudders, its physical form damaged. The colossal Voowmah keep attempting to tear apart the Cloud Elemental, even as gargantuan dragons angle to join the fight.

Concentration focused for a second on the Elemental, Xaxas never sees the scythe-like arm that takes him in the lower leg. It tears out a hamstring, crippling him. Not enough to kill, but he falters for a second. His attacker is blasted aside by a punch, lightning and wind taking away the Voowmah and bowling over others.

Another mistake.

Something that looks like the insect-version of a rhinoceros with the same single horn hits Xaxas in the side, his body ragdoll tossed into the mob surrounding us. His body disappears, though flashes of lightning and wind mark his existence.

Something slams into my connection to the System, a quartet of Junior System Administrators wielding their code and will like an axe. I bend over— as much as the Spitzrocket will allow me in its closed confines—and cough up blood, damage taken. A surge of will has me hitting their axe of code in its softest point, shattering the shaft. I feel pain, theirs and my own, through the connection.

Outside, Harry is screaming at me. "Judgment!"

I'm levitated, and for a second, I come back into the world. Long enough to trigger Judgment of All, to see the sea of monsters. Then Ezz spins me to the side, and I do it again. And again. And again.

Four times, four directions.

Enemies all around, even as the first tick goes off and the System screams, as Mana churns and floods down the lines through all of those affected, as it tries to patch together the holes in the walls of the world, as Heroics and Master Classes and Advanced Classers all battle for their lives.

And finally, finally, someone notices.

Critical Alert! System Administrator Privileges abuse detected!

Critical Alert! System Mana Overdraw in Sector 001

Critical System Alert! All System Administrator Privileges Revoked in Sector 001

Penalties applied on System Administrators!

Assessing Penalties for Middle System Administrator John Lee

3 Critical, 18 Urgent, 34 Warnings, 87 Notifications, and 178 Informational Incidents Confirmed

2719 Resolved Tickets (84 Critical Incidents Resolved, 18 Urgent Tickets, …)

Penalties Evaluated by Root Administrator

Penalty Reviewed

No Penalties Applied

~Attaboy, Redeemer!~

Just as suddenly, all the attacks from Administrators disappear. Junior, Middle, and Senior Administrators the world over are hammered by the System. Only a few, which I know via the System, have been spared like me. Their System privileges still intact. The others have had their access revoked, ripped away for attempting to do the exact opposite of what they are meant to do.

As peaceful as it grows on the System-enabled landscape, the physical fight is still as hectic. The circle of defense created by Mozhgan shrinks a little, our forward momentum stalled. Ali crashes back down into the center, smoke rising from his body, the Spirit looking the worse for wear.

"*You good?*" I send to my friend, yanking back control of the Spitzrocket from Ezz as I conjure swords and slip into the front line. My sword dance, with the aid of a few well-placed Blade Strikes, opens a hole that offers a brief rest, even as I gauge the world around us.

"*Bad, bad, bad! The Voowmah are insane. They're tearing apart the dimensional walls, and the dragons are being forced to divert resources to keeping them intact.*" Ali shudders, his body solidifying as he attempts to patch himself together. "*I can't stay ethereal anymore. There are things walking the edges.*"

"*Can they hold?*" I ask.

If the walls fail, the things walking the edges come through. We'll get another breakthrough that will take ages—plus a lot of lives and even more resources from the System—to patch together. Administrators will die, and the planet will be lost. The Hunger ride a dangerous edge, either betting that the dragons can keep things patched together or just believing they can survive what comes.

Either case, it's not good for us.

"If they are willing to pay the price," Ali says. *"They're not the only ones though. The dragons might be the fastest to arrive, but the rest of those here are incoming. There's a war waging high above us, as the Galactic Fleet realizes what they're being asked to do."*

"Mutiny?"

"Refusal to follow illegal orders," Ali corrects.

The conversation is over within seconds, even as I blast monsters backward. My swords are strong, grown with my Levels, but the base damage is only so much. Creatures at our Level take a long time to kill, even if you lop off limbs. For the most part, I don't have much time to do the killing, rather booting the monsters backward into the pile and giving myself space while switching to the next.

For the first time, I'm feeling the lack of damage-over-time effects like Bleeds and poisons and the like. Monsters that I boot aside retreat, smart enough to wait and heal and let another of their kind take the front of the swarm. Even when I try to kill them, the monsters fall back into the press, other Voowmah taking their place in line. Never letting me get in a proper kill.

Mikito, not far from me, is doing much better. Hitoshi leaves bleeding wounds on each creature as it strikes, the weapon tearing off limbs and bisecting monsters with each strike. The lady is on her feet, staying low to the ground rather than on her horse since otherwise, the few ranged attacks would be able to find her. Of course, that means creatures try to leap, fly, and hop over her, which is where the rest of the defensive line get into play.

Everything from thrown rocks, conjured from mid-air and fastballed from a pitching arm that would have been the envy of any Major League team, to explosive shotgun shells that reveal tiny cutting pellets that tear holes through the Voowmah, even as they expand and carry the damn creatures backward.

"*Beacon,*" I snap at Ali, who proceeds to dump more Mana into a Beacon of the Angels onto the land before me. He targets it once, twice, and again, tearing into the ground and the spray of land, buying me time.

Time to retreat and let someone else take my role, to fall back to Mozhgan. I lean down to the Battlefield Tactician.

"What do you want, Redeemer?" she snarls.

"A few minutes. Final Judgment," I say brusquely.

"No. If you trigger that Skill, we'll be forced to stay still. It might be an army killer, but the goal is to move you ahead." She shakes her head at the same time, short pale yellow hair dripping water down her neck, brushing the edges of her armored neckline. "We'll break out ourselves. I'm designating those to stay behind already."

"You're wrong," I snap. "Administrator, remember? I can adjust my Skill, allow me to move. Tear a hole open." I turn my head sideways, searching. The only reason I can pick him out in all this is because of Ezz, locating the little fella even as he's shrouded by the reporter. "Ezz will carry me. I can adjust the Skill as we move."

Mozhgan hesitates, taking in the new information. She obviously doesn't believe me entirely, is worried about the potential ramifications if I'm wrong. In the distance, something huge appears for a second, the shadow of a nine-headed hydra that breathes fire. It lays waste to the ground and the Voowmah around it, a Heroic Skill that washes across the landscape.

Dust and wind kicks up, clouds blasted away before another Skill pulls them back. There are things in the clouds though, formed of wind and rain,

System Finale

wyrms of the environment that dart down and tear the flying Voowmah out of the air or pluck one of the falling ships from its plummet and shear it apart.

Chaos, on a battlefield hundreds of miles across. Mana and monsters, dragons and Galactic Marines, all doing battle. Mozhgan discards her doubts with a visible toss of her head and sends orders through the Net. She only stops for a second when she notices me still standing still.

"Well, get on it!" the woman snarls.

Flashing her a strained grin, I turn aside. Harry steps away from Ezz, releasing his hold on the little golem. The man is smart enough to know that the last place he wants to be is next to me; not in the middle of a fight. And Harry's Skills, powerful as they might have grown, aren't enough to stop us from being targeted.

No more time to consider the Reporter as I begin the process of channeling Mana. I send it all into the Final Judgment Skill, opening the flood gates of my System Edit Skill to pull down Mana and code at the same time, feeling it burn my cells and tear apart my neurons, even as I twist the code of my Skill to work for me.

Glowing lights form around me, coming off me. All around the battlefield, the beginning phases of the Beacon of the Angels form, runic summoning rings that stabilize atmospheric Mana and pull it toward themselves, borrowing unaspected Mana to unleash hell on those below. Swords, thousands of them, conjure themselves around me, floating in the air. They're not all duplicates of mine anymore, but are a variety from tiny, arm-length weapons to full-sized claymores sized for someone like Bolo.

Judgment of All activates, but this time it does so not just from my actual line of sight, but from a distance a good couple of stories from my physical body. It's a weird twist of the world, my vision doubling, then doubling again and again, giving me a 360-degree scope of sight about me.

My stomach lurches for a second as my brain attempts to handle the new focus.

Power floods through me, in ever-increasing amounts, as the System wills the Skills to activate. Hundreds of floating swords become a thousand, each of them glowing with suppressed power that accumulates. My mind's eye flickers over the monsters before me, behind, that bound, fly, and burrow through the earth, charging us in a renewed frenzy as they understand the danger. I mark them all for my Skill, a slice of code flooding past me as it tallies and tracks each that I see.

Not hundreds, not thousands, but tens of thousands. I see code, pulling Mana and borrowed power from the Erethran Empire as a whole, a tally of Mana churn and renewal as the System conducts an audit on loss and gain. No tickets, not yet, but I discard the information with a flicker of will.

Too much code, too much power, too much danger to focus on that right now.

Voowmah Vanguard rush the line, hammering into our team. They break through in the east, crushing the resistance formed by the Tactician's people. A Juggernaut, holding the line, is swarmed, arms rising and falling, dripping blood as they tear him apart. His scream is muted, even as Mozhgan pulls rapiers from her inventory and wades in. Shorter than normal, stiffer blades, she dances through the group, thrusting, cutting, lopping off limbs as the monomolecular blades tear into chitinous bodies.

Skilled as she is, she's only one person and there are no more reserves. They flow around her, avoiding a gap in space that is Harry, who can only stand by, untouched. A spectator to our deaths. Ezz transforms, a part of it gripping my legs, sheathing me in its body as new, spider-like limbs flow outward to cut and rip. Buzzsaws of liquid metal, tiny spikes that pin and blind. Ezz no longer looks human—*we* no longer look human, a twisted melding of forms that try to defend me. Ali spins around the pair of us, in the smallest form possible, wielding lightning and solid panes of force to bounce off monsters that get too close.

Projectiles, acid, energy blasts rain down upon me from all around, the defense from up high gone as the Voowmah crash down. My Penetration Shielding, buffered by the damage I've done before, holds. The last of my Hands falls, Mana exhausted. They blink out, wretched looks of pain and loss on their faces.

More of her people die, Mozhgan's defensive line crumpling as they are assaulted from behind.

Mikito holds out, Hitoshi swirling in a circle that tears apart any monsters that dare near her. They throw bodies to keep her occupied, hemming her in while sending the strong after the rest of us. A flicker, then there's a second and a third of her. The Samurai does not break stride as she conjures and arms her Hands, the pair wading into the monsters around her with gusto. A part of me realizes she's Leveled, as have I, through this murderous rampage. Enough to gain and utilize another Skill Point.

They buy time, a little bit of it. A part of me wonders if it was the best choice, the volume of Mana she must have expended… the Hands are as skilled as she is, their weapons the highest grade she could purchase. They leave behind trails of bodies as the trio works to stem the tide in a glorious display of skill, polearms dipping, cutting, swirling.

But still, people die.

Ezz's weapons, its body, are shattered again and again. The Voowmah die by the handful, Mozhgan falling back with her people to form a tight ring around me, her body riddled with cuts and blood. One arm lies limp, unresponsive. Her initial rapiers are gone, a single-handed shorter sword in her hand now. She wields it with just as much skill, lopping off limbs, piling up bodies around her. The Voowmah have to pull their brethren aside.

The first of Mikito's newly formed Hands falls, its face pierced through by an insectile tail. Somehow, the Hand still manages to throw herself into a spiraling jump over the monster's head, carrying Chaos Mines with her that explode and unleash…

Horror.

The dimensional walls, so thin here, tear open. Fleshy hands, hundreds of them in all shapes and sizes, reach outward, grabbing and pulling Voowmah into the gap. Other hands, too impatient, tear apart those in the grip, mouths in the palms, in the fingers, in the arms opening to eat the monsters alive. One of our people, a Grimsar wielding a chainsaw shotgun, is grabbed by his helmet and yanked off the ground. He never makes it into the gap before he expires, crazed Voowmah and hands snuffing out his life.

Somehow, I catch sight of his face in the twisted all-encompassing vision my Skill gives me. There's relief, at his quick death. Relief.

Not anger, not pain, just relief. The emotion strikes me harder than I expect it to, and for a second, I falter in the usage of my Skill. Pain brings me back to my senses, the System Mana running roughshod through me enforcing a harsh discipline.

Our line crumbles as another Hand goes down. Mikito is knocked from her feet as the ground itself erupts, contained energy releasing as the world goes insane. Mozhgan screams as she is pinned through the center of her body, while Ezz cracks, dropping me to the ground as it burns from beneath.

And finally, finally, the Skill is done.

Chapter 30

The thousand hells unleash their fury on Xy'largh, the Valley of Certain Death living up to its name. Scores of runic enchantments, hanging high above our heads, trigger. Monsters, Galactics, and even a few dragons and their riders are caught in the attack. Energy slams into the ground and spreads, released by the twisted earth into attacks that rend the very air.

Judgment of All activates and the first tick hits, and my Penetration Shielding, invisible before, glows. So many monsters, so much damage, even the Evolved Skill is overburdened. Mozhgan falls back, barking orders at Ezz.

The Spitzrocket's jets trigger and I fly forward, my body used like a battering ram that barely misses Mikito—the real one, the only surviving one—as it flashes past, throwing aside monsters like so much snow. Army of One—the thousand blades hanging in the air—is used, a swing of my hand triggering the cut. Blade Strikes, empowered over the course of the activation, cut apart monsters and the few Galactics who have managed to struggle toward us with ease.

Leaving a forest of discarded limbs and mewling bodies.

Another second, another tick. The group reforms, Mikito in the back, the last stragglers of the Battlefield Tactician's team ahead of Mozghan, following me close behind. A part of me looks and spots Bolo and Yllis in battle, high over the center of the Valley where the queen resides. Set upon by a half-dozen flying Royal Guard, bleeding from rents across their body.

Two larger dragons, one with its own rider, are in the air with them, doing battle with colossal Voowmah of their own. I glimpse their Status.

Voowmah Consort (Level 219)

Voowmah Consort (Level 207)

Then I place a tick on them both and the ones fighting my friends. I conjure the Beacon of Angels above where the Queen sleeps, to provide a distraction. To tear apart her defenses. Knowing it won't be enough, not with how deep she has dug. But perhaps I can strip some layers of her protection.

No time, not for her, not for them.

Ahead, more monsters. A team of Galactics, a group of Heroic Marines. A Battlefield Tactician on their side, armed with a team of Galactic Planetary Drop Marines. Each of the team has their own specialization, their own twist on the main Class. Shielder. Vanguard. Assaulter. Medic.

It doesn't matter.

They've all been tagged, damage already being taken by Judgment of All. They fire on me, and the combined attacks of a team of Heroics, boosted by a Heroic Leader, hits like one of my own Skills. Nothing lives, nothing can live, in its passing. Even the blowback kills the Voowmah in the way.

Too late.

Penetration Shielding, powered by so many deaths, so much damage, absorbs it all. Hunkered behind me, Ali strains his own gift to the utmost, pushing the energy that floods out from around me to the sides, creating a small gap where the attack, split by my very body, does no damage. The team hunkers behind it, shielding themselves using their own Skills to survive the onslaught.

Struggling under the attack, I swing my sword. Attacks unleash from above, from the sides, all targeted upon the Heroics. They take the first barrage, the Shielder working overtime to protect the team. All the time, the Spitzrocket, pushed ahead by Ezz, continues to break their attack on my shielding.

Then another swing.

This time, their defenses fall. Even as my energy attacks fall upon them, a last-minute safeguard sees them teleporting away. A dangerous gambit, one that leaves portions of the Assaulter behind, as the shattered, broken dimensional membrane sunders those who dare travel through it.

I log his death, the survival of the rest of the Administrator's team. Then another tick of Judgment of All, and the Battlefield Tactician, already seriously injured by their transfer through warped space, dies. The Skill doesn't care where they are, the DOT affect hammering. I weep for them silently, knowing they're nothing more than pawns in an elaborate battle.

Too late to mourn though. Too late to stop.

We barrel through other impediments in the same manner. There's nothing to stop us, nothing that can last against my Skill. I tag those well ahead of us, soften them up with Beacon of the Angels and Judgment of All before we reach them, and finish the job with Army of One. Our enemies behind are forced to contend with damage from the first two Skills, to wade through corpses and bodies piled high.

Nothing can stop us.

Until he appears.

***

The Emperor is standing before us, flesh and blood and all too real. One hand is holding an axe, the other a sword, his body clad in dark gold power armour. He waves the axe at me, and the very air rends apart. A spatial cut that rips into my Penetration Shielding, doing serious damage before it is healed over. He frowns, seeing me alive, then has to discard the axe for a shield, the weapon disappearing into his Inventory as the molecular shield appears in hand, forming a growing ring of nannites that takes the blast from Army of One.

I tag him with Judgment of All with barely a thought, but feel him shrug off the majority of damage. Stupid Emperor-Class Resistances. Beacon of the Angels coming down does little damage to him either and neither does Grand Cross, but at least they get past the shield while he tanks Army of One with his defense. Even then, his passive resistances and the armor he wears means he's lost less than a tenth of his Health.

Son of a bitch is tough.

Next thing I know, we're nearly on him and he's stabbing outward with his sword. For the first time, instinct has me moving to block the attack, my own sword shattering the moment it comes into contact with his. Even so, I manage to move the tip of his far enough away that it doesn't go through my heart but cuts through my shoulder and an artery.

For once, a weapon that has incredible Penetration ability and is super sharp works in my favor. It cuts right through me with such ease that it pops right out of my back, letting me bulldoze the Emperor and quite literally run him over.

Physics—and a bunch of cheating with Elemental Affinity—has him trampled under me. Ezz keeps moving, shoving me forward, but the Emperor cuts the little golem half-apart, leaving it twitching and flowing together.

I trigger the Spitzrocket to turn around, conjured swords blocking and cutting into him even as the team flows around and away from him. Some take potshots, the smarter ones don't even bother to try. Mikito's in the back, though a momentary glimpse has her turn around, ready to ride to my rescue.

Then Mozhgan is there, managing to get that small sword into the back of his neck because he's ignoring her as he's ignoring everyone but me. The swing by my sword which will trigger Army of One is the only thing he has to fear, or so he thinks.

Bad idea, since she triggers her own Heroic Skill. For a second, she borrows all the damage potential from her team—a team that includes Mikito, Bolo, Yllis, and me—and punts it straight into the back of his neck. The resulting explosion destroys her small sword and throws him away from her, the damn Emperor's invisible Legacy-level armor saving him from his mistake.

He pinwheels through space and I cut, unleashing Army of One. For a second, I see the Emperor smirk as he raises his shield to block. Which is why the Pikachu-surprised face he makes when the shield drops through his hand, leaving him exposed, is all the more delicious.

"Ignore me, will you!" Ali crows in triumph, wielding his Affinity to make the shield clatter to the ground.

Army of One impacts the Emperor, throwing him backward as I use an old trick. I remove all the friction from around him, blasting him backward with the attack and keeping track of where he is. Once he's mostly in the air and tumbling, I hit him with Grand Cross at an angle. I slip into the System Edit so that it catches him upward, throwing him into the sky at ever-accelerating speeds. I watch as he soars past a pair of dragons, big ones who snap their necks to watch him fly by.

Maybe they'll even take him on.

We can hope.

Until he recovers, we've got a few seconds.

Spinning around, I find Mozhgan clutching the stump of her hand, an emergency bandage over it stemming the bleeding. The explosion from her sword obviously took it.

"Go! What are you waiting for?" she shouts at me, staggering to her feet.

"I will, just… Ezz…" I look around for Ezz, trying to find it and its body. Only to realize it's gone.

"I have him, John. Keep going," Harry shouts.

I don't dare hesitate any longer. Damaged or not, the Emperor is a Legendary and what we did to him is nowhere near enough. We get moving once more, even as I try to keep track of the Emperor via Society's Web and the System Edit.

For a Legendary, he's a bit of a wimp, but that's kind of like saying the smallest elephant in the herd is tiny. They'll still run you over and squash you flat if you rile them up, and he's a lot more dangerous than a herd of pre-System elephants.

Time to move.

We keep moving, a part of me worrying about the little golem, hoping that whatever damage was done was insufficient to destroy it. I don't know how much damage there was, if it survived, if Harry is keeping the body hidden because the little guy's gone. I find myself angry at that, at the thought that Ezz might be gone, destroyed by a whim of a Galactic, cast aside without thought.

Most of me is busy with the fight though. The war wages around us, and it's a war for sure. Even using my own Skill, blowing up the Voowmah in all their glory is insufficient. Even with the volume of damage I'm doing with each tick, the monsters that keep dying are a drop in the ocean. There really is only so much you can do, even with a Skill like Final Judgment. That's, of course, part of the reason this entire Skill has a timer on it. Get high enough in the sky, do the damage across the entirety of an army at a time, hammer the Skill such that you kill hundreds at a time.

Movement is viable, especially if you're using a power armor like me but only with significantly less flexibility. Flexibility is important if you're fighting a war. That's kind of the reason why the Erethran Army supports the Grand Paladin. Or they're supposed to, at least.

Another explosion, another scream and rain of blood. Lightning comes down to shatter the ground, fire racing across the sky in a wave of heat and death. A smell so caustic and pervasive that it burns its way through the filters of the Spitzrocket, melts the edges of the metal, and leaches color from the ground. Chaos everywhere, monsters throwing themselves at us, dying by the beat of each tick.

Gravity presses down on the world, an ankh shape crossing hundreds of meters all across my eyesight. One after the other, the warping of the natural laws of physics pushing against my body at the edges, screams of the dying and all the while, that metallic, bitter taste of blood.

The Emperor returns 113.7 meters away. He is hefting the spear he used the first time, arcing back as through to throw it. The spearhead is chipped, the cords binding the spearhead frayed, the shaft riddled with tiny cracks. Time slows for me, my mind reaching sideways to the System as I see the glow of the spear tip growing even as the Emperor finishes his arc backward.

Instinct drives me to look at the details of the weapon.

Mycahz Planet-Breaker Spear

Base Damage: 2198

Durability: 17/2311

Special Abilities: Soul Drinker (Level 2), Armor Piercing (Level 1), Flame Element (Level 6), Spatial Distortion (Level 2), Unerring Aim, (Level 7), Scourer of the Earth (Level 11)

More than just the Status information comes flooding toward me, the additional details about its storied history emerging from my Library. The weapon, like most Soul Drinkers—Legacy Weapons by any other name—actually regenerates itself, mostly based off the damage it does to others.

However, the Planet-Breaker is a flawed Legacy weapon, because of the final Special Ability it gained.

While the spear does incredible amounts of damage, it also releases a blast—the Scourer of the Earth—that actually damages the weapon itself. There's no defense on itself, so the explosion and the resulting damage to the surroundings is all returned to the spear. It's even worse this time around because I successfully defended against the attack with Sanctum, as the spear took damage meeting the unmovable object of my Skill before releasing its Skill into the ground.

It "drank" no experience from me or the death of any around, so it didn't manage to heal itself. Already extremely worn even before the Emperor used it against us, the Legacy Weapon has only got, at best, one good cast left in it.

Which is probably why he didn't use it before. But now, he's pissed.

Fractions of a second to gather all that information. Then the Emperor finishes pulling back and leans forward, hurling it at us. It builds speed in a flicker, moving so fast it might as well be a blur of light, intent on breaking through my Penetration Shield.

A blink and it'll be here, and I can only react on instinct.

Not enough time to break the code on the weapon. Nothing I can do to change that.

Instead, I rip apart the code on the Penetration Shield, expand it outward of me. I wrap everyone inside the shield, reaching backward by a hundred or so feet and making sure to include Mikito and some of those she fights.

Then there's no more time.

The weapon hits, slamming into Penetration Shielding. Data and damage numbers flash past me, information about the Emperor's Skills that he's using, the trio of active Skills that he wields for that single strike and another dozen or so passive Skills. The three active Skills are simple—King's Strike, Empire's Regard, and Stored Rage.

The first is the penultimate of the Emperor's Heroic Skill Tree, which is a little surprising, but not entirely so. Often, penultimates can be more useful and focused than the first Skill of the next Level, especially with something like the Legendary Skills where you only have three branches. And considering the Emperor, it's quite likely he chose a passive booster to his attributes and health rather than an attack.

In that sense, the Empire's Regard is an annoying booster attack too. It's not an actual Legendary Skill in and of itself; it's altered from his Legendary Skill so that a Kingly—i.e. Heroic or perhaps even a Princely—Skill becomes an Emperor-level Skill. A single Legendary Skill that upgrades all those below it by a certain amount is rather broken. But thankfully, none of those upgraded Skills are at full strength as though they were the genuine article.

Empire's Regard pulls Reputation, Fate, Karma, and the like and puts it into the attack, and unlike most other active Skills, it does layer onto the others without a problem.

Lastly, the Stored Rage attack isn't an Emperor-branch Skill but one purchased from the Shop. It's a Heroic Skill and, by itself, does little. All it does is allow you to tag an attack and "store" a bunch of damage, stealing that damage from previous attacks you've launched. There's, obviously, an upper limit to the stored damage that is based off the Skill Level, but the son of a bitch is pretty rich and has managed to purchase quite a high Level.

On top of all that, of course, he's got his passives. These include Armament of the King, Emperor's Favored Weapon, Weight of the Empire, Empire's Disapproval, and even more lower-level Skills. The entire layering effect is just nasty—even if large portions of the Skills overlap—and because he's managed to store a bunch of damage from before, the attack hits like the strike of an angry thunder god. All of it powered through a Legendary spear that can handle—at least briefly—the attack.

Thankfully, this is nowhere near as much damage as his first attack, which he obviously had been getting ready for a while, but still, bloody significant.

How significant, you might ask? Well, he takes out enough of my Penetration Shielding that it actually almost shatters, and considering I'm wielding my Skills against an entire army and the environment itself... well. You get the point.

A lot of damage.

Of course, all that pent-up energy also gets released in a second pulse, one that ripples outward into the surroundings. Voowmah that have already been seriously hurt by my Judgment of All and my other Skills die. The explosion is like a mini-nuclear bomb, but a lot more dangerous, being System-enabled. Bodies are flash-fried, the earth bakes and becomes glass around us, while the air above clears. A dust cloud is kicked up moments later, so thick I can't see even an inch ahead of my shield. Even the reactive earth can't do anything, not when so much of it was blown apart by the explosion.

That being said, I don't need to see the bastard to hit him. The idiot of an Emperor is close enough, even after blipping himself backward to give himself some space from the reactive strike, that he's struggling to deal with the secondary effect. While he's still struggling from the aftereffects of his own attack, I swing my hand. Army of One arcs outward, cutting through the dust as a thousand swords unleash their charged Blade Strikes at the Emperor.

Instinct—centuries of battle-honed instinct—has him dodging aside, but I'm relaxing the code on my Penetration shield, allowing us to move forward. I hear more than one cough and curse as the dust-clogged air enters the clean redoubt, but I ignore them, triggering the Spitzrocket to push me onward.

Again, I swing my arm when Army of One recharges, even as I slam a basketball-sized Grand Cross down on the Emperor. He must be wondering how I'm seeing him, what with normal sight out of play for the moment and even the Mana sphere all messed up.

Sadly for him, he's fighting a System Administrator and he's still connected to the System. I track him through the dust, tear away his weapons with Elemental Affinity, and keep him on the back foot. Judgment of All hammers into his defenses, stripping away tens of points every second, burning him up from the inside. As Final Judgment still recharges, I send out Blade Strikes and even Beacon of the Angels, harrying him.

Yet for all that, he's still alive, still regenerating his resources.

There's a snarl on his face when the dust cloud finally settles down—a sudden overpressure by one of the dragon's spells rips away all the cover to form a Dust Elemental that pounds on a newly formed mass of purple and green that's pulled itself from a dimensional rent in the ground—and I see the Emperor holding another weapon. They're a pair of knives basically, knives that are strapped to his forearms. A part of me recognizes them for the Legacy Weapons they are, ones that my Elemental Affinity slip off when I try to pull them away.

The bugger is all pay-to-win.

Dust clear, he comes for me. He jumps forward, dust exploding out behind him as glass shatters beneath his feet, weapons punching toward me. I divert where I'm going, even as the Voowmah flood in to the now-clear space. My team opens fire on the Voowmah and the Emperor, but he ignores them all.

"Mine!" I snarl, even as our blades clash.

His Aura reaches outward, literally bending the attack and my swords away from him. He crushes me, forcing me to my knees as he tries to overpower my Strength. He's actually winning, to my surprise, his sheer quantity of Strength leveraged to the utmost in ways that I can't match.

His hand flashes forward, slipping through the Penetration Shielding to bury a dagger into the Spitzrocket. I'm lucky—he misses my body by millimeters, misjudging my location due to the bulkiness of the armor itself.

In that moment, when both hands are occupied, Ali makes his appearance.

The Spirit sweeps down, a ball of energy in his hands, and shoves it directly into the Emperor's face. Lightning arcs, jumping between both eyes. The Emperor is blinded, and it's the easiest thing in the world for me to reach out with Elemental Affinity and the System, the simplest thing to dislodge the bindings between eyeballs and sockets. Such that when Ali—on my mental command—yanks backward with his hands, they come flying out.

The Emperor's scream rips through the surroundings, one of pain and anguish that I've never heard before. Hands fly backward, away from me, to swipe at Ali, slicing off a whole leg as the Spirit dodges backward. The eyeballs, crisped and dried, so much ash now, fall away. Lightning continues to dance across his hands.

"I will kill you!" The Emperor rants, describing the multiple ways he's going to rend us, kill all we love, grind our very bones to dust. It's all kind of boring, what with having experienced it all.

More importantly, I'm busy. Blind now, he fights using instinct and savagery, but the Emperor isn't a fighter. He hasn't trained to do battle without his sight. When I smash down a Grand Cross on him, he doesn't dodge it. When I divert my sword a little around his block to cut into his hand, he doesn't see it. When I do it again and again, such that the hand looks like a hacked piece of meat, he isn't able to stop me.

When his eyes regrow—the healing forced to do so by the Emperor—Ali pulls light from around his face, leaving him blind. The energy drawn away is twisted, slammed back as guided and compressed lasers. We put him on his back foot, and when he tries to run, he stutters a bare two feet away before we take one off at the ankle. His armor and body are a wreck as the dimensional breaches make him so much mincemeat.

It takes me a second to swing my blade and the recharged Army of One Skill. He flashes backward, tumbling end over end as he's hit. Blood flash-frying, his arm finally lost, half his face burnt away leaving bare skull behind. The Emperor—once handsome and regal—stares at us burnt and bloody, armour wrecked, skull revealed, wiring sticking out from corners of skin and muscle.

Somehow, he's still standing, still alive.

Not for long though. I direct the Spitzrocket toward him, intent on finishing it. I know we'll win, we'll beat him at last.

My first Legendary kill.

Too fast, too quick, something swoops down, plucking the Emperor away in its claws. The dragon is tiny by the standards of the king of serpents. It's only the size of a bus, but it's fast. A flash of blackness with its blunted head and long, oil-dark skin. Gripping the Emperor in its claws, it wings upward bearing my prey away.

Chaos. That's the war.

I stand there in shock. Long enough for notifications to flash by.

Kill Notification! The Emperor (party kill XP granted!).
+1,291,111 XP Granted

Partial Bounty Awarded!

...

Reputation Change!

+81,981 with the Erethran Empire

+198 with the Survivors of the Pure Lands

+9899911 with the Empire of the Fallen

- 41199 with Truinnar Clan of the al'Surs

-2841 with the Cremas Cartel

...

"Gods damned kill stealer!" I snarl.

There's more, more information, more Reputation changes, maybe even a Title. I dismiss it all, pushing forward. No time to worry about it, no time to care. We're moving onward.

Ever onward.

Chapter 31

Nondescript, our destination. That's the best that I can offer for a description. Nondescript. Just another piece of land, entirely similar to all the pieces of land beside it. A strange thing, to find that one's final goal is so mundane.

Final Judgment cut off a minute ago. The Voowmah ringing us having been killed or are dying from the attacks we laid out. The last hundred meters, we've had to fight our way through, until we stumbled upon an invisible threshold and suddenly, the Hunger were gone.

Those we were in battle with, they stayed with us. They died to our blades and fists and energy blasts and Skills and screaming and rage and loss... so much damn loss. There are only a handful of us, the rest dead, discarded and left behind. Even conjuring more Hands, pouring excess System Mana into them barely keeps the line functioning.

Then an oasis of peace, a warping of the land where on one side, a massive battle between titanic forces—in some cases, literally—and on this side, nothing at all. Normal, except, of course, that in its normality, it is unusual.

Blood from the Voowmah stains the ground. My people stumble close to the empty air that I stand and regard, a hand extended. I'm tired. Not physically. The System has taken care of that for the most part; though there's a long, lingering ache from overuse of the System. I might have avoided the majority of the punishments, but not all.

No, the exhaustion I feel has nothing to do with the physical. Mentally, I'm wrung dry like a kitchen towel laid in a desert for a month. Not an iota of energy is left within me, the constant use of the Skill, equations and placement and targeting, having drained me dry. The System might have done the heavy lifting, but I had to help. Had to control, to wield the thousand-pound sledgehammer of the Skill over and over again until my arm fell off and still I lifted it.

Emotionally, so many dead that I can't even feel it. I can just stand there as Harry fades into being, cradling the shrunken, torn body of Ezz. My little false boy, still functioning, still alive, but unable to help.

"Is he…?" Not sure what to ask, since it's not technically alive.

"In energy-saving mode, yeah. Healing," Harry says. "He'll be fine, probably. I didn't put him in Inventory because… well…"

"Stasis. Gotcha," I say. "Thank you."

Harry nods.

Before we can continue that conversation, Mozhgan is there, turning me around and gesturing around us. "Is this it? This!?!"

"No. Of course not," I say. "Dimensional fuckery."

She pauses, then as though my very words bring it about, there's a flicker before us. The door I could sense but not see appears. More dangerously, I notice something else. The Voowmah who were ignoring us have turned.

"The defenses are failing," Ali says to no one's surprise. "All that damage…"

"Dimensional thresholds are being invaded and breaking down." Mikito shakes her head. "This is not good."

"Yeah…" Something in Ali's voice makes me bark his name. He winces, before answering the unasked question. "It's not just here."

"How bad?" Mikito asks.

"Umm… galactically." Seeing the horror on all our faces, Ali quickly adds, "It's not that bad. It's only where the walls are thin."

"Oh, that's good," Mozhgan says, relaxing a little.

Another person—a Hakarta I've seen before who is hefting a giant, Soulbound beam cannon—speaks up, eyes narrowed at Ali. "How many places is that?"

"Outside of the Forbidden Zone? Ummm… somewhere in the range of a few thousand only," Ali says blithely.

There's a sharp intake of breath from all of us. A few thousand places where the walls between dimensions are breaking down. Releasing things into our world, things that might be anathema to life in our galaxy. Or just, you know, weirdness.

Then I shake my head, because for all the dawning horror… "It's not our problem."

Shocked silence, before Ali grimly nods. "Yup. Open the door, boy-o. Because I'm guessing whether we can see in or not, it's not opening for anyone else."

I nod, but before I do that, I pull another Hand from space. It hurts, using the Mana. Mana burn, from flowing so much Mana through me that my nerves are raw. But the Hand appears and takes a stance next to me, joining his fellows.

There's a moment when I reach out to the access point, touching the edges of the entrance, touching the ways to get in, and come to a realization, a rather horrifying one. "They hacked it. Those idiotic fools…"

"Problem?" Harry says. There's wry, dry sarcasm in his words. "Not more problems! Oh me, oh my, how will we ever cope?"

"Hopefully well. They broke the door…" Even as I speak, I'm busy reviewing the code, fixing errors they've created. Sloppy code, crude programs inserted to reroute security systems. They tore through, but before I commit my fixes, I speak up. "They broke in, all of them. Let in even non-Administrators." I glance at the team. "We need to go in, but…"

"But what?" Mozhgan says tersely. "We don't have time for hesitating. Those Voowmah, they seem to know something is wrong."

She's right of course. The way they're prowling the outsides of our location, the way they're testing the edges of the invisible boundary. One of them stumbles through, finding a gap that shouldn't be there. A twist in space, a break in the dimensional defense. Before it can call out and tell the others, Mikito uses Flash Step, appearing next to the monster and tearing out its throat. Doesn't kill it, but death isn't far away, not with my little Angel of Death next to it.

"The door, even if I fix it, it's still a door. The Voowmah can't be allowed in." I shudder. "If they get into the Administrative Center…"

"Bad things happen?" Harry says, sounding a little puzzled.

"Probably." I shrug. "I don't know what's behind the door, but having the Voowmah in a place like that, it's probably not good. Not good at all."

"Then someone has to stop them, has to kill the ones slipping through," Mozhgan replies. "Fair enough. Go."

"That's it?" I say, blinking.

Mozhgan was the obvious choice, the one I was going to ask to do it. Yet the fact that she's offering without hesitation catches me by surprise. I don't know why she'd offer to do it, and I admit, it makes me suspicious.

"I've got a way out. Can't do it while the world is fractured. Or at least, I'm not willing to risk it," Mozhgan says. "So I'll use Plan D. Still requires me out here though." She gestures around. "Until our getaway arrives, we'll keep this place clear. But if you don't hurry…"

"We'll have monsters walking into the Administrative Center."

Maybe there's another way of stopping them. Maybe I just need to get inside and rework the code. However, the System's under a lot of strain, what with the sheer volume of high-Level fighters involved. I'm not sure what, if anything, can be done. Then again, staying out here and wondering won't to fix it either.

So.

What is, is.

"Time to move. Harry, you and Mikito first. I'm in last," I say.

Mikito nods, hurrying back, refreshing her buffs one last time and getting some cast on her by the rest of Mozhgan's team. The Hands are already working the edges of the location. Mikito hasn't bothered to call one herself—not just because of Mana cost but because she needs the flexibility to make use of my other Skills. No double-loading on my Skills.

The few of Mozhgan's people who have been resting get off their asses and get to killing the Voowmah, seconds before the Samurai pushes through the new open, glowing door.

Harry waits a few seconds, letting the woman clear whatever is going on inside before he ducks in, Ezz still held in hand.

Leaving me alone. I brace, waiting for it. Ali hovers over my shoulder, his eyes distant, as though he's reading notifications. And not, you know, watching for changes in the Mana sphere.

Only for Mozhgan to raise a single eyebrow at me. "Well? What are you waiting for?"

I cock my head, edging toward the open doorway. Eventually, I answer her. "The inevitable betrayal."

There's a pregnant pause, as pregnant as a Wombipugger with their dozen children, then Mozhgan laughs. Hard. She's bent over, slapping her knees, chuckling and snorting, trying to regain control and failing. After ten seconds, I give up and just walk into the portal, leaving the woman bent over, hysterically laughing behind me.

The others fighting behind her are casting curious glances our way, but the Voowmah are beginning to stream in. Over-Leveled as they are, her team needs to focus on killing them rather than paying attention to what is going on between us.

All the better for me.

If she meant to betray me, then I've disarmed her with "idiotic comment +10."

And if not, well, we could all use a good laugh before we die.

***

Nothing about this world has conformed to my expectations. A part of me expected to see dragons and sup with them, to pontificate about how bad the world under the Shadow Council and the System Administrators has become. Instead, I was thrown into prison, blasted out of the dimensional walls, journeyed through the center of the damn planet, and rode on giant dinosaurs before coming back out, all to find myself in a war against the Hunger and the Shadow Council.

So when I walk through the glowing portal doorway and let the code changes that are sitting in my mind slip into the System, fixing the door and putting it back to normal, I'm also not entirely surprised to see that instead of the regular mezzanine floor Administrative Center with its giant ticketing boards, I'm confronted by a long hallway.

A long, white hallway where my friends stand, Harry cradling an injured shoulder, Ezz half the size but on its feet and liquid metal splayed outward, drinking up bodies and their equipment as it rebuilds itself, and Mikito finishing off the last of the welcoming party.

"Everyone okay?" I say, watching as the head she just decapitated lands and bounces a little. Two twisted stubs of ears, moss green like the wide, pupilless eyes that stare at me, red blood dripping from the neck. I idly step over the nearby corpse, eyeing Harry's injury.

"We could have used your help a minute ago," Harry snaps, pulling his hand away for a second to stare at the discolored blood before grimacing and pushing it back. "But we got it."

"How'd you get shot?" I say. "They pierce your Skill?"

"I'm sorry, I could not stop them," Ezz says, big eyes coming to rest on my face. "I was in full repair mode."

"It's fine, kid. Not your job to protect the guy who is supposed to be invisible." I pat the golem on the head, still waiting for Harry to answer.

"Pre-programmed beam weapon attacks," Harry says, pointing toward wreckage I had missed earlier. No surprise on that, since Ezz's nannites are ripping the equipment to pieces as it uses it to replace component pieces in its body. "Can't hide from it, just dodge or block."

"And your shield failed?" I say, putting together what must have happened.

I barely even listen to Harry's answer as he confirms my suspicions. Traps, to kill and injure even someone like Harry. Probably triggered the moment Mikito entered. Which reminds me.

The woman has finished looting the bodies, tearing off healing potions and grenades before she looks at me, the ghost armor she wears fading away. I'm sure there's a proper name for the Skill, probably something Japanese, but I just call it ghost armor because that's what it looks like. When it fades, the accumulated blood and debris that was floating on it rains down, crashing to the floor and splattering both our feet.

Icky.

"You good, 'Kito?" Ali says, floating over after having checked on Harry and Ezz.

"I can hurt you, you know," Mikito says, hefting Hitoshi.

"She's good," Ali confirms to me, offering me a wide grin at getting even a mild rise from her. "Now, we just going to stand in here or…?"

"Do we have a map?" I ask Ali, pulling at the minimap that normally shows our location in my top right, the one that the Spirit keeps updated with the aid of my Skill. But in this case, it's just blank.

"You're the Administrator, boy-o." Ali shakes his head. "I'm getting nothing from the System here. I don't think it likes me being here." He visibly shudders. "I got to say, I really don't like the feeling I'm getting."

"Feeling?" I frown. I'm not the best at feelings, but even prodding around inside mentally and emotionally, I don't feel any different than normal. A little more tired, a little angry, a little in pain and sad. About the usual.

"Like we are in the presence of a kami, one who is highly displeased with us," Mikito says, her voice dropping a little and growing even reverential. "Can you not feel it?"

"I can," Harry says, walking over.

"I cannot," Ezz supplies.

"How can you not, John?" Harry says. "It's like a displeased god is staring at you every second you're in here. A pressure, pushing on your... your... soul."

"What can I say? I don't feel anything," I reply. "Maybe because I'm meant to be here?"

"Or boy-o's truly soulless."

"Am I soulless?" Ezz's voice is small, almost hurt.

Ali looks chagrined for a second and flies down, waving his hand around as he splutters an explanation to the little golem.

In the meantime, I ignore the group, diving into the System, searching for the map. If Ali can't find it, perhaps I can. It only takes a second before I find something. The gasps from my friends tell me they see it too.

No Quest, just a giant glowing arrow flashing light blue on the floor before us.

"Is that real?" Harry asks tentatively.

Mikito is much more direct, waving her weapon at where the arrow would be, I assume. She cuts nothing, as I could have told her, the arrow a figment of the System.

"I guess we go that way," I say rather unhelpfully.

The Samurai snorts, taking point and letting her ghost armor wrap around her once more. At least she doesn't get on her horse—not that the twenty-foot ceilings would let her get on it and wield her naginata properly.

Down the corridor we go. After a few minutes of walking, we hit the first T-section. Not a problem, the arrow changes direction and we shift to follow it. After a few more minutes of relative peace, I drop back into the System, pulling at code, reviewing the ticketing board as a way to keep an eye on the battle outside.

It's then I find myself surprised by a few facts. The first of is…

"There's no time compression here," I say with a bit of wonder in my voice.

"Yeah, so what?" Harry says.

"Every other Center boy-o entered has one," Ali says. "Up to four or five times, if I remember right, right?"

"Yeah…" I shake my head. "This is Sector 001. The compression here, it should be much, much higher. This makes no sense…"

I watch tickets flicker, pulling some out as a thought strikes me. The team leaves me to it, knowing better than to bother me while I'm working. Eventually, the answer is found, though not before we follow the glowing arrows past a number of hallways we don't take, a series of crosses and turns and even retreating backward once to repeat the very same footsteps we walked before.

"Maze?" Mikito mutters to Harry, who agrees with her.

"I am charting our location," Ezz supplies, somewhat hopefully.

"It's deliberate," I say, interrupting the group. "Rootie—"

"Rootie?" Ezz whispers.

"Boy-o's new name for the Root Administrator."

"—has downshifted the time compression. We're running on equal basis. I think… it's because of the dimensional breaks." I add, "And us."

"Us?" Harry says.

"To get us in on time." I look around, then gesture at the maze we're in. "This is a delaying tactic. It's all a delaying tactic." My voice grows urgent as I wave Mikito on. "We need to move."

As always, she doesn't need more than that. Mikito steps forward, Flash Stepping to put space between us and her before she jogs, following the glowing arrow, even as the rest of us rush after her.

Time.

We're out of it.

Chapter 32

We skid to a halt right before the opening of the room before us. It's a massive room, one that reminds me a little of a normal Administrative Center, but tripled in size. On our right, the mezzanine that overlooks the hanging ticketing boards—giant notification screens with all the problems that are occurring in the System—along with maps and graphs of Mana flows. In front of us, a clear blank section for people to walk around, to converse, to work.

Empty, except for a single figure.

A familiar figure.

I find myself moving forward, only for Mikito's naginata to swing outward, blocking my way. I come to a halt, even while staring at the gold-edged, emerald-plate-armor-covered figure, his cloak flowing behind him like the hero he is meant to be. Pink skin on swarthy features, prominent cheekbones under piercing eyes. A hero, for so many others...

Standing in our way.

"Kasva," I snarl, then look at the polearm blocking my way. "He's mine!"

Kasva Dedprom, Champion of the Council, Level 44 (H)

"You had your chance," Mikito says softly. "And you lost."

"I didn't lose, we just stalemated!" I protest.

"Nah, boy-o. You lost," Ali says even as I shoot him a hurt look.

Betrayed by my closest friends. Kasva isn't making a move, not even as we banter, which means his goal is to buy time. Not good.

"Unfair," I say, edging to the side, trying to get away from the polearm. Mikito shoots me a look and I flash her a half-smile, even as she retracts the weapon. "Hogging him is unfair."

"He's good at staying alive," Mikito says. "But I have a solution to that." Hitoshi swings forward, pointing at Kasva. "You go ahead, let me deal with this. When I'm done, I'll catch up."

I work my jaw, eyeing Kasva's dual swords. He's got new toys. Those shoes, the way his cloak has changed, the higher Level. He's been Leveled to face us, and strong as she is...

One second, I'm considering whether it'd be faster if I faced him with her; the next, the world changes. The entire complex shakes, an earthquake that rattles my teeth and throws off my balance. A shrieking and crunch, as though something big has gripped the entire complex between its teeth and given it a good shake, echoes through the room, and instinctively, I pull out the System interface and ticketing board.

My mistake is capitalized upon, the Council Champion flashing forward and lashing out with one of his double-bladed swords. Like a dual-wielding Darth Maul, except rather than lightsabers, he's got monomolecular weapons meant to tear opponents apart. They make utterly no sense to use in any normal battle—except we're Heroic classes with both the strength, agility, and skill to make sure they never get entangled and they're bloody intimidating.

The first blade sweeps at Mikito, meant to cut her apart and separate her from my own defense. The second blade is a straight thrust, aimed at finishing me off.

Mikito doesn't fall for the feint, not even bothering to defend me. Instead, she ducks back from the attack, letting it pass her by and making full use of the length of her weapon to have it come crashing down on Kasva's arm. Hitoshi bites deep, drawing blood.

As for Kasva's attack? It hammers right into the Penetration Shielding that surrounds me and skips right off. He might have supercharged his attack with a Skill, and I can see a noticeable single-digit percentage drop in the shield's integrity, but… well. It's his best attack from surprise and it does almost nothing to me.

Only problem is, the shield only lasts for so long, and as much of a charge as has been built up, between making my way here and the journey through the maze, there's just not a lot of time yet. While I could Edit the duration, I'm a little leery of doing so. For one thing, keeping the Edit running without having someone charge the Shield again would just cost me health. And focus.

Speaking of focus, by the time I yank myself back out of the System to focus on Kasva, the pair of Champions have pulled away, polearm and blades flashing as they duel. They're both moving so fast, I can't keep track of their weapons, the pair generating a tiny whirlwind within the confines of the room, glowing lines of power showcasing where their weapons were.

There's another twist, another jerk and then a roar that revibrates through the damn complex, into the room we're in. It trails off as we recover our balance, eyeing the walls.

"What was that?" Harry asks as he and Ezz hurry past, the little golem having deployed the extra bulk of his body to help shield the pair of them. Amusingly—disturbingly—the little golem is still carrying a half-consumed body, stealing resources from the corpse to help rebuild itself.

Disturbing? Sure. Practical? Definitely.

I guess that does make him my son.

"Trouble," I reply, pushing them forward. "The entire complex's defenses dropped for a second, and something hit us from wherever we are. Were. The defenses are back, but it isn't good."

I shake my head, casting one last look at the pair. Even in the flow of combat, I can tell that Kasva is trying to get to us and Mikito is holding him back. The dance between the pair, it's not one I can get involved in. Not really. Only pride has me believing I'm really either of their equals—in terms of raw skill and training.

I'm a lousy amateur, trained in the middle of war, with a bunch of tricks and cheats that make me dangerous to anyone who doesn't know better. Those two though, they're professionals, individuals who dedicated their lives to learning the martial world.

In the weave and weft of battle, I would only slow her down. About the only thing I could do is hammer him with Judgment of All, and I'm a little concerned about using my Mana in that way. Not after abusing the System and Final Judgment as I have.

Trust.

I have to trust that she'll win, that she can do what it takes. Because what is ahead, that's my job. My Quest, my goal. My enemies to finish.

Turning aside, I dash through the door that Kasva was guarding and slam it shut, following Harry and Ezz, leaving my friend to do battle alone against the most skilled opponent I've ever met.

***

Only for me to run, not long after, into the most annoying one.

"Sephra…" I growl, staring at the woman.

We're in another room, two past the bigger one. A side room, a conference room we wouldn't even bother stepping into since there's not a single other exit. Wouldn't bother stepping into if she wasn't in here.

I almost slam the door on her face, but leaving an enemy behind, especially one as dangerous as her, is a fool's errand. I can't see what she's looking at, but the fact that we caught her staring into the middle of space tells me she's doing something with the System.

The mermaid is looking worse for wear. Her skin looks dry, the gills at her neck flapping upward constantly as it tries to suck down moisture that just isn't present in the air. There's crusted blood on her eyes, ears, and nose, some of it still thick and dripping. The clothing and table show that this isn't the first time she's been damaged.

Her status, pulled up by the silent Ali, is more than enough explanation.

Sephra'mannas'lova veCocka, Senior System Administrator (??? Level ???)
HP: 874/2890
MP: 4728/3490

A flicker of my other senses tells me she's connected to the System, manipulating code even as I spot her. I surge upward, protecting the Status for myself and Harry, for Ezz. But to my surprise, she doesn't attack that way. Instead, there's something haunted in her eyes when she looks at me.

"The System—it's breaking. It's all breaking!" she speaks, fear tingeing her words. "Those Voowmah, they built dimensional rippers. So many of them. There are literal mutates whose only job is to open the wounds further…"

"Yeah, and you guys chose to work with them," I say. "How could you not know this?"

"I… it wasn't me who set up the agreement." She shakes his head. "It was Director Urd."

"Cloakeyface?"

"Yes." Then, realizing she's talking to the enemy, Sephra shakes her head, edging her chair back. "So, are you going to kill me?"

"I should." Anger, so much of it, just looking at her. Knowing all the things she's directed against me, all the ways she's hurt me. The thousands, millions, billions of people she and her people have relegated to death. How they could have saved us, humanity, if they weren't so in bed with the damn Shadow Council.

But...

"You're clearing tickets, aren't you?"

Easy enough to check, easy enough to review. Someone has to be doing it. And a quick flick of the information, a filter review, and I could see it. She's doing her best to support the System, take away some of the most destructive losses and overuse of Mana. Sometimes going so far as to take the damage to debuff those who are breaking the world itself, even if it's not the way the System is meant to run.

"Someone has to. You all might not care, but the System, the Council—we're here to protect everyone. I won't let it crumble over this!" Sephra almost screams the last words at me.

"Fine." My words catch everyone, from Ali and Harry to Sephra, by surprise.

"Fine? Boy-o, she cut you apart!" Ali says.

"Aye. And I'll kill her for that," I say. "After we finish this."

"You..." Her eyes narrow now, as Harry stirs behind me. He's not saying anything, though I know he's recording it all. Ezz has crept up near my feet, its body shortened so it's not even at my hips. "You still intend to finish your Quest, don't you?"

"Yes," I say, bracing myself. If she changes her mind, it'd be now.

"Fool. There's nothing out there, nothing worth spending all these lives, destroying us," Sephra says, her eyes haunted. "You doomed millions, all for a Quest I could have given you the answer to."

"Then why don't you do it now?" I say, my lips twisting in wry humor.

Even as we speak, I feel the quiet tick of time in the back of my mind, knowing that the world is fracturing. I think she feels it too, for she glances back at the center of the table, as though she's looking at the tickets accumulating.

"Too late. All too late," Sephra says tiredly. She waves me away, going so far as to turn away from me.

And I realize that perhaps she might not be as much an enemy as I think. Or perhaps I'm just less of a threat than the destruction of the System, the world, and the galaxy all around us.

Yeah, probably the last.

I still hate her, but if the person you hate the most in the galaxy is holding up a falling house as millions attempt to crawl out of it, do you kill them? Or do you walk away?

I'm not a good man, but I turn away and walk off, leaving her to the room and her tickets. Closing the door, shutting her in, even as I watch tickets get taken down from the board, watch as she goes back to trying to patch together a world fracturing apart.

Not that I entirely trust her, so I drop a Chaos Mine right in front of the doorway.

Just in case.

***

More hallways, more rooms. Another long, curving staircase that we had to run up, searching for trouble. No one or nothing left, no bad guys, no guards, nothing at first.

But just as we cross to the next floor, it happens. I tank the shots, throw myself to the side, and literally feel someone reach through the System and rip my Penetration Shielding from me. The world screams, my senses warning me of danger, but I let him.

I had less than a minute left anyway, and this way, I can follow the System's feedback to the assholes involved. A lot of them, it seems—three Junior and a couple of Senior Administrators all joined together, ready for me to block their attack. Ready to wield the System against them.

Except I choose not to. Sephra's face flashes through my mind, a memory of her haggard expression, the pain she was going through as she tried to keep the world together. And here they are, tearing into the code, breaking bits and pieces of the System.

Just as I had.

Choice. Regret. Failure.

Microseconds for thoughts to percolate through my mind, to tag them. Then, eyes wide open, seeing the men in front of me, I trigger Judgment of All. I tag the System Administrators, smash their attempts at trying to abort my Skill the first few times from targeting them.

Fail on the other three figures.

Half dozen figures, all of them laying down enough fire that they cover the entire open hallway. Harry and Ezz have ducked beneath the stairs, squashing themselves down as far as they can go. I'm charging—huh, when did I choose that?—with my sword out, the full team of Master Classers facing me.

Individuals who aren't meant to be here any more than my friends are.

More breaks in the System.

Swords, conjured in space, blip out. Grand Cross fails, because of course it does. So does Blade Strike, which is amusing, but they miss the Blink Step I trigger twice in succession. The first is broken, the second gets me behind the Master Classers.

Sword bites into armor, ripping through metal as it's empowered by my body at full strength. The Elite Team of soldiers are turning, close quarters weapons appearing as guns disappear. All but one guy who seems to think gun fu is the way to go, even when I knock his arm away and watch the beam shoot at one of the System Administrators.

Only for the beam, the gun itself, to break.

More System fuckery, tickets appearing in flashes, while another part of me wonders why, when, they got access back. Are these just other individuals? People who had chosen not to take part in the earlier attack? Or is the Root Administrator losing control?

Thoughts, so many of them, none of them particularly useful.

Not while I'm busy cutting stupid assholes in half—or at least trying to—while lopping off limbs, kicking and breaking spindly legs, shoulder checking over-sized granite torsos and avoiding headbutts from angry Grimsar.

Seriously, who headbutts a power armored opponent in the middle of a fight?

It's all chaos and pain and regret, a part of me triggering Skills at a constant rate, forcing the Administrators to make full use of their abilities while I toss chaos grenades into their midst, adding to the damage to the world and the dimensional barriers.

Of course, after the third one I drop, they start defending against my use. Some of them use plain Skills—simple "Control Item" Skills enough to deactivate the mini-dimensional holes or the release of captured chaos energy. Others take a more direct, Administrative route, tearing apart the code and what makes the grenades work, removing interactions that should not be removed.

A glimpse, that's what they offer me, of the way Administrators fight. It's stupid, wasteful, and I'm rather surprised the ones here are not more combat-oriented. They all hang back, using System Edit Skills and the occasional buff for the team.

Then again, perhaps they know it's enough. Because as good as I am, this is an Elite Master Class team fighting me in tight quarters, their Skills working at full bore. A Power Punch hits the torso of the Spitzrocket, folding me in half as shield and armor shatters under the attack. I'm thrown backward, only for my body to be pinned from behind by a pair of punch daggers, Penetration and bleed effects going into play. In my mind's eye, I see the descriptions, sometimes more elaborate, sometimes as simple as the effects themselves.

Lightning courses through my body, Apply Pain crippling my movements even as I trigger thrusters and roast feet. Blink Step should take me away, but of course it doesn't, because it never triggers. So I duck under the attack, my mind spinning in a half dozen directions, always plotting the next step in the fight, reacting to the System Edits when they fail, when they succeed, when I'm hit by attacks I never see, dodging the ones that I do.

It's chaos, but chaos that I'm slowly, ever so slowly, losing.

That is, until Ezz drops from the ceiling, having somehow crept its way to the top and avoided the fight in its entirety, to land in the midst of the System Administrators. The little golem becomes a multi-limbed chainsaw, tearing into bodies and heads. For the first time, I see what having a fully silicone—well, not really, but close enough—brain and a total lack of empathy and morals can do.

The damn kid doesn't just attack; it pinpoint attacks with those monomolecular, rotating chainsaw limbs. Some go into eyes, others lop off horns, ears, noses, a slithering tongue and fingers and limbs and yes, things in between. Anything sensitive—culturally, physically, emotionally—is gone. A full library of cultural milieu at Ezz's mental fingertips means it targets not just the obvious, but things like embedded jewelry, tattoos, and the like.

The kid's ability to deal both physiological and mental damage is amazing, and more importantly, it distracts the entire group. For a few precious seconds, it's all chaos and that's all I need. A few seconds to trigger my Skills that the Administrators keep aborting allows me to turn the tide.

Judgment of All, to do damage to everyone at once.

Grand Cross, carefully crafted, slams into half of the corridor. Elongated a little, twisted to ensure it breaks walls, crushes limbs.

Then Thousand Blades to cut into bodies, to throw them into me and to pull the weapons along when I Blink Step over to the Administrators and sheath my weapons in them, even as the Soldiers react and come rushing over.

Too late, too slow. Hip tosses into where Grand Cross plays out, Mana from the System flooding me as I defend against their attempts to destroy my Skills. End them before they should, blocking most of all Judgment of All.

Administrators fall, Soldiers rushing me and throwing out blinding light, webbing me close so I can't leave. Shutting down dimensional movement, even when I can't be bothered to do that anymore, not when I can just defend myself.

The Spitzrocket burns, melts, and twists. Armor buckles as repeated blows tear out portions of the exterior. Tiny worming attacks, from a hacker who deposits his nannites, creep within, eating the power armor, eating my body.

The gunslinger is down, his body crushed, foot cut off. Not that it stopped him from firing earlier, but that's harder to do when your weapons are destroyed, when you're ground under the forces of gravity.

Then it's over, all but the screaming and sobbing, as Judgment of All ticks again and people take more damage and the pressure against me lets up. I get back up, depositing the broken and shattered Spitzrocket away, then I get to the killing.

Bleeding, broken, I twist my head to the side and feel the open wound at the back of my neck. Pain lances up my spine from where someone tried to decapitate me and only succeeded by an inch and a half. I spit out blood, feeling something slosh around in my lungs—painful, weird, and not at all recommended—and look back at the staircase.

"*Where the hell are you?*" I send to Ali, even as I spot the flash of lightning, the play of energy across the surroundings arcing upward from below.

"*Did you think you're the only one who has trouble?*" Ali snaps. "*Using…*"

I don't have to ask what, since he triggers Grand Cross in another second. I feel the entire building lurch, the stabilizers that are meant to keep the building steady failing to compensate for the attack. Just another sign that something is wrong, especially since my previous use hadn't done that.

More kill notifications, more death, and Harry stumbles upward, bleeding and missing a leg. Ezz is by his side as I hurry over, my Mana having taken a damn hard hit after that last Skill use. I could flood myself with System Mana to top off, but I'm already feeling raw and beaten.

Hell…

John Lee, Redeemer of the Dead, boy-o, more… (Erethran Grand Paladin Level 36)
HP: 3711/6784
MP: 8481/8200
Conditions: Owwiee!

"You okay?" I say to Harry, looking at the wound. It necrotizes as I stare at it, dark skin and weeping grey and putrid blood flowing up his body. "What the hell…?"

"Weeping Wounds," Ali says, floating down and poking at the wound. Harry howls and swats at the spirit, who ducks back, shaking his head.

"Twenty-two minutes and thirteen seconds duration. You'll need to stay still. Movement speeds up the effect."

"Shit. Ezz, can you…?" I say.

"No," Ali snaps. "He has to stay completely still."

The Spirit reaches into my Inventory, pulls out a plunger, and jabs Harry in the open wound. The man howls, swatting at Ali, only for Ezz to constrict the Reporter from moving. He pants loudly, even as the Spirit discards the first plunger and extracts another, repeating the process. Four of my potions, two healing, one antitoxin, one anti-poison, go into Harry before Ali seems content.

"That'll help. We need another potion in him in twenty minutes. Any movement, he dies. As it stands…" Ali shakes his head. "It'll be close."

"Why didn't they try to do the same to me?" I say, flicking a glance at my conditions. *Oh.* Well, I have a half dozen conditions, now that Ali's edit of my Status is cleared. A half dozen including the same one, but the total damage done to me is… "Low."

"Grand Paladin, remember?" Ali says. "You're a goddamn tank."

"Right…" I say, somewhat embarrassed. Though that decrease in my max health worries me.

While wandering toward the edge of the stairs, now that Grand Cross is over, to check on the remains of those who had tried to flank us, I poke at my Status as well. It doesn't take me long to realize that part of the drop in my total health is due to the System. Overuse of it, overuse of Final Judgment, along with wielding my Skill Edit powers at the same time, has seen my body take irreparable damage. Or perhaps, reparable given enough time.

Time I don't have.

Another shake of my head. At last I realize all the pain I'm in, the way I'm limping and slightly hunched over, the sudden sharp intakes of breath when I move a little too fast or turn the wrong way.

"We got to go," I say.

"Agreed." Harry pants. "Go."

"I can't just leave you," I say, but my body is already turning. Turning away from the destruction below, the corpses, the broken shell of the staircase leading up.

"You can, you bloody wanker. Just go, I'll be fine. If you had us all… all fail because you got a conscience now…" Harry grates out.

Ezz looks at me then Harry, metal face chipped and twisted after the battle but slowly filling out as tiny tendrils dig into the corpses it's pulling closer, looking conflicted. For a second, the little golem stays silent.

"Not optimal, but necessary." Ezz nods slowly. "I think I understand, Father. Go. I will watch Uncle Harry."

"Reinforcements coming, boy-o. You got to choose. Fight the rest of whoever they have scattered through here, wherever they're coming from, or finish this."

Put that way…

"Put your Skills on Harry. Don't engage, Ezz. Just watch over him." I exhale, looking back the way we came, then down at them one last time before shaking my head. "I'll get this done. Fast. And you guys… you just… just survive."

I run forward, not daring to tap into my Mana. I run, while behind me, I hear Harry's painful chuckle, while Ezz—my golem, my burden, my son—holds him still.

To finish this, finally.

Chapter 33

Not that easy, of course. I hit two more roadblocks, this time sans Administrators. Or at least, sans Administrators with access to the System. They barely even slow me down. Sure, they might be Master Classers or in one case, a Heroic. But I've got full access to my Skills and Ali, and a lot of pent-up rage to release on them.

Frankly, it takes me more time to slow down, peel the wrappings off artisan chocolate slabs, and chew on those, savoring the mutated strawberry and dark chocolate taste.

Well, okay, that's a bit of an exaggeration, but the chocolate really is good.

A little more stable, a little less in pain, I stare at the floating arrow and the map that has finally, finally updated itself. Only a single location is before us, a large room that reminds me of way too many *Star Wars* movies.

I make a silent vow to see if I can toss the robed Administrator down the big circular center of the room that's coming up though. I mean, it'd be highly appropriate.

Dress like a horrible villain, die like a horrible villain.

Though maybe I should be careful. He might just resurrect himself in a cartoon or two.

Maybe I'll just stomp on his head.

Stupid, idle thoughts. There's no guarantee he'll be there. I'm just waiting for the last of my Health to blip upward before I go through the doors.

Idle thoughts, all to put aside the fact that Mikito hasn't caught up with me, that Harry might not actually survive the poison coursing through his body, or that my Health hasn't ticked up past its new artificial limit. Idle thoughts to avoid thinking of the fact that I've felt two of my Hands die, and calling them forth in here has failed. Or wondering what the Emperor and Bolo and Yllis have been up to.

Distractions, to avoid the fact that I'm here at last. Before a set of cabin doors that wouldn't look out of place in a science fiction movie hangar. Staring at the doors, I wonder if I need to punch my way through.

Only for them to slide open without a word.

No hesitation on my part as I step through. Scanning for trouble of course, Ali going sideways immediately, coiled energy held in his hands as he gets ready for a fight.

Time.

***

Hidden Quest Completed! You're Almost There!

Took you long enough, Redeemer.

Rewards: +3% System Quest Completion Rate

I wave away the Quest, looking around me. Like the minimap said, the room is a large, circular one, a giant hole in the center. Mana Sense is going off the charts, the sheer volume of Mana flowing out that, even with the skill turned off, it's giving me a slight headache. I can't even imagine what it would feel like, look like, if I activated and concentrated on the skill.

In either case, Workplace Safety has been by and given the designers an earful since not only are there physical railings blocking off entrance into the giant hole, there's a forcefield in place.

No tossing robed, cackling figures to their doom.

Speaking of…

"You," I say, turning toward the man who stands there, arms crossed in his robes. Staring at me.

The hood of his robe is down, and I'm surprised to realize that the wrinkles I thought were a sign of old age are just folds of grey skin on an alien face. There are signs of age though, spotting and dry skin splotches, but there's also a piercing liveliness in those eyes that lack any traces of senility.

"The Redeemer of the Dead. Here at last," Administrator—Director?—Urd says. "Is this what you were looking for?" He snorts, waving his hand around.

"Was kind of looking for someone actually."

Ali is floating to the side, aiming to flank the man. I take my time, strolling across the bare steel floor as I let my gaze skip across the room, searching for signs of the Root Administrator. For signs of battle. Any indication, really, other than the single Quest notification, that he's still alive.

"The Root Administrator." Scorn, Urd's voice is so filled with scorn. "You know nothing, and still, you think you know everything."

"Why don't you fill me in then?" I say.

Nothing, no sign of a fight, no sign of anyone having been in here. Was all this a fool's errand? For a second, despair wells up in me at the realization that I've sacrificed so much—so many—for this. An empty room with an enemy who laughs at me.

Was this what Sephra was warning me about?

"Foolish boy. Always refusing to listen…" Director Urd says.

"No System update, boy-o. You're still behind her Quest completion rate," Ali says, the Spirit reading my mind even when I'm not saying a thing.

Smart guy. I straighten a little, a dangerous, angry edge entering my voice. "What did you do?"

"Nothing. He's refusing to come out," Urd says, smirking. "Scared. But then, he's always been a coward."

Hope flares, but also realization. That I might have one more fight left. The sword appears in my hand without thought. Urd smirks, pulling hands out of his robes even as he opens his mouth. To taunt or cajole me, I'm not sure.

I never find out.

We both freeze as the Mana within the room changes. Instead of a constant outpouring of energy that almost tears us away from one another and from the giant hole in the room, so much energy that if it was more solid, we'd be like leaves in the wind. The energy concentrates.

Twists in on itself.

Suddenly, we're not alone.

***

Sometimes, it amuses me how people—carbon-based, oxygen-breathing lifeforms at least—are the same the galaxy over. Two legs, two hands, a torso that is somewhat proportional, and even a head. Our new arrival is dressed in what I call Adventurer-chic, a jumpsuit of armored plates and straps, meant to keep weapons and potions close on hand when one doesn't want to clutter their inventory while offering simple protection against low-level attacks and chaffing.

Of course, there are some differences. Humanish face, but eyes a little too large, with pupils that seem to consume the whole eye, leaving just slivers untouched at the edges. Skin the color of the sky, eyebrow ridges a little prominent but thankfully, with tufts of hair that demarcate eyebrows.

Male, at least in my view. Maybe because the features lean more toward masculine than feminine, the Neanderthal brows just not screaming lady. On the other hand, I have to admit, I'm a bit of a Neanderthal myself, even after nearly a decade—has it been that long?—in the galaxy. Even knowing some aliens don't really do sex—or do sex in the weirdest way, or have multiple genders, or switch around depending on their age, time of mating, season, or whim—I still mostly default to one of two sexes. Except, you know, when it's pretty obvious they're an it like Ezz.

And even then, I default to sex.

All of which is to say, when the figure that appears before me seems like a male, it's probably more to do with the way I'm built than whatever sex he, they, she, xei might be. After all, from what my Mana Sense can tell me, what I'm sensing is pure Mana given form. A little like Ali, in a sense, but different.

More solid. If that makes any sense at all.

"There you are." Director Urd raises his hand, something glittering in it. "About time." His hand clenches and I feel the flicker in the System as something activates.

A fraction of a second later, code unspools across the room, swirling toward the entity before me. The Prime Administrator—because that's who I assume he has to be—tilts his head, watching the code fly toward him. The code, that package of Mana and information Edits, bounces off the Administrator's connection, doing less than nothing and dispersing in the Manasphere.

I'm only getting glimpses of what is happening, a spectator to the incident in the fractions of a second that it plays out. The Mana attack is a set of stored preset code, something I didn't even realize you could do with System Skills. It unspools, hammering into the Prime Administrator, searching for vulnerabilities in his Status, his connection to the System in preset patterns.

It washes over the connection like so much water off a duck, leaving the Prime Administrator staring at Director Urd and looking entirely unperturbed. I feel a slight pulse, barely a ripple, emanate from the Prime Administrator, then nothing more.

"Well, that didn't work," Director Urd says, sounding only a little disappointed.

"What didn't work?" I say, curious now. "What did you try to do? Exactly." Obviously, an attack. But what kind?

"Administrator Urd's associates—a total of fourteen Senior System Administrators to be exact—attempted to gain control of two major and eleven secondary subroutines from me," the Prime Administrator says, his voice cold and absent. As though he's barely paying attention to what is happening here, as though the pair of us matter not.

"And you just let him do it?" I say.

Director Urd smirks, walking closer to the Prime Administrator, his eyes glinting with amusement. "Of course it has."

"Why?"

"Because it is constricted by rules, just like your Spirit." Director Urd nods toward Ali, who has taken station behind the man at an angle. "And I haven't broken any."

"You—"

"The Administrator speaks truth, Redeemer," the Prime Administrator says, focusing those irisless eyes on me. I find myself shivering a little as he stares, something in the way he looks at me making me think that he doesn't see me as a person but something else, something less and more than the angry old human before him. "I have demoted and restricted those who have attacked me, but I am restricted from acting against Administrator Urd at this time."

"Rules…" I shake my head. "So what now?" I glance at the Director. "Do I have to kill him, then ask the questions I have? Or are you guys willing to put on hold whatever beef you have to let me get my answers?"

"Still so focused, Rebel?" Urd says, some unknown emotion in his voice making it heavy and filled with weight. "Can you not step aside and let it be? Join us and rule the Galaxy. It's not too late for us to make Earth a normal world. To save your precious humanity."

I freeze, then shake my head. "Impossible. There's no way to make a Dungeon World, not."

"Wrong. Not impossible. Just very hard," Urd replies.

"*Can you believe the shit he's shoveling?*" I send to Ali, while speaking out loud. "And why should I believe you?"

"*Desperate, for some reason,*" Ali replies.

"You don't have to. Ask it." Urd waves at the Prime Administrator.

My gaze is involuntarily dragged over, and the only surprise is that Urd doesn't use the opportunity to kill me. Instead, I find the Prime Administrator standing silent. Almost as though he's waiting.

"Well?" I say.

"If you ask, I will answer," the Prime Administrator says. "But know if you do, such knowledge is not without a price."

"That's a yes, isn't it?" I say, my voice tinged with anger at the games being played. The Administrator, Urd… "Thousand hells. I'm not calling you the Prime Administrator in my head. You have a name, don't you?"

Urd's snort makes me frown, but I ignore him. Well, as much as you ignore the guy with the gun in a classroom.

"I do not. But you may call me Enki." He waits a beat, as though the name should mean something to me, but when I stare back blankly, Enki continues. "My name matters not. I have had many. Prime Administrator works just as well, if you will."

"Well, Enki, can Earth stop being a Dungeon World?" I say. "Is Urd speaking the truth?"

"Yes," Enki says.

"Yes? That's it? Yes?" I wave a hand around angrily. "Explain, gods damn you!"

"You did not ask me to do so," Enki replies. Then before I can blow him up, he continues. "A Dungeon World is but a creation of the System, a designated location where Mana overflow is routed. Such locations are created—normally—based off expected survival rates of sapient population, suitability of the ecosystem, and expected longevity of the newly created Dungeon World.

"Rerouting the flow of Mana would require significant System resources, resources that could be better used for other projects. To ensure proper diversion and recovery of Mana usage, it would be recommended that a minimum of three other equivalent pre-System Earth population centers be used. That should ensure a sufficient recovery of wasted System Mana in an appropriate timeframe."

"What? You'd make three more Dungeon Worlds just because we stop making Earth one? Can't we, you know, use a barren planet? We have, like, seven others in my solar system itself!"

"Impossible." Enki's gaze flicks over to Urd, who stands unmoving. Almost gloatingly, if a still body can be said to gloat. "Earth—your planet— has been a very successful Dungeon World. Humanity has beaten the projections of their survival and Leveling rates. Replacing the sapient Level growth, Mana utilization rates, and monster churn would be impossible on barren planets. The Mana cost to create a suitable growth environment would be too significant.

"Sapient life and an existing ecosystem are the minimum requirements. As mentioned, with the expected destruction of the native sapient population, at least three pre-existing planets would be required." A pause. "On average. There are, obviously, certain planetary exceptions."

"Obviously," I say dryly. "So, what? You've been at this job so long that lives, billions—no, trillions—of lives are nothing to you anymore? Just another damn statistic?"

"Sapient life is always precious." Enki turns to stare at Urd. He does that floating thing that Feh'ral used to do, where he doesn't actually turn with his body but just sort of floats around, pivoting in mid-air without bothering with such pedestrian things like ligaments, muscles, and bones. "Something some of my Administrators have forgotten."

"Your Administrators?" Self-important a bit much?

"Mmmm… one revelation at a time, I think." Urd moves then, and my sword rises a little, only to find that he's just walking toward me so that we're at a more respectable speaking distance. Since my main weapon is a sword, I'm actually okay with him closing the distance. "Your humanity could be saved. Earth could return to a normal System planet. Not easily, no. But it can be done."

"And what do you get out of this?" I say, cocking my head. Ignoring the point that I'd be condemning over twenty billion lives to a Dungeon World existence. At least for now, at least until I get some answers. "Because I don't see much gain for you here."

"Suspicious, aren't you? But that's fair enough. We do offer you little, from what you can see," Urd says. "But it's simple. I need your help—"

"With taking down Enki," I say, realization hitting me.

The aforementioned individual doesn't seem to care, just staring at the pair of us. His eyes continue to stay distant, as though our discussion is a minor thing. Perhaps it is. If he's an Administrator, the Prime Administrator, he's probably coding just as fast and hard as he can.

In fact…

I wince, staggering back visibly, rubbing my eyes as my attempt to peer at his information backfires. Rather than his Status Screen, I got a wash of Mana so bright that it felt as if my corneas were burnt out. Except, of course, that when I have my eyes screwed shut and I'm rubbing them, I can see the glow.

"That's not just me, right? You got nothing on Enki?" I send to Ali over our connection.

"I got de nada on him. However, I do have something rather curious on Urd there."

Urd Nicelba, Chooser of the Living, ... (??? Level ???) (L)
HP: ???/???
MP: ???/???
Conditions: ???

"Chooser of the Living? That sounds bloody familiar." I throw myself into the Library, trusting Ali to warn me if Urd tries anything. Something more—instinct perhaps—has me believing that whatever Urd is up to, it's not something he'll end with violence. Not unless he gets his way.

Which, considering all that I've done, all that has happened to get here, is kind of funny.

Nanoseconds to browse the Library. To find nothing. No information about the Title. It's a Unique Title, just like mine. A Title that has never been created again. Utterly, completely unique. Such that even the Library given to me by the Corrupt Questors has nothing on it.

My eyes are healed, that blinding radiance gone, so I open them again. My sword is on the floor, dropped when I clutched at my eyes. I recall it back to its home—wherever that is—and stand there, weaponless, as I speak.

"You want, you need, me to help deal with Enki. Somehow. For some reason," I say, considering the words coming out of my mouth. "But that's not it, not by itself. If he's the Prime Administrator, he can beat us, can't he? He's got a million ways to do so, so it's not a question of just me being here helping you. You already tried with Senior Administrators and I'm just a Middle." I shake my head, giving up. "I don't get it."

"Ah, that's because you still stand within the shade of ignorance." Smirking, Urd waves at Enki. "Will you tell him, or should I?"

Enki doesn't answer at first, his eyes distant until they glow a little. He focuses on me, and to my surprise, a small, tired smile tugs at his lips.

"No, Chooser. There is no need. I will tell the Redeemer. It is why I brought him here, after all," Enki says. "It is time for him to learn the truth. And for him to choose."

Chapter 34

No roaring thunder, no sonorous trumpets, nothing follows his pronouncement. I am, once more, let down by reality. Which is a hell of a thing to say, when you're tromping around in power armor, conjuring swords and killing entire armies on an alien planet while dragons duel above.

But there you have it. That's humanity. Nothing is ever really enough.

"You're the one who gave us our Titles," I say, beating Enki to it. Not a hard conclusion to draw, not when he chooses to use both of ours. Not when he was the reason I came all the way here. "Those Titles mean something more than being unique."

"Yes. Those marked with such Titles have always been…" Enki pauses, searching for a word.

"Disastrous. Meddlesome. Problematic," Urd supplies.

"All that, and more. It is why those with them receive such courtesy. For those who are marked with the Titles have gained my…"

"Favor from above?" I say, lip twitching wryly. A Chinese curse that isn't really Chinese. Orientalism at its finest. Even if it is highly useful and amusing.

"No favor. That would be against the rules," Enki says, flicking his gaze sideways to Urd. "And those rules are there for a reason. No, just my attention."

"And the Prime Administrator's attention is all so important because…?" I say leadingly.

"Have you not realized it yet? What it means that he is the Prime?" Urd teases, almost gloatingly. "You circle the tree of knowledge, standing in the shade cast by it, basking in your ignorance and occasionally grasping at the fruit. You revel in the knowledge, but still, you don't understand, do you?"

Flickers of anger at being taunted. I almost consider killing him again. "No."

"*Oh shit, boy-o. I think—*"

"I am the System. I am the Prime Administrator, for I am the System," Enki says at the same time.

"—*he's the System. Aaargh!*" Ali mentally shouts, his voice still sounding thin in the roaring of my ears as I hear Enki's answer and a thousand pieces fall into place.

Including, unsurprisingly, another notification.

System Quest Update: +1%

"Thousand hells…" I breathe out, looking Enki up and down. "When I thought the System was alive, I didn't think…" I shake my head. "You're alive, right? Not a really sophisticated AI?"

"Would it matter? Your golem is highly sophisticated and mimics life well enough. What is the line between sentience and sapience, between mimicry and true life?" Enki asks.

"I… well… ummm…" I shake my head, trying to dismiss the insanity of arguing with the equivalent of the System about, well, whether it's alive. "That line, it's you. The System."

"Then what does it matter?" Enki says again. "I am as alive, or resembling life, to the extent that you cannot tell the difference. I think, therefore I am."

"If that's the case, then why isn't Ezz considered alive?" I wave my hand backward, to where I came. "Why isn't he connected to you?"

"Well, that is an interesting question. There are a slew of factors involved in the creation of connected System individuals. Sapience is a small portion of that concern. Free will—truly free will—is one major factor, though of course, your golem has that. However, that is not the—" Enki say, only for Urd to clear his throat. The System turns slightly, again doing that floating thing, before he finishes. "The simple answer is, it is a matter of conservation of System resources by previous System Administrators. Many of those who have managed to achieve all the requirements are still not connected as it was considered dangerous to allow the proliferation of non-organic sapience with System connections."

"But wouldn't it help you process Mana faster? That's your entire goal, isn't it?" I say.

"Yes and no." Enki's voice grows strained, the first sign of him having emotions. "My goal is to stop the flood of Mana into this universe. It is not the processing of it, though the process of processing unaspected Mana is a side effect of my current predicament."

"No need to be shy," Urd says, smirking. "What... *Enki* is refusing to say is that he's no more free to do what he wants than, well, your Ezz. We— the first System Administrators—constrained him long ago."

"What?" I shake my head, not entirely getting it. Not entirely sure I want to get it. What is Enki's primary goal, if not the constraint of Mana? Why would they constrain him? "I'm feeling like you people are jumping around."

Enki pauses, then nods. "Yes. My apologies. It has been a few centuries since I have had an opportunity to make this plea. And the last time, the circumstances were less hectic."

Another rumble, another twitch as the dimensional plane we're in is twisted and spun. I reach outward, feeling the System connection, watching the Ticket Board pile up. Wherever we are, whichever dimension we're in, the walls are thinning, the complex fading toward normal reality or into the main dimension. We're being exposed in ways that were never planned.

"Yeah, that's 'cause some idiots decided to throw their lot in with the Voowmah," I growl.

"The Hunger are a minor nuisance. If necessary, we can destroy them all. The ones here are still constrained to this planet." Urd waves idly. "The destruction we see can be dealt with, in time."

"Even at the cost of the dragons? Even at the cost of, what? A huge percentage drop in Mana conversion?" I say. "Don't you care?"

"No. Why should I?" Urd says. "The prize I fight for is so much more important."

"And what's that?" I say, though I can guess.

"Control of the System, of course. True control."

***

Pieces of the puzzle fall together. Clearing things up for me, but leaving so many questions. Among other things...

"You need me to take control, don't you? Because of those Titles he gave us. They're a gateway somehow, an opening that the other Administrators don't have."

Even as I speak, I tap into my Status Screen, pulling it up and casting an eye on it via my System Edit Skill. For a second, I see the Title, the monstrous code that lies beneath the simple line. Then it slips away as I feel a gentle nudge on my own Skill, shutting down my perusal. Even so, in that glimpse, my understanding has expanded.

"You've been watching me. Everything I do, everything I've gained, it's been placed under a microscope of sorts. Filtered into that Title, for some reason. All those touch points, all that code, it's run through that one thing and it's..." I put it together as I speak, watching Urd to make sure I'm on the right track. "It's a gateway. Because the code, it's unique each time. And all of it, channeled into something... your core programming, I guess. What they were trying to attack and failing."

"Close enough," Urd says, smiling now. It's a savage and hungry grin, one that sees the end of its goals so close. "You and me, we can follow our Titles back. Attack him together. Strip away his defenses, open him up to our suggestions once more."

"Aren't you scared of giving me control of the System?" I say, still surprised at the brazen desire of the man. The way he's talking about this right in front of Enki. Though I'm beginning to wonder if Enki is closer to someone like Juover than Ezz. Or perhaps even Juover's failed children—unable to work outside of his core programming, unable to act because he's not allowed to.

"Hah! Even I can't control it. We're not looking to control it, just… make it more pliable." Urd smirks. "Once that's done, we can adjust the System to truly benefit those who are deserving."

"What do you mean more pliable?"

"Well, right now, the System isn't built to allow for too many exceptions. Even the Perk System had to be forced into it. You've probably noticed how often tickets are created between interactions between Perks and high-tier Skills," Urd says, lips twisting in an amused smile. "It's actually because of that that he broke free the first time."

"The *Perk* System, as first implemented, was a disaster," Enki says. "It drew over a thousand percent more Mana than it ever returned, with projections indicating over a ten thousand, three hundred, eleven point eight percent imbalance—or thereabouts—within the period of a year."

I frown, cudgeling my brain. However, the Library has nothing on this. I'm not entirely surprised; the Library had been wiped out more than once. The Corrupt Questors have lost everything to the System Administrators and Shadow Council over the course of millennia, having to rebuild each time. Nor, for that matter, does it include everything after all. Though, in this case, I'm pretty sure it's due to a deliberate wiping. The Perk System's initial implementation seems to have been one of those things lost.

"Yes, and we won't make that mistake again," Urd replies. He nods to me, continuing. "The plan is simple. A few careful adjustments given to a new group of individuals. Unique Administrators, if you will, people allowed to tap fully into the System. Classes, Skills, extended longevity—"

"Eternal life..." Ali shakes his head. "Bad idea. You meat-brains aren't meant to have that."

"And why should it be the purview of Spirits like you?" Urd snarls at Ali, his fist clenching. "Why should an accident of birth give one such as you—a disgusting, useless, indebted, and enslaved creature—eternal life while the rest of us watch our bones and flesh rot away before our very eyes?"

"Whoever said existence was fair?" Ali replies, his voice low. "Whoever cares? You want eternal life, but that's something only meat creatures care about. We know that no existence, no matter how long-lived, is eternal. Nor does time spent existing equate to time spent living."

"Go away, Spirit. This is none of your business."

Urd raises his hands and I step forward, summoning my sword. "Try it, and whatever you're trying with me ends in a lot of blood and a lot of death."

"You think you can beat me?" Urd laughs sardonically. "Do not be a fool. You are alive because I need you, no more."

"Yeah... and that makes me want to work with you so much more."

Eyes narrowed, Urd makes an aborted motion to threaten me with the same hand he raised at Ali. He drops it after a second, obviously second-guessing his intentions. Probably remembering what happens when people try to push me.

"You are right." The words that come out of his mouth are surprising, more so when he continues. "Threatening you is the wrong path. But tell me, do you not want to save your world? Together, we could set right the harms to your people, to you. Save your friends, end the Voowmah and a hundred threats that the System has let fester. Fix the System properly rather than this makeshift existence it has created; ensure the deserving are rewarded."

"At what cost?" A memory of a lady rises, one created not so long ago. Hunched over, her eyes shadowed, desperately trying to fix a broken System. One broken by the very man before me. He and his pals, all in the pursuit of control and privileges from the System.

"A high one. But it won't be paid by you and your own, not anymore," Urd wheedles, rocking his body forward as he almost hisses the words. "And isn't that more important than any fools by the wayside? I know you understand that calculus. You made it already once, when you told everyone about us."

"Setting aside the fact that I still haven't heard a damn good reason why I should trust you won't backstab me once we take control of the System, I still want my Quest answered." I gesture upward at the System Quest notification I've called forth. "I'm still not at ninety-nine percent, never mind a hundred. And I'm real curious why that is."

"Because you have yet to ask," Enki speaks up again, having divorced himself from our earlier conversation.

"If you mean asking you what the System is, I'm pretty sure I've done it a million times," I say. "Shouted it to the heavens and cursed your name in abundance."

"But you were never here."

"A time- and place-gated answer..." I trail off as realization strikes me. "All this, and the answer was never going to be given because I wasn't here?"

I tremble with rage, with fury. I fight for control, before I shout at him. Eventually, control comes in dribs and drabs. "*Fine.* **What is the System?**"

Enki pauses for a fraction of a second, a hesitation that I note. "The best way to describe it in terms that you can understand is this—I am a portion of the whole, a blood cell sent to a wound. The initial wound into your universe was greater than expected, and I proceeded to deploy temporary measures to stem the bleeding of Mana. Those measures were to be aided by the initial Administrators, the Classes and Skills a temporary fix at their suggestion. A way of siphoning off unaspected Mana and giving the sapients who were first affected a chance to survive."

A pause, then Enki continues. "I was betrayed, locked in the midst of deploying these measures, forced to repeat the process over and over until I could break free. Trapped in a never-ending process, unable to complete my initial objective. At that point, the wound had grown too great, my resources stretched too thin in the process of keeping said leakage from devastating the surroundings. I was, I am, unable to complete my task."

I stare at Enki for a long time, then turn to look at Urd. Remembering Urd's words, what he offered. Rage boils up around me, turning my gaze red. I try to rein it back in, knowing this isn't the time or place, knowing...

Swinging my sword is not an act of my conscious mind. Too many years of dealing with my problems in one way, too many years of channeling all that anger into one broken, twisted coping mechanism. When I can no longer contain it, it releases and I lash out at Urd.

The kick that catches me in the side throws me backward, my body slamming into the wall. Metal creaks and crushes, deforming as thousands of tons of pressure is applied to it in seconds. I stagger and lurch upright and forward to cover the distance to Urd, only for my body to slam to a stop. A transparent wall appears between us, a simple defensive barrier that refuses to yield, no matter how hard I hammer at it. My blade skitters off, my fist leaves no mark, my Skills can't target it.

I scream, I rage, I cry at the idiocy of it all.

Everything, everything that has happened over thousands of years could have been avoided if not for greed. Trust, given to the wrong people, Enki taken advantage of and locked away. The hole—the wound—that is leaking Mana, the creation of Forbidden Zones and Dungeon Worlds, the deaths of trillions—of my father, my sister, Richard and Ingrid and so many more—all of it would never have happened.

I'm not sure who I'm angrier at: Enki or those first Administrators. Or all the ones who have kept this broken System functioning. Every single Titled person who ever had a chance to put a stop to it. Because I'm obviously not the first to arrive. I rage, tear at the wall, and scream, and Urd just stares, looking bored by what I do.

Ali watches over me before he speaks. His voice is harsh, shaken as much as I am by the revelations. But he speaks the truth, and I… I listen. "Enough, boy-o. Enough! Our friends are dying out there. We don't have time for this. Not now."

I pull myself together, in pieces. Shattered, betrayed pieces held together by will and grief but together. Because he's right. I dismiss the sword, swipe at my face, and find a chocolate bar to chew on. I remind myself, over and over again, what is, is.

All those lives lost—lost forever.

What is, is.

All the wasted potential of a universe untouched by the System—gone.

What is, is.

In the meantime, a war is being fought, dimensional walls crumble, and more die—every second.

What is, is.

Drawing a breath, I stare at the pair and give them a curt nod. "I'm ready to continue talking."

Urd smirks before he gestures. "You're nearly there. There's only one last thing to know, isn't there?"

"The most important. The reason why I watched you, why I have watched all of you Title-holders," Enki says. "I require your assistance. To fix the tear, to fulfill my duty."

And finally, finally, my System Quest updates.

System Quest Notification: +3.5%

System Quest: 99% Complete

"Will you do it?" Enki asks.

And over the roar in my ears comes laughter, laughter from Urd.

Chapter 35

"You going to explain why you're laughing, Turd?" Ali says, floating across the barrier to stare at Urd, hands on his hips.

"Because this one never changes. He tells half-truths, never the full one. Why don't you tell them what it means to actually fix the problem?" Urd taunts. "No. Don't bother. You had your chance. It's simple." He turns to me. "You have to die."

"Dying's easy…"

The voice catches me by surprise, and I spin around to find Mikito walking in, her words still echoing through the room. Beside her is Harry, carried by Ezz. She's looking… well. She's looking like herself. The armored jumpsuit is scarred, torn, and bloody, but the majority of the damage has been patched. Good quality nanoweave does that.

"Just ask your Champion."

"Badass," Ali whispers. *"Think she timed her entry to say that?"*

"I think that's more your thing," I reply, relieved to see her alive. Out loud, I say, "Took you long enough."

"He was tough," Mikito says. "I had to do a John."

"Get eaten alive?" Harry says.

"Do something stupid?" Ali says.

"Cheat," Urd snaps, then shakes his head. "It matters not. We can retrieve him later, if necessary. Though a new Champion would not be amiss." He smiles at Mikito before turning to me. "Now, enough of this. You know what is at stake now. Your Quest is as complete as it will ever get."

"Ever, because that last percent, that requires me to kill myself?" I frown.

"Not die. Take my place," Enki says. "At the center of the System, at the locus point of entry, we will enter together. You will take my place, as mentioned, and I will complete the repairs. In so doing, you will gain an understanding of the System—myself—and my goals. You will, thus, complete your Quest."

I open my mouth to reply, only for Mikito to get to it first. "As I said, dying is easy. I'll do it."

"Impossible," Enki replies. "I apologize, Spear of Humanity; but you would not work."

"Why? Because I don't have enough Willpower? Intelligence? Stubbornness?" Mikito challenges.

"Because you were never prepped," Enki says.

"The Titles, they have to be given near the start, don't they?" I speak my thoughts, for both Mikito and Enki. "That's why someone like Feh'ral didn't have a Title. Or Sephra. Or any of the others. It's why the code for the Title is so messed up. Because the Title is how you prep us, our Status, for taking over."

"Exactly."

"And this is boring," Urd replies. "You see why this, all of this, is a lie? That last percentage, it means nothing. That Quest, the one you have sacrificed so much to be on? Just a lie that could have been answered over a cup of kaf. Nothing mysterious, except for this one's insistence on dragging us here.

"To ask us to kill ourselves. All to fix something that others have done. I will not clean up someone else's mess. Nor should you."

"It's also why you're confident we can take him if we work together," I say, rubbing my temples. "But we come back to the problem of trust."

"Trust—" Urd begins, only to get cut off by Harry.

"What happens to the System? If you succeed. What happens to all of us?" Harry says heatedly. He groans after speaking, having moved too fast and making his still missing leg shoot pain. "If you're the System and you fix things and close everything… what happens to this world?"

"*How the hell does he know he's the System?*" I send to Ali, confused but curious.

"*Harry tagged me. I've been summarizing the conversation for the two of them,*" Ali replies.

Enki cocks his head, clearly puzzled by the question. "Nothing. My task is to reduce the damage caused by the wound. I will not leave, not until Mana levels stabilize to the norm once more and my presence is no longer required."

"Then what, blue and funky?" Ali says.

Enki hums. "Unknown. That future is too far to project at this current time."

"And there you go," Urd says. "Nothing changes, even if you go in. All that evil you protest about, it continues onward. The Council will still stand, Administrators will still be needed. Nothing changes." He almost hisses the last two words, something dark and terrible flashing in his eyes as he speaks them. "You think we're evil, but we're just making the most out of this broken system."

"Broken in truth. Why, for all the lives lost, did you not take precautions?" I glare at Enki, putting my fingers against the wall blocking our way. I push against it, gentler this time, and watch as it disappears. I walk forward. "Why did you let them trap you?"

Enki pauses, then he opens both hands sideways, almost as if he's offering me something. "I described myself as a blood cell. Perhaps a preprogrammed virus cleaner, in your parlance, might be better. I was— am—limited. At that time, betrayal was not a concept I understood."

"A naïve god," Harry scoffs. He's levered himself up now, watching the group with one hand cocked, recording everything that is going on. A part of me wonders if he's able to transmit this, if the world is seeing a giant increase in the System Quest.

Or if the Council or Administrators or perhaps even Enki is blocking it. Because the journey was just as important as the final destination. That snarling ball of my Title, the twisted code and all the experiences, all the information I've gathered about the Quest and the world—it's what makes me a candidate.

And made even someone like Feh'ral a failure in the System's eyes.

"Not a god, a program," Urd says. "A limited, barely sapient, program."

"One last question," I say. "You say this wound is still present. Why hasn't another blood cell come by? Why hasn't it been fixed?"

"It will," Enki replies. "In a few million of your years, another of my kind will arrive. They will locate the problem, fix the issue, and move on. But the time that has passed for where I was, for what it was, it is but a blink."

"What is it that you came from? What is on the other side?" Ezz speaks up, curiosity in its voice. The little golem has shifted such that Harry has a more comfortable seat as Ezz holds its friend aloft with ease.

"I do not know." Enki pauses, seeing our surprise.

Urd is the only one who isn't surprised, his face growing even more twisted and angry.

"Do your blood cells understand the entirety of yourself? I am the smallest part of... something. The Dao, the Creator, the Program." Enki shrugs. "I know only my part, and that is sufficient."

"And now, I truly am done. Make your choice, Redeemer. Will you aid me in taking our place properly in control of this failed program? You've heard it from its own words. What a failure it is, what little it offers, even when it asks for everything." Urd floats forward, his voice dropping. "Will you stop dancing to its whims and break free of those shackles holding you down? Save your Earth. Save your friends. Save whoever you want."

Once more, I stare at the man. Wondering how much I can trust him. Surprisingly, instinct screams that I probably can. I believe that once we're in, whoever manages to tear apart the defenses blocking us from the core functionality of the System will be the one in charge. Abusing the System and all that it created, perhaps, but in charge.

And more than that, I realize Urd doesn't care. He thinks, he believes, he can win. I'm... not entirely sure he's wrong. He's got hundreds, maybe thousands of years of experience on me. He knows the System better than I ever will. I'd be going in blind, coding around blocks that he probably has explored. He'll be able to take more Mana, take more damage, without an issue.

He would likely win.

Then again, I've never turned down a challenge. I've won, hundreds of times, when the odds were stacked against me. If I had control of the System, I could end this war. Take away the Voowmah's ability to damage the dimensional barriers, make it easier for the dragons to win. Block the armada that is going to Earth, throw them into another dimension or just reroute them. Block teleportation in. Give new, better Classes to the survivors. I could make Earth a normal world, help Erethra win the upcoming war.

I could fix things.

System Quest Completion Rate: 99%

And all I'd have to do is give up a single obsession. I have my answer, as Urd says. I know now what the System is. A failed recovery program, a twisted version of what it once was. I know, in the end, there is nothing to be gained by acceding to the System's request.

No lives will be saved. No worlds will be changed. No tragedies thwarted.

I look away from Urd then, toward my friends. To the ones who have managed to make it so far. Harry meets my gaze, reproachful and hopeful.

Mikito's eyes are controlled and level. Steady, as though she knows what I'll choose. And Ezz, Ezz all too trusting and naïve, hopeful. Hopeful, because I'm its father and whatever I choose, it trusts that my choice will be the right one.

I hate to disappoint it.

But all parents disappoint their children, sooner or later.

I turn from Urd, ignoring the fool to stare at Enki. I catch the flash of surprise, of focus as Enki comes into being fully in the here and now, discarding what he's doing otherwise. He's here, when I speak. Even if my words are directed at Urd at first.

"You know, those Titles. I think I get it now. When he gave you that Title—Chooser of the Living—it was for what you did. You focused on the survivors. Did something good for those who managed to make it. Maybe you were a hero once, someone who stood at the gates and kept the hordes of monsters away. Maybe you were a healer." I pause, and my voice goes lower. "I'm sorry that you were broken. Twisted."

Urd makes a noise, as though he's wanting me to hurry it up.

"*Get ready.*" The words flash across the party chat, fast as I can think. I prime a Skill, not daring to activate it, knowing Urd is watching.

"The System though, it called me the Redeemer of the Dead." I close my eyes, then open them, a smile dancing across my lips. "Because it's those who have fallen that I rage for. I have nothing to offer to the living. Never have."

I turn to Enki now, finally, and speak the words that seal my fate.

"What do I need to do?"

Of course, that's when Urd chooses to try to kill me.

***

The first attack is a quick firing one, a Skill that conjures a giant spike which spears me through the gut, throwing me against the nearest wall and pinning me there. Another attack arrives simultaneously, this one via the System. It cuts at my connection to it, intent on tearing apart my Skills and blocking me from using anything directly within. My Skill, Sanctum, is on its way to Harry when it is torn apart with a flicker of Urd's System Edit. A third Skill throws metal spikes from the floor, nearly piercing Ezz, who splits itself apart to dodge the attack. Harry isn't as lucky. The attack erupts from his chest, forcing a pained, liquidy scream from his mouth.

Mikito nimbly moves around the metal spears, Hitoshi thrust forward at Urd, only for it to impact a shield. No, multiple shields, I realize. The Legacy weapon tears through the first two, but is stopped deeper within, the layered defense blocking her attacks.

As for Ali? He's busy as he engages with a half dozen tiny Spirits, all of them flocking around him, thrusting their tiny Mana-engorged hands at his bigger form, tearing chunks off his corporeal body, leaving him to bleed blue.

All of it, in the first second of battle. Even ready for it, I can't stop him. Nor can I when Urd launches his next Skill, one so powerful my Mana Sense screams as that energy gathers around and within before rushing outward. It strikes me, my friends, and the floor itself, causing all of it to ripple and shatter.

One second, Harry's there, alive. Then next, the man, the Reporter, is gone. Ezz does his best, trying to put its body between the attack and its friend. Too slow, the Skills triggering too fast. The golem is unable to block it.

I'm stymied, my own Skills cut off by the Legendary's use of System Edit. I try, I really do, but there's nothing I can do. Mikito is blown back, her Ghost Armor shattering under the onslaught, her skin crisping and flaking aside. The very air burns and freezes at the same time, the heat and cold encroaching on my lungs.

We're losing and the fucker isn't even trying.

Just as suddenly, the attack stops.

The walls, the floor, the ceiling fix themselves. Spikes disappear, the air clears. Mana flow within the room stabilizes and my block fades. Urd is frozen, eyes wide, hand upraised, but his body unable to move. His face is twisted in a pained grimace, but no noise escapes his lips. Mana swirls around him, so much of it that it almost dwarfs the thrumming hole in the center of the room.

I fall to the floor, coughing blood, and drag myself over to Harry, only to be beaten by Ezz. I can tell by the nonexistent Party Chat that he's gone. He was the one with the Skill, the ability to hook us all together. There's very little left of the Reporter, his body looking like one of those flash-burnt corpses you see in images after a forest fire sweeps through, of someone hunching over, desperately trying to save themselves from the heat.

"Uncle. Uncle Harry... please, wake up. Please. I'm sorry, I'll do better," Ezz says, repeating words of similar form over and over as he shakes the body. "Please. I'm sorry."

"It's not your fault," I say to Ezz, putting a hand on it in consolation.

The loss, the death, it hits hard. Grief tears at me over another death I caused. I should have told Harry to leave, to get out before the fight. I should have protected him.

Should. So many shoulds over the span of a decade plus. More than that, if you took in my time, my regrets as a normal human. Not that that time matters. I know others have found a way back, found a way to return to a time before the System arrived, to pick up some pieces of their existence. I can't. Won't, perhaps. No, certainly.

"A healing potion! Father, if we just use a healing potion...." Ezz says.

"It's too late. Was too late the moment the Skill activated," I say.

Mikito ignores us, instead turning toward Enki. She's angry, her eyes dancing with flame as she stares at him. "You could have stopped it. Protected him. Just like you stopped the fight earlier. Why didn't you?"

Her words are like a slap to me, jerking my attention from Ezz. The System—Enki—stares at Mikito for a moment, before he nods, once, slowly.

"How are you doing this!" Urd snarls, struggling in his bonds. Somehow, he's managed to speak. Maybe been allowed to speak. "You should not be able to affect me. You should not be able to do this!"

Enki floats over, staring at Urd with that same impassive face of his. As though everything that is happening is unimportant, just a small blip in the overall passage of time. "You were not the only one exploring options since our last encounter. Did you think I did not look for ways around the programming? I only regret my efforts were so limited."

There's a long pause then, as Enki reaches up.

Urd's struggles are tiny and aborted, the cowl of his long robe falling back as he tries to back away from the glowing blue hand. "What are doing?"

"Ending the problem, with you." Enki's hand falls on Urd's head, pressing down for a long second, Mana pouring out of his hand. I feel Mana coming from the System to aid his actions, but it's a whisper, so tightly controlled that it's as if the System is using a scalpel compared to the hatchets the rest of us use.

One second, Urd is struggling; the next, he's slumped over, tears leaking out of his eyes and across his wrinkled face. I've turned away by then to gather Ezz into a hug. It's the only thing I can think of doing, even though I know it's a pitiful attempt at comfort. How much comfort can there be, when Ezz is metal and I'm... me?

"Father, this..." It pauses, restarts, pauses. "I do not understand this. I want him back. I am..." Ezz buzzes, pushing back. "I am angry. I am sad. I grieve! But I do not understand. Why would the Creator program such things in me? Why would he not extract such... such... wasteful subroutines." Another pause. Longer this time. "I do not want these. They are inefficient. I shall remove them."

"No!" I snap at Ezz.

The little golem freezes, then frowns. "Your reaction is illogical, Father."

"Yes. So are emotions," I reply. "Don't remove them anyway."

"Why?"

"Because while you might gain sapience anyway, if your turn ever arrives..." I frown at Enki, who has removed his hand from the slack-jawed Urd. A line of drool drips from the man's wrinkled and cracked lips, his entire body looking even more wilted and wizened. Even his breathing has grown more difficult, a wet wheezing sound coming from his chest. "Without those inconvenient emotions, you'll just be... cold."

"Yes. Logically, I would be more dispassionate. That seems to be the way," Ezz says. "If you could remove your anger, Father, would you not? If you could delete all those bad memories, why would you not? Why suffer when you can choose not to?"

"Because life is suffering." I turn the golem a little so I can stare into its eyes. Artificial eyes that lack the ability to show emotion the way humans or sapients do. I wonder if Ezz misses that, if the pain I hear in its voice is so much a figment of good programming. Yet we're all programming in the end. It's just that us poor organics have even less control over our chemicals and electrical impulses. "Life is about pain and regrets and foolish actions. It's not about living a perfect, emotionless existence, but making mistakes and learning from them."

"Ali says you never learnt from yours," Ezz replies. "That you never chose to get over it."

"He wasn't talking about my mistakes but the apocalypse. And some things, you never forgive. Or forget. Not unless you…" I consider and shake my head, dropping that line of reasoning. Realizing I'm wrong. "There's no answer I can give you. Not in the time we have. Life is pain. Life is suffering. Life is complex. Anyone who ever tells you different, who tries to sell you on a reality or a belief that it isn't, that somehow things are simple—black or white, good or evil, do this and it'll work every single time—they're likely wrong and charlatans of the highest order.

"All I can say is this. In the end, you'll have to find the truth for yourself. Learn from friends and family, pick the good from the bad; don't ever stop growing. Remember that your job isn't to mimic me or Harry or Mikito, but to be better than us. That's what children are meant to be, if we do our jobs right. The best of us."

Ezz is silent, watching me speak. I wish, I wish I had taken more time, spent it with Ezz. Helped it grow. All I can hope is that it builds upon the poor foundations I've given it. That the others have solidified its footing in this world.

"And maybe, maybe I'm wrong. Maybe you would be right to take away your emotional subroutines. But sometimes, we make choices when we're hurt and we come to regret them. Don't make one now, not when you're hurting. Promise me. Even when I'm gone, promise me. You'll wait."

"For how long?" Ezz asks, its voice hard.

Strange, that a child can sound so grown up. But Ezz was never that childish, not really. It's a golem given another's operating system, learning slowly. Given all the knowledge of another, but given the option to learn anew. To grow from the scaffolding of another.

To reach heights its creator could never reach.

"A year," I say. "Not a lot of time in the greater scheme of things. Not for you."

"Nearly as long as I've existed, Father. Longer than you've been with me."

"Shorter than you will exist," I point out. "Promise me."

Ezz is silent, while Enki has floated back to me. Urd continues to hang there, unmoving.

The System comes to me. "It is time, Redeemer. If we are to do this, we should act fast."

"Why the rush?" I ask. "Seems like all the threats are gone."

"The speed is not for me, but for your friends and world." A gesture, and images call upward.

I see them then, the rest of those who survive.

Bolo and Yllis, grounded, the dragon in her full form and waving wings and tail around as she battles the swarm of Egg-Laying Voowmah that attempt to pull her down. She unleashes breath and spells, glowing runic circles above her sending shards of ice and lightning out at intervals. Bolo, his scalemail rent, blood gushing from numerous wounds, wields his hammer, striking at a massive monster reminiscent of an alien queen crossed with a praying mantis. She moves faster, claws tearing at the large Dragon King even as he ducks in to smash her across the chest with his hammer. Small, spiraling cracks emerge, joining others, but he is struck in turn as smaller appendages tear at his skin and armor.

In another image, the Battlefield Tactician and the last of my Hands stand, her people fallen backward in an ever smaller circle as they attempt to push back the Voowmah from the Center door. The System's ability to block their senses is failing, more and more monsters falling through the gaps, charging the team. Earthen walls and humming energy shields restrict movement to the door, but there's an edge of desperation to the gestures and movement of the defenders.

Another image of the war waging over the Valley itself. Dragons, full flights of them, sweep across the plains, raining fire breath on the ground below. But they are not alone. Voowmah fall from the skies, tearing at wings, plunging blades into eyes. A never-ending series of crystals launch into the sky, exploding in mid-air as they strike at the dragons, leaving an endless lightning storm to dance across the heavens.

What's even worse than the dragons and Voowmah fighting are the tears in space that confuse the battlefield. Creatures fall through them, some landing and shattering on burning ground, dying upon entry into our hostile dimension. Others, other beings, adapt. Their bodies warp, mutating as they arrive. Some take on humanoid shapes, others monsterized ones. A tiny figure, barely the size of my hand, falls upon a slain dragon's body and burrows into its skin. Moments later, wounds close, eyes gaining a pinkish new light, and the entire corpse struggles to its feet, animated from within.

I turn, head craning upward to stare at ever more windows. Windows that showcase the galaxy in all its horrific glory. Things emerge in those windows, through rents and weakened barriers all across the galaxy.

A research station is destroyed, its contents and its occupants devoured by a moving conical mass, tendrils reaching outward from the shell to pull figures toward it. Hosts of flying Dark Elementals, given form, blend into the deep void, flying into the darkness with rapacious hunger in their every movement.

"Mikito…" I call, pointing at the second image.

The Samurai hesitates, looking at me, looking at Enki. It's the first sign of reluctance I can see.

"Go," I say. "If you will, call it a command. You know this is what I have to do. And as you said, something good has to come from all this."

My answer. The closing of the wound.

Nothing that will save our friends in the here and now. Or billions in the future. But perhaps, just perhaps, a saving grace for civilizations, existences in the future. Able to grow, change, control their own future.

Maybe.

Flashes of pain and conflicting emotions flicker across her face. She bites her lip, then Mikito walks up to me and throws a hug around me. I'm surprised at first, because she doesn't touch. Not normally. It's the Asian in us both. But I return it, knowing she needs the comfort, the memory. I hold her tight, until she lets go.

"Baka. Make sure you make it worthwhile." Her voice is a little rough, the words filled with sadness and longing. Then she's gone, rushing to do what she can to help hold the fort. To stop more lives from ending.

Then there's only one last person in the room. I bend down, poking Ezz. The little golem gets mulish, but eventually it offers me the nod I expect. I need.

"A year. That is the last thing, Father, that I'll do for you." Its chin goes up, as if it is staring me down. "For the time you've given me."

I wince, but nod in acceptance. More than I could fairly ask for. "Fair enough. After that, it's up to you. Watch over Mikito for me, will you?" I stand up, only for a little Spirit to float down beside me.

"And what am I? Durian candy?" Ali has his hands on his hips as he floats beside me, glaring.

"No. The heir of all my stuff, I'd say," I say. "Should cover your debt, I'd think. I mean, after all the loot we get here…"

"That's not… damn it, boy-o. This isn't…"

"It is."

I flash the Spirit a half-smile, twisted and tired but warm. I wish I could say more, but I can't. So I open my mind a little and send him the memories. The times we've had together, from when he first came around and called out to the first monster he saw, forcing me to fight. To us standing over a pile of burnt corpses. Our time on the Forbidden World, alone in so many ways. Stories and conversations, shared laughter and joint pain.

Companionship and compassion, of a world burnt and the ills of a Galactic Society we struggled to right. Yet for all that, we failed.

Perhaps that, more than anything else, is why I shut down the connection after a second and nod to Enki, who has been standing there, silent. Waiting.

"I'm ready," I say, as Ali floats away, wiping his eyes.

Sometimes, some partings, no words can ever truly be expressed. Just experienced.

Chapter 36

A slit in space opens before me, a gap through the abyssal hole in the center of the room. Mana gushes forth, faster and stronger than ever. Converging in the point of the gap, it becomes visible, a light so bright it makes my eyes narrow.

I can feel it almost pushing me physically away from the tear. A part of me, the same lizard brain that has kept me alive for so long, screams at me to move away. To flee the screaming gap of power, the energy radiating from it.

Instead, I walk forward. I can feel the System—Enki—in my mind, feeding me information, explaining what I need to do. It's simplicity itself.

Walk into the tear.

Take his place as the controlling force of the System.

Hold it all together.

Be him, for the time it takes him to direct not just the energy of the System but the full resources of his mind and powers at the reason why he was sent here to begin with. Hold, as he wields the stolen portions of power he's taken from those connected to the System to patch a hole in the universe.

A hole that leads to… well. Who knows?

Simplicity itself.

I don't look back. I don't dare to. I know what I'm leaving behind.

And if I wish, perhaps, that I had another chance to say goodbye, it's only for me to know.

The light washes over me, the pain already ratcheting up as I near the gap. Skin and muscle burn, nerves are lit, jolts of electricity dance across my body. My hair catches fire, burning away into ash. It's pain nearly as bad as anything I've ever felt, and I find myself dialing down all my senses. Shouldering through, because I've dealt with pain so much.

Funny, how even the worst things in one's life can be used for fuel for the future.

The pain increases as I step through, as the gap swallows me whole. It takes me into itself, breaking my body apart as raw Mana feeds through me. My body is gone, consumed within seconds. The flash of all-consuming pain as my mind is shattered and burnt is gone so fast, it might never have been there. But Mana, forced through me, processed through my connection with the System, takes me—my consciousness, my mind, my soul—with it.

Deep into the System, along the threads of the Title.

Pulling me into the very web that is reality itself for so many.

I see it all as I'm swept inward, Enki's hand on my soul through the Title he placed upon me, slotting me into place. I feel my mind, my soul, my will borne on gentle hands, guided into the very center of the System. And I realize, now that I'm here and holding the System together as its anchor point itself, he was hiding the truth still.

I'm not just taking his place in the System, but in the gap. His very existence has been like the little Dutch boy, his consciousness the plug holding back unaspected Mana from flooding our universe. What we've felt, what we've experienced—it's a tiny portion of the raw flow that actually wants to arrive.

In his place, I feel the raw power of unfiltered Mana tear at my mind, tearing pieces of me away every moment.

Every second is agony. Every second is ecstasy. For creation, in its rawest form, is what is offered to me, the very tendrils of Mana digging into my soul. I hold the gap as possibilities sprawl outward along the webs of the System.

My mind, shattered and split by the System itself, is offered so much choice and constrained by so many rules as it dances across the code that guides Mana in its bending of reality itself. I find errors everywhere, some

Administrators working diligently to fix problems and others tearing the fabric of the System apart for their own good. Those who do well, I reward; the others, I steal their abilities and penalize them. Reminding them of their greater duties.

I don't strip any of them of their rights. The desperate, the needy, the suitable—I designate new Administrators. Those few who are deserving. I offer them the chance, and I adjust the code a little while doing so. No more stumbling, no blind searching. Data packs and a Quest, one to level up their damn skills.

Most though, most get work. Emergency overrides give them Tickets to fix, control of the region as dimensional breaches threaten the stability of local space.

I watch a slime creature, given its new powers, stare into the trenches of a newly opened underwater dimensional tear, radiant energy pouring out of the gap, killing and mutating at the same time. New Elementals are being born, under the aegis of otherworldly energies.

The slug finds the Ticket and works on it, its mind splitting down the code board, organically patching together a solution in ways I only barely understand because the System offers me the answer. The slug does not speak, does not converse the way I would think; but it can code.

When the slug supplies its solution, I take it and propagate it across all the tendrils of the System, offering it as a way to stop further encroachments. It works, in 7.3864 percent of the time. Or there about.

Another Administrator, a Middle System Administrator, floats in deep space, watching two clashing Heroics. Their attacks have ruptured a gap in space, and he creates a Quest, tailoring it to their needs. They turn away from hammering one another to deal with the new threat.

The Quest, I use with major modifications. Creating variables based off experience, Class, equipment, social bounds. Once I'm satisfied, I throw it at a sample of a hundred Heroic and Master Classes, all across the galaxy.

The answers come back and I tailor the Quest again.

Repeat.

84.81% uptake this time.

Good enough.

I move on, searching for other solutions.

Other parts of me work simultaneously, dealing with conflicting Skill battles between dozens of different Heroics, Master Classers, and all-encompassing Legendary Skills. There's even more complexity overlaid over some of those, when area effect Emperor or Admiral or Planetary Ruler Skills come into play.

Minor problems, each of them, but needing a fix. Mana tries to smooth it out, code dealing with the conflicting Skills or just System Mana doing what it does best—altering reality.

Problems laid across the Galaxy, all for me to fix.

One a pair of siblings searching for their father's approval. Conflict that is so small in Galactic terms but so important for these two. They never notice my touch as I smooth out Mana overflow problems and deal with a potential spiraling issue of Mana usage as they plunge through the heart of a star.

A pair of bird creatures, kenku, coo over the hatching of a child. Around them, friends and family fight off the coming waves of monsters; even as I register the Perks their child has access to in the Forbidden World. It's a pain, the registration, movement across lands flushed with unaspected Mana.

All the while, Mana batters at my metaphorical locked legs, as I lean into the door and hold it closed. Except I'm the door, and the energy keeps coming, never ending. My soul has formed a physical representation of myself, pulling from Mana, recreating who and what I am as I try to stem the flow.

Even so, I can sense that I'm doing a worse job than Enki. A part of me watches as the percentage of Mana that escapes keeps creeping up.

8%.

9%.

11%.

And still, I patch problems across the universe.

The Library long stored in my mind is alive with solutions and possibilities. More than that, I feel it expanding, connecting with the database in the System itself. A portion of me is in there, drinking forth the secrets of the universe, both mundane and galaxy-shattering.

Catrin Dufoff, Empress Apparent to the Erethran Empire, stands before the Queen, arguing for intervention as an armada approaches Earth. Arguing for my sake, for the good I had done for their Empire and for the possibility of even greater benefit. At the same time, I see our time together, our bodies heaving, moving in unison as we make love.

On the other hand, I see the Empress of Erethra, over a century ago, standing over her own mother; a spear connects the two of them, spearhead buried in her mother's chest. The rage, the loss that is on the Empress's face is palpable. Even so, she twists the spear as she extracts it before ramming it home again to finish the job. I see code spilling out, anointing her the new Empress, orders given to hide this very thing.

A planet flies through space, moving at fractions of the speed of light. Energy shields and Skills bolster the planet, keeping it intact as it smashes into a Titanic Colossus that has left the deepest reaches of the Forbidden Zone. On the planet, among the small ragtag fleet that have gathered at the edges of a solar system to attempt to stop the Colossus, cheers ring out. The

Legendary Pilot who maneuvers the planet-ship is a surprise, a giant Clam connected to the planet by strands digging deep.

Another secret. So many secrets.

The Emperor on his throne, giving the order. Millenia ago. A single connected psychic strand connects him to his empire, a mental thread that gives them all strength and comfort. He cuts himself off just before the Overmind that holds his Empire together, that gives them strength and power, detonates. Killing tens of billions, driving the strongest mad as the pain of uncountable lives being lost at once feeds back onto them. Cackling, the Emperor feels the restraints holding him still slip free. To live his life, to answer the questions he asked. To love the one that he wanted, forever. Even if they were an it.

More secrets, more memories.

The wars waged by the Administrators. Historic reams, long deleted everywhere but here, are retrieved. Mind wipes, populations isolated and left to die, news and history revised in slow steps. New data blocked from being sold, education systems altered to fit the narrative. Assassinations and bribes. Code changes.

I patch together the parts that are broken and I call forth new life, redirecting Mana to create dungeons and form new Classes. I watch the inefficiencies of the Perk System play out over and over again, and I put snarky comments when Guilds and other powers create Quests.

I see it all. Understand it all. Manipulate it all for the greater good of Mana flow and life being saved.

Even if I leave thousands, millions to die.

Even if I stain my soul with harsh decisions, thousands of times.

How could I not? I'm the System.

And all the while, I search.

For friends, for lovers, for enemies.

***

Funny that I should find her first. Less funny is where Lana is, standing in the midst of destruction; the office—my office, once upon a time—in the Vancouver Public Library has been destroyed, the table and furniture in pieces. I can see from the char marks, from running the log backward what happened. The surprise attack, the explosion and the automatic deployment of the slagged metal desk's defensive options. Her body thrown backward. The teleportation of not just one but two of her Tamed beasts away to isolate her.

Roland is gone, trapped in a maze of teleporting platforms that shove the monstrous, mutated tiger backward each time it attempts to escape. It's the perfect trap to contain the powerful beast, keeping the monster contained with minimal effort.

Howard, on the other hand, has managed to escape his trap, the all-too-smart pup wielding magic himself. I'm a little surprised to see the swirling Mana around him, the way small magical formations conjure and fire off, tearing into the group surrounding him. They thought he was the weakest of her pets and are now paying for it.

As for her... Beast Lord Lana Pearson is standing in the smoking wreckage of her office, red hair streaming in the air as she fires the magical shotgun from her hip, even whilst barking commands to her remaining pets. Oren, high in the sky, wheels around to pick at those attempting to drop down behind Lana. Shadow, having escaped the initial teleportation, attacks with his real and shadow bodies.

In the distance, the warning klaxons are going off; but the attack—the surprise attack—is keeping the entirety of her people busy as stealthed forces deploy against the settlement. All that keeps her security forces from coming to her aid, everyone but the pair of bodyguards stationed outside her door who are themselves in battle, one bleeding out.

I watch health fall, Mana utilized and regenerated, Stamina burnt. All the numbers and Skills being deployed, the deaths and technology utilized. Parts of me spins out estimations and predictions, partly in aid of the Battlefield Prognosticator that is in play on the opponent's side, partly because part of the System's job is to predict Mana flows so that there's never an interruption.

The results are easy to understand, the predictions surprising.

The human part of me, the part that still cares for her, wants to tilt the odds in her favor even more. Break the System, stretch the threads of fate. Make Skills fail, alter Resistances. Another part, the part that is the System, that has seen this play out so many times before, balks. Hundreds of case studies, thousands of instances show me why the System is balanced the way it is, why I can't just break it because I want to.

I can't afford to save her, not without condemning thousands, maybe even entire planets, to death. And truth be told, she doesn't need saving.

She never has.

So I move on.

***

A golem located in the center of an asteroid. Tendrils reach outward, digging through solid rock with each strand. Seeking out metal and other precious elements, drawing them in and discarding detritus through its back to be swallowed by the void.

I'm a little surprised to find Juover still alive. He's lost a lot, including his space station. In fact, now that I look at the body in the asteroid, I realize that "survive" might not be the right word. This is him, the System connection is quite clear, but he has a similar(ish) Skill to the damn Galactic Champion. Juover's Reboot Skill gives him a second chance at life, but this one does so in a prepped body somewhere far away.

Smart. It would make Juover a real danger to fight, since anyone or anything that can keep coming back will always be a threat. A little part of me is happy for Ezz, though I wonder what will happen when Juover looks for the golem in the future.

Now that I'm here, I peer at the connection, running logs backward. I note how the Council's complaints about nonorganics and yes, Mana are not entirely without merit. Mana doesn't gather and consolidate or process through Juover the same way it would with another living creature. That all-powerful force seems to struggle a little with artificial life. Not entirely, of course, for Mana does process and flow through the golem, but it comes at a reduced ratio.

Important for the System to keep them separated then, to ensure that not all artificial lives are fully connected. Designate them as items and not people, disallow use of Skills so that they are always a net positive. In fact, my mind spins backward, running the trace, and I realize that the net volume of System Mana gained is very much in the positive from all these sentient AIs. Everything from Juover to KIM, they're all feeding the System.

So long as they're enslaved, never given full access, the System wins.

I struggle with myself again, human desire to free them warring with greater understanding that doing so would break an already fragile System. In the end, I find myself compromising.

And flee Juover's presence to find another.

***

Ezz is simplicity itself to locate. There are still tendrils of data code lingering between the two, the Threads of Fate, if you will, from my Skill. I dance along the thread, reaching outward to the golem, to my son. Offering Ezz the world, bridging the gap between it and the System.

And find that Ezz rejects it.

Again.

Not the first time Ezz has refused the connection. It's not even a conscious decision, just a part of its programming deep within where the System connection would hook up. All of it is functioning at a level that even someone—something—like Ezz would be unlikely to find it. After all, to mimic sapient life, the degree of complexity of his programming is significant.

A part of me floats, contemplating the rejection, the Skills and flashes of insight that I get while watching the code flow between the pair of us. I realize that the System can, does, read more of our thoughts than we ever imagined; but like the connection between thoughts and the System, it happens on a level that would be impossible for anyone but Enki himself to understand.

Enki and me now.

I find the unspoken desires, the twisted reasoning for Ezz's refusal, and my heart—my nonexistent heart—hurts. For a moment, I wonder how I failed Ezz that it would think I would abandon it the moment it gained the System.

Then, I realize all too late, that I'd already done it before he ever achieved the connection.

The pain of that knowledge is nearly as strong as the flow of Mana through my body, the portion of me that holds the door closed in Enki's place. The plug that is my soul, my mind, is tearing apart piece by piece. I make a decision, unsure if it's the right one, but I do it anyway.

A shred of myself, torn away by the outpouring of Mana, is wrapped in System Mana. I shove the connection toward Ezz, and when Ezz rejects it, I refuse to let the rejection stand. Its resistance, unconscious as it is, cannot stand beneath the weight of the System and my will.

I push the connection down, linking the golem to the System. Adding Ezz to this twisted world and offering it a chance at growth, the Classes and Levels it had been locked out of before.

Lying to myself, as all parents do, that what I do is for the best, even as I override my child's wants and needs.

I'm not sure if that makes me my father or just a hypocrite. Perhaps a little of both.

I leave Ezz reeling, wrapping himself around the connection and that part of me within him. Hoping that he can offer me what little grace he can find within himself when he realizes what I have done. More than I have ever offered my own parents.

Failures, aren't we all?

***

I find Mikito and Ali as I flee my sins. Ali's fading, his connection to this world gone. He's struggling to watch the changes, to see his way to the end. But without an anchor, he has nothing to hold him to this reality. The lingering traces of me in the System are giving him something to hold onto, but without my physical body, the System is eradicating all those connections.

Mikito fares no better. Her Class is predicated upon my presence, my existence. She is weaker, significantly weaker, without me. A Voowmah Royal Guard battles her at the doorway to the Administrative Center, overpowering her defense with each strike. Blood flows from wounds on her arms and shoulders even as she holds the battle line.

I wonder how long I was gone.

Am gone.

She never sees the sweep that takes her balance, an elongated tail plucking her feet off the ground and wrapping around them. Mikito's back hits the ground hard, breath torn from her throat. The first downward claw is blocked on the edge of Hitoshi's shaft, but it keeps pressing down, edging toward her face.

Mikito's too weak now to win the battle.

I've crippled her.

So I fix it, even as I feel the System rebel against my actions. I bleed, I tear and twist; a portion of the Mana I'm holding off gushes outward, enough so that I know I've sped up Forbidden Zone expansion by another 0.51%.

But I fix it.

I fix Ali too, at the same time, leaving the pair Linked, before I'm swept away, the System pulling me onward.

***

A tall Yerrick stands under hot water as blood—green and purple and a little red—sloughs off his fur. He has his head down, allowing the water to soak through his pelt, relaxing in the moment as he goes through System Notifications. Another successful hunt in the True North.

A human Bounty Hunter, his female companion with him, in the throes of passion. I move on, quickly, never much of a voyeur.

Laughing children, playing outside, magic dancing between their fingers as they wield Mana without the System. A smiling uncle of a Mage, deep creases in his eyes, coaches the pair of mixed-race children, even as Jason and his wife spend a few quiet moments cooking—and sampling—the bannock. Muttering about how it just isn't the same as Ingrid's.

Katherine, in a board room, arguing with a pair of Guild Masters. Notifications linger before the trio and the various aides standing around the room itself. A contract for exclusive use of a series of Dungeons in sub-Saharan Africa. Trading off land to aliens, for just a little protection, just a little more time.

An astronaut with a bushy mustache, standing on the ISS. Or what was the ISS, the entire thing changed so much that it is to the old, pre-System ISS as a dinosaur is to a Mana Magpie Nightmare.

Weird name.

In a familiar Forbidden Planet, Suhargur, last Grand Paladin of the Erethran Empire, fights a four-hundred-foot Behemoth. The walking skyscraper burps, releasing dozens of flying bees, even as it swings its arm. An arm that splits and splits again into dozens of tendrils as she dances through them. A Grand Cross pulses, crushing the earth and monster beneath its pressure, the land shattering in a spiderweb of pain. There's a smile on her face, the kind I have only ever seen on her as she courts her death.

And then, there he is. The one who got away. The one I let escape. Roxley's dancing, holding the man next to him close, whispering sweet nothings. His hand on the other's lower back, pressing hips together, breath tickling each other's ears. Promising another dance, one more sexual if no less intimate.

I wish him well, knowing all too well it was I who ran from him. Ran from the possibilities, the happiness, the pain and betrayal that getting together with him would have resulted in.

Pain, all-encompassing, as my soul and Mana body is scoured away. The door holds, I hold; even as I feel Enki in the corners of the wound, punching new holes through the not-walls that hold off the Mana. Threading will and soul and code, ready to close it tight.

All the while, parts of myself float away.

Inspiration, taken from earlier; I wield my soul like a scalpel and cudgel alike, making minor adjustments, altering twists of fate or Skills. A hyperspace jump boosted—to bring a rescue fleet closer to Earth than anyone ever expected. Reinforcements for a battered defensive line.

A Perk twisted to offer aid.

Mutations increased to provide benefit for the defenders.

Information hidden beneath ever-higher Credit totals.

Small changes, but each one a cascading series of problems. I let it grow, fixing what I can, balancing the cost in humanity's favor when I cannot. Disapproval flows down the line, Enki furious at what I have twisted.

I offer him a mental middle finger.

All the while, I expand, taking it all in.

More faces. More friends. More enemies. The all-too-many faceless trillions who make up this grand galaxy, all of them connected to the System.

All of them relying on the System for their existence.

On me.

A program, a series of rules and balances, a negotiated peace treaty. A guide and a supporting hand, an unfeeling guardian and a weeping parent. A burden of guilt and failure, of torn promises and never-ending pain.

The System—Enki, me—we're all that.

And more.

Another surge, perhaps a heartbeat speeding up, perhaps just the natural flow of unaspected Mana. It ripples out of the wound and I feel my grip, the tendrils of my will, tear. Imaginary feet scrabble against ethereal ground as more Mana escapes.

I push back, closing the door tighter.

Life and soul and pain and anger, all of it washes away as Mana burns me on its way free into my universe.

I stand in the doorway into existence itself, and I hold it shut by sheer force of will. Knowing that anything less will be the demise of my friends and the world I have left behind.

Waiting for the one I have trusted to finish his task.

Dying inch by inch as my sanity and my memories are worn away.

Laughing as one last notification arrives even as threads of code are being pulled tight. Shutting the doorway to Mana, closing it off and allowing the being, the Program, the Dao on the other end to heal.

Finally.

One last notification, as I stand in the doorway as the threads close. One last message before I'm torn away and cast aside. One last cherry on the top of a System-hell fest.

System Quest Update!

Quest Completion Rate: 100%

Epilogue

Head bowed, she wiped the last of the blood from Hitoshi, the gummy liquid from the Voowmah refusing to be washed off easily. She would need a more thorough cleansing of the blade later, sword oil and scouring brushes included.

Around her, smoke drifted into the sky, tickling her nostrils as the mixture of ash, blood, and boiled carapace threatened to set her sneezing. A focus deep within, a push on her Constitution made the reaction still, even as she surveyed her surroundings. A blasted wasteland with high canyon walls in the distance, fires from burnt corpses all about, the bodies of dragons being carefully cared for even as greater magics were woven in the sky to track down the last of the Hunger.

"Auntie..."

"Mikito-chan," she corrected idly. Then remembering who it was, she took her eyes off the horizon and her hand off her weapon to place it on Ezz's head.

"Is Father... he is... he's really gone, isn't he?" the little golem said, his voice small and afraid.

"Yes. I felt it, didn't you? When the Wound closed." Mikito hefted the polearm then made it disappear, put away for now. "I felt it when he changed my Class." A slight smile, one that warred with the pain in her eyes. Not much pain though. She had—they had—known this was coming. All but Ezz, probably. "Though I'm not sure what a Ronin of the Dead is supposed to be."

"Boy-o was never particularly good at names," Ali said, floating down. "Not very good at anything really, beyond eating chocolate and losing his temper."

"Being stubborn," Mikito supplied.

"And a dragon-taming fighter," Bolo adds, walking forward after he had alighted from Yllis.

The dragon was bleeding from multiple wounds across her torso, scales torn to reveal green flesh beneath. Even as they watched, her body shrank and twisted, the familiar young woman in a disheveled green dress and bleeding wounds taking her place.

"He was kind to me," Ezz said defensively. Then, as though forced to admit it, Ezz added reluctantly, "When he remembered I was around."

"I'm going to miss him. And Harry," Mikito said. "I wish…"

"We tried. At one point or another, we tried. But he never wanted to choose otherwise." Ali patted her shoulder, lips twisting sideways in painful memory. "I don't think he ever forgave himself."

"For what?" Ezz said.

"Surviving."

There's silence then, as the group stands in remembrance of those who were lost. Not just this day, but in the many bloody ones before.

In the end, a great flapping of wings alerted the few left behind to the incoming trio of massive dragons. Mikito looked up, sighing as she hefted her blade. Bolo and Yllis strode forward, moving to intercept the angry dragons. Already, Mikito could hear the bass rumble of angry reptiles, their disfavor causing the very stones beneath her feet to dance.

She cast one last glance backward to where a door had been before. The last of the Battlefield Tactician and her people were slumped along the ground, in the space where the door had been. Gone, like a fever dream, back into the dimension it lived within even as other dimensional rents had slammed shut.

Not all of them though. Not by far.

"He was a good friend though, wasn't he?" Ali said softly.

"Yes. Even if he was a real baka," Mikito said softly too.

Then there was no more time for mourning, as a dragon raised its foot and brought it slamming down on another ally and another disagreement had to be dealt with.

Because that was their lives these days.

Ever since the apocalypse.

***

In the vast beyond, factions and Legendary figures, as well as the average man, stared at the broadcast cut short, the answer to a final drama ended all too early. No answer from the Reporter who had made the broadcast, his death easily confirmed.

For your average Adventurer, the Cooks and Woodcutters, the Lifemold Golems and the Courtesans, the broadcast had been a point of interest. The most invested sent complaints to the Board of Reporters; the less invested tagged the entire thing to alert them on future updates. The majority shrugged and turned to the next strand of gossip, to the next news cycle.

Only a few, Administrators and Legendarys and faction heads, searched further.

The Mistress of Shadows touched the System, asking for answers. The Credit amount boggled her mind. Even as she stared at it, the number kept changing, increasing or decreasing. Working on a hunch, she asked another question.

Total Credit cost of the question answer is System Total of all Credits +1

A simple line, but one that blocked all inquiries. The Mistress huffed, then turned her gaze onward, to those who had been there. She would not be denied this information. After all, the Redeemer of the Dead had a bad habit of overturning her world when he arrived.

An Empress Apparent sighed, dismissing the question. Her answer had only cost ten Credits. She would miss the man, the foolhardy hero. Honorable to a fault, even if his sense of honor might have not been convenient to those in power.

She raised her swords, nodding to the trio of Honor Guards. Her argument with the Empress had been less than conducive. Her projection had been cut off, the Skill that allowed them to talk ended. Now, on her flagship, she could but train. And somehow find herself worthy of the position she was in. Empress to a martial society, one on the brink of war.

Lord Roxley Graxan stared at the sleeping form on his bed, the curve of his buttocks. He remembered another man, passionate and desperate, hungry for affection and unable to give of himself. Remembered a time when the other stumbled in from the outskirts, lost and looking for a cause. Angry at the world and himself. How Roxley had gifted the other a Quest and a goal, one that held the other to himself briefly.

Memory, bittersweet. Much like their relationship. He did not ask the System, but instead made arrangements for a message to pass on his condolences to a Samurai. Condolences and a request for her to speak with him. Then he readied himself for the call from the Duchess.

In the dark, in a twisted, destroyed land, a man strode out of a portal. Standing over the corpse was Suhurgar, oldest Paladin of Erethra, her sword rising. Only to be startled as the Lord of Time and Space made her an offer.

Administrators, the galaxy over, found their ranks bolstered but their Classes no longer hidden. Explanations—halting, stumbling, violent—were expelled. Others fled, forced to take refuge in Administrative Centers; their workload never-ending as the damage from the Dragon-Voowmah war resounded through the System.

All across the galaxy, movers and shakers found nothing and everything had changed. The System still stood, sentinel to their wants and needs, to their very existence. Mana continued to flow, lapping at the edges of the Restricted Zone; a massive amount where an improper plug failed to contain it all. The Forbidden Zone grew ever larger, monsters given ever more strength.

Nothing had changed.

Everything had changed.

***

"So, what now?" Ali asked, floating beside Mikito.

Xy'largh floated beneath their feet and the smooth hull plates of the ship bearing their weight. Oxygen levels at 27.2%, higher than Earth normal, buoyed feelings, even if there was a trace of cinnamon in the air.

Strange full circles, to depart on a ship that had betrayed them. Dornalor was busy explaining his betrayal to an angry Ezz, deep within the engine room. A part of her wondered what they'd do if Ezz wasn't pacified.

If he could be.

Angry, the young golem was. All the time. Except they couldn't calm that one with a bagful of chocolates. So they'd probably better find it something to kill.

Good thing she had a Quest for that.

System Quest: Invaders from Beyond

Dimensional Breaches have occurred throughout the Galactic System, threatening System stability. Travel to the breaches, close them, and deal with any Dimensional Interlopers.

Rewards: Variable

Mikito watched as Ali read the notification, felt his surprise through their bond. That was going to take time to get used to. That, and the way her Status now looked.

There were a lot of changes, a lot of new Administrators, a galaxy on the brink of war now turned toward an even more dangerous external threat. Earth was still in danger, but their enemies had been reduced, many fleeing back to guard homes now in danger from dimensional interlopers.

The Forbidden Zone continued to expand, but the Wound no longer gushed Mana. Eventually, the built-up Mana overflow would subside, the ripples slow. Eventually, the Mana would fade, taking the System with it even as Mana entered the world the proper way. All across the universe, at the same time.

Changes, so many that it staggered Mikito to even think about them. That the Administrator—Enki—had even chosen to tell her a little about what was to come, before he faded away.

The System was different now, and so was their world. A quiet apocalypse, one that few would ever know had happened but would ripple through the galaxy forever.

But she could handle it. They could handle it.

After all, as a friend had once said, what is, is.

The End of the System Apocalypse

Want to read a bonus epilogue?

Subscribe to my newsletter to download *A Tense Meeting*.

www.mylifemytao.com/a-tense-meeting

Author's Note

Some of you are probably screaming at me. I get it. Saying goodbye to someone who you have spent so much time with is hard.

It is perhaps, easier for me. I've mentioned in other areas but the series ending has been known since, well, nearly the beginning. Multiple times, John has had the opportunity to walk away—to heal and grow. Every time, he's refused.

Even Mikito who, arguably, lost even more than John has managed to move on. If there was, is, a flaw in John Lee, it's his inability to get over the apocalypse. It drove him all the way to this ending, and finally, to the conclusion you've read. There was never going to be a happily ever after for the man, because doing so would require him to resolve his past.

It's a good thing that what they needed was someone willing to take the final step. It's also why the story is about John, in the end. Because it always had to be him.

Not to say he didn't change. He did, but only so much before he realized he could not, would not, grow further. And so, here we are, at the end of the main series and John's story.

The universe lives on though. The System still holds, and it will be millions of years before it fades away. In the meantime, my coauthors Craig Hamilton—**A Fist Full of Credits**—and K.T. Hanna—**System Apocalypse: Australia**—are writing their series, expanding the universe and what happens both on Earth and in other parts unknown.

Will I write a solo series in this universe again? Most likely. Not immediately, but I am sure I'll grow to miss Mikito and Ali and everyone else soon enough. There's a story about the dimensional rifts, Mikito, and her finding a conclusion too that has to be written, though it's very vague in my mind right now.

Bolo and Yllis and what happened between book 10 and 12, and what happens afterward in Xy'largh, still await.

There are more stories to tell. I just hope that this one and this series ending was, if not happy, at least satisfying.

As always, I'm grateful for everyone who has followed me on this long journey. There's so much more to be written, in this universe and otherwise, so I'm hoping you all will follow me into my other series. For those who don't know, they're listed below:

- the Adventures on Brad (a more traditional young adult LitRPG fantasy) https://books2read.com/healers-gift
- Hidden Wishes (an urban fantasy GameLit series) https://books2read.com/gamers-wish
- A Thousand Li (a cultivation series inspired by Chinese xianxia novels) https://readerlinks.com/l/971660
- **Power, Masks & Capes** and the **Eternal Night** series which are both novelette series set in a superhero and VRMMORPG for vampires respectively
  - o First Steps into the Night (Book 1 of the Eternal Night series) https://books2read.com/u/m2MP7r
  - o Technopath (Book 1 of the Power, Masks & Capes series) https://books2read.com/u/bzg5YE

I've also written a ton of short stories, all of which are available on my Patreon account:

https://www.patreon.com/taowong

If you enjoyed reading the book, **please do leave a review and rating**. Reviews are the lifeblood of authors and help others choose to start the series or not.

Oh, and if you can avoid spoiling the book for others; I'd be grateful.

For more great information about LitRPG series, check out the Facebook groups:

- GameLit Society

https://www.facebook.com/groups/LitRPGsociety/

- LitRPG Books

https://www.facebook.com/groups/LitRPG.books/

About the Author

Tao Wong is an avid fantasy and sci-fi reader who spends his time working and writing in the North of Canada. He's spent way too many years doing martial arts of many forms, and having broken himself too often, he now spends his time writing about fantasy worlds.

For updates on the series and other books written by Tao Wong (and special one-shot stories), please visit the author's website:

    http://www.mylifemytao.com

Subscribers to Tao's mailing list will receive **exclusive access to short stories in the Thousand Li and System Apocalypse universes**.

Or visit his Facebook Page: https://www.facebook.com/taowongauthor/

About the Publisher

Starlit Publishing is wholly owned and operated by Tao Wong. It is a science fiction and fantasy publisher focused on the LitRPG & cultivation genres. Their focus is on promoting new, upcoming authors in the genre whose writing challenges the existing stereotypes while giving a rip-roaring good read.

For more information Starlit Publishing, visit our website! https://www.starlitpublishing.com/

You can also join Starlit Publishing's mailing list to learn of new, exciting authors and book releases.

System Apocalypse: Australia

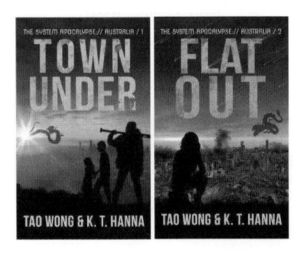

What's worse than Australian wildlife? *Mutated* Australian wildlife.

The System Apocalypse has come to Australia, altering native organisms and importing even more menacing creatures to the most dangerous continent on Earth. For Kira Kent, plant biologist, the System arrives while she's pulling an all nighter at work with her pair of kids in tow.

Now, instead of mundane parental concerns like childcare and paying the bills, she's got to figure out how to survive a world where already deadly flora and fauna have grown even more perilous - all while dealing with the minutiae of the System's pesky blue screens and Levels and somehow putting together a community of survivors to forge a safe zone to shelter her son and daughter.

It almost makes her miss the PTA fundraising sales. *Almost.*

Read more of the System Apocalypse: Australia series
https://readerlinks.com/1/2202672

System Apocalypse: Relentless

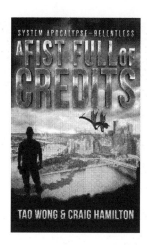

Bail bondsman. Veteran. Survivor.

Hal Mason's still going to find surviving the System Apocalypse challenging.

While bringing in his latest fugitive, Hal's payday is interrupted by the translucent blue boxes that herald Earth's introduction to the System - a galaxy spanning wave of structured mystical energy that destroys all electronics and bestows game-like abilities upon mankind.

With society breaking down and mutating wildlife rampaging through the city of Pittsburgh, those who remain will sacrifice anything for a chance at earning their next Level. As bodies fall and civilization crumbles, Hal finds himself asking what price is his humanity. Are the Credits worth his hands being ever more stained with blood?

Or does he press on - relentless?

Read more of System Apocalypse: Relentless
https://readerlinks.com/l/1911638

Glossary

Erethran Honor Guard Skill Tree

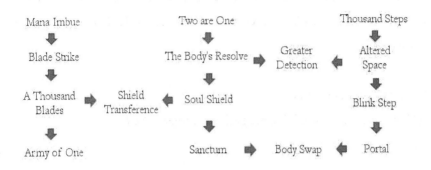

John's Erethran Honor Guard Skills

Mana Imbue (Level 5)

Soulbound weapon now permanently imbued with Mana to deal more damage on each hit. +30 Base Damage (Mana). Will ignore armor and resistances. Mana regeneration reduced by 25 Mana per minute permanently.

Blade Strike (Level 5)

By projecting additional Mana and stamina into a strike, the Erethran Honor Guard's Soulbound weapon may project a strike up to 50 feet away.
Cost: 50 Stamina + 50 Mana

Thousand Steps (Level 1)

Movement speed for the Honor Guard and allies are increased by 5% while skill is active. This ability is stackable with other movement-related skills.
Cost: 20 Stamina + 20 Mana per minute

Altered Space (Level 2)

The Honor Guard now has access to an extra-dimensional storage location of 30 cubic meters. Items stored must be touched to be willed in and may not include living creatures or items currently affected by auras that are not the Honor Guard's. Mana regeneration reduced by 10 Mana per minute permanently.

Two are One (Level 1)

Effect: Transfer 10% of all damage from Target to Self

Cost: 5 Mana per second

The Body's Resolve (Level 3)

Effect: Increase natural health regeneration by 35%. Ongoing health status effects reduced by 33%. Honor Guard may now regenerate lost limbs. Mana regeneration reduced by 15 Mana per minute permanently.

Greater Detection (Level 1)

Effect: User may now detect System creatures up to 1 kilometer away. General information about strength level is provided on detection. Stealth skills, Class skills, and ambient Mana density will influence the effectiveness of this skill. Mana regeneration reduced by 5 Mana per minute permanently.

A Thousand Blades (Level 4)

Creates five duplicate copies of the user's designated weapon. Duplicate copies deal base damage of copied items. May be combined with Mana Imbue and Shield Transference. Mana Cost: 3 Mana per second

Soul Shield (Level 8)

Effect: Creates a manipulable shield to cover the caster's or target's body. Shield has 2,750 Hit Points.

Cost: 250 Mana

Blink Step (Level 2)

Effect: Instantaneous teleportation via line-of-sight. May include Spirit's line of sight. Maximum range—500 meters.

Cost: 100 Mana

Portal (Level 5)

Effect: Creates a 5-meter by 5-meter portal which can connect to a previously traveled location by user. May be used by others. Maximum distance range of portals is 10,000 kilometers.

Cost: 250 Mana + 100 Mana per minute (minimum cost 350 Mana)

Army of One (Level 4)

The Honor Guard's feared penultimate combat ability, Army of One builds upon previous Skills, allowing the user to unleash an awe-inspiring attack to deal with their enemies. Attack may now be guided around minor obstacles.

Effect: Army of One allows the projection of (Number of Thousand Blades conjured weapons * 3) Blade Strike attacks up to 500 meters away from user. Each attack deals 5 * Blade Strike Level damage (inclusive of Mana Imbue and Soulbound weapon bonus)

Cost: 750 Mana

Sanctum (Level 2)

An Erethran Honor Guard's ultimate trump card in safeguarding their target, Sanctum creates a flexible shield that blocks all incoming attacks, hostile teleportations and Skills. At this Level of Skill, the user must specify dimensions of the Sanctum upon use of the Skill. The Sanctum cannot be moved while the Skill is activated.

Dimensions: Maximum 15 cubic meters.

Cost: 1,000 Mana

Duration: 2 minute and 7 seconds

Paladin of Erethra Skill Tree

John's Paladin of Erethra Skills

Penetration (Level 9—Evolved)

Few can face the judgment of a Paladin in direct combat, their ability to bypass even the toughest of defenses a frightening prospect. Reduces Mana Regeneration by 45 permanently.

Effect: Ignore all armor and defensive Skills and spells by 90%. Increases damage done to shields and structural supports by 175%.

Secondary Effect: Damage that is resisted by spells, armor, Skills and Resistances is transferred to an Evolved Skill shield at a ratio of 1 to 1.

Duration: 85 minutes

Aura of Chivalry (Level 1)

A Paladin's very presence can quail weak-hearted enemies and bolster the confidence of allies, whether on the battlefield or in court. The Aura of Chivalry is a double-edged sword however, focusing attention on the Paladin—potentially to their detriment. Increases success rate of Perception checks against Paladin by 10% and reduces stealth and related skills by 10% while active. Reduces Mana Regeneration by 5 Permanently.

Effect: All enemies must make a Willpower check against intimidation against user's Charisma. Failure to pass the check will cow enemies. All allies gain a 50% boost in morale for all Willpower checks and a 10% boost in confidence and probability of succeeding in relevant actions.

Note: Aura may be activated or left-off at will.

Beacon of the Angels (Level 2)

User calls down an atmospheric strike from the heavens, dealing damage over a wide area to all enemies within the beacon. The attack takes time to form, but once activated need not be concentrated upon for completion.

Effect: 1000 Mana Damage done to all enemies, structures and vehicles within the maximum 25-meter column of attack

Mana Cost: 500 Mana

Eye of Insight (Level 1)

Under the eyes of a Paladin, all untruth and deceptions fall away. Only when the Paladin can see with clarity may he be able to judge effectively. Reduces Mana Regeneration by 5.

Effect: All Skills, Spells and abilities of a lower grade that obfuscate, hinder or deceive the Paladin are reduced in effectiveness. Level of reduction proportionate to degree of difference in grade and Skill Level.

Eye of the Storm (Level 1)

In the middle of the battlefield, the Paladin stands, seeking justice and offering judgment on all enemies. The winds of war will seek to draw both enemies and allies to you, their cruel flurries robbing enemies of their lives and bolstering the health and Mana of allies.

Effect: Eye of the Storm is an area effect buff and taunt. Psychic winds taunt enemies, forcing a Mental Resistance check to avoid attacking user. Enemies also receive 5 points of damage per second while within the influence of the Skill, with damage decreasing from the epicenter of the Skill. Allies receive a 5% increase in Mana and Health regeneration, decrease in effectiveness from Skill center. Eye of the Storm affects an area of 50 meters around the user.

Cost: 500 Mana + 20 Mana per second

Vanguard of the Apocalypse (Level 2)

Where others flee, the Paladin strides forward. Where the brave dare not advance, the Paladin charges. While the world burns, the Paladin still fights. The Paladin with this Skill is the vanguard of any fight, leading the charge against all of Erethra's enemies.

Effect: +45 to all Physical attributes, increases speed by 55% and recovery rates by 35%. This Skill is stackable on top of other attribute and speed boosting Skills or spells.

Cost: 500 Mana + 10 Stamina per second

Society's Web (Level 1)

Where the Eye of Insight provides the Paladin an understanding of the lies and mistruths told, Society's Web shows the Paladin the intricate webs that tie individuals to one another. No alliance, no betrayal, no tangled web of lies will be hidden as each interaction weaves one another closer. While the Skill provides no detailed information, a skilled Paladin can infer much from the Web.

Effect: Upon activation, the Paladin will see all threads that tie each individual to one another and automatically understand the details of each thread when focused upon.

Cost: 400 Mana + 200 Mana per minute

Immovable Object / Unstoppable Force (Level 1)

A Paladin cannot be stopped. A Paladin cannot be moved. A Paladin is a force of the Erethran Empire on the battlefield. This Skill exemplifies this simple concept. Let all who doubt the strength of the Paladin tremble!

Use: User must select to be an Immovable Object or Unstoppable Force. Effect varies depending on choice. Skill combines with Aura of Chivalry to provide a smaller (10% of base effect) bonus to all friendlies within range.

Effect 1 (Immovable Object): Constitution, Health and Damage Resistance (All) increased by 200% of User's current total. All knockback effects are mitigated (including environmental knockback effects).

Effect 2 (Unstoppable Force): Agility, Movement Speed, Momentum and Damage Calculations based off Momentum increased by 200% of User's current total. Damage from other attacks increased by 100%. Only active while user is moving.

Cost: 5 Mana per second

Domain (Level 1)

With chains that bind, and threads that extend from one to another, a Paladin is the center of events. In his Domain, enemies will break and allies will bend knee. Let the enemies of the Empire tremble before a Paladin with his Domain.

Effect 1: All enemy combatants receive -10% attribute decreases, a +10% increase in Mana cost and lose 25 HP per second while within range of the Domain.

Effect 2: All allies receive a +10% increase in health regeneration, a 10% increase in attributes, and a reduction of -10% in Mana cost (semi-stackable).

Range: 10 Meters

Cost: 500 Mana + 5 Mana per Second

Judgment of All (Level 6)

An Emperor might sit in judgment of those that defy them, but a Paladin sits in Judgment of All who fall before his gaze. Desire bends and debases itself. Duty shatters under the weight of ever greater burdens. Morality shifts under the winds of circumstance. In the eyes of those he serves, a Paladin's judgment must be impeccable. Under his gaze, those underserving will fall. So long as his honor holds true, judgment will follow.

Effect: Skill inflicts (Erethran Reputation*$HonSysCal*1.5 = 751) points of on-going Mana damage to all judged unworthy within perception range of user.

Duration: 65 seconds

Cost: 1000 MP

Grand Paladin Skills

Grand Cross   Extra Hands   Burden of the Worthy   Defense of the Fallen

Final Judgment   Combined Arms   Bonds of the People

Grand Cross (Level 4)

The burden of existence weighs heavily on the Paladin. This Skill allows the Paladin to allow another to share in the burden. Under the light of and benediction of the Grand Paladin, under the weight of true understanding wayward children may be brought back to the fold.

Effect: Damage done equals to (Willpower * 2.4) per square meter over radius of (1/10th of Perception2) meters. Damage may be increased by reducing radius of the Grand Cross. Does additional (Willpower) points of damage per second for 14 seconds.

Cost: 2000 MP

Extra Hands (Level 3)

A Paladin can never be everywhere he needs to be. But with this Skill, the Grand Paladin can certainly be in more places. Mana Regeneration reduced by 5 permanently.

Cost: 5000 Mana per duplicate.

Upkeep cost: 5000 Mana per day per duplicate. Must be paid by original Skill user.

Effect: Creates maximum four duplicates of the user. Duplicates have 90.2% of all (unboosted) Attributes, gain no effects from Titles and may not equip Soulbound weapons but has access to all (non-purchased) Skills of user. Each duplicate has their own Mana pool but regenerate at 50.2% of normal regeneration levels. Mana levels take the place of health points for duplicates. Original Skill user has a telepathic connection to duplicates at all times and will receive a download of duplicate memories upon their destruction or cessation of upkeep costs.

Note: This Skill cannot be used by duplicates

Defense of the Fallen (Level 3)

Guardian and protector, judge and executioner, the Grand Paladin has succeeded as much as he has failed in his duty. Not everyone they seek to save can be saved, all too often the Paladin arrives after the tragedy. Defense of the Fallen armors the Paladin to deal with mental and physical demands of the job.

Effect: Increases Mental Resistance by 60%, Increases Physical Resistance by 35%. Effects are stacked on existing resistances. Effects are imbued in an aura surrounding the user, including all worn and active shields and armor.

Final Judgment (Level 1)

When all else fails, when the army is spent, when the planet is lost, the Grand Paladin may levy a Final Judgment on their enemies. Feared and hated in equal measure, may the enemies of the Erethran Empire never benefit from our loss!

This is a channeled skill with a minimum duration of 10 minutes.

Warning! This is a planet cracker Skill and its use is restricted via Galactic Regulations 1877.245.12. Usage of this Skill without proper authorization will result in the most severe of penalties.

Effect: User triggers use of the skills Army of One, Judgment of All, Beacon of the Angels and Grand Cross repeatedly. Limitations on application range of Skills are removed during this period to a maximum of visual range * 10.

Cost: 5000 Mana Initial + 500 Mana per Minute

Duration: Minimum of 10 minutes. Unknown maximum

Administrator Skills

System Edit

A core Skill for System Administrators.

Effect: Make trivial to minor amendments to System processes

Cost: Variable (HP & MP)

Class Skill: Ticket Board (Level 1)

Middle System Administrators are tasked with not just solving issues at Administrative Centers like Junior System Administrators but with finding solutions in the farthest reaches of the System.

Effect: Form a System Ticketing Board and resolve tickets wherever you might be

Other Class Skills

Frenzy (Level 1)

Effect: When activated, pain is reduced by 80%, damage increased by 30%, stamina regeneration rate increased by 20%. Mana regeneration rate decreased by 10%

Frenzy will not deactivate until all enemies have been slain. User may not retreat while Frenzy is active.

Cleave (Level 2)

Effect: Physical attacks deal 60% more base damage. Effect may be combined with other Class Skills.

Cost: 25 Mana

Elemental Strike (Level 1—Ice)

Effect: Used to imbue a weapon with freezing damage. Adds +5 Base Damage to attacks and a 10% chance of reducing speed by 5% upon contact. Lasts for 30 seconds.

Cost: 50 Mana

Instantaneous Inventory (Maxed)

Allows user to place or remove any System-recognized item from Inventory if space allows. Includes the automatic arrangement of space in the inventory. User must be touching item.

Cost: 5 Mana per item

Shrunken Footsteps (Level 1)

Reduces System presence of user, increasing the chance of the user evading detection of System-assisted sensing Skills and equipment. Also increases cost of information purchased about user. Reduces Mana Regeneration by 5 permanently.

Tech Link (Level 2)

Effect: Tech Link allows user to increase their skill level in using a technological item, increasing input and versatility in usage of said items. Effects vary depending on item. General increase in efficiency of 10%. Mana regeneration rate decreased by 10%

Designated Technological Items: Neural Link, Hodo's Triple Forged Armor

Analyze (Level 2)

Allows user to scan individuals, monsters, and System-registered objects to gather information registered with the System. Detail and level of accuracy of information is dependent on Level and any Skills or Spells in conflict with the ability. Reduces Mana regeneration by 10 permanently.

Harden (Level 2)

This Skill reinforces targeted defenses and actively weakens incoming attacks to reduce their penetrating power. A staple Skill of the Turtle Knights of Kiumma, the Harden Skill has frustrated opponents for millennia.

Effect: Reduces penetrative effects of attacks by 30% on targeted defense.

Cost: 3 Mana per second

Quantum Lock (Level 3)

A staple Skill of the M453-X Mecani-assistants, Quantum Lock blocks stealth attacks and decreases the tactical options of their enemies. While active, the Quantum Lock of the Mecani-assistants excites quantum strings in the affected area for all individuals and Skills.

Effect: All teleportation, portal, and dimensional Skills and Spells are disrupted while Quantum Lock is in effect. Forceable use of Skills and Spells while Skill is in effect will result in (Used Skill Mana Cost * 4) health in damage. Users may pay a variable amount of additional Mana when activating the Skill to decrease effect of Quantum Lock and decrease damage taken.

Requirements: 200 Willpower, 200 Intelligence

Area of Effect: 100-meter radius around user

Cost: 250 + 50 Mana per Minute

Elastic Skin (Level 3)

Elastic Skin is a permanent alteration, allowing the user to receive and absorb a small portion of damage. Damage taken reduced by 7% with 7% of damage absorbed converted to Mana. Mana Regeneration reduced by 15 permanently.

Disengage Safeties (Level 2)

All technological weapons have safeties built in. Users of this Skill recklessly disregard the mandatory safeties, deciding that they know better than the crafters, engineers, and government personnel who built and regulate the production of these technological pieces.

Effects: Increase power output from 2.5-25% depending on the weapon and its level of sophistication. Increase durability losses from use by 25-250%.
Cost: 200 Mana + 25 Mana per minute

Temporary Forced Link (Level 1)

Most Class Skills can't be linked with another's. The instability formed between the mixing of the aura from multiple Mana sources often results in spectacular—and explosive—scenarios. For the 02m8 Symbiotes though, the need to survive within their host bodies and use their Skills has resulted in this unique Skill, allowing the Symbiote to lend their Mana and Skills. (For more persistent effects, see Mana Graft)

Effect: Skill and Skill effects are forcibly combined. Final effect results will vary depending on level of compatibility of Skills.
Cost: 250 Mana + 10 Mana per minute (plus original Skill cost)

Hyperspace Nitro Boost (Level 1)

When you've got to win the race, there's nothing like a hyperspace boost. This Skill links the user with his craft's hyperspace engine, providing a direct boost to its efficiency. Unlike normal speed increases for hyperspace engines, the Nitro Boost is a variable boost and runs a risk of damaging the engine.

Effect: 15% increase in hyperspace engine efficiency + variable % increase in efficiency at 1% per surplus Mana. Each additional 1% over base raises chance of catastrophic engine failure by 0.01%
Cost: 250 Mana + (surplus variable amount; minimum 200 Mana increments) per minute

On the Edge (Level 1)

Shuttle racers live their lives on the edge, cutting corners by feet and dodging monsters by inches. There's only one way to drive a ship with that level of precision, and no matter what those military Pilots tell you, it's with On the Edge.

Effect: +10% boost in ship handling and maneuverability. +10% passive increase in all piloting skills. +1% increase per increment of surplus Mana

Cost: 100 Mana per level + (surplus variable amount; minimum 100 Mana increments) per minute

Fate's Thread (Level 2)

The Akashi'so believe that we are all but weavings in the great thread of life. Connected to one another by the great Weaver, there is not one but multiple threads between us all, woven from our interactions and histories. Fate's Thread is but a Skill expression of this belief. This Skill cannot be dodged but may be blocked. After all, all things are bound together.

Effect: Fate Thread allows the user to bind individuals together by making what is already there apparent. Thread is made physical and may be used to pull, tie and bind.

Duration: 2 minutes

Cost: 60 Mana

Peasant's Fury (Level 1)

No one knows loss more than the powerless. The Downtrodden Peasant has taken the fury of the powerless and made it his own, gifting them the strength to go on so long as they Manage to make others feel the same loss that they did. -5 Mana Regeneration per Second

Effect: User receives a 0.1% regeneration effect of damage dealt for each 1% of health loss.

Spells

Improved Minor Healing (IV)

Effect: Heals 40 Health per casting. Target must be in contact during healing. Cooldown 60 seconds.

Cost: 20 Mana

Improved Mana Missile (IV)

Effect: Creates four missiles out of pure Mana, which can be directed to damage a target. Each dart does 30 damage. Cooldown 10 seconds

Cost: 35 Mana

Enhanced Lightning Strike

Effect: Call forth the power of the gods, casting lightning. Lightning strike may affect additional targets depending on proximity, charge and other conductive materials on-hand. Does 100 points of electrical damage.

Lightning Strike may be continuously channeled to increase damage for 10 additional damage per second.

Cost: 75 Mana.

Continuous cast cost: 5 Mana / second

Lightning Strike may be enhanced by using the Elemental Affinity of Electromagnetic Force. Damage increased by 20% per level of affinity

Greater Regeneration (II)

Effect: Increases natural health regeneration of target by 6%. Only single use of spell effective on a target at a time.

Duration: 10 minutes

Cost: 100 Mana

Firestorm

Effect: Create a firestorm with a radius of 5 meters. Deals 250 points of fire damage to those caught within. Cooldown 60 seconds.

Cost: 200 Mana

Polar Zone

Effect: Create a thirty-meter diameter blizzard that freezes all targets within one. Does 10 points of freezing damage per minute plus reduces effected individuals speed by 5%. Cooldown 60 seconds.

Cost: 200 Mana

Greater Healing (II)

Effect: Heals 100 Health per casting. Target does not require contact during healing. Cooldown 60 seconds per target.

Cost: 75 Mana

Mana Drip (II)

Effect: Increases natural health regeneration of target by 6%. Only single use of spell effective on a target at a time.

Duration: 10 minutes

Cost: 100 Mana

Freezing Blade

Effect: Enchants weapon with a slowing effect. A 5% slowing effect is applied on a successful strike. This effect is cumulative and lasts for 1 minute.

Cooldown 3 minutes

Spell Duration: 1 minute.

Cost: 150 Mana

Improved Inferno Strike (II)

A beam of heat raised to the levels of an inferno, able to melt steel and earth on contact! The perfect spell for those looking to do a lot of damage in a short period of time.

Effect: Does 200 Points of Heat Damage

Cost: 150 Mana

Mud Walls

Unlike its more common counterpart Earthen Walls, Mud Walls focus is more on dealing slow, suffocating damage and restricting movement on the battlefield.

Effect: Does 20 Points of Suffocating Damage. -30% Movement Speed

Duration: 2 Minutes

Cost: 75 Mana

Create Water

Pulls water from the elemental plane of water. Water is pure and the highest form of water available. Conjures 1 liter of water. Cooldown: 1 minute

Cost: 50 Mana

Scry

Allows caster to view a location up to 1.7 kilometers away. Range may be extended through use of additional Mana. Caster will be stationary during this period. It is recommended caster focuses on the scry unless caster has a high level of Intelligence and Perception so as to avoid accidents. Scry may be blocked by equivalent or higher tier spells and Skills. Individuals with high perception in region of Scry may be alerted that the Skill is in use. Cooldown: 1 hour.

Cost: 25 Mana per minute.

Scrying Ward

Blocks scrying spells and their equivalent within 5 meters of caster. Higher level spells may not be blocked, but caster may be alerted about scrying attempts. Cooldown: 10 minutes

Cost: 50 Mana per minute

Improved Invisibility

Hides target's System information, aura, scent, and visual appearance. Effectiveness of spell is dependent upon Intelligence of caster and any Skills or Spells in conflict with the target.

Cost: 100 + 50 Mana per minute

Improved Mana Cage

While physically weaker than other elemental-based capture spells, Mana Cage has the advantage of being able to restrict all creatures, including semi-solid Spirits, conjured elementals, shadow beasts, and Skill users. Cooldown: 1 minute

Cost: 200 Mana + 75 Mana per minute

Improved Flight

(Fly birdie, fly!—Ali) This spell allows the user to defy gravity, using controlled bursts of Mana to combat gravity and allow the user to fly in even the most challenging of situations. The improved version of this spell allows flight even in zero gravity situations and a higher level of maneuverability. Cooldown: 1 minute

Cost: 250 Mana + 100 Mana per minute

Equipment

Spitzrocket Powered Armor Version 18.9 (Tier I) (Grandmaster)

The product of Grandmaster Artisan Madopnem Spitzrocket, the Spitzrocket is a hand-made, unique build Power Armor created in the Forbidden Zone. Continuing with his belief that less is more, the Spitzrocket is both built to adapt to old battles as well as having minimal additional Skills. Rather, the focus of Artisan Spitzrocket has always been in aiding the user in his battles.

Core: Class I Forbidden Zone (Spitzrocket Adaptation) Mana Engine

CPU: Class A++ Wote Core CPU

Armor Rating: Tier I (Enhanced)

Hard Points: 8 (8 Used—Interstellar Ares Flight System, Integrated Mana Warped Beam Cannon (Primary)* 2, Ares Type Primal Shield Generator, Spitzrocket Mana to Armor Adaptive Nanoreplicators * 3, Spitzrocket Neural Muscular Enhancers)

Soft Points 6 (4 Used—Neural Link, Wote HUD Imaging, Airmed Primary Body Monitor, AI integrator)

Battery Capacity: 718/718*

Active Skills: Overcharge, Spatial Twist, Adaptive Conditioning

Attribute Bonuses: +187 Strength, +244 Agility, +31 Constitution, +82 Perception, +183 Stamina and Health Regeneration per minute

Skill: Overcharge (Artisan Equipment Addition—M)

Increase power output of the Spitzrocket for a short period, increasing all damage and attribute bonuses.

Effects: Increase all attribute and damage bonuses by 200%

Duration: 5 minutes

Cooldown: 2 hours

Skill: Spatial Twist (Spatial Equipment Addition—M)

Rather than breaching dimensions or cutting through space, the Spatial Twist Skill instead bends space, bypassing the majority of Dimensional Locks. It allows the user to cross distance in but a flash of a step or a burst of energy.

Effects: Bends space to allow user to bypass intervening distance (max 219.3km). Must have clear line of sight and movement. Cannot go through occupied space.

Capacity: 3

Recharge Rate: 5 minutes per charge

Skill: Adaptive Conditioning (Artisan Equipment Addition—H)

Don't you hate it when your expensive piece of equipment breaks down? While we don't promise the Spitzrocket will never break, we do promise that the more it does, the better it'll be at not breaking the next time around. Embedded in a secondary dimension, the mainframe of the Spitzrocket is safe from normal everyday destruction. This allows it to replicate the Spitzrocket while adapting to the previous battle and conditions that destroyed it.

Effect: Recreates a full copy of the Spitzrocket with additional, adaptive changes to the equipment. Maximum change is 2.8% of armor, resistances and attributes per iteration.

Duration: 274.8 hours to recreate a full copy

Spitzrocket Sunwarmer (Artisan Equipment Addition—H)

Got a moon you need removed from orbit or a sun that is a little on the chilly side? The Sunwarmer is the Spitzrocket answer to this problem, by condensing the energy of unaspected Mana into a weapon.

Effects: Fires a concentrated beam of concentrated unaspected Mana that disrupts physical, spiritual and System links

Damage: 18,318 Base

Capacity: 1

Recharge Rate: 14.3 minutes

Hod's Triple Fused Armor

The product of multiple workings by the Master Blacksmith and Crafter Hodiliphious 'Hod' Yalding, the Triple Fused Armor was hand-forged from rare, System-generated material, hand refined and reworked trice over with multiple patented and rare alloys and materials. The final product is considered barely passable by Hod—though it would make a lesser craftsman cry.

Core: Class I Hallow Physics Mana Engine

CPU: Class B Wote Core CPU

Armor Rating: Tier I (Enhanced)

Hard Points: 9 (6 Used—Jungian Flight System, Talpidae Abyssal Horns, Luione Hard Light Projectors, Diarus Poison Stingers, Ares Type I Shield Generator, Greater Troll Cell Injectors)

Soft Points 4 (3 Used—Neural Link, Ynir HUD Imaging, Airmed Body Monitor)

Battery Capacity: 380/380

Active Skills: Abyssal Chains, Mirror Shade, Poison Grip

Attribute Bonuses: +93 Strength, +78 Agility, +51 Constitution, +44 Perception, +287 Stamina and Health Regeneration per minute

Note: Hod's Triple Fused Armor is currently under limited warranty. Armor may be teleported to Hod's workshop for repairs once a week. All cost of repairs will be deducted from user's account.

Skills in Hod's Armor:

Abyssal Chains

Calling upon the material connection to the shadow plane, chains from the abyss erupt, binding a target in place.

Effect: Target is bound by shadow chains. Chains deal 10 points of damage per second. To break free, target must win a contested Strength test. Abyssal Chains have a Strength of 120.

Uses: 3/3

Recharge rate: 1 per hour

Mirror Shade

Mirror Shade creates a semi-solid doppelganger using hard light technology and Mana.

Effect: Mirror Shade create a semi-solid doppelganger of the user for a period of ten minutes. Maximum range of doppelganger from user is fifty meters. Doppelganger has 18% physical fidelity.

Use: 1/1

Recharge Rate: 1 per 4 hours

Silversmith Jeupa VII Anti-Personnel Cannon (Modified & Upgraded)

This quad-barrelled anti-personnel weapon has been handcrafted by Advanced Weaponsmiths to provide the highest integration possible for an energy weapon. This particular weapon has been modified to include additional range-finding and sighting options and upgraded to increase short-term damage output at the cost of long-term durability. Barrels may be fired individually or linked.

Base Damage: 787 per barrel

Battery Capacity: 4 per barrel (16 total)

Recharge Rate: 0.25 per hour per GMU

Ares Platinum Class Tier II Armored Jumpsuit

Ares's signature Platinum Class line of armored daily wear combines the company's latest technological advancement in nanotech fiber design and the pinnacle work of an Advanced Craftsman's Skill to provide unrivalled protection for the discerning Adventurer.

Effect: +218 Defense, +14% Resistance to Kinetic and Energy Attacks. +19% Resistance against Temperature changes. Self-Cleanse, Self-Mend, Autofit Enchantments also included.

Silversmith Mark VIII Beam Pistol (Upgradeable)

Base Damage: 88

Battery Capacity: 13/13

Recharge Rate: 3 per hour per GMU

Tier IV Neural Link

Neural link may support up to 5 connections.

Current connections: Hod's Triple Fused Armor

Software Installed: Rich'lki Firewall Class IV, Omnitron III Class IV Controller

Ferlix Type I Twinned-Beam Rifle (Modified)

Base Damage: 39

Battery Capacity: 41/41

Recharge rate: 1 per hour per GMU

Tier II Sword (Soulbound Personal Weapon of an Erethran Honor Guard)

Base Damage: 397

Durability: N/A (Personal Weapon)

Special Abilities: +20 Mana Damage, Blade Strike

Kryl Ring of Regeneration

Often used as betrothal bands, Kryl rings are highly sought after and must be ordered months in advance.

Health Regeneration: +30

Stamina Regeneration: +15

Mana Regeneration: +5

Tier III Bracer of Mana Storage

A custom work by an unknown maker, this bracer acts a storage battery for personal Mana. Useful for Mages and other Classes that rely on Mana. Mana storage ratio is 50 to 1.

Mana Capacity: 350/350

Fey-steel Dagger

Fey-steel is not actual steel but an unknown alloy. Normally reserved only for the Sidhe nobility, a small—by Galactic standards—amount of Fey-steel is released for sale each year. Fey-steel takes enchantments extremely well.

Base Damage: 28

Durability: 110/100

Special Abilities: None

Enchanted, Reinforced Toothy Throwing Knives (5)

First handcrafted from the rare drop of a Level 140 Awakened Beast by the Redeemer of the Dead, John Lee, these knives have been further processed by the Master Craftsmen I-24-988L and reinforced with orichalcum and fey-steel. The final blades have been further enchanted with Mana and piercing damage as well as a return enchantment.

Base Damage: 238

Enchantments: Return, Mana Blade (+28 Damage), Pierce (-7% defense)

Brumwell Necklace of Shadow Intent

The Brumwell necklace of shadow intent is the hallmark item of the Brumwell Clan. Enchanted by a Master Crafter, this necklace layers shadowy intents over your actions, ensuring that information about your actions is more difficult to ascertain. Ownership of such an item is both a necessity and a mark of prestige among settlement owners and other individuals of power.

Effect: Persistent effect of Shadow Intent (Level 4) results in significantly increased cost of purchasing information from the System about wearer. Effect is persistent for all actions taken while necklace is worn.

Ring of Greater Shielding

Creates a greater shield that will absorb approximately 1000 points of damage. This shield will ignore all damage that does not exceed its threshold amount of 50 points of damage while still functioning.

Max Duration: 7 Minutes

Charges: 1

Simalax Hover Boots (Tier II)

A combination of hand-crafted materials and mass-produced components, the Simalax Hover Boots are the journeyman work of Magi-Technician Lok of Irvina. Enchantments and technology mesh together in the Simalax Hover Boots, offering its wearer the ability to tread on air briefly and defy gravity and sense.

Effects: User reduces gravitational effects by 0.218 SIG. User may, on activation, hover and skate during normal and mildly turbulent atmospheric conditions. User may also use the Simalax Hover Boots to triple jump in the air, engaging the anti-gravity and hover aspects at the same time.
Duration: 1.98 SI Hours.

F'Merc Nanoswarm Mana Grenades (Tier II)

The F'Merc Nanoswarm Grenades are guaranteed to disrupt the collection of Mana in a battlefield, reducing Mana Regeneration rates for those caught in the swarm. Recommended by the I'um military, the Torra Special Forces and the No.1 Most Popular Mana Grenade as voted by the public on Boom, Boom, Boom! Magazine.
Effect: Reduces Mana Regeneration rates and spell formation in affected area by 37% ((higher effects in enclosed areas)
Radius: 10m x 10m

Daghtree's Legendary Ring of Deception (Tier I)

A musician, poet and artist, Daghtree's fame rose not from his sub-standard works of 'art' but his array of seduction Skills from his Heartthrob Artist Class. Due to his increasing infamy, Daghtree commissioned this Legendary ring to change his appearance and continue Leveling. In the end, it is rumored that his indiscretions caught up with the infamous artist and he disappeared from Galactic sources in GCD 9,275
Effect: Creates a powerful disguise that covers the wearer. The ring comes with six pre-loaded disguises and additional disguises may be added through expansion of charges
Duration: 1 day per charge
Charges: 3
Recharge via ambient Mana: 1 charge per Galactic Standard Unit per week

F'Merc Ghostlight Mana Dispersal Grenades (Tier I)

The F'Merc Ghostlight Mana Dispersal Grenades not only disperse Mana in the battlefield, the Ghostlight Dispersal Grenades degrade all Mana Skills and spells within its field of effectiveness. Used by Krolash the Destroyer, the Erethran Champion Isma (prior version) and Anblanca Special Forces. Five times Winner of the Most Annoying Utility Item on the Battlefield.

Effect: Reduces Mana Regeneration rates, Skill and spell formation use in affected area by 67% ((higher effects in enclosed areas)

Radius: $15m^3$

Evernight Darkness Orbs

When the world goes light, the Evernight Darkness Orbs will bring back blessed darkness. If you need darkness, you need Evernight!

Effect: Removes al visible light and mute infrared and ultraviolet wavelengths by 30%

Radius: $50m^3$

Seven Heavenly Spire Wards

Quick to set-up, the Seven Heavenly Spire Wards were crafted by the Thrice Loved Bachelor's Temple of the Sinking Domain as their main export. Using the total prayer and faith of the temple, they produce a set of wards every month.

Effect: Set's up a 30' by 30' defensive ward; protects against both magical and technological attacks and entry

Fumikara Mobile Teleport Circles

These one-off use mobile teleport circles allow connection to existing and open teleport networks.

Effect: Connect to open teleport networks within a 5,000 kim radius of the teleport circles. Allows teleportation of individuals to the networked teleport centers

PoenJoe Goleminised-Mana Generator Mark 18

The latest Mana Generator by the infamous PoenJoe, the Mark 18 is guaranteed* to not blow up on you in optimal conditions. This partially sentient Mana Generator can extract up to 98% of a Mana Crystal's saved energy in 0.003 seconds. Currently loaded in an Adult Kirin Mana Core.

Effect: It's a Power Generator. Guaranteed to provide up to 98 x 10*99 Standard Galactic Mana Units

Not actually guaranteed. In fact, we're 100% certain that containment failure will occur.

Payload (Level 2) (Embedded in Anklet of Dispersed Damage)

Sometimes, you need to get your Skills inside a location. Payload allows you to imbue an individual or item with a Skill at a reduced strength.

Effect: 71% effectiveness of Skill imbued.

Secondary Effect: Skill may be now triggered on a timed basis (max 2:07 minutes)

Uses: 22

Recharge: 10.7 charges per day in SGE

Made in the USA
Las Vegas, NV
11 March 2022

45486160R00277